LAST STAND

Deb watched the five vampires flow into the auditorium, casting a pall through the warm light like silent, oiled snakes. She'd lit the candles intentionally, preferring to see those who came for her, their faces, their number, their expressions—did they still have *souls*? She wished she could search each pair of eyes to see if any visage of humanity remained.

And so here they were at last, her future, her *fate*. Two women, three men. She would have little time to defend herself; startled by the flickering light, they were already splitting up, moving with frightening speed.

"Come on in," Deb called cheerfully. Beneath her deadly calm she felt the comforting pull of the shoulder strap as she hoisted the Streetsweeper into position. The noise of the shotgun pumping slugs into the magazine drowned out most of her next words.

"I've been expecting you!"

She opened fire.

Don't miss other spine-tingling horror novels from Bantam Books:

By Ray Garton
Dark Channel

By Alan Rodgers
Blood of the Children
Fire
Night

By John Saul
Brainchild
Creature
Darkness
The God Project
Hellfire
Nathaniel
Second Child
Shadows
Sleep Walk
The Unloved
The Unwanted

By John Skipp and Craig Spector
Book of the Dead (eds.) (Winner of the Bram Stoker Award)
Still Dead: Book of the Dead 2 (eds.)
The Bridge
The Light at the End
The Scream

AfterAge

Yvonne Navarro

BANTAM BOOKS

NEW YORK · TORONTO · LONDON · SYDNEY · AUCKLAND

AFTERAGE

A Bantam Book/September 1993

All rights reserved.
Copyright © 1993 by Yvonne Navarro.
Cover art copyright © 1993 by Alan Ayers.
No part of this book may be reproduced or transmitted in any
form or by any means, electronic or mechanical, including
photocopying, recording, or by any information storage and
retrieval system, without permission in writing from the publisher.
For information address: Bantam Books.

ISBN 0-553-56358-0

Published simultaneously in the United States and Canada

Bantam Books are published by Bantam Books, a division of Bantam
Doubleday Dell Publishing Group, Inc. Its trademark, consisting of the
words "Bantam Books" and the portrayal of a rooster, is Registered in
U.S. Patent and Trademark Office and in other countries. Marca Reg-
istrada. Bantam Books, 1540 Broadway, New York, New York 10036.

PRINTED IN THE UNITED STATES OF AMERICA

RAD   0 9 8 7 6 5 4 3 2 1

To my sister Debbie,

who would've gotten a charge out of this whole thing. Life goes on, but you will always be an irreplaceable piece of its magic.

Special thanks to:

My Mom, for telling me I could do this in the first place;

Rick McCammon, for not laughing in 1984;

Dave Silva, for publishing (and paying me for!) my first short story;

Ann Kennedy, for a vision of what "Victory's Ode" could be;

A big possum hug to Kathy Ptacek, for giving me my first pro sale;

My Dad, not only for his technical teachings and patience, but for helping me pull things back together;

Jeff, for his endless support and encouragement when I needed it most;

Wayne, for Advanced Weapons 1.01 and just for being a buddy;

Roger Coleman, formerly of Mountain View, California, for help with the "medical stuff";

Joe Lansdale, for a turn in the right direction when I was at wit's end;

My agent, Howard Morhaim, for following his intuition;

A wonderful bunch of friends who took me into the fold with tireless advice and support and love: Beth, Brian, Dave, Mark, Peggy, Andrew, Harry, Kathleen, Amy, Kurt, Marthayn, Augie, Jeff J., and again, the Waynester;

And Tams, for her unfaltering "I never had a doubt" attitude.

Most of the quotes from Revelation in these pages have been blatantly, shamelessly, and conveniently paraphrased ... but the real words are still frightening enough to twist your dreams.

Prologue

PROPHECY . . .

In the time before, many had prophesied, wailing loudly of the damage being done to God's good world: the Ten Commandments, they pointed out, were not just being ignored; they were being *mocked. Remember,* God's seers said as they drew themselves up knowingly behind priests' vestments and holy white collars:

The meek shall inherit the earth.

But those who inherited the earth were not meek at all.

I

March 23

The Survivors—
Life in the Land of the Living

1

REVELATION 11:8–9
And their dead bodies shall lie in
the streets of the great city. . . .
and shall not suffer their dead
to be put in graves.

A quarter of an hour until dawn, and Alex Nicholson
could see a woman on the street below.

He woke early, during the gray, pre-safe time before
the sun topped the downtown buildings and filled the
streets with light. As always, he stood shivering at a window while he scanned Clark Street from thirteen stories
up, looking for movement, birds, whatever might catch
his gaze. This morning his eyes widened as he saw the
female come from around the corner of City Hall. At first
he thought she was one of *them*, but she drifted east
across Daley Plaza as if she were out for a morning stroll,
back when 5:45 A.M. had been a time ruled by joggers
and health freaks. Even at this distance he could see her
hands reach to pry at a pale knot atop her head; a moment later a fine sheet of hair fell to her hips, then
streamed behind her in the spring wind like bleached
corn silk, barely visible against the startling white of her
dress. There was no hurry in her step and for a moment
she lifted her face to the sky, as if to welcome the soon-
to-rise sun.

He stared in dismay as she headed straight for the
subway entrance.

All drowsiness fled. "Stop," he hissed. "It's too early—
get away from there!" His knuckles gripped the metal
ledge until the fingers went bloodless. What the hell was
she doing? She must be mad! His thoughts spun desperately. He could grab a weapon and start down, but it'd
take him seven minutes—five at least—just to negotiate

the stairs and throw back the bolts on the doors. By then the sun would be up—

She was parallel to the stairs sinking to subway level now and Nicholson felt the hairs on the back of his neck rise.

"Watch out!" he cried uselessly. Her head swiveled to the left as a figure darted from the stairs and clutched at her wrist. From Nicholson's vantage point, she didn't seem to resist as she was dragged into the stone entryway; for an incredible moment he could have sworn she embraced her attacker.

In three seconds she was out of sight.

In another five he was pounding down the stairs, a wickedly sharp machete gripped in one fist while he struggled for balance as he leapt down four and five steps at a time. Each second was precious; there wasn't enough time to drain her, he reasoned wildly, it was too close to sunup. But there *was* time to drag her somewhere and tie her for later. If it got her into the tunnels, she was finished. He'd never been foolish enough to explore the lightless underground, even during the day. He tried to speed up, every footfall jolting purposely buried memories closer to the surface of his mind, releasing phantom screams and pernicious shadows from beyond the crumbling walls of mental safety. Breath rasping, he reached the first floor and fought with the tight metal bars across the stairwell door. They grated and screeched as he wrenched them loose, the unoiled hinges screaming their alarm. His senses heightened in the stairwell's blackness, and he could smell his fear for the girl on the sweat squeezing from his pores as he finally tore open the steel fire door.

After the darkness of the hallway, the mild gray light of dawn spilling into the lobby nearly blinded him; he stumbled, then found his footing and raced for the main doors. *Too long!* he thought frantically as he fumbled keys into the locks. For the first time, he regretted welding shut the building's underground entrances, but his good intentions could be contemplated later. Right now, he clenched his teeth in frustration as his fingers tangled and his hold on the keyring jittered. *I'll bet she's—*

Then he was out and running across the plaza, his grasp on the machete precariously slick. He skidded to a stop at the top of the stairs and peered below, then turned away in revulsion; the smell sliding up his nose reminded him of dead frogs in long-ago biology classes.

There was no sign of the woman. The bloodsucker that had attacked her was crumpled on the stairs, a mass of slowly disintegrating flesh; where its mouth had been was a maw of blackened skin and fused stumps that might have once been fangs. Insane red eyes blinked against the light and fastened on Nicholson as it tried to crawl away. In them he saw pain, rage, and hate, and the legs kicked as Nicholson covered his nose in disgust and raised his machete. In another moment, the thing's head thumped down the concrete stairs into the shadows, leaving bits of flesh and sticky fluid in its wake as the mouth still worked hungrily. At Alex's feet, the fingers twisted and reached reflexively and he backstepped, watching until the sun did its work and nothing was left but a tarlike puddle.

Where one of the hands had been, Nicholson saw several strands of fine white hair; he plucked them from the gooey remnants with the point of his blade and held them up. Still clean, they sparkled like silver threads in the brightening sunlight before the breeze flung them away.

Where was she? he wondered numbly.

What was she?

2

●-●·●-●·●-●

REVELATION 20:6
... On such the second death hath no power.

●-●·●

Another few minutes and it would truly be a glorious morning, Jo thought. The air remained night-chilly, but the sky was beginning to lighten as she walked; above the tops of the skyscrapers surrounding her, the sky was still a dark, navy blue, the color of the uniform her adopted father had worn years ago as he dressed to go to his job as a policeman. To her right she could see five or six blocks east, past the elevated tracks where the sun was painting the dawn pink and pale blue above the lake.

The wind increased and she reached to pull the band from her hair. An instant later the tight mass atop her head came free, falling to her hips in a straight silvery mass. She fingered a strand curiously for a moment, then dropped it; two years ago her hair had been light brown. The color had changed seemingly overnight—no, that wasn't true. A chunk of her memories was *gone*, cut from her mind like a wedge of pie; the resulting gap bled a fiery faith into her soul that she could not ignore.

The wind—God's breath—caressed her face and raised goose bumps on the skin beneath the high collar and long sleeves of her white dress. She cut diagonally across the intersection of Clark and Washington and headed east again, facing the hard lake breeze. Her hair floated behind her and she raised her eyes to the pinkening sky, knowing that the sun—another of the Lord's wondrous creations—would rise above the buildings within minutes. She let her sixth sense lead her, following like a blind person at the mercy of a guide. Her eyes scanned the windows of the buildings, but the plaza was wide and empty; here and there pieces of paper fluttered in the growing breeze. She wondered idly how the trash had gotten there—it might be new, she thought hopefully, brought outside by human hands. Then again . . . .

Jo was no longer alone, she could *feel* it. No eyes had watched earlier when she'd stopped on LaSalle and brushed her fingers against the engraved brass eagle plaque on the American National Bank Building. Eagles, huge creatures of the air flying without mechanical parts or fuel, had always fascinated her. Now she paused opposite City Hall and looked across Daley Plaza to the Picasso statue that resembled a metal horse dying a slow, rusting death. Something whispered from within the subway and she moved toward the shadowed steps of the Dearborn underground as if in a trance, unbuttoning her collar invitingly. Beneath the translucent skin of her throat her pulse increased, visibly throbbing as it gave out the warm scent of lifeblood.

Four feet from the stairs, her face turned toward the dirty creature as it leapt. Clawed fingers wrapped around her wrist, freezing through the thin cotton material as it yanked on her; still, she followed without resisting. At the top of the steps she met its surprised eyes without flinching and opened her arms, stepping forward and exposing her throat. Fangs gleamed like pearly scissors in the dark pit of its mouth; the beast's arm slipped around her waist and pulled her down the steps almost tenderly. Held against its icy, half-starved body, her warmth was like a furnace, and she knew it would not be able to resist a quick taste before sunup. Her pulse thundered in her head as the fangs closed on her neck; she welcomed them.

Bright, white light and pain, like being washed in the lake of God's holy sun.

Another dress in charred tatters, and her last one, too. Jo sighed and walked up LaSalle toward the river; her unmarked throat ached nastily and she was a little lightheaded, but the crisp air would clear that away soon. Right now she needed more clothes and she skipped childlike across the bridge at LaSalle and Wacker and pushed through the unlocked revolving doors into the Merchandise Mart. Her stomach growled and she glanced at the cigar stand in the lobby and the twisted metal gates that had once closed off the Walgreen's Drug Store. There was still food here, old candy bars and snacks, but there were also others who needed the nourishment—such as it was—more than she. The knowledge brought a flaring of despair to her head, and her mind turned quickly away from the black thoughts.

On the sixth floor Jo wandered into a women's wholesale store and shook out an armful of white dresses in a size five without regard for style. Beneath a counter supporting an open cash register with a drawer still full of dusty bills, Jo found a shopping bag and put the dresses inside, then touched the money thoughtfully, trying to feel the old vibrations of the people who'd once held it. When nothing happened, she picked up the bag and made her way back to the first floor.

Passing an empty cookie stand in the massive lobby, Jo stopped and held her breath for a moment, listening. This building, she knew, was never silent; the space left by the sound of her breath was filled instantly with the faint moans and crying of the Damned imprisoned two floors above, growing louder now as they sensed her presence. Tears filled her eyes and she hung the shopping bag over one thin arm and clapped her hands over her ears.

Not enough . . .

She fled into the blessed warmth of the spring sun.

Jo left the ruined dress on the sidewalk under the Lake Street elevated tracks, unconsciously shedding it like an old and ill-used skin. Soon the sunlight would warm the day, but the morning air was still chilly on her naked shoulders and she turned into the black building on the corner of Lake and LaSalle. In her pile of garments she found a dress cut from a heavier material and slipped it on. There was a Greek restaurant off the lobby, door still unlocked from her last visit; inside the restaurant's shadowed pantry was a plastic jar of her favorite tangy black olives—a strange breakfast, but she liked the garlicky flavor and was sure this was one of the foods eaten in ancient, biblical times. The supply was almost gone; soon she would have to look elsewhere for her treat.

Outside again, she stopped at a corner bench and sat, eating the rich olives and spitting the pits into her palm. Before returning to St. Peter's, she would detour and drop them in the small patches of soil surrounding the trees along the river's edge; even if they didn't grow, maybe the squirrels or birds would want them for food. Her thoughts returned to the Merchandise Mart. The need to free those within was strong, but the means still eluded her. It would come—but *when?* Sometimes frustration filled her so intensely she would drop to her knees and beg God for His answer, right *now!*

But He was always silent, and she knew He would wait as long as He wished.

A bird, a tiny sparrow, landed on the sidewalk at her feet and gave a cheerful peep. "Psalm Thirty-seven," she whispered; the bird cocked its head as if in understanding and hopped closer. She nodded. "Verse seven."

Rest in the Lord, and wait patiently for Him.

She closed her eyes and napped for a time; while she slept, the sparrow flitted to her knee and preened itself calmly.

3

●━●━●━●━●━●

━●━●━

In the third-floor hallway of the Merchandise Mart,
Howard Siebold stared around nervously. Was everything
okay? Yes, he thought so. For a minute everybody had
squealed at once, though he couldn't figure out why.
He'd finally beat on one of the old radiator pipes with
the tranq pistol he sometimes carried and screamed
"Shut the fuck up!" The yowling had died as quickly as it
started, but it left his senses jangling and his ears ringing,
and he wasn't positive they'd stopped because of him.

Time for a check anyway, he thought as he heaved his
three-hundred-pound bulk from a chair beneath the window in his "office" and tossed the old girlie magazine on
the table amidst crumpled candy wrappers and potato
chip bags. Sweating immediately, he trudged the shadowed length of the hall and peered into each small, bare
room along the way. The doors had been removed long
ago, and his practiced eye took in everything. Chained at
the ankles to keep them from reaching the windows, the
men and women within crouched on dirty blankets and
stared at him with sullen, hate-filled eyes. He grinned at
the women until most dropped their gazes, filing away
the faces of those who glared back with the most
defiance—these he would visit before Rita took over at
the end of the day shift.

Howard grimaced when he thought of Rita, a bad spot
in his otherwise uncomplicated existence. The others ignored him, but he knew this particular vampire regarded
him as little more than wasted food, although Anyelet

would never allow Rita to harm him. That dead bitch should learn to appreciate him, he thought sourly—at least he could watch over things during the day without rotting. He passed one room and its occupant, a still-muscular young man caught a few days ago, lunged toward him. The chain around the man's ankle stopped him short, but the prisoner sneered openly when Howard flinched. "Come on, *big* man," he taunted as Howard passed. "Let's see how you do in a fair fight, you traitorous piece of *shit!*"

Howard bunched his fists but kept going, cursing himself for showing fear. Now the man would heckle him every time he passed until Howard found a way to shut him up—and hell wouldn't hide Howard if he lost his temper and killed the bastard. He itched to go back and kick the son of a bitch in the balls, but that would be just as bad. He gritted his teeth as the guy called out again, then paused at the room holding a young woman whose hands were still bound, a new one dragged in last night. Like the others she'd been stripped, and Howard's eyes swept her speculatively, noting only a few bruises marring the whiteness of her skin. He stepped inside, licking his lips. In spite of her expression of dread, her lip, tinged blue from the cold, curled in contempt, and Howard's smile faltered and changed to a silent snarl when she spit.

He pulled off his belt and knotted it around his right fist. A smart-ass, he figured. She'd probably heard the crack made by Mr. Mouth down the hall. Well, he'd purge her thoughts quick enough; the colors of respect were black and blue, and like a dozen others before her, she was about to learn the many shades of appreciation. As she backed away, he grabbed the chain that circled her ankle with his left hand and yanked her off her feet. The woman landed heavily on one hip and her yelp of pain changed to screams as his arm rose and fell.

Taking his pay in midshift would be too easy. He'd rather have a little fun first.

4

●━●·━●·━●·━●·━●

REVELATION 20:12
And I saw the dead, small and great.

●━·●·━●

Standing in the echoing pastel halls of Northwestern Memorial Hospital, Dr. William Perlman listened carefully. For a moment, he'd thought he'd heard something—ghosts? Maybe. He believed in them, oh yes, although eighteen months ago he would've laughed at anyone suggesting such a thing.

Of course, eighteen months ago the word *vampires* had meant Dracula and Christopher Lee.

Perlman was a tall man and the last ten months had taken its toll: his once-well-fed frame weighed a thin one-forty now that he had to forage food from the supermarkets and stores along the Gold Coast. Like his wife, Mera—who had disappeared over a year ago with their small son—he had taken their lifestyle for granted. He ached for Mera and what he had teasingly called her classic "Jewishness"; he often wondered if she would—or could—ever come back. And what would he do if she did?

He tucked his shirt into painter's overalls and pulled a comb from his back pocket from out of habit, running it through thinning hair the color of faded stone. Last night before bed he'd rinsed his face and found himself fascinated by his own flesh: living muscles expanding and contracting, oxygen-rich blood pumping through arteries, millions of fragile capillaries beneath the layers of skin. With a pang he'd also acknowledged that his body was dying—slowly and naturally—but dying nonetheless. He didn't want to die, ever. He wanted to live for a hundred years, or a thousand—

But not like that.

He touched his fingertips to the new crevices around

his eyes and across his forehead, lines that he'd never noticed before. Mera had always kept her face bland, hiding her joy or sorrow in an endless attempt to outwit the wrinkles. Studying himself, he wondered if she hadn't been right; the once-deep smile lines around his mouth had all but faded over the past year. Perhaps his cherished Mera had finally been successful in her search for eternal youth. . . .

He shook the thought away. Workboots clomping loudly in the deserted building, Perlman smoothed his bright red shirt and checked his pockets before unlocking the delivery door and slipping into the alley off Chicago Avenue. He glanced around cautiously, then pulled the door shut, hearing the reassuring *click* as the sturdy lock engaged. With the lake only a block away, the air was clear and vigorous as it fogged from his lips. A short jog west on Superior and he reached the crosswalk, looking up the instant the sun crept above the Barclay Chicago Hotel. In a microsecond one sun blossomed into a thousand as the rays caught and reflected on the rows of mirrored windows in one of the buildings bordering Michigan Avenue's west sidewalk. Perlman's breath hitched at the spectacular sight.

He pulled his gaze from the near-blinding display and light motes danced behind his blinking lids as he debated his direction. First, he decided, something to eat, a shot of carbohydrates and protein to bolster his daily vitamins. He turned north, staying on the east side until Water Tower Place rose in front of him, its proud white marble scoured clean by the spring rains and lake winds and almost painful to view. He tried the glass doors futilely and peered inside; he could see little besides shadows and the muted shine of chrome-edged escalators climbing into the dimness.

Shrugging, he turned away; shattering the doors would only open the Tower to nature's destruction. A glint of metal caught his eye and he returned and squatted by the doors, nose pressed against the glass as he struggled to see. There was a wide strip of tarnishing brass at the bottom, a toe kick, and just inside he could barely glimpse the edge of some sort of locking rod; at night it would be invisible. Hope rose in him and he touched his palms to the glass tentatively. Were there people inside? Even just *one*? He spent five minutes knocking on the thick glass and bruising his knuckles before he gave up, resolving to keep a closer eye on the Tower; the metal rod was much the same as the one he used across the entrance at Northwestern, though with glass doors it was only the sly illusion of an abandoned building.

Perlman slipped into Walgreen's through a door he'd carefully jimmied some months ago; inside he saw further evidence of life in the food section where the shelves had been rifled for supplies, though nothing was wasted by vandalism or carelessly ripped packages. He had food at the hospital and now took only to satisfy his immediate appetite; two cans of sardines and a small box of stale Ritz crackers. Outside he sat on the curb, ate, and watched the sun climb a little higher in the sky, letting his eyes wander repeatedly to Water Tower Place and its imagined occupants. As usual, his hunger died after a few bites; he stubbornly finished the sardines and crackers, then pocketed the other tin before dropping his garbage into a rusting trash can on the corner. More habit—it was amazing that such an ingenious, predictable man such as himself had survived in this back-assward world.

Perlman chewed the last bite of oily fish and swallowed it with difficulty, then stood, stomach fluttering uneasily. Tied in the hammer loop of his overalls was a coil of strong polypropylene rope; in his bulging pockets were duct tape, a heavy Mag Lite flashlight with good batteries, a Schrade Lockback hunting knife and four thick plastic garbage bags. He could get the two-by-fours he'd need from the construction sites along Michigan Avenue. Then it was just a matter of searching a few dark storerooms and basements until he found what he wanted.

He was about to blow his predictable life to hell.

Knife in hand, Perlman sawed a generous length of rope and braced himself to enter the three-flat on the corner of State and Pearson. It hadn't taken long to choose, and he was certain there were scores of others around that would have been suitable. He'd doubled back to the construction site at 700 North Michigan, a massive jumble of open ironwork and granite slabs that would be forever incomplete. There he'd picked two sturdy lengths of wood, carrying them on his shoulders before finally stopping in front of this forbidding three-story brick. His eyes swept the structure, noting that the basement, second- and third-floor windows were shut tight against the elements. The upper floors might be simple coincidence, but boards had been leaned over the basement windows and the first floor's destroyed picture window told another tale; Perlman shuddered as he imagined the family that must have cowered inside and their terror at hearing it shatter, then looking up to see—

He blinked and forced himself back to the present. Bad enough that ragged drapes fluttered in and out of the opening as though the building were breathing; now he was reliving by proxy the horror that had probably occurred there. He was breathing in fast, shallow gasps and he forced himself to slow down before he hyperventilated. He was not particularly brave and what he was about to do pushed beyond limits he hadn't known existed.

At the top of the stone steps, Perlman stopped and cut four generous lengths from the roll of duct tape, patching the sticky strips together so that they formed a square sheet—his first protection. Bile crept up his throat and his hands began to tremble as soon as he touched the knob; if it had been anything but the sticky tape in his hands he would have dropped it. Swallowing, he pushed through the unlocked door into the foyer.

It had once been an expensive building. There was a metal stop on the bottom of the entry and Perlman toed it into position to keep the door from closing; the door itself, inlaid with large panels of rich stained glass, threw the hall into colorful shadows. To his right was another open door beyond which he could see stairs leading to the upper floors; mild daylight filtered from the grimy windows on each landing, enough to discourage anything from hiding in the empty apartments. But the door on the left held his attention. Once inlaid with the same stained glass as the others, now it was impossible to tell if the window was even intact beneath the plywood stacked in front of it. When he moved the wood, he found the doorknob still in place though it was only a formality; gouged into the wood where a small lock had been were deep grooves. When Perlman touched the knob, the door swung open all too obligingly.

A heavy smell of dampness and decay saturated the air. Beneath the stench Perlman's senses detected something worse as he descended the stairs and tried to breathe through his nose. The hall's watery light carried only a few steps before he reached for the flashlight; its glow was little comfort in the deepening blackness. Nerves screaming, his leg jarred when the steps ended unexpectedly and he swung the flashlight in a jittery arc around the room to make sure he wasn't standing on top of something he wasn't yet prepared to meet. He was taking an incredible chance. He knew almost nothing about what vampires could or couldn't do, when they could do it—*nothing*. Perlman's survival these past months had been based on two principles: stay well hidden at night and stay out of dark places. For all he knew, the cursed things could rise during the day as long as the room was dark. Well, he'd soon find out.

He played the light around more slowly; the basement was smaller than he expected and the beam picked up everything from cardboard boxes and newspapers to a bicycle slowly corroding in the dank air. From his position it was easy to see across the room, where a set of weights had been scattered at the foot of a beat-up antique wardrobe whose wood was even blacker than the mildewy wall behind it, and Perlman's heart skipped. He'd been half-hoping not to find anything; then he could run safely back to the hospital and its white-walled security and firmly pledge to try again another day. He'd never been a procrastinator, but fear was doing odd things in his head and he looked longingly at the staircase with its faraway dribble of daylight before forcing himself to cross the floor, clearing a path from the stairs to the wardrobe.

The sounds he made as he pushed aside a bundle of magazines seemed as loud as a symphony, and he wondered if they could hear in their sleep. By the time he was standing within a few feet of the cabinet, he was shaking so badly he almost couldn't breathe; each step made the air in the basement thicker and so filled with evil that he didn't want it in his lungs anyway. The hair at the back of his neck, stubby from his awkward homemade haircuts, was standing so high he could have been moving through a field of static electricity. His hands, pale, slender, and defenseless—a surgeon's hands—shone in the backglow of the flashlight. Could he actually go through with this?

Clutching the tape and rope, he watched in absentminded horror as his other hand pulled open the wardrobe's door.

Thick, vile air spilled out. His heart pounded fiercely in his chest and at first he thought his blood pressure had escalated so dangerously that he'd lost his eyesight, because even with the flashlight he couldn't see anything inside the cabinet. Then he realized he was gazing at a filthy blanket nearly as black as the wardrobe's interior. Before his courage could flee, he yanked the blanket aside.

"Oh!" he whispered as he stared face-to-face with a child of about four years old. The boy's naked, dirty skin was a deep, emaciated gray, and twined on his sunken chest were sticklike fingers from which sharp, blackened nails curled. Unwittingly, Perlman's gaze met the vampire's; beneath bloodless, translucent lids, unholy brown eyes sparkled up at him.

Daddy? The sweet voice in his mind was that of an innocent preschooler. *Please hold me. I'm so coooold....* Behind Perlman's eyes formed a vision of this child as he had once been, and for an instant he imagined he'd found the boy alive, skin pink with health but shivering, brown eyes gazing at him trustingly. *Daddy ... please help me*, it said, and Perlman's heart nearly broke.

His body moved on its own and he began to bend, intending to pull the poor, tiny body into his warm arms. Beneath the pitiful cries swirling in his mind, Perlman

sensed a building eagerness that caused his pounding
pulse to stutter.

He stepped forward and reached—

Another step—

His right foot cracked into a twenty-pound weight lying just under the front of the wardrobe and he cried out
as sanity-bringing pain rocketed up his foot and ankle.
His face—which had been only a half foot from the
boy's—jerked up and away as his fingers fumbled with
the tape and slapped it over the creature's face. The agony climbing up his leg was an immense thing competing
with the voice that still rang in his head—a voice that
had gone from childish cajoling to fading screams of rage
as he leaned back against the wall and panted for breath.
When he realized that he'd almost become a human pac-
ifier for this miscreation's daytime nap, the sardines and
crackers he'd eaten earlier exploded from his throat in a
smelly, wet mess across the weights at his feet.

His leg almost buckled as he took a step and Perlman
wondered what damage he'd done to his foot. Moisture
trickled into his eyes and he swiped at it with the back
of his hand as he pulled out two of the garbage bags and
tucked one inside the other; grimacing, he leaned back
into the wardrobe and tugged the bags over the vampire's head and skeletonlike torso. As he worked the plastic around the frigid body, the voice tried to squirm into
his mind again and he purposely ground his foot into the
floor, hissing through his teeth as the pain cleared his
thoughts. Even with a busted foot it didn't take much to
lift the boy from the wardrobe and draw the other bags
around it from the feet up.

The child weighed little and normally Perlman could
have simply tossed him over a shoulder and gone on his
way. As he tied the plastic tightly around the boy he was
grateful that he'd brought the two-by-fours, though he'd
done so because he'd assumed his captive would be an
adult and considerably heavier. Now he placed a wood
piece at each side of the creature and ran the thick duct
tape around and around, twisting and circling until he
was certain the body wouldn't slide down and scrape
against the ground as he dragged it. With the extra

length of wood at one end, he could pull it down the street like a travois.

He was never so relieved to see daylight as when he finally hauled his burden down the porch steps of the three-flat. Each time the wood bumped from one riser to the next Perlman felt the vibration run up his arms and travel to his injured foot. His head ached, his stomach churned, and his foot throbbed, and to make matters worse, when he crossed the street and came out from beneath the tree shadows into the sun, the thing in the garbage bags began to try and wriggle free. With the amount of tape and rope wrapped around it, Perlman thought the boy could have undulated for a week and not gotten loose, but it was a spooky thing to witness and he tried to hobble faster and get the vampire back to the hospital as quickly as possible. The way it was writhing it seemed the sun's rays were going through the dark green plastic as though it were mesh. It had felt like hours inside but the sun, springtime bright and strong, had just reached its axis and Perlman relaxed, knowing he could still count on hours of daylight.

But he wondered what tonight would bring.

5

REVELATION 6:12
. . . and the moon became as blood.

Deborah Nole's teeth ached from being ground together for the last three hours, yet every time she tried to relax, her teeth started chattering; in the empty auditorium the sound was machine-gun loud.

Dammit! Why was she awake? Exhaustion usually made her sleep through the night, oblivious to her usual fear of the dark and the creatures that now owned it. Tonight her eyes were open uselessly in the blackness, lids stretched wide as if they could re-form into extra ears with which to search the cavernous room for sounds. She could detect nothing, and she was pretty good at it. More than *pretty* good—she'd managed to stay alive when countless others hadn't. But the heavy drapes that hung between her cot and the back wall could be a double-edged benefit: while her own sounds were muffled from the hundreds of empty seats surrounding the stage, the stealthy steps of an intruder would likewise be easy to hide. What time was it? Frozen in the same position for so long her arms had gone numb, Deb was afraid to even finger the light on her wristwatch and she could no longer feel the reassuring pressure of the twelve-gauge next to her. For all she knew the shotgun was balanced on the edge of the cot and would clatter to the floor if she reached for it.

How long? This was driving her insane; she had to know what time—wait! Her breath hitched at an imagined sound and the muscles of her arm unlocked automatically as her hand slid down and closed around the stock of the Winchester. Her stomach tightened, then acknowledged the fullness of her bladder, a sure sign that she'd made it to another dawn.

Her lungs emptied in relief and she grasped the gun and sat up, still shaking as she groped for the matches and oil lamp; a few seconds and a warm, welcome glow lit the backstage alcove. She took the lamp and climbed the carpeted steps around the banisters, caution returning at the first entrance as she pushed the bar down and felt the lock release. As she eased out of the Arthur Rubloff Auditorium, weak daylight filtered down the stairs from the dining room on the second floor. The building's noises had still terrified her a year ago, but eventually Deb had learned to recognize the daily creaks and groans as the sun brought the temperature up and caused the old mortar and stone to expand. But Deb listened for other noises, such as the stealthy steps of someone who'd managed a way inside. Although she daydreamed about it often, she really didn't know what she'd do if that ever happened, and it had been six months ago in October since she'd last seen a living person outside. His name, he'd said, was John, and he was as ragged and thin as they came. She'd greeted him eagerly and together they'd gathered another cot and blankets, more food and fresh clothes. After months of cowering alone, this man was a godsend of potential security.

Back then she'd been sleeping in the Morton Lecture Hall, yet in spite of her loneliness she was no fool; her 9mm pistol had stayed hidden in the deep pockets of her jacket, and John hadn't known about the sawed-off shotgun until she'd blown half his chest away when she caught him undoing the locks on the basement hall's entrance after he'd thought her asleep. Only the worst type of human could walk the night hours and she knew he would have returned in a few hours—if that long—and even her miniature arsenal wouldn't have stopped the creatures he would've brought with him. She'd spent the remainder of that night sitting in the dark and listening to the blood drip from John's cooling body. How long had he known about her? Long enough to alert others to her refuge before she'd met him? Maybe blood creatures already crawled through the rooms above. Combined with her terror was the guilt of having taken the life of an-

other human; as wretched as John had been, killing him
seemed almost unforgivable when so few *real* people still
walked this earth.

Almost.

In the morning she had wrapped the body in a sheet
and dragged it out, intending to throw it in the lake. Despite her sturdy build, the distance had proved too much
and she'd settled for hoisting it over the concrete barrier
on Monroe and dropping it to the railroad tracks forty
feet below. Guilty conscience or not, the corpse made a
satisfying thud as it hit; if there were others like him, she
hoped they'd see the justice in his death. She'd cleaned
up the mess and locked the hall permanently from the
inside; perhaps the man's ghost would be trapped there,
too.

A quick examination now showed her the entrances
were unscathed, and she finally felt safe enough to return
to the auditorium and use the Port-o-Potty. As she
changed from one heavy cotton jumpsuit to another, an
ache spread through her stomach and she flinched. She'd
have to go to the library soon and read up on ulcers; the
mirror showed the same clear blue eyes and curly black
hair spilling down her shoulders, but the growing pain in
her gut mocked her healthy appearance.

Deb pocketed her keys and let herself out the Michigan Avenue doors, testing them to make sure the latches
caught. A year ago she would've never guessed locks
would be such an important part of her life. Standing on
steps leading down to an empty world in the morning
was nearly as frightening as the coming of each dusk. She
had worked in the Art Institute since graduating from
college and had seen it overrun with employees and
visitors—maybe that was why she had chosen to live
here; good memories, the images of a thousand people
and times captured on canvas, in photographs, bronze,
and marble. Outside, nothing moved for as far as she
could see: no people, no cars—not even a single squirrel,
once so common along the boulevard and in Grant Park.
Only the birds remained; safe in their ability to fly, God
alone knew where they roosted. She wondered longingly
if the animals in the rural areas had fared better.

If she closed her eyes and concentrated, she could still remember mornings at her parents' house not so long ago, still hear her little sister Janet calling her to *Get out of bed, Mama's got breakfast on the table!* Dad's laughter booming out of the kitchen at some wisecrack made by seventeen-year-old Mark. And Mom . . .

The familiar loneliness settled heavily around her, amplified in silence broken only by the occasional twittering of an unseen sparrow. She hoped the sparrows and pigeons would become more plentiful as spring progressed, but for now most probably still huddled high atop the skyscrapers. A few more weeks and maybe the silence wouldn't be so damned . . .

loud.

6

REVELATION 3:2
Be watchful, and strengthen the things which remain. . . .

"What's he doing?"

The man, his white hair the only testimony of age, shrugged as they looked to the sidewalk from a window high in Water Tower Place. He could think of no logical response as the teenager pressed one cheek against the window in an effort to see better.

"Should I go down?" C.J.'s eyes, usually so hard and suspicious in his unlined face, brightened with the prospect of contact with someone new. Although he smiled to himself, Buddy McDole's expression remained outwardly bland as he watched the thin man below struggle with a small stretcher on which he had obviously tied a vampire. Even from here McDole could see the plasticlike covering ripple as the sleeping creature instinctively tried to escape the sunlight. But the man had done his task well; the vampire wasn't going anywhere—at least not until tonight.

The guy was limping badly and McDole's first impulse was to send someone down to help. They'd certainly seen him enough—many times before the sentries had alerted McDole to the knocking at the main doors this morning. It had been a point in his favor that the stranger hadn't broken in, and if it weren't for one nagging question, McDole might have indeed sent C.J. to greet him—probably scaring the shit out of him in the process.

But . . .

What the hell was he doing with a vampire?

7

REVELATION 3:10
I will keep thee from the hour ...
of them that dwell upon the earth.

"Up and at 'em, Beau," Louise told the little dog. "Time to move out." Beauregard's ears perked, though the cataract-filmed eyes never wavered. She scratched the tiny graying head, wondering how much he really heard.

This morning's hotel was the top apartment of a four-story walk-up in East Rogers Park in the fancier section along Sheridan Road just north of the park, not far from where she'd been a student at Senn High School. New sunlight blazed across its front room through the triple picture windows; the chilly air was warming and old Beau crawled from her lap and stretched unsteadily, working the stiffness from his pencil-thin legs. Copying him, Louise crossed her arms and massaged the night tension from her shoulders, then stared out the windows at the Lake Michigan shoreline and the calm, deep waters. Two miles south there would still be ice chunks bobbing in the colder waters of Montrose and Belmont Harbors, but if the weather stayed warm, the ice would disappear in another two days ... she smiled. Warm weather at last! More important than that: shorter nights, longer days. More hours in which to ... what? Louise shook her head and wandered back to the bedroom to gather her sleeping gear from the dusty bed. It would take another twenty minutes to pack up and haul the furniture away from the front door so they could leave.

Breakfast was a can of peaches for her and a packet of burgerlike dog food for Beau. It wasn't until she automatically carried their trash to the kitchen that she realized they'd shared the night's hideaway with a corpse.

The peaches tried to come up but Louise locked her throat until the urge passed, then opened her clenched fist and dropped the garbage in the wastebasket. The dried-out body, curled in a fetal position, was crammed into the space between the refrigerator and stove by the back wall. Either the eyeballs and lids had rotted away or cockroaches—those indestructible insects—had feasted before moving on to a fresher kill. It was impossible to tell what had killed the person or whether it had been a man or woman—something Louise didn't care to know anyway. What counted was that they'd been lucky: the corpse had *stayed* a corpse.

Her scalp tightened at the enormity of her carelessness—in her haste to find shelter, she'd barricaded herself and Beau in an apartment she hadn't checked thoroughly, only glancing hurriedly through the rooms before dusk. Her luck had held—*this time*. Being trapped with a bloodsucker was *unthinkable*. How could she have done this?

Her legs carried her back to the bright front room before they began shaking. When she sank onto a once-plush leather sofa, Beau tilted his grizzled face toward her, then padded across the carpeting until he bumped her ankle, where he curled up with a contented snuffle. But even the comforting sunlight couldn't overthrow the knowledge of the cadaver one room away. The kitchen, she now realized, had no windows. She had stupidly not seen the body to begin with; it was even more unlikely she would have noticed it had it been intentionally covered by something to block out the sunlight, and she was alive this morning only by the wildest of odds—*Jesus!* She and Beau had developed a pattern this last year: wake, eat, and wander, always looking for better things to eat and better places to sleep. They stayed put only during the heavy snows when footprints made travel impossible. In the small buildings they frequented, it could be easy for the vampires to pinpoint the prolonged presence of warm flesh, so they moved on. And on. Easing into a comfortable routine with the coming of spring's longer hours and the thinning vampire population, Louise had pushed the travel time to the limit the last couple of weeks, stretching each day as far as she could.

Then . . . last night. How many other bodies hadn't she noticed over the last month?

She stared moodily at her roughened hands. Long-fingered, pianist's hands, her grandmother had always said. What would the old woman say now? These thin fingers had sewn canvas sleeping bags, hammered ten-penny nails and learned to load a rifle, even once used an ax to sever a night creature's head—back, she thought in disgust, in the days when she'd checked their sleeping quarters more carefully. Perhaps the constant running had become too much and she had developed an uncon-scious death wish . . . still, she'd strangle the dog and put a bullet through her own head before she'd become food for one of *them*.

Her gaze traveled to the bony wrist beneath her baggy sweatshirt. Maybe she and Beau just needed a rest, some-where safe to call home for a couple of months. Or . . . why not? A home to safeguard over the summer and hiber-nate in during winter, when the frigid temperatures and snow— the earth's tattling white carpet—left no alterna-tive but seclusion. A place in which to fatten up and where poor old Beauregard wouldn't have to bump into different furniture every night. But where? Louise rose jerkily and went back to the picture windows. From there, it was easy to see the city sprawling to the south through the glass, the hundreds of trees in Lincoln Park still bare of the season's coming growth. With each block the buildings grew, from small brownstone flats to the bigger buildings holding twenty-four, then forty-eight apartments, until the tall condominium complexes crowded along the curve of the Drive. Her eyes followed the sweep around the lake, then stopped on the far-off cluster of skyscrapers fringing downtown. Her brow fur-rowed.

Downtown. . . . Maybe the place she needed was in one of those huge office buildings, in some lawyer's suite with a thousand windows to let in the light, a newer one where the sealed glass was practically unbreakable. She and Beau could sleep in the center at night, where they couldn't be seen if one of those creatures crawled up the side of the building—or could they even climb that high?

The possibilities seemed suddenly endless: walls of windows; up as high and safe as she wanted. There were even sporting-goods stores in the north loop, which meant easy access to supplies and warm gear. She looked again at her grimy, improbable survivalist's fingers, then back at the skyscrapers sitting silent sentinel over the city. Each past month had been a bleak little eternity; now, hope finally flared. If she, of all people—seventeen-year-old Louise Dorsett and a feeble dog almost as old as she was—had lived, maybe others had, too.

Nothing was impossible, right?

God knew that was certainly true.

8

●•●●•●●•●

REVELATION 2:28
And I will give him the morning star.

●●•●●

At noon Nicholson found the white dress he thought the
woman had been wearing. After donning warmer clothes
and locking up, he'd spent all morning searching for her;
he hadn't seen people for months, and the few he'd
glimpsed in the fall had disappeared during winter's long
grip on the city. He had spotted no one since the snow
melted; if they hadn't frozen, no doubt they'd become
vampires. The number of vampires had dropped, too; the
cold made the weaker ones sluggish, and dawn often
caught a bloodsucker that had stupidly wandered too far
from safety. Every so often Nicholson found their smelly,
liquefying remains.

But the woman was another matter. He wanted desperately to find her—to *talk* to her, dammit! Now that he
knew she existed, the thought of being alone yet another
day was unbearable. Fascinated, he examined the dress
lying on the sidewalk at Lake and LaSalle, four blocks
northwest of the attack. There was no blood on it. He
touched the charred collar curiously, then sniffed it.
When he'd been twelve, he and a few buddies had
picked through the remains of a burned-out apartment
building, nosing around the crumbling ruin of wood and
ashes, furniture and rags. The cindery smell of this collar
brought the memory back clearly. Had she been wearing
it when it burned? The dress was a tiny thing and he was
still amazed that a woman with her *own* blood flowing in
her veins, not blood stolen from another at the expense
of a life, had worn it just today. He draped the garment
over his shoulder and glanced around; no sign of her
now. Maybe she was hurt and had gone back to wherever
her home was. The enormity of downtown suddenly

loomed; like himself, if the woman didn't want to be
found, she never would be. He could search for . . . forever, really—even if she wasn't *trying* to hide. Besides
that, what could he do? Take out an ad in the personals?
How about a big sign on the sidewalk? His lips pulled
into a small, bitter smile. That was good; for starters it
could say *Vampires: This Way to Dinner!*

Dejected, he headed back toward the Daley Center
and eyed the buildings towering above the empty streets;
the machete hanging from his belt made a dull, lonely-
sounding slap against his leg with each step. It occurred
to him that in the vastness that was downtown there
could be ten, twenty, or more people sequestered away at
night like him, foraging for supplies during the day and
purposely avoiding contact with others out of paranoia.
There were literally hundreds of buildings within walking distance of the Daley Center; if only a fraction had
people holed up inside . . . an entire *community*! Possibilities whirled again and he doggedly tried to cap them.
Time enough for grandiose plans; a more intelligent start
would be to pay more attention to his surroundings instead of wandering around in this fog of self-pity. Maybe
he just might find some of these people he was actually
beginning to believe existed.

Nicholson was so accustomed to solitude that he never
really expected to find anyone. As the hours passed, he
grabbed a flashlight and weak batteries from Woolworth's
and went to Marshall Field's to find something out of the
ordinary to eat. Nicholson's tastes were pretty conven-
tional and he existed on whatever he found in the restaurants close to the Center; his groceries had initially come
from the basement cafeteria of the Daley Center, which
he had investigated after welding shut the doors that led
to the subway and the Bank of Tokyo Building. The cafeteria had turned up items like Minute Rice and jars of
Cheez Whiz, a quick fix on his small campstove and a
feast compared to his early diet of Spam and sardines. In
time he'd discovered the gourmet section on the seventh
floor of Field's, and he went there now, climbing the
stilled escalators effortlessly on legs conditioned from

endless trips up the Daley Center stairs. This morning Nicholson had eaten dry cereal chased with bottled water—he couldn't stand powdered milk—but here he could browse among shelves stacked with oddities. He fetched a bag from behind the counter and let his beam pick out the easy-to-cook delicacies: saffron pasta, canned white clam sauce, dried romano cheese, cans of Pepperidge Farm soup. He studied a can of bacon-lettuce-and-tomato-flavored soup doubtfully. *Canned lettuce?* His mind supplied a picture of crisp green leaves and his mouth watered; he tossed the can in his bag.

As he added a box of melbas and reached for a jar of currant preserves, a hushed noise made him freeze. He snapped off the flashlight by reflex; how comfortable he'd been within that small circle of radiance! Cursing the sudden dimness, Nicholson soundlessly replaced the jar as his eyes struggled to adjust. Straining to hear, he worked the machete loose, bent his knees, and crab-walked to the front of the aisle, where a generous swath of daylight bled around the doorway from the windows above the abandoned fish-fry section. Weapon in hand, he peered into a well-lit dining room crowded with tables. He could easily slip down the escalator, and if anyone moved, he could—

What am I doing? Nicholson exhaled and tried to relax his grip on the machete. The noise hadn't come again; it was probably nothing—the building shifting, a bird flying in through a broken windowpane. More importantly, if someone *was* there, he wanted to *meet* them, not leave.

Didn't he?

"Hello?" The hoarse greeting escaped his mouth before he could change his mind, sounding like a huge, living thing as it echoed through the dining room. He cleared his throat and tried again, voice wobbling. "Is anyone there?" *Come out with your hands up!* he thought a little hysterically. He opened his mouth to chuckle, then a figure darted past and fled down the escalator.

"Wait! Please!" He damned his inattention as he jumped to his feet and followed, adrenaline shooting his pulse into a frantic drumbeat. The escalator vibrated as he took the steps three at a time, slowly gaining, the shadows changing wildly from floor to floor as Nicholson slowly closed the distance on a person almost as tall as himself. "Why are you running? Come *back!*" His heart sank as the figure jumped the last six steps to the first floor; in another two seconds there was a clang as one of the doors was yanked open—an entrance Nicholson had never tried—and the person bolted into the loading alley that divided the building's ground level. Nicholson charged through the doors, glimpsed someone turning the corner onto Randolph, and grinned. His leg muscles bunched powerfully as he stretched to the full stride that had won him ribbons in high school, and it only took a quarter of a block to see it was a dark-haired woman.

He was so surprised he nearly lost his footing. Jesus— had his wild thoughts been correct after all? Had he spent the winter burrowed into that huge building when he could have been with other people? Excitement flooded his bloodstream and his legs worked harder; she'd have to pull a miracle to get away now.

Thirty feet ahead she slewed around the corner onto Wabash and Nicholson sprinted after her, his faster momentum carrying him into the turn on a wider angle. He faltered, confused, when he realized the sidewalk was empty.

"Hey."

Nicholson whirled at the feminine voice coming from one of the Wabash Avenue entrances. He smiled and stepped forward, then jerked backward as he saw a dull splash of silver and realized the machete he still clutched was useless against the pistol aimed at his chest. Her tone was filled with acid.

"Freeze, you son of a bitch, or I'll blow you all the way to the lake."

9

REVELATION 13:11
And I beheld another beast coming up out of the earth....

We need transportation.

At midmorning Louise and Beau were still in Rogers Park, and she finally realized foot travel downtown would take all day and leave little time to find a place for the night. She checked her watch. No more mistakes—the sun would set at about six and she intended to be safely cloistered by then, even if only temporarily. Holding Beau in the crook of her arm, she shifted her backpack and looked around. There were plenty of parked cars and people occasionally hid keys under the mats; or Western Avenue, with its stretch of auto dealerships, was fourteen blocks to her right. In a couple of hours she and Beau could be cruising in a Thunderbird, or maybe a Park Avenue.

She discarded the idea quickly. Closer to downtown it would likely become a game of motorized checkers as she tried to negotiate dozens of abandoned autos. They might end up on a bridge leading into the Loop and find it so thoroughly blocked that she'd have to dump the car and hunt for a new one, look for keys, worry about fuel— forget it.

A bicycle? Louise stopped thoughtfully in front of a small shop advertising Schwinns and eyed the dusty window display. She could get one with a basket so Beau wouldn't have to ride inside her jacket during the twelve- or thirteen-mile trip. When she tried the knob, the door pushed open without resistance. The shop was in an ornate, turn-of-the-century building, and as she stepped inside Louise realized uneasily that it was deep and dark. The daylight struggling through the twisted display of detached wheels, handlebars, and bikes extended only

about twenty feet and was weakened further by the
grime-encrusted window; the shadows beyond deepened
steadily to black, and she'd learned to avoid lightless
places even during the daytime. Louise prudently decided to make her selection from the stock closer to the
window.

Nothing she saw had a basket, but Louise put Beau on
the floor so she could inspect a gold Schwinn twelve-
speed with a jumble of gears and derailleurs at the back
chain. Hefting it, she found it heavier than expected—
she wasn't much of a cyclist but she knew that two hours
on this along bumpy streets and she'd be worn out. Unsure of his surroundings, Beau trembled and rubbed
against her ankles for security; she used the toe of her
shoe to push him gently aside as she set the Schwinn
back in place. Next to it was a metallic blue one with the
name *Nishiki* stenciled on the crossbar, a bike she
guessed weighed only fourteen or fifteen pounds—not
bad.

Beau tangled around her ankles again as she swung
the frame up and down a few times, and Louise opened
her mouth to scold him when she realized she could feel
him shaking all the way up to her thigh. She glanced
down in surprise and saw the dog staring toward the
back of the store.

Beau growled softly. In the stillness the sound was
stunningly loud.

Equally shocking was the quick, whispering noise of
shifting from the pitch-black rear of the store.

Her head snapped up as an alarm shrieked in her
brain. The Nishiki still suspended from her hands,
Louise stood paralyzed as the sound, a gentle slithering,
came again. Like something *crawling*. Her elbows unlocked and Louise soundlessly lowered the bike, then
bent and snatched up the dog without taking her eyes
from the rear of the room. Blood pounded furiously in
her temples, each fear-drenched pulse catapulting
through her body in time with the tension running
through Beau. He growled again.

"*Shhhh!*" she hissed. Her gaze flicked back to the ancient wooden door. Its spring had pulled it shut behind

them and now she recalled hearing the click of the latch
as it had closed. It was stupid not to have propped it;
now she'd have to press the old-fashioned thumb plate
and pull open the door. If something sprang at them in
the meantime—

There was a muffled *thump* as something fell to the
floor.

No more time to fuck around, Louise thought clearly.
Get the hell out of here NOW!

She bolted, hands fumbling between a frantically
squirming Beau and the door handle. For a sickening instant it stuck and Louise thought they were trapped, picturing with sudden, brutal clarity a hideously decayed
beast leaping onto her back and tearing at her throat as
she beat at the door glass. Then she heard a rattle as the
antique mechanism lifted and she yanked on the door so
hard it slammed against the inside wall; she leapt
through before its rebound and sprawled on the sidewalk, twisting sideways to avoid crushing Beau. Clutching the dog, she scrambled backward on her butt as the
door crashed shut.

Her heart lurched and she heard herself moan as
something inside pummeled the door, shattering its old
window. A hand, clawed and shriveled, swiped from the
jagged opening that had been the beveled glass pane, but
the deep recesses of the doorway couldn't block the sun's
rays and the creature screeched as light crossed its fingers and the tips split and sizzled. By the time Louise
had sucked in her breath for a scream, the monster had
gone, retreating to its hiding place at the rear of the
building.

Gasping, Louise pulled herself up and hugged Beau
furiously. As he licked her face and wagged his stubby little tail, she staggered along Clark Street, putting distance
between her and that gaping doorway while her heartbeat calmed and her breathing slowed to a soft wheeze.
A few blocks away she collapsed onto a bus stop bench;
farther north, the bicycle shop's sign swung mockingly in
the slight breeze.

She was jolted almost senseless. Unearthing a bloodsucker was always a chance in a dark building housing a

back room and this building's age and mustiness had masked the usual stench, but it had always been safe as long as the totally dark areas were avoided. It was incomprehensible that the creature's hunger was so great it would sleepwalk and risk the sunlight in an attempt to attack. If it had been cloudy, would the loathsome thing have followed her right onto the sidewalk? No, of course not—the sun would have destroyed it.

Wouldn't it?

Her legs were still pudding but she finally forced herself to stand. Perhaps she was too eager to get all the way downtown today. This morning had already drained her, and riding a bike for miles would exhaust her and still leave the task of finding a safe place to spend the night. It might be better to work toward the Loop gradually; at a couple of miles each day they could walk there in a week—

Vespa—The Scooter of Steel!

Her eyes widened as the silver lettering on the display window they were passing abruptly registered. Turning back to the glass, Louise could see a well-lit showroom filled with brightly colored motor scooters, and she ruffled Beau's ears and grinned. "Bingo!' she told him. "I should've thought of this months ago! Why walk when we can ride?" His tongue lolled and he yipped at Louise's voice; already he seemed to have recovered from the cycle-shop incident.

The door was firmly locked and she eyed the huge windows doubtfully. Breaking one would be stupid—a scooter wouldn't roll three feet before getting a flat. A larger exit would probably be through the service area at the unlit rear, but she didn't want to chance it. So she'd have to try and jimmy the glass door—*if* it wasn't a deadbolt. Louise found a crowbar in the open garage of a gas station a block away; as she bent to retrieve it, Beau stiffened in her arms and her eyes stopped on a small, filthy door in the far corner—the washroom. Closed tightly; she could easily guess its occupant. She darted from the garage before there could be a repeat of this morning.

Back at the dealership, the lock held stubbornly and she realized that it was either smash the glass or scrap the notion of taking a scooter. The thought of giving up after all this effort pissed her off, and instead she dug Beau's leash from the backpack and tied him back at the bench, then returned and beat furiously at the door with the crowbar until it shattered. Inside, she rummaged through the desks and turned up a box of ignition keys, each labeled in the dealer's code. Still, the sun wasn't at its peak, so she had plenty of time to find a key for one of these things, roll it out, and learn how to drive it. Louise scanned the rows and chose a scooter that was bright yellow.

She'd never been particularly patient, and Louise was gritting her teeth by the time she finally found the right key. The little yellow machine didn't have a fuel gauge, but unscrewing the gas tank cap showed her it was full. Getting more meant siphoning but she wasn't looking for extended transportation, just a way to get downtown. She used a desk blotter like a shovel to clear the broken glass before rolling the Vespa outside. Although the seat was cushioned and fit her rump comfortably, it was heavier than anticipated and Louise realized that this was not at all the glorified bicycle she'd believed. It was a *machine*, with a suspension system and brakes, and it was *fast*, provided the battery was still charged enough to turn over the engine. If she could get it running and head back to Lake Shore Drive, they might be downtown in half an hour.

Everything was marked: front and rear brakes, headlight, an accelerator much like a snowmobile's, with which she had at least some experience. She took a nervous breath, twisted the accelerator a few times, turned the ignition key to ON and pulled the starter cord.

Eighteen tries later she was ready to give up when a loud whine spliced the air on her last yank. The noise bounced off the buildings then subsided to a jarring buzz that made her head ring, and she resisted the urge to clap her hands to her ears, afraid the motor would die if she let up on the gas. She grinned as she saw Beau wriggling excitedly next to the bench. When Louise was sure the Vespa's idle was steady, she untied Beau and let him sniff the scooter and sneeze a few times. She would have to zip him inside her heavy jacket; he weighed only six pounds and she hoped her warmth would be enough to keep him from getting a chill. The first blocks were choppy; while she got used to the Vespa, Beau cowered inside her coat as everything around him moved at an almost-forgotten speed, but by the time they putted up Hollywood Avenue to its eight-lane spread into Lake Shore Drive, the ride was smooth and holding at about twenty miles an hour. They were finally on their way.

The cool air became cold as it whipped the hair away from Louise's eyes and plastered it against her skull. She could feel Beau burrowing deeper for warmth, and although her face and hands quickly lost heat, her jacketed torso stayed comfortable. Already the scooter was closing the distance on the huge buildings that had seemed so far away.

"*Yeah!*" she yelled, her pulse hammering with excitement. The wind snatched her voice and tossed it away. "We're rolling now!" The buildings at their right grew larger with each passing block, the flats and apartment buildings giving way to the encroaching condominium complexes and skyscrapers.

And the Vespa carried them toward the heart of the city.

10

REVELATION 2:13
I know . . . where thou dwellest . . .
even in those days.

•••

"Place is turning into a regular city, ain't it?" C.J. grinned
crookedly at Buddy McDole as they stood again at the
window overlooking Michigan Avenue. "Must be the
warm weather bringing 'em out, like the birds." C.J. had
been outside earlier, and for the first time this year he'd
heard the sparrows twittering wildly, as though today was
the last day such racket was possible—which could always
be true. Each morning that he didn't wake up dead—
literally—surprised him. Now this woman rode boldly
along Michigan Avenue on a sick-sounding motor scooter.
C.J. studied her, puzzled; either she had only one huge tit
or there was something stuffed into the front of her jacket.

McDole, as usual, kept his thoughts to himself as he
watched the scooter's exhaust send puffs of white into the
air, something the older man hadn't seen in quite a while.
Another survivor, he thought, warm weather bringing
them out, like the boy had said. He guessed spring would
reveal a lot of people they hadn't discovered, and more of
the ones they had—like that fellow this morning. While
he'd known the man stayed at Northwestern, C.J. had sent
Tala, a whip-thin eleven-year-old who ran like a gazelle, to
follow in case the guy changed his habits; thirty minutes
later she'd returned and reported the man had taken his
prisoner into the hospital through a rear entrance.

McDole was impressed and worried at the same time.
Although folks often went out alone, they *never* hunted
in groups of less than three because of the danger of getting mesmerized, yet this guy had found and captured a
vampire alone. But why bring it back instead of kill it?
McDole hadn't seen any weapons; it was pure-d amazing

that someone would go vampire hunting with no protection. Maybe the man had survived so far by blind luck; if that was the case, he was in for a monumental surprise at nightfall.

He turned his attention back to the woman below. There was no way to follow without being seen or heard. A lone woman who had survived the winter *and* the vampires was special, all right. Their group was mostly tough outdoorsmen and a sprinkling of once-whitecollars with more than average common sense. Two of the seven women in the group were over fifty, elderly in this new and dangerous age. With the exception of Tala, the others were older than C.J.'s seventeen and had no interest in him. The lithe quickness of the woman on the scooter hinted she was quite young and no doubt C.J.'d picked up on that.

But right now it was past midafternoon and he had other things to worry about. One of the women, Evelyn, was pregnant, and coming close to her time. McDole could think of no good reason for a healthy-looking man to hide in a hospital unless he was a doctor, and it was time they found out.

"I want you to go out," McDole said.

The teen brightened and his eyes flicked toward the receding scooter. "After her?"

"To Northwestern. Take Calie with you." C.J. raised his eyebrows and McDole nodded. "Find the guy we saw this morning, find out if he's really a doctor and what he's doing with that vampire. Go with Calie's instincts as far as telling him about us."

"But what about that woman?"

"A doctor's more important right now. If she's made it this far on her own, she'll last one more night. You can look for her tomorrow."

"Shit. She'll be long gone by then." The boy folded his arms sullenly, then shrugged, his brief rebellion already faded. "Never catch her now, anyway. I'll go find Calie."

The hair along his forearms prickled and McDole knew Calie was there before she spoke in his ear. "Hi, boss." Her breath smelled like Juicy Fruit.

He frowned at her greeting, but her grin never wavered and he finally smiled. Calie was odd, all right; he tended to think of her as a girl, but in reality she was over thirty and endowed with a strange sixth sense that could judge a person's trustworthiness inside of five minutes. Beneath short brown hair, her friendly, pixielike face was the smiling equivalent of a professional poker player's, and she brushed her teeth more than anybody McDole had ever known—probably to counteract the constant chewing gum. The woman had the sweet, innocent eyes of a teenage receptionist, and it had been Calie, not him, who had formed the first tentative alliances that had developed into this small underground, offering comfort and drawing the shell-shocked and sometimes-unpredictable survivors like C.J. together one by one, searching out their hiding places in the early months with an instinct no night creature would ever possess. Her implacable calm and inexhaustible strength had buoyed them all through some of the darkest, most unimaginable times . . .

Yet she insisted on calling *him* boss.

C.J. waited by the stairwell door with a crossbow under his arm as Calie pulled on a heavy denim jacket. "What're we doing?" she asked.

"We've been watching a man living at Northwestern," McDole told her. "I figure he might be a doctor, something we really need with Evelyn's baby about to drop. I want you guys to get in there and talk to him, see what he's all about."

"No problem," she said. She glanced at C.J. as she zipped up and her eyes narrowed. "What else?"

"He took a vampire back to the hospital with him this morning," said McDole. "We want to know why."

"A vampire?" Calie said wonderingly. "That's different."

"He may not realize what he's getting into. He might need help tonight—*if* he can be trusted."

"I'll find out," she said. Before McDole could reply, their footsteps echoed down the stairway. Calie's sixth sense would locate the man easily, but what if *he* didn't trust *them*? He might refuse their help, or even run.

McDole went back to the window and peered out. A

few wispy clouds floated in from the west, but farther out he could see a heavier accumulation. The cloud cover would cause an early dusk and slip their friend at Northwestern into unexpected danger.

"This is where he goes in." C.J. indicated a locked metal door in an alley behind the hospital. "If we break it down, it'll leave him open to an attack tonight."

Calie looked around calmly. "We'll find another way, then. It's a big building; there's bound to be a side door that we can nail shut again."

"What about the windows?"

"Probably locked," she answered. "Come on."

They circled the building silently and after a few minutes Calie relaxed and let her attention wander as C.J. carefully searched. Eventually he picked up a stick and poked behind a dumpster. "Here," he said suddenly. Grunting, he rolled the dumpster aside to reveal a wire-covered window at ground level. He rattled the covering experimentally. "It's loose enough for me to get at the screws."

"I know," Calie said from behind him. Her eyes were big and soft and brown, like a placid doe's, and C.J. stared for a second then dragged his gaze away. His skin crawled a little, but it wasn't the nasty feeling he got when he found a bloodsucker; instead, it was the delicious sensation of having experienced something *magical*, like déjà vu. He pulled a screwdriver from one pocket and attacked the metal frame; the first few screws were awkward, then the work went faster. Behind the metal covering, the dusty window was still locked.

Calie nodded at C.J.'s worried glance. "Break it— there's no other way in. We'll board it up and reinstall the cover later. With the dumpster in place, it won't look any different." She held out her hand and C.J. realized she'd picked up a brick even before he'd gotten the last screws loose. "Use this."

C.J. took the brick and bounced it in his hand a few times, feeling like a vandal. He could feel her staring at him again and he tossed the brick through the window just to give her something else on which to focus her at-

tention; the glass cracked and fell inward with a muted
tinkling. He kicked the loose pieces away from the window's edge, then squatted and felt around the sill until
he found the lock. A few careful maneuvers and they
stood inside. They were in an accounting office, surrounded by rows of desks like those C.J. had once seen
in the traffic court office when he'd gone to pay a speed-
ing ticket. Thick dust shrouded the furniture and the
dark computer screens, making everything, even the paper strewn at each station, a solid, dull gray. Each desk
was a portrait of its vanished owner; the one closest to
the window was army-neat but for the shards of glass
that had left skittering impressions in the grime across its
top. Across from it was another whose surface was lost in
untidy documents and jumbled office supplies, in the
middle of which perched a framed photograph showing a
bride and groom. The smiling woman looked a little like
Calie.

"Come on, C.J." She said the words softly, but he still
jumped. "Let's go find our man."

"Okay," he whispered, then cleared his throat and tried
for a normal voice. "Lead on." She stepped around him
and he followed her to the door and into the hallway. Although they were in a first-level basement, it wasn't as
dark as expected; faint light spilled onto the pale linoleum from doorways on each side down to a stairway at
the far end. She turned left without hesitating, as though
she knew exactly where to look.

C.J. figured she probably did.

Ten more minutes of mazelike corridors and stairs and
Calie raised a finger to her lips, then pointed to a left-
hand door in a dead-end hall. C.J. had tracked their
course and they were in a nearly pitch-dark branch of
the fourth floor; all the doors here were closed except the
one Calie was indicating, and the only light from behind
came from a window made of thick glass blocks in the
stairwell. They could hear someone moving around, and
C.J. was relieved to see that at least they would confront
the man in a well-lit room. On the other hand, the guy
had stupidly bottled himself into a potential trap.

He and Calie eased silently into the room. The guy's

back was turned and he didn't hear them; C.J. was so surprised that the fellow had lived this long he let a reckless, caustic *"Knock, knock!"* pop from his mouth around a big, shit-ass grin.

The guy jerked and spun, eyes bulging with shock.

"Hi, Doc," Calie said matter-of-factly. Then her gaze dropped and she gasped.

The doctor had slashed his wrist.

11

●■•■■•■■•■■

REVELATION 13:4
And he worshiped the beast, saying . . .
Who is able to make war with him?

■■•■■

"Chow time!" Howard Siebold bellowed. "Hot food today!" Pushing a battered grocery cart that canted to the
left, he shuffled down the corridor at a little after eleven.
It would've been a helluva lot easier just to toss them
boxes of dry cereal at six A.M. and be done with it, but for
some reason the dweebs wouldn't eat in the dark. Since
the Mistress got pissed if they didn't get fed, Howard had
to screw up the best part of his day by cooking, and now
he paused by each small room and slopped an army-style
helping of congealed, steaming rice into a large paper
cup. He'd been feeling creative today and had tossed a
couple of envelopes of beef flavoring into the pot; he
thought it tasted pretty good and these worms were
damned lucky to get a meal that had taken two cans of
Sterno to cook. He filled another cup with heavily sug-
ared grape Kool-Aid and dropped a handful of saltines
atop the rice. He figured that ought to cover everything:
calories, starch, and protein. The Kool-Aid even had vita-
min C.

The woman he'd beaten this morning cringed when
she saw him and cowered against the wall. Howard
chuckled when he saw the nasty red welts from his belt
stippling her skin, some already darkening to bruises. He
liked to see them like that, spirit broken and bowing to
him. Two years ago it had been him sniveling before people in command, asshole businessmen in leather chairs
and corner offices—

*("Howard, I generally avoid making suggestions re-
garding personal hygiene, but I'm afraid if you want to
continue employment, it will be necessary for you to . . .*

*shall we say, trim down. Unfortunately, you don't present
the professional image we need to maintain.")*

—handing down orders like they were God and sticking polished noses into his private life. And where were
they now? Dead, if they were lucky; if not, they were
probably undead and starving, and that suited Howard
just fine. Better, in fact.

His smile faded as the woman at his feet ignored the
food and curled into a ball. Her back was a mass of colors
and he wondered if her contempt had goaded him too
far. It wouldn't hurt if she didn't eat for a day or two—
most didn't—but Rita . . .

He shrugged and pushed the cart on. It was done now
and he wasn't going to worry about it. He hadn't hurt her
permanently, and she wouldn't be breeding material for
another couple of weeks anyway. Then a beating would
be the least of her worries. Besides, the last door on the
right guaranteed his favor for a while.

A few rooms down, the guy who had given him a hard
time earlier was dozing on wadded blankets in the corner
and Howard quietly put the food down and backed out;
his frustration was vented, and he didn't bother with
grudges. Howard pitied him; initiation was over and tonight the prisoner's life would become one built on two-
week cycles. In four hours the man would provide two or
three vampires with a small meal, and every week they
would feed on him again . . . *for the rest of his life.*

Howard shuddered. He had no illusions about himself,
and the last of his conscience had disappeared when he
and a companion had been caught—neither had been
very adept at life on the streets—and the Mistress had
offered him The Deal. He had instinctively refused, but
that had changed as he watched his partner twist beneath
the mouth of one of those ravenous, deadly creatures.
Licking the last drop of blood, the female vampire he
now knew as Rita had leered as she chopped the head
from the limp body, then tossed it outside for the sun to
fry in the morning. Population control, the Mistress had
told him blandly. How easily she had seen the dark part
of his soul, giving him the things that had always been
unattainable. He became the caretaker of what had

started as a carefully guarded food supply, spending this last year in a haze of fulfillment as he endeavored to turn the Mistress's "pantry" into a breeding center.

The vampires had tried to make the captives breed, but the men and women refused to couple. Howard didn't care; he had plenty of drive and no reservations about privacy, age, or physical condition. The Mistress didn't worry so long as he didn't kill or permanently injure anyone, and Howard was finally able to indulge every grotesque fantasy he'd ever imagined and invent a few he hadn't.

Mankind, he figured, was doomed anyway. The vampires were superior in strength, and although starvation and the sun were whittling away at them, they still outnumbered humans by a staggering ratio. Their terrifying hypnotic ability was the final, crushing factor in the hopeless war against the pathetic members of his own species, and Howard's utmost priority was to avoid being someone's meal when he died. The memory of his friend's convulsing body remained fresh, and he had to make sure the vampires found him valuable for decades to come.

The prisoners had finally quieted, most concentrating on the food, others napping in the scant warmth of the springlike day. The last room, the brightest and warmest, was a small corner office with double windows. For the woman inside, Howard assembled a minifeast: besides the rice and Kool-Aid, he added canned green beans and a pile of greasy preserved sausages. So far she was his only success, and it was easy to ignore the look of loathing as he hand-fed her, his bloated fingers almost tender. Her own hands had been tied behind her since last week when he'd caught her trying to punch herself in the stomach, and she ate only because she knew he would pulverize the food and force her if necessary. Again, Howard didn't care.

She was five months' pregnant with his child.

There were no heroes left and Howard Siebold was a happy man.

12

"Drop it." Deb pointed at the man's weapon as she came out of the doorway. *"Do it now!"*

"Okay," he said in a respectful voice and eased the long knife he'd been clutching to the ground. Deb had seen those things only in old Tex-Mex westerns, and in real life the machete seemed twice as large as her vague memories. "My name's Alex," he said suddenly. He hopped from foot to foot and started to shove his fluttering hands into the pockets of his jacket.

"Don't move!" she snapped. He could have anything in his pockets and her knuckles had gone dangerously white around the handgrip of the H&K. "Keep your hands where I can see them!"

He froze and they eyed each other suspiciously until he finally managed a shaky smile and nodded appreciatively at the gun. "Were you a cop?" he asked. "I used to work construction myself, welding. Was just about to go into business for myself, when—well, you know."

Deb looked at him numbly. Now what? She felt confused and . . . *hungry* for the sound of someone else's voice. "Why were you chasing me?" she demanded.

He looked genuinely surprised. "Why *not*? You're the first person I've seen in months, and you ran away. So I went after you."

The logic was inescapable and she lowered the pistol slightly; he looked relieved and stood patiently as she studied him. He was disheveled and tall, though not as tall as her, with shaggy brown hair and a day-old beard. Without the machete he didn't seem at all menacing, and the look in his brown eyes was a mixture of yearning and disbelief. Deb's mistrust slipped another reluctant notch.

"What's that?" Tied loosely around his neck was some kind of burned white scarf. Deb tensed momentarily when he undid it and held it up for her to see.

"A dress," he said. "I found it this morning."

"So?"

For the first time she saw frustration cross Alex's features. "It means there's someone *else* besides us." He swept the air with his hand. "There are other *people*, maybe a lot."

"How can you be sure?" She motioned to the tattered material. "That mess probably came off a vampire."

"It didn't," he insisted, and Deb's eyebrows raised at his conviction. "I *saw* the woman wearing this dress early this morning. A vampire dragged her into the subway. By the time I got outside, she was gone, but I did find the vampire . . . *dying*." His fingers spread the fabric and she saw that it had a high, old-fashioned collar. "It looked like his mouth had been blasted with a torch."

"Really?" Despite her nervousness, Deb couldn't help her interest. The pistol uncocked as her grip relaxed and she slipped the gun into her pocket, keeping one hand on it for reassurance. He offered her the garment and she took it gingerly, frowning. "I don't think I understand."

"Sure you do," Alex said confidently. "The vampire bit her and died because of it. But I don't know where she went. You haven't seen anyone, have you?"

Deb shook her head and tossed the dress back, watching it flutter as he snatched it from the air. "Only you. How come I haven't seen you before? Where've you been?"

"I live in the Daley Center. You know where that is, right?" She nodded. "And as far as not seeing each other—chance. A big city, not enough people, that's all. You never did tell me your name."

"It's . . . Deb." His eyes were fixed on her and she blushed. "What are you staring at?"

He laughed and she jumped at the sound. He sounded so . . . happy, so *alive*. She tried to hide the tiny smile creeping along her lips.

"Because you're a real *person*! Isn't that great?"

Weapon forgotten, he spun giddily and skipped down the sidewalk a few steps. "Two people! And probably more, don't you think?"

Deb picked up the machete and examined it in the sunlight. The razored edge gleamed. "What good is this thing?"

He made a face, then grinned. "It's a lot more effective at decapitation than your gun." She turned the blade handle-up and tossed it; he caught it with an ease that showed more than a few hours' practice and snapped it onto his belt.

"I don't carry the gun for vampires," Deb said in a low voice. "I carry it for people."

The confusion on his face was obvious. "What?"

She gave him a stony look. "Not everyone can be trusted—Alex," she said. "You've got a lot to learn."

He scratched at his beard, then retied the dress like a muffler. The two began to drift back toward State Street. "You lost me. I can't imagine why not."

"I want to live as much as anyone," she told him as they settled into a stroll under the warm afternoon sun. "But there's a limit to what I'll do to stay alive. Some people have no limits." She told him the story of John, partly as a warning and partly to point out his own naïveté. "So I killed him," she finished. It felt strange to confess her crime to another human being, and she kept her eyes trained on the sidewalk so she wouldn't have to see the accusation on Alex's face. "I shot him and dumped his body on the railroad tracks. I felt guilty for a long time, wondering if I'd murdered the last man I'd ever see." Deb finally lifted her chin and met his stare. "But I wasn't sorry. That doesn't make sense, does it? Maybe I just got over it."

"Sounds like you had no choice," Alex commented. "Bargaining with vampires." He shook his head. "Unbelievable. But I'll tell you something." He brought the fingers of one hand into a hard fist. She realized that the determination shining from his face matched her own fierce will to survive, and the bitter residue of her mistrust thinned a little more.

"We've got to find that girl, Deb. I just *know* she's the key."

"The key to what?" Alex's expression faded to bewilderment, then dreaminess as he peered to the western sun that was beginning its slow descent toward night.

"The key to . . . *everything*."

Four hours of searching proved fruitless, but Deb didn't mind; it was amazing how quickly she and Alex became companions. Frightening, too—she felt she was sliding into trust too easily, setting herself up for some monstrous disappointment. There was a bond here, something missing from the man she'd killed last fall, who had been first a surprise, then a reason behind her bad dreams. She hungered for company, yet the concept gave her the jitters.

Purposeful at first, after a few hours and a scrounged-up lunch their hunt turned lazy and meandering. Rather than lead *and* deliberate Alex's trustworthiness, Deb simply followed until predictably they ended up in Daley Plaza. She sat gratefully on one of a group of granite benches surrounding a tree, her eyes following the spindly branches and noting the buds that were appearing at last. Off to the right were a couple of matching granite trash containers with still-legible blue-and-white signs bearing a circle of stenciled arrows and the legend CHICAGO RECYCLES. *Will it?* she wondered. Will *mankind* recycle? Two years ago there'd been hundreds of pigeons in the plaza and the benches had been mounded with bird droppings. Today not a single bird strutted at her feet.

Somewhere beyond the steel-and-glass buildings the sun moved toward the horizon, draining the day of light and safety. More than in the slowly spreading shadows she could see the coming sunset in the tenseness of Alex's shoulders and the way his eyes flicked along the streets, testing each dimming doorway like the fleeting movement of a snake's tongue tasting the air. Closer to home he became a little more relaxed; behind the mask of tinted windows a bed or sleeping bag waited, offering safety and warmth during the coming night.

"It's getting late," he finally said.

"Yes." Deb stood, thinking of her own safe place and her shotgun—the cold steel of protection. "I have to go."

"Stay with me tonight," he said suddenly. She looked at him wordlessly and he reddened, like a kid caught doing something dirty. "Not like that," he added hastily. "Just . . . so there can be *two* of us, you know? I can't remember the last time there was *two*."

Unfortunately, Deb could. Still, it was a tempting invitation that offered many things, perhaps even intimacy, but the memory of the Winchester's thunder across the nothingness of Morton Lecture Hall during the night remained a bloody mark in her mind. "No," she said at last, avoiding his eyes. Alex's scrubby face drooped with disappointment. "I'm sorry. You know the old line: I'm just not ready for that yet." She risked meeting his gaze, then regretted it when she saw the loneliness reflected there.

"I don't suppose you'd let me walk you home?" he asked hoarsely.

Deb shook her head. "It's too late to be safe. But I'll meet you somewhere tomorrow. How's that?"

"Yeah?" Alex brightened. "That'd be great. Where? When?"

He's so *innocent*, she thought. Either I'm being utterly duped or this man's never been burned in his life. She opened her mouth to ask where in the building he stayed, then decided against it. He'd tell her without a second thought, and God forbid something should happen to her tonight. Then this silly, trusting man would probably be her first victim.

"Field's," she finally decided. "The doorway where you caught me. Or I caught you." She grinned.

"First thing in the morning?" he asked.

"Right after sunup," she promised. Deb turned away, then paused. "Don't follow me, Alex," she said softly.

He shoved his hands in his pockets and nodded mutely. She wasn't ready to trust, and as she headed south along Dearborn, she glanced back every quarter block to make sure Alex was still at his corner. Three blocks away she veered east, knowing that even if he tried he could never catch her now. She'd planned on sprinting the next few blocks, but she felt fairly comfortable with Alex's honesty and she relaxed her stride; she supposed she could trust a *little*. Her booted steps echoed through the streets but she made no effort to be quiet; within fifteen minutes she was at the Institute and unlocking the door, then quickly going through her evening scrutiny. Normally she dreaded night—too much time lying motionless in the blackness, waiting out the hours until dawn. Tonight, though, she felt exhausted, not merely from over-exercise but from the excitement of meeting another human being. Anxiety tried to twist into her stomach and she mentally shoved it away; Alex was self-sufficient and had survived this long without a hitch; there was no reason to doubt he'd be waiting at Field's in the morning.

She picked out a can of chicken spread and a box of crackers to make a small evening meal. Sitting on the main steps, she ate and watched the light fade behind the buildings to the west, thinking about Alex and wishing that the chicken-smeared crackers were pieces of steaming Popeye's chicken. In a few minutes she was finished. There was another half hour of light left, but chores still needed to be done: pack away the garbage and lock the auditorium doors, clean and reload the shotgun. As she reached to pull the door closed, shock spasmed her fingers.

Somewhere in the maze that was downtown, Deb could have sworn she heard a woman's faint scream.

13

REVELATION 19:13
And he was clothed with a vesture dipped in blood. . . .

"My God," Perlman breathed. The bloody bandage pressed against his wrist slipped unnoticed from his fingers. *"My God!"*

He was looking at *people*, for the first time in—why, since he couldn't *remember*! And there they stood, a woman and a man—teenager, really—not six feet away! The woman, his height and about thirty, had short hair and brown eyes that stared right through him. The teenager was lean and hard, a born street fighter wearing an olive tee shirt under an army jacket from which the sleeves had been ripped; tense muscles bunched beneath the coffee-colored skin of the young man's arms. His odd, tawny eyes were emotionless beneath thick black hair, but some kind of metal weapon hung loosely from one hand and Perlman had no doubt his visitor could use it with deadly speed.

Those few words of surprise; then all Perlman could do was stare soundlessly.

After a few seconds, the teenager reached into a breast pocket and withdrew a cigarette. Without taking his eyes from the doctor, he lit it one-handed from a book of matches.

Voice hoarse, Perlman said the first thing that came to mind. "Those things will kill you."

The boy grinned. "Lots of things'll kill you, mister." His features, Perlman realized, were delicate and almost pretty; his face didn't match the vaguely dangerous physique. "Matter of fact"—the youth arched an eyebrow—"you're dripping on the floor."

Perlman glanced absently at the blood trickling around

his fingers in a slow but steady flow. "What? Oh—this is nothing."

"Did you cut yourself?" the woman asked.

"Miscalculated, that's all." Perlman pressed a square of gauze over the small puncture. "Nothing a little coagulant won't fix."

"So you *are* a doctor," the teenager said. "We—"

"My name's Calie," the woman cut in. "This is C.J." She smiled slightly, trying to put him at ease. "He won't tell what the initials stand for. What should we call you?" The boy pulled on his cigarette, undisturbed by the interruption.

Perlman wiped at the bloody floor with a length of paper towel, his sore foot making his movements awkward. His hands were shaking, too—he was just an all-around mess. "William—Bill, I mean. Bill Perlman." He wadded up the towel and tossed it at an open plastic bag on the floor. "I . . ."

He gave up then, unable to do anything but stand there with a huge, stupid smile plastered across his face.

"We saw you drag the bloodsucker back this morning," C.J. said matter-of-factly. "Did you kill it?"

The three of them were in the large room that Perlman called home, and having company for the first time made Perlman aware of just how *un*inviting his living quarters were. He and C.J. were sitting on the sofa, a leatherette thing Perlman had found in a waiting room; beside it was an end table sporting a defunct brass lamp and a metal table on which sat a camping stove and two clean pots above a small stock of fuel, plastic water jugs, and some groceries. Folded neatly in the corner were his winter supplies; two kerosene heaters, heavy sleeping bag and blankets, a case of kerosene canisters. The newest addition was the hospital bed he'd dragged in last week, finally having had enough of the couch. He suddenly realized how ridiculous it looked, with its metal gates and the sheets he'd so carefully folded military-style. Calie was ambling around and . . . *touching* things with a faraway expression; when she stopped and smoothed the bedsheets, Perlman couldn't help flushing. C.J. didn't notice Calie's behavior—or did she act this way all the time?

Bill remembered C.J.'s question. "No." He bent back to his task of applying a topical coagulant to the puncture in his wrist. "I put him in a closet. But he's still tied up."

Both C.J. and Calie looked unsettled. "I don't know, Doc," Calie finally said. "Those things get stronger at night."

The doctor wound a fresh bandage in place. "I think it'll be okay. He's just a child, probably no more than five years old." Calie and C.J. glanced at each other and C.J. rolled his eyes. "What's the matter?" Perlman asked.

"For a doctor, you ain't very smart," C.J. said. "You ever heard of research?"

"Maybe you're just too sympathetic," Calie pointed out. "Your 'little boy' will rip you apart at nightfall unless you get rid of him." She frowned then, and her eyes darkened. "That vampire in there isn't your son, is it?" A muscle in C.J.'s jaw twitched.

Perlman shook his head, squelching the momentary pain the idea brought. "Of course not. But I don't want to kill him—*it*. I haven't been out much, and this is the first one I've been close to. I want to experiment on it."

C.J. whistled. "That's original." He peered at the doctor. "Say, you ain't some kind of Nazi, are you?"

Perlman had to laugh. "Not hardly. I'm as Jewish as they come." His smile was gone as quickly as it had appeared and his expression turned intense. "But I'm going to find a way to kill them off.

"Before I die, I swear I'm going to stand on Michigan Avenue at midnight and see the stars."

"Well, Doc, let's see what you've got." C.J.'s weapon turned out to be a crossbow, and now the teenager had it loaded and ready to fire as Perlman led them into a room and motioned to a closed door.

"He's in the closet," the doctor explained. "I put him in there temporarily so I could take care of my foot."

"Yeah," C.J. said. "I was going to ask you about that."

Perlman undid a heavy padlock on the closet door. "I

jammed my toe when I . . . was pulling him out of his hiding place. It was pretty uncomfortable."

"That's not all that would have been uncomfortable," Calie said softly at his back. He grimaced, then opened the door to reveal a small supply closet and the travois, its occupant still tightly bound.

C.J. snorted. "What the hell is this? *Duct* tape?"

"There's rope, too," Perlman said defensively.

The teenager slung the bow across his shoulders, grabbed the handles of the stretcher and dragged it out. Perlman had chosen this room specifically because it was dim, but the thing beneath the plastic shifted restlessly, as if even the shadowed light caused it pain. Then it was still.

"I hate to bust your bubble," Calie said, "but I'd guess this would've held him about sixty seconds. And the closet even less."

Perlman gaped at her. "But he's so little—so *thin!*"

C.J.'s face was scornful. "You're gonna find out these things are nothing like that." He turned his wrist so they could see the time on his watch. "I hope you've got someplace else to keep it. Otherwise you're in deep shit in about three hours."

"But I do!" Bill said eagerly. "In the basement, next to the G.I. lab. I just didn't take him down because of my foot."

"Let's go, then," C.J. said, hefting the travois effortlessly. He gave Calie an exasperated glance as he ambled after the doctor. "I can't wait to see this."

Perlman didn't notice. He hobbled in front, easing the weight on his foot with a cane as he led them to a flight of stairs. "This way. You'll see I'm better prepared than you thought."

C.J. smirked and turned the stretcher to skim it down the stairs like a toboggan as they followed. Two flights below, the doctor pushed through double doors into a huge equipment-filled room. An eye-watering amount of daylight spilled from a high row of northern windows with open shades and the creature began a frenzied squirm under its dark covering.

"Quickly!" Perlman slid a two-inch iron rod free of its

slots in a metal door and swung it inward, then pulled a flashlight from a wall hook and snapped it on, illuminating a flight of stairs sinking into blackness. "Down there." C.J. needed no further prompting and within moments had the stretcher down and through another open metal door, finally resting it against the back wall of a small empty room. Then he backed up and looked around curiously as the vampire quieted.

"Fallout shelter," Perlman explained. He pointed to a pattern of crisscrossed streaks on the back wall. "I pulled down the shelves and threw out the old rations. Most of it was dust anyway. I wanted a clear, secure space and this seemed perfect. The door is nearly impossible to break and I added iron bars at the top and bottom for extra strength."

"The door certainly looks strong enough," Calie agreed. "But a trapped vampire might just rip right through the walls."

Perlman waved at the room with a childlike pride. "This was built to withstand a bomb strike." His eyes found Calie's. "The inner walls are steel-sheeted and it's a fireproof building. All the floors and ceilings are reinforced concrete, and the supporting walls are concrete blocks built on steel rods."

"What's that?" C.J. motioned to a small screened box high at the juncture of two walls and the ceiling.

"A battery-powered light and home video outfit. In the morning I'll be able to see how he acted during the night."

"If it doesn't get out and kill you first," C.J. muttered. "Speaking of which, we gotta fix that window."

"Window?"

"We took off a metal screen and broke a window to get in," Calie told him. "You won't be safe if it's not fixed."

"I never thought to ask how you got in," Perlman admitted sheepishly.

"Yeah, well, you'd better *start*, Doc." C.J. crammed another cigarette into his mouth angrily. "We've only known you an hour and you've already pulled some dumb-ass moves."

"Never mind, Dr. Bill." Calie put her hand on Perlman's arm and he jumped. No one had touched him since Mera. "C.J. always gets antsy toward evening. But it *is* time to get moving."

"Okay," Perlman said hastily. "Just leave him, I guess. Or should we untie him first?" He regretted the question as soon as C.J.'s withering stare found him. "Right. Let's just close it up. I'll come back later and turn on the camera."

"I'll tell you what," Calie said. "You lock up here and we'll go fix the window. Then you can let us out."

"Sounds good to me," the doctor said.

C.J. took a pull from his cigarette, then crushed it out. "We'll be back in half an hour."

Perlman reluctantly watched them go.

For an unsure quarter of an hour Perlman thought they weren't coming back. Perhaps they didn't want anything to do with him—he must have seemed like a maniac, dragging a vampire into his hiding place and stuffing it into a closet, and they only knew part of his plans. It was fortunate that they'd left him alone for a while, since he was just about explained out and C.J. had been painfully accurate in his assessment of the doctor's scant forethought. As he made his final arrangements, locked up the "vault" and readied the light and camera, it dawned on Perlman that Calie and C.J. were a total mystery to him. Where had they come from? Were there others as well?

"Hi." His heart stuttered briefly at the unexpected sound of Calie's voice. "We're back." Her smile was reassuring, but C.J. looked even more apprehensive. Perlman checked the time; they were down to under an hour before sunset.

"We thought you might like to stay with us tonight," Calie said. Her dark eyes were purposely wide and guileless. "C.J.'s not convinced your little prison will hold the prisoner."

"What?" Sudden doubt welled: in all this time, Perlman had never seen these people. Why now? And just *where* did they live? C.J. was a hard-ass, but Calie looked safe—and he felt fairly certain she could be trusted.

Then again, his decision-making today hadn't been very sound. "I don't know," he finally said.

"It'll be all right," Calie offered as C.J. peered out one of the windows. Thick clouds obscured the late afternoon sky, leaving only about forty-five minutes of good light. "Just start the camera a little earlier. You really need to be out of here. That kid's going to wake up hungry."

Perlman looked at the floor.

"Come on, Doc," C.J. asked impatiently. "What's it going to be? If you're not coming, you need to lock up behind us. We wait any longer and the vamps'll be on us like hounds."

"He's coming." Calie's voice was incredulous. He met her deep gaze unwillingly and had the troubling sensation that she had just read his mind. "Our man needs a full meal and rest tonight. Right?" C.J. frowned at her from his post at the window.

"The doctor has to replenish the blood he gave to the vampire!"

"This is where you'll sleep," Calie said as she showed Bill into a cubicle sandwiched between two larger rooms. He looked around doubtfully; it was closet-sized, and although there was a thick sleeping bag, pad, and pillow on the floor, he couldn't help remembering the comfortable bed at Northwestern. Even the vampire's vault was bigger than this. "I know it's small," she continued, "but I'm right next door and C.J.'s around the corner. We can find you something better tomorrow, but I thought you'd like to be near us tonight." She waited.

"It's fine," Perlman heard himself say. He was still reeling—there were at least twenty people in this place! Never had he imagined that many people were still alive in Chicago, much less in a single location—and he had been at the outside doors only this morning! Calie had come up with a bowl of warmed ravioli and insisted he wolf it down to help replace the blood he'd lost. The meal and the habit of bedding down at sunset warred with his excitement; Perlman didn't know whether to collapse from exhaustion or skip with exhilaration.

"When will I meet the others?" he asked. "They acted kind of . . ."

"Funny?" Calie smiled and pushed him down on the sleeping bag. He wanted to resist, but it felt good to get off his injured foot. "It's too close to dark for niceties. They'll be more hospitable in the morning. Then you can meet the boss."

He looked up with interest. "The boss?"

"McDole," she said. "He's the one who told us to go and get you."

"Really?" Bill felt a brief rush of alarm. "He *knew* where I was?"

"Don't worry," she added at the chalky expression on his face. "We know about almost everyone in the area—everyone alive, anyway."

"You mean there're even more besides the ones here?" He couldn't believe it.

"Yes."

Perlman frowned as he carefully tucked his legs into the double-wide bag Calie had provided. "Then why doesn't everyone get together? Wouldn't it be safer?"

"Not necessarily." She studied the chewed ends of her fingernails. "So we wait and see, like we did with you."

"I don't understand," he said sleepily. He snuggled into the warmth of the overstuffed bag.

Calie bent and adjusted his pillows. "I'll explain everything tomorrow. Tonight, you just sleep. The only thing you need to know right now is . . .

"You're safe."

14

REVELATION 3:8
Behold, I have set before thee an open door,
and no man can shut it. . . .

The city overwhelmed her.

Louise felt like Jonah, looking into the mouth of the
whale and about to be swallowed alive by some great,
hungry, and unfeeling monster. That is, if the smaller
monsters didn't get her first.

The Vespa was not the great idea Louise had thought,
and by the time she reached Belmont it was running like
shit. Chugging down the off ramp toward Broadway, she
and Beau spent most of the afternoon coaxing the scooter
toward downtown, figuring that if the Vespa did quit,
they'd be close to the smaller, near north buildings that
could be searched quickly before evening. She thought
about looking for another scooter, then realized with disgust the one major thing she'd forgotten: while she was
surrounded by cars and motorcycles, they all ran on gasoline that had gone stale a year ago.

But at last they were struggling southward along Michigan Avenue with the cheerful yellow Vespa coughing
and jerking like some kind of ancient, sickly lawn mower.
Poignant Christmas memories resurfaced with each
block: twinkling Italian lights entwined in the trees
stretching from Oak Street Beach to the river and beyond; holiday shoppers hurrying through the snow; sleek
black carriages parked along the boulevard with drivers
huddled next to old-fashioned lanterns while horses
snorted in the frigid air and stamped their hooves at the
curb. She wondered what had happened to the horses.

The Magnificent Mile didn't look magnificent anymore. Beneath the declining sun, it looked empty of everything except spreading malevolent shadows. How

much daylight was left? She watched the sky anxiously as they continued south; inside the front of her jacket Beau fidgeted, his dry little nails raking yet another throbbing furrow across her belly despite her heavy flannel shirt. Her chest and rib cage probably matched the striped pattern on the material.

The Vespa died just over the Chicago River and Louise was almost grateful. Next to finding shelter, she wanted nothing more than to get Beau out of her jacket and away from her raw skin. She set him down to pee and hopped up and down to get the circulation going again in her legs, blocking his way to the curb and the six-inch drop to the metal grating of the bridge, where forty feet below the water flowed a dull, quiet green. She still recalled how the City used to dump a hundred pounds of kelly green dye into the river before every St. Patrick's Day parade.

Louise scrutinized the buildings along the river's edge, then decided she would feel more comfortable if she were surrounded by buildings on all sides. In the direction from which she'd come was North Michigan Avenue and a jungle of never-to-be-completed construction sites interspersed with skyscrapers and smaller one- or two-story buildings, but southward and a little to the west were a myriad of huge buildings.

Her direction decided, she picked up Beau and started walking rapidly. It was interesting how differently she viewed the downtown buildings than she had in past summers, when she and friends from her Rogers Park neighborhood had often ridden the L train to the Loop to catch a morning matinee at the Chicago Theater. She turned west on Lake Street, glancing at the old theater as she crossed the cobbled width of State Street (*that Great Street!*). A few years before everything went crazy, a group of developers had renovated the theater and started booking some big names. The final headliner still screamed across the marquee: WHOPPI GOLDBERG—A MILLION LAUGHS! At street level a scarlet curtain covered the glass inside the ticketmaster's booth. What horrors lie curled beneath the velvet seats inside?

Louise shuddered and Beau whined as she increased

her pace, almost jogging. At Dearborn she went south
again, leaving the elevated tracks and its dim stretch of
street behind as she hurried away from the decrepit
movie houses and low-slung buildings along Dearborn
and Randolph, winding her way to the southwest high-
rent district. By Monroe, Louise was running and she finally paused to catch her breath in front of a massive
white skyscraper.

One Xerox Centre boasted bright white stone and
looked as good a place as any. Louise felt herself sliding
on the edge of panic as she realized it was past four—by
now they should be inside and settled for the night.
Buildings towered on all sides and the sky was thick with
gathering clouds, another bad break. Rain would chill
them good in the dropping temperatures and the cloud
cover would bring an early dusk . . . and terrible danger.
She stuffed Beau loosely back into her jacket and circled
the building, but every door she tried was tightly locked.
Dammit! She needed more time! Breaking the glass
would be a fool's move, yet she didn't have time to de-
vise a more subtle entrance. She had to find someplace
quickly, and though they might unwittingly share it with
sleeping vampires, any one of these skyscrapers was big
enough to house both with a minimum of risk—*if* she
could get in without leaving an obvious trail.

Beau was scrambling around the inside of her jacket
like a caged rat and she resisted the urge to rap him on
the nose. It was fear that was spooking him, the same
fear that was making it impossible for her to think clearly.
Jesus, what a mess they were in this time, that same ridiculous presumption that everything would work itself
out backfiring on her yet again. Before now, her worst assumption had been toward the end of the month of disappearances a year ago, when she'd gone traipsing off to
Elmwood Park to stay with her friend Cindi. Louise had
spoken to the girl only the evening before, yet the small
suburban bungalow where Cindi lived was unlocked and
deserted, the house—the entire empty *neighborhood*—
permeated with an ugly undercurrent of sleeping evil
that had grown stronger with each flick of the clock toward evening. She and Beau had run out of light then,

too, and that was the first night she'd learned to hide.
Riding the eerily empty Metra train back to the city the
next morning had only been the start of a daymare of discovering her mom and stepfather missing and their
apartment a mirror of that same pervasive corruption,
with the Chicago Police Department depleted to only a
fraction of its former size and so overrun with disappear-
ance reports that they could do nothing but advise her to
call it in next week.

But there had been no next week for the city.

The clouds split for an instant, showing the deep, painful blue preceding sunset; Louise knew there was no
more time to waste. She turned, heading west toward the
last feeble daylight sliding behind the skyscrapers. Her
stomach knotted angrily; there was food, a few tools, and
an all-but-useless gun in her backpack, but there was no
time to eat. There was a hunger far worse that she didn't
want to experience. At Clark she went north again, remembering the older government buildings in that direction. They had windows that could be forced open with
her hammer and screwdriver, then closed up again with
a few nails. City Hall had a high-level first she might be
able to reach. She forced herself to jog and conserve energy that might be needed later, though the adrenaline in
her blood was making her ears ring. A lifetime ago she'd
read an animal-rights pamphlet on people in the Philip-
pines who strung captured dogs from trees before killing
them, claiming the adrenaline made the meat taste better. If that was true and her luck ran out, she'd make a
tasty treat for some bloodsucker tonight.

Louise was swerving across Madison when something
went wrong with her feet and she fell. She had a split
second to realize that her rubber soles had caught the
edge of some sort of street grating, then her hands shot
forward and one knee came up to break her fall. There
was no chance to turn; to keep from crushing Beau her
hands took most of her weight, like dropping face-
forward into a brutal push-up. Agony flared as a hundred
tiny metal teeth bit deeply into her palms and fingers,
then she was rolling sideways, back onto the cold concrete in a fetal position as she cradled her shredded

hands. There was a faraway stinging in her knee and a
hard ache in her shoulder joints, but it was *nothing* compared to the pain pulsing up her arms. Inside her jacket
Beau gave a frenzied bark and dug a fresh furrow across
the side of her left breast, his scrabbling paw slicing bare
skin when it slipped into her shirtfront.

Louise groaned and sat up, fumbling with her jacket
zipper so Beau could climb out; when she saw her hands,
she almost sobbed aloud. In the last ten seconds their situation had plummeted to desperate. Both her hands
were a mass of split, bleeding cuts, the deeper ones along
the base of her palms dripping with blood. Even if she
found someplace within the next quarter hour, the
bloodsmell alone would leave an easy trail. The pain was
enormous and she shook her head and tried to think
around it. There was an extra shirt in her pack; she could
wrap—

Beau jumped from her lap and took off.

For a second Louise just sat, staring dumbly as the dog
scrambled up Madison, wondering how he could even
see where he was going. Then she panicked. That silly
mutt was the only thing she loved in this world; she blot-
ted out the pain, clambered to her feet, and chased after
him.

"Beau, *heel!*" Five feet and new pain rammed her, this
time from her knee, a minor stinging that rocketed into
a throbbing jolt every time her weight shifted to that leg.
Louise didn't care; that dog meant everything. She'd
crawl after him if she had to. If Beau heard he gave no
sign, and Louise was still stumbling behind him when he
ran full-tilt into a small riser of stone steps. He yelped
and stopped, his watery eyes blinking as his old body
panted with exertion. Louise snatched him up with
blood-soaked fingers, then collapsed on the stairs.

"Are you crazy?" she gasped. "Where were you going?"
Hysteria edged her voice as she hugged him. Beau's tail
wagged furiously; he yapped and wiggled again, but this
time she held him close as she checked the darkening
street. She felt like a bleeding piece of meat in the midst
of piranha-filled waters; in only fifteen minutes the fish
would begin to bite. But defeat didn't fit into her life, and

she hung onto the dog and pushed unsteadily to her feet. Around her were lots of small shops at street level—risky, but better than out in the open. In the heavy dusk she could see LaSalle off to her right, while directly behind her—

—were the doors to St. Peter's.

There was no time to weigh options. She scooted up the steps, wrapped bloody fingers around one of the ornate handles and pulled. Unbelievably, the door opened on silent hinges and she stepped through, moving quickly past the dim foyer into the main room. When the door swung closed behind her, the abrupt blackness almost made her cry out. She took a few tentative steps instead and one wet hand found the cold and not-at-all-comforting side of a wooden pew. Fading light still shone through the vividly stained glass windows above, as though an immense kaleidoscope were suspended just out of reach. In a few seconds she could make out the vague shape of a huge cross at the altar.

Ten more minutes would bring total darkness. Louise's only experience with a church had been months ago, when she'd explored St. Ita's on Broadway and found it filthy and desecrated, the altar smeared with dried waste, the icons torn from the walls and smashed. She'd had no way of knowing if that ruined place of worship could still offer shelter, and hadn't risked staying in another of the huge, dark buildings that dotted the cityscape. If the church in which she now stood could not protect her, she was doomed.

The weak light from the stained glass windows four stories above changed visibly as darkness fell over Chicago. Nestled in her arms, Beau was quiet and calm, a good sign. Feeling her way pew by pew up the aisle, Louise slid stiffly onto the front bench, feeling the deepening cold seep into her butt and the backs of her legs immediately. The temperature had dropped drastically and she set Beau on the floor for a second and eased off the backpack; a little fumbling and she drew out a blanket and pulled it around her shoulders. Now it was time to wait; her hands were tacky with blood and the smell surely surrounded her. Ultimately, if the night beasts could enter St. Peter's, they would find her no matter where she hid. She reached toward her feet, searching the darkness for Beau.

There was a quick scraping in the black void in front of her and a match burst into sudden, blinding light.

"Welcome," said a childishly sweet voice, "to the House of God."

The Hunger—
Life in the Land of the Dead

15

●━●∙●━●∙●━●∙●━

REVELATION 1:18
I am she that liveth, and was dead;
and, behold, I am alive for evermore. . . .

●━●∙●━●

Anyelet opened her eyes and the oceans of the world
were made of blood. She stood at a pulsating shore and
gazed upon the red vastness even as need rose in her
body and her mouth began to fill with thick saliva. In a
moment her fingers had undone the iron clasp at her
neck and the velvet cape fell to the sand like a sheet of
black oil. The air, heavy with bloodsmell, played across
her collarbone and breasts, caressing her bared skin with
a lover's icy, intimate hand; waves of blood swelled and
ebbed before her, leaving wet, crimson shadows in front
of her feet.

Anyelet's deep red hair whipped heavily in the wind
but the piercing gaze never blinked. Eons ago those eyes
had been clear green; time had deepened them to a black
so dark they seemed like twin pits within skin that
glowed white in the deep dusk, the veins beneath blue-
smudged trails of emptiness. She ached with fierce Hunger as she stepped forward, easing her foot into the hot
bath of fulfillment as her lips parted in anticipation.

The sole of her foot met cool, dry sand. Anyelet looked
down impatiently and saw the ruby liquid receding, as if
the traitorous moon had suddenly pulled in the tide. She
tried again, and again, but with every foot she gained the
ocean receded an equal distance.

She closed her eyes and concentrated. Cold and beautiful, Anyelet spread her arms wide and felt power course
through her as she reached, her mind's eye picturing her
fingers locking as she enfolded mankind into her deadly
grip. Her pain bled to agony, the collapsed arteries and
veins becoming razor-studded snakes twisting within her

body. Her eyes flew open and she gazed over the world she had so easily conquered, now a withered, dried-out sphere bearing no trace of the oceans of plenty she had envisioned. Fresh fever surged and her back arched, crushing the imaginary world against her chest until it began to disintegrate. Still her fingers would not open. She threw back her head and screamed as bits and pieces of the globelike form cascaded down her breasts and rib cage, then began to stretch and re-form against her rigid torso. It had been an eternity since she'd felt fear, but terror returned easily to her memory as her hands finally unclasped.

Too late. There was no escaping the starvation-blackened arms that now trapped her. The form was taking shape, smothering her in its foulness as she beat at it with fading strength, the creature sucking away her energy in great, thirsty gulps.

Anyelet gagged helplessly and her head lolled, exposing her throat and its trail of barren arteries. Loathing filled her as this nightmare being opened a pus-encrusted mouth in which two rotted fangs slid forward.

No! she howled frantically into its mind. *There is no food for you here!*

Hideous laughter rang in her ears. The beast's head shot forward with a speed that she had never possessed and the cracked lips fastened greedily on her neck around its filthy teeth.

Anyelet's stomach convulsed as the artery in her neck gorged and blackness began to radiate from her throat. Despair enveloped her as she realized her captor wasn't *feeding*.

It was pumping its filth into her body.

Night had arrived with arms open, like an old friend bringing comfort.

With it came The Hunger.

Anyelet's fingers stretched, opening like the petals of a black-red rose, the sharp nails dragging along the underside of her satin quilt, an old habit that soothed her and made her feel secure. She thought briefly of the nightmare, then dismissed it. She didn't need a portent to know the situation was harsh, but with Siebold's assistance things should slowly improve. She flung the quilt carelessly aside and rose, moving to light a couple of cut-glass oil lamps. The last of the sun was sinking below the horizon; even through these stone-and-steel walls she could feel its fading heat still trying to sear her flesh in her place of rest. She smiled complacently. The sun would never set its golden sight upon her again.

The lamps spread a rich glow as she scanned her closet. Her gaze stopped on a magenta silk pantsuit, an outfit Rita had found at Marshall Field's. Seeing Anyelet in it would please her dark companion and she pulled the suit from its hanger and tossed it on the bed, then let the floral nightdress in which she'd slept drop to the floor. Naked, she crossed to the woodstove in the center of the room, a huge, windowless storeroom in the sub-basement of the Merchandise Mart. She could hardly wait for spring and the rising temperatures that would finally warm the ice in her body. The stove, vented only to keep smoke from permeating the room, did a passable job until about two hours before she woke each evening; now its surface was barely warm. No matter. Rita would arrive soon, and wrapping in the covers was worthless since she had no body heat to build beneath their surface.

Anyelet turned at a slight noise and saw Rita glide into the room. Beneath a striking copper robe, the taller woman's skin gleamed like polished mahogany in the lamplight as she crossed to the stove and tossed in a bundle of prefabricated logs. That done, Rita swept a hairbrush from the nightstand and stepped behind her. Anyelet's eyes closed contentedly as Rita began to pull the brush through the red spill of her hair. A log crackled as warmth began to rebuild. Behind her, Anyelet felt Rita finish and lay the brush down, then move to stand in front of her. Opening her eyes, she met the depthless dark brown of Rita's almond-shaped gaze. The tight cut of Rita's hair emphasized her sharp cheekbones and full lips; four-inch daggers hung from her ears and followed the long line of her neck to the jutting ridge of her collarbone.

Rita spread her fingers wide and drew her hands through Anyelet's hair, combing it back from her temples to her shoulders. She stopped for a moment, then eased her fingers down to rest just above the swell of Anyelet's breasts. Rita, normally so sharp-tongued, spoke for the first time since entering the room.

"Is there something else I can do for you?" The offer was tempting. The pleasure Rita could bring was almost excruciating and the coldness that ached between her thighs eased at the thought.

But The Hunger was agony.

Anyelet sighed. "Maybe later, Rita. I must have food."

Rita nodded and stepped away, returning with the billowy pantsuit. A few minutes later the two women stepped into the blackness of the outer corridor, neither bothering with a light as they made their way along its length.

Five floors above, the Damned began their nightly screams.

16

●—●—●—●—●

REVELATION 2:23
And I will kill the children with death. . . .

●—●

The child screamed his rage at the steel-bound walls that held him prisoner, then threw himself at the vaultlike door.

Neither walls nor door acknowledged his tantrum.

In his other life, Tommy Gilbert had not been a particularly bright boy. That he had survived this long in his new existence could be attributed to his youth—now everlasting—and the fact that as a child he focused on instinct rather than intellect. The dark hours had been his friend ever since the Saturday night he and his twin had awakened to Mom and Dad—mysteriously absent all day—standing over them with hellish, hungry grins. Amos was smarter but never very healthy, and as their mother drained the smaller of the sons she had carried in her womb, so too had she drained away his life— permanently. Though Tommy had loved Amos after a fashion, he'd felt nothing but disdain the following evening to discover his brother had become only stiff, decomposing flesh. Forgotten now, at the time there'd been a cry of envy from deep in the darkness that had swallowed Tommy's soul.

His captivity now was incomprehensible. Tommy didn't know or care how he'd gotten here. The Hunger was overwhelming and the bloodsmell was driving him insane. He needed—

Bloodsmell.

Where was it? He crouched in the corner and fought the urge to claw at the walls again, knowing it would only frustrate him. He hadn't seen electric lights in over a year and the harsh glow burned his eyes. Tangled at his feet was the rope and duct tape that had held him for only a few seconds, while smashed plaster left concrete block and steel rods exposed around the room. Now the boy's eyes searched the rubble more carefully, then followed the line of the door to the ceiling of the tiny room.

There! Suspended from a hanger about seven feet above the floor was a small plastic bottle of blood.

A millisecond later it was down and he was fumbling with the cap, which was nothing more than the pull-type kind that bicyclists used. His prison wasn't warm but it wasn't cold either, and the blood was a cool fifty degrees, maybe not the same as fresh but awfully close. He sucked the last drop out, then split the plastic lengthwise with a dark fingernail, his blackened tongue cleaning the inside like he was licking the middle of an Oreo cookie. For months he'd been living on subway rats, though the wily rodents were scarce and hard to catch and the tunnels full of others who wanted only to pull him apart for sport after making sure nothing worthwhile flowed in his veins. The blood—barely more than a pint—was a rare feast.

Stomach half-full, he tossed the bottle aside and curled up to sleep and dream of dark and evil innocence.

17

REVELATION 12:11
And they loved not their lives unto the death.

After all this time, Vic Massucci still felt screwed up when he woke at dusk instead of daybreak. He supposed he always would.

I am a vampire, he thought. On the heels of that: *How disgusting.*

He sat up on the folded blankets, then stood and groaned as his muscles twisted into place. For a minute he just stood in the dark like a massive, shaggy beast, waiting for the sleep to ease from his mind, knowing that The Hunger would roar in to drive the last cobwebs from his tormented brain. He wondered how long he would have to bear this, and his mind immediately obliged with the answer.

Forever.

He lit the candle stuck onto a saucer on the rim of the small sink, but its glow did nothing to relieve his despair as feeble light crawled into the recesses of the water and supply closet that he called "home." He plugged the drain and splashed an inch of water into the sink from a five-gallon plastic jug, then dampened a washcloth and brought it up, looking reflexively at the wall to the mirror.

But the mirror was gone, pulled from the wall when he'd claimed this room as his own. He could have left it—to look in a mirror didn't hurt or frighten him, an idea just as ridiculous as the notion that vampires had to sleep on the earth. Why would anyone, alive *or* undead, spend half their existence lying in dirt? Still, his eyes sought the space where his thirty-five-year-old mind expected a mirror to be. He found nothing, hence the reason he'd taken down the mirror. It was just too damned eerie to *know* you were standing there but not see anything, plus it did weird shit to him optically. Two seconds of staring and he started feeling dizzy; ten would put his ass on the floor.

Vic wiped his face then ran the wet rag around his neck and forearms. Sometime during the day a mouse had left droppings on his shirt; he curled his lip and pulled it off, choosing another from the hangers along an overhead pipe. The shirt was an expensive Ralph Lauren polo and it fit well, the white cloth molding snugly to the massive muscles in his chest and arms. In another time it would have shown off his gardener's tan; the thought that now it just made him look like a ghost made Vic laugh aloud as he tucked the shirt into his slacks, but his mirth died quickly. *Gardener,* he thought bitterly. *Yeah, that's me.* He had no business here; he belonged in the sun, surrounded by greenery and living things. He'd grown up an Italian boy from the northwest side and in his heart he hadn't changed. Even the engraved card in his wallet still read *Vito "Vic" Massucci, Specialty Gardens, Inc.* Unfortunately the living things of this earth could no longer bear his hand; how could he be happy when the most important things in his life now blackened at his touch?

He left his room and descended the stairs, feeling his leg muscles bunch as they worked faithfully. He had been at the peak of his weight lifting when immortality had put a timelock on his body. Even his strength hadn't saved him then.

Anyelet . . .

Just thinking her name made him ache with conflicting emotions. In the tough public high school he'd attended, rumor was if you popped a girl's cherry, she'd put out for you forever. Anyelet had caught him outside his Elston Avenue greenhouse on an icy fall night as he was covering his hybrid roses because of a frost warning. With her lips against his throat to teach him the true meaning of cold, his struggles had been feeble tremblings and *he* had been the virgin. If there was any truth in that crude saying, it explained why he still found her irresistible, though he fought her mental hold at every turn and

would have killed her for what she'd done to him had he
not feared her so much.

On the third floor, he paused and watched Howard
Siebold with narrowed eyes, dreaming about encircling
the man's fat neck with his powerful hands and squeezing until Siebold's face turned black. It had been three
nights since Vic had eaten and The Hunger uncoiled in
his stomach at the smell of the chained men and women;
as he struggled with himself, more loathing for Siebold
surfaced in Vic's thoughts than he had previously thought
possible. While it was monstrous that Vic himself fed on
the human race, Siebold was filth, a traitor and purveyor
of devastation to his own kind. And for what? A few de-
mented sexual fantasies. The Hunger clawed at him
again, warring with his revulsion and hatred; he folded
his arms and spat loudly on the floor, knowing Siebold
would be forced to clean it up tomorrow. On his way out,
the fat man turned to glare at him. Vic's black-flecked ha-
zel eyes glittered in the wavering light and Siebold's
tongue flicked over his lips nervously; he quickly scurried away.

Reluctantly Vic made his way down the hall. Howard
had fashioned red and black magnets to indicate which
prisoners had replenished their blood level and could
give a hungry vampire a meal. Vic had ignored The Hunger so long that his body screamed for one of the larger
males; still he ground his teeth until he felt them slice
into the bloodless flesh of his bottom lip and kept walking. Finally he stood at a cubicle where a red magnet
clung to a disconnected door hinge. Inside, a woman
cowered against the wall at the sight of his six-foot-four
height, her skin mottled with yellow and black bruises.
Besides that, Vic thought in irritation as he tossed back a
spill of his unkempt hair, she was probably cold. In keeping with Howard's eternal depravity, she, like the others,
had been stripped to the skin.

He turned the magnet to black and stepped inside.
The woman threw herself as far out of reach as her chain
would allow and opened her mouth to scream, but the
sound trailed away to a sad moan as Vic locked eyes with
her. He grabbed a dirty blanket from the floor without

breaking the gaze and tossed it around her shaking shoulders.

"Don't be afraid," he whispered. "I won't hurt you." *Much*, his mind whispered derisively. He cringed at the thought.

The woman was young, in her twenties, and her terrified blue eyes rolled back in her head as she moaned again. "Please," she whimpered. "No more. . . ."

"Shhhh," Vic murmured. With the blanket bunched in one fist, he pulled her into his arms, forcing The Hunger to wait. "Look at me," he commanded softly. Head rigid, her unfocused eyes met his.

The first thing he saw was that her name was Giselle.

Then he saw everything else.

The vicious arcing of the leather belt, the searing agony each time it kissed her flesh, even Siebold's promise of better things to come as his thick fingers worked himself to orgasm over her beaten body.

Rage made Vic hiss and bare his teeth; The Hunger saw its chance and took it.

With his fangs sunk into the softness of her throat and the sweet richness of hot copper filling his mouth, one small thread of sanity remained to control The Hunger before it could destroy the woman whose warmth he rocked in his arms like an infant . . .

While The Hunger obliterated everything else.

18

●─●━●─●━●─●

REVELATION 19:8
. . . She shall be arrayed in fine linen, clean and ~~white~~:
for the fine linen is the righteousness of saints.

●─●━●

"Please," Jo said, extending a hand toward the girl on the front pew. "Don't be frightened. You're safe here." The shaky light from the votive candle showed that her visitor was terrified, although already the little dog had come to scamper around Jo's ankles. The girl, a bedraggled teen-ager, scrambled from the bench, her eyes dark orbs of terror darting frantically from her pet to Jo. But for the dog, Jo knew the girl would have run out the church doors and into disaster.

"Look," Jo lifted the small terrier, "he likes me." She smiled reassuringly as the dog, its cataract-covered eyes blinking with happiness, wriggled and tried to lick her face. "He wouldn't come near me if I wasn't all right. What's his name?"

The girl hesitated, then answered cautiously. "Beauregard." The words came through gritted teeth as she fought to control her fear. "Beau, for short." She flinched at the volume of their voices in the cavernlike hall. As she pushed the hair from her eyes, Jo saw dark liquid leaking from her palms, like the stigmata of Christ.

"You've been hurt!" She lowered Beau to the floor and steadied him until he found his footing. "We need to clean you up or the smell of blood will have the vampires battering at the doors all night." She motioned to the right, at the dark shadows beyond the altar. "I've got bandages in the office. I'm Jo. What's your name?"

"Louise." The girl took a few steps but seemed reluctant to come closer. "Do you live here? In the church?"

"Of course." Jo tilted her head. "What safer place could there be?"

"There are lots of churches that aren't safe anymore." Louise glanced around again and missed Jo's puzzled look. "It's so *dark* in here. Doesn't that make you nervous?"

"Not at all." Jo gestured at the altar and its carefully polished holy objects. "This is a place where God's children can come for safety and solace anytime. There is no evil here, in either daylight or darkness." Her hair floated around her white dress like a shimmering veil and she swept it aside and picked up the matchbook again. "But if it makes you feel better, I'll light more candles. If you like, I'll light them *all*."

Back in the vestibule something scraped against the front doors. There was a quick, sputtering hiss like the pop of a dud firecracker, then a muffled, enraged howl. Louise whirled, but Jo never faltered as she touched a flame to another six candles. Beau's ears perked at the noise, but he didn't bark, and Louise was too exhausted to move away when Jo took her elbow kindly. "I'm sorry that scared you." Her voice was soothing as she urged Louise toward the back, leaving little Beau to follow the sound of their voices. "But they really won't stop unless we bandage your hands." Louise looked shell-shocked and weary, and Jo's heart went out to her. Both Louise's hands were crusted with dried blood topped with droplets of fresh red. Still, Jo couldn't help smiling. "I'm glad you came tonight," she said earnestly. Her arm came up and she gave the older girl a quick, sisterly hug.

"It's time things got started."

The nave was ablaze with candlelight. Louise couldn't believe it; she kept imagining a whole group of bloodsuckers knotted on the steps by the church entrance, having a friendly little conference about how to get inside. The easiest way would be to lift something really heavy—and oh, God, they were *so* strong!—and simply ram one of the doors with full strength. With a door busted—

"It wouldn't matter, you know." Jo's gentle voice floated from the circular area at the rear of the altar, where she was rummaging in a chest topped by a velvet cushion. "They still couldn't step over the threshold of a holy place."

From where she sat, Louise had to squint to see Jo's face and her smile amid the wildly flickering candlelight. "You read minds?" Louise asked incredulously. Directly across from Jo, Beau snoozed on another velvet settee, oblivious to the occasional scrabbling sounds at the front doors.

Jo made her way back to where Louise rested. "Of course not. I just assumed that's what you were thinking. Look." She held up bandages, adhesive tape, and a bottle of scarlet liquid—Mercurochrome.

"Do churches always keep medical supplies behind the altar?" Louise asked dryly as she reached for them.

Jo pushed her bloodied hands aside. "I'll do it, and no, that's just where I put them for emergencies. Handy, too—I don't think you would've made it to the back offices, and certainly not the kitchen. That's in the basement." Trying to descend the stairs earlier had nearly made Louise pass out; two fuzzy seconds later she had found herself held by Jo's slender but very strong arms, and she flushed with embarrassment at the recollection.

"It's been a long day," she muttered.

"I'll bet." Jo set a plastic bowl of water on the pew next to Louise. "Let's take a look." Louise reluctantly held out her palms. Both were scored with small, deep gashes; some still bled while others had stopped simply because the flesh had swollen the cuts shut. The skin was a colorful combination of blue, black, and yellow.

It's the candlelight, Louise thought grimly as Jo dipped a soft cloth in the bowl and began to carefully sponge the wounds. *They won't look that bad tomorrow.* Aloud she asked, "Where'd you get the water?"

"It's river water," Jo answered. Louise's eyes widened and she started to pull away, but Jo held her firmly. "Don't worry. It's been blessed."

"Blessed?" Louise eyed the bowl doubtfully. It looked clean and it *had* been nearly two years since any of the factories had operated. Still. . . .

" 'I will wash mine hands in innocency,' " Jo quoted. "Psalm Twenty-six." She pulled Louise's hand closer to inspect it; it looked raw but she couldn't see any more dirt. She spread a towel on her knees and rested the injured hand on it while she opened the bottle of antibacterial. Louise hissed as the medicine sank into the gashes and pain lanced up her wrist.

Jo looked at her in concern. "I'm sorry it hurts, but this red stuff should keep it from getting infected."

Louise gave the girl a taut smile. "Just get it over with." Jo bent back to her task, but Louise could see Jo's dread in the tense set of the younger woman's shoulders. At last it was over and Jo taped clean gauze around both of Louise's hands. "I can't move my fingers," Louise complained. "Can't we fix it differently?"

"You don't *want* to move them for a while." Jo pressed the last pieces of tape in place. "Otherwise you'll open the wounds." She pulled a small packet of aspirin from her pocket. "These will help the pain. I'll get you some drinking water, then we'll look at your knee."

Louise watched her go, noting the way Beau followed the sound of her footsteps across the floor with sleepy snuffles before laying his head back on his paws. The girl was ... what? Some kind of angel? With her hip-length platinum hair and that white dress she was almost too bright to look at. Had she lived all these months in St. Peter's? It seemed likely since the church was still sanctified. On the one hand Louise was overjoyed to find someone else alive; on the other, it was a crushing disappointment to realize the girl had been staying here all this time but had found no one else.

Or had she?

Jo returned with a cup of water, and Louise took it and swallowed the aspirins without hesitating; everything below her wrists was nothing short of twitching agony. Like her hands, her knee was swollen and stiff, but her jeans had kept the wounds from being as deep and Louise thought it would heal fairly fast. Besides the cup, Jo had brought a small pair of scissors to cut away the edges of the torn fabric.

"Hey!" Louise protested.

"I'll get you another pair tomorrow," Jo soothed. She

swabbed at the bruised knee, then carefully applied the Mercurochrome.

"So," Louise said, "you live here by yourself?"

"No," Jo answered immediately. Louise's hopes rose, then fell again with Jo's next quote. " 'For he hath said, I will never leave thee, nor forsake thee.' Hebrews, chapter thirteen, verse five." Jo sat back. "All finished."

"Is there . . ." Louise found it difficult to push the words from her mouth. "Is there anyone else? Anyone at all?"

"Of course." Louise gaped and Jo tilted her head. "Did you really think God would let His children be exterminated?"

"I—I didn't know," Louise whispered. It was impossible for her to comprehend this girl's faith, and for a terrible instant she wondered if Jo might simply be slightly . . . *daft*.

"There are quite a few other people." Jo rose and gathered the remnants of gauze and tape, then put the bowl of blood-tinted water aside; tomorrow she would pour the water down a storm drain outside. "Mostly downtown, where it's easier to find food and there are bigger places in which to hide." She glanced at Louise. "That's what you were looking for, wasn't it?"

Louise nodded.

"I've seen people now and then, though they've never seen me. There's a group in Water Tower Place on Michigan Avenue, another in the Civic Opera Building. I'm surprised no one has explored St. Peter's." She looked wistful. "I really thought I'd have company before now."

"Then why haven't you spoken to them?" Louise asked in amazement. "Wouldn't you be safer?"

Jo shrugged. "They've built little communities, and while they have strength in numbers, that can be a weakness, too. I'm quite safe here and besides, I have other things to do. And there're more."

"*More?*" Louise was grinning now; she couldn't help it.

"There're a lot in the Building of the Damned." Jo's face lost its youth for a moment, her voice suddenly sounding very old and troubled.

"The what?" Louise asked in confusion. She felt like

someone had stuck a pin in her party balloon. "Building of the Damned? Where—?"

"It's a bad place," Jo said simply. She turned away, then swung back, her hair spilling over one arm like a silvery waterfall. Louise again had the eerie impression she was talking with some kind of angel. "Have you eaten?"

Louise shook her head and started to ask about Jo's strange statement, but Jo cut her off. "Come with me. I'll fix you and Beau something quick, then we'll rest. Sunlight is too precious to sleep through.

"Besides, dawn comes earlier for me."

Louise rose unsteadily and followed Jo into the recesses at the back of the church. What had she just said?

Dawn comes earlier?

19

REVELATION 9:8
And they had hair as the hair of women,
and their teeth were as the teeth of lions.

REVELATION 17:6
And I saw the woman drunken
with the blood of the saints,
and with the blood of the martyrs. . . .

●●●●

"You disgusting maggot, you're not even fit for food!"

Rita ached to split the man from throat to crotch, but Siebold had retreated four or five doors away to what he believed was a safe distance. The snail would live to see another of his precious sunrises; she couldn't risk Anyelet's anger by killing him. Anyelet, who watched impassively from the stairwell, was the only reason Siebold still breathed.

"Look at this woman!" Rita gestured furiously at the pale, shivering form. "Not only did you beat her senseless, you made her available for a feeding the same night!" She gave a feline snarl. "Her second night here, and she's already half dead!" Rita stepped inside the room and tossed another blanket over the terrified figure on the floor, noting that the woman was too weak to even pull away. She stormed back into the hallway toward Siebold, who squawked and lumbered farther away.

"Rita."

Anyelet's honeyed voice stopped her. Little could be seen of the Mistress beyond her glittering eyes, like burning stars in an ebony sky.

"He's a fool," Rita said sullenly. "We don't need him—there are other ways to deal with the humans during the day."

Anyelet didn't answer; instead, she turned her displeased gaze on the cowering Siebold. "Howard," she said, "you are useful to us. Yes?" Anyelet smiled and Rita could see the redhead's wet fangs gleam. How she would love to see Anyelet tear out that slug's throat—better, she would gladly do the job herself. "But you are becoming careless in the ways you take payment—"

"But you said I could do anything!" Siebold exclaimed. Spittle flew from his lips and Rita's mouth twisted in revulsion. "Anything at all!"

"No one said you could *kill*, you idiot!" Rita snapped.

"I didn't—" Howard began with exaggerated patience.

Anger overruled reason and Rita crossed Siebold's "safe" distance before the pig could blink; one hand, fingers filled with incredible strength, wrapped around his throat ahead of his would-be scream. Her talonlike nails sank into his neck and she pushed her face close, mouth stretched in an evil smile; beneath the smell of his body—a combination of filth, old sweat, and beef broth— the scent of blood pulsed fast and strong, fired by the jets of adrenaline pounding through his bloodstream.

"But you *wanted* to, didn't you?" she demanded through a terrible grin. Siebold's hands fluttered ineffectively around her back as her nails sank deeper. "Didn't you?"

"That's enough."

Rita stiffened at Anyelet's voice, then grudgingly eased her fingernails from their crescent-shaped depressions in the fatty folds of Siebold's flesh. Before she released him, she rubbed her face affectionately against Howard's cheek, her earrings swinging like sharp holiday ornaments. "You lucked out," she murmured. *"This time."* In the second it took her to step back, he gasped as Rita's other hand found his crotch and gave him a swift, cruel squeeze. His bulging eyes followed her as she glided away and held up the hand that had encircled his neck; the tips of the first and middle fingers glistened with his blood. Rita flicked her tongue over the nails as he watched, then grimaced and spat the red-tinted wetness at his feet. It was a pleasure to see the flush of anger on his florid, oily face—almost better than his fear. Then again, she decided, anyone could frighten a cowardly animal. Better to slaughter it.

Anyelet moved out of the doorway. "You may go, Howard."

"But I thought . . ." He glanced longingly at the quivering female prisoner, his voice a thin whine. "I wanted—"

"Not tonight." Anyelet turned her back on Siebold's sulking figure and addressed Rita. "The woman must be fed tonight, by force if necessary."

Rita nodded. Her eyes flicked distastefully to Siebold, scuttling away like some kind of giant, mutant cockroach. "What about him?"

Anyelet grimaced at Siebold and the heavy man finally retreated up the stairs. "He's becoming a problem," she allowed finally.

"I could eliminate him," Rita offered eagerly.

"Soon. First we must find another breeder."

Rita trailed Anyelet as she moved leisurely down the hallway. "That could be difficult."

"Perhaps." Anyelet stopped at a doorway and turned its magnet to black. The man inside looked drawn but still healthy, though Rita thought he was nothing special, pale brown hair over paler-still skin, crystalline gray eyes above smudged blue circles of weariness. She'd certainly seen handsomer men. Still, Rita ground her teeth as Anyelet chose this same man yet again. Why?

"But perhaps not."

Rita watched with jealous fascination as Anyelet entered the room soundlessly and offered her hand to the naked figure crouched on the floor. The sense of struggle between her and the man was almost palpable as Anyelet willed him to rise and step into her opened arms. When he finally did, Rita could see that the man had a full erection and his breathing was coming short and fast through parted lips.

"Please," he whispered hoarsely. "Don't."

The words were still hanging on his lips as Anyelet's cold, silken hands slid down his body and he shuddered and let her pull him close. His eyes rolled up when her lips trailed the line of his jaw and brushed his neck. Mouth not quite touching his skin, Anyelet raised her eyes to Rita. "And do you know why?" she asked. She nuzzled the man's neck softly.

"Because . . ." Rita hesitated. "Man will always think of himself first." She looked on resentfully as the prisoner's thin arms slid around Anyelet's waist.

Anyelet smiled, then sank her teeth deep into the offering of white flesh. Her victim's hands spasmed with pleasure and reached to pull the Mistress closer as Rita averted her gaze and slipped away from the dark lovers.

Stephen Rhodes wanted to moan aloud, to pray, to call out to God for release. There were a lot of things that he wanted, as a matter of fact. High on the list was sleep, without the dreams of Anyelet that tormented him every night. But he didn't dare call out. There had been a time, months ago, when he had tried to pray in this place. The beautiful black vampire called Rita—he had learned all their names—had shown him the stupidity of vocalizing his faith by hurling him repeatedly across the small room that was now his home.

But he still believed, oh yes. And God would surely damn him for eternity.

A lifetime ago Stephen had been a second-year Jesuit student at Loyola University. He planned to be a priest, to lead God's flock—or that much of the populace as he could get his holy little hands on—straight to salvation. Then, the seminary had been luxurious compared to his expectations: he had always pictured himself living in a dim cell with a hard, narrow bed and thin blanket, rising at four A.M. to join his brothers in prayer as he lived out his days in stark, unfailing service to God. How ironic that he spent his days and nights in just such a room now, without even the comfort of the imagined cot. And in his monkish fantasies, he had always been fully clothed.

He shivered and fumbled around the floor, trying to find the blanket. His mind provided a new fantasy: instead of the dirty blanket, his searching fingers found a knife, unknowingly dropped by that horrible man who guarded them during the day and regularly raped the women and some of the men. The knife was sharp and long and gleaming in the meager light thrown from the candles in the hallway. It was righteous and clean, and Stephen knew it would cut deep. But though Stephen was a weak son, he was a faithful one and suicide was unthinkable. Instead, he smiled at Anyelet as she glided into his room, then quoted a line of Scripture, his voice, clear and strong, spilling into her ears before she could stop its burning impact.

"If thine hand offends thee, cut it off."

And he castrated himself.

Instead of the dream he longed for, Stephen's feeble hand closed around a corner of the blanket; he struggled to roll his freezing body into a cocoon within the material, his chain dragging against his raw ankle. How much blood had she taken tonight? And the time before, and before that? He cursed himself for trying to estimate how long he had been here, knowing he was only gauging the nights before she came again. His neck was an unhealing wound, and when that became too thick with scabs, Anyelet found other places to put her lips, sometimes in the bend of his elbow, once high on his inner thigh as she sought the femoral artery.

This time Stephen did moan out loud. The memory made him burn with need, though it had only been a few hours since her visit. He wouldn't have thought there was enough blood in him to manage it, but he was growing hard again, desire building as he remembered her lips against his neck, the touch of her frigid fingers sliding down his hips and thighs, reaching under to cup his testicles as she fed—

"No!" He fought to a sitting position. Anemia made him dizzy and he coughed, trying to clear his perpetually congested lungs. He wanted to throw off the blanket and use the chilly air to clear his head, but the ache in his chest warned against such a foolish act. How could he crave that female abomination when the women of his own kind had never attracted him? He had planned to be a *priest*—how could he surrender so easily to the unholy lust that she awoke? I will be strong, he told himself. The next time Anyelet comes I won't respond. She—

"Stephen."

His head jerked up. For a second he thought his earlier fantasy had come true: there she stood, a silhouette in the doorway backlit by the faint glow of candlelight. His fingers spasmed around a knife that wasn't there, then he realized he wasn't dreaming at all.

"No!" he rasped. "Go away! You've already—"

"I didn't come to feed, Stephen." Her voice was velvety as she slithered toward him.

"*Go away!*" he sputtered again. He scrambled away, hating himself for crawling along the floor like a terrified lizard until the chain stopped his flight.

Anyelet knelt in front of his cringing, pale body. He tried to resist looking into the black pools of her eyes and made the mistake of gazing at her lips—so red and moist—instead. He wrenched his eyes away and squeezed them shut. Another stupid mistake.

"*I came to reward you.*"

Something cool and silky fluttered against his cheek and the skin of his shoulder where the blanket had fallen aside. He reached to push it away—some kind of gauzy fabric—and found his damp hand encased in one of hers. "You what?" he whispered. He opened his eyes and saw his wrist encircled by her fingers, watched with nearly orgasmic dread as she pulled his hand up and curved it around the cold whiteness of her naked breast. When she released him, he hated himself for his failure to pull away. As Anyelet tugged the blanket from him, Stephen's eyes drank in her unclothed figure, felt his traitorous hands wander lightly across her exposed flesh in defiance of his conscious will.

It was strange, he thought disjointedly, to be feeling this. In the rare moments of his youth that he had wondered what it would be like to touch a girl, he had always imagined her skin would be warm. Perhaps the breasts and thighs of a *real* woman would be, but the creature with which he now joined encased him like a sheath of ice. As he pulled her arctic length closer and caressed her coldest places, it didn't matter that she still fed upon him, though this time she took warmth instead of blood. She had gotten into his mind somehow, and nothing mattered but the desire.

Forgive me, Father.

He cried the words in his mind, where the she-beast that possessed him couldn't stop them.

Forgive—

Rapture.

20

●◐●◑●◐●◑

REVELATION 9:5
And to them it was given that
they should not kill them,
but that they should be tormented. . . .

●●◑●

"I'm hungry," Hugh announced.

The others ignored him and went on about their business, carrying on conversations, planning forays for food or whatever; Hugh stayed in the corner and waited for a few more minutes, until his weathered face sagged into confusion. He was hungry—shouldn't someone feed him? Where was Tisbee, and why didn't she have dinner ready? And besides that, where the hell was that boy?

In another second, he spied Vic Massucci and sprinted across the lobby, grabbed Vic's arm and ground his teeth into it, his yellowed fangs ripping through the skin and searching uselessly for a full blood vessel. But Vic's earlier feeding had long been absorbed; the bodybuilder looked at him with a pained expression and shook him off easily, swatting Hugh away like an annoying housefly. "Cut it out!" Vic snapped. He rubbed his arm automatically, though the bite had hardly stung and his flesh was already closing.

Hugh stumbled away, tripping among the plush furnishings until he found the far wall and pressed against the bamboo-textured wallpaper in wonder. He swept his gnarled fingers in wide circles along the wall, round and round, and began singing softly to himself. "Swe-e-et emoooo-shun," he crooned. "*Ba*-dap, *ba* da da da da." There were shadowed, moving things with him here, but they held no warmth or food and thus were of no use. But the music was a different thing: it was always there, always a comfort, always feeding energetic pulses through his hot and ravenous brain. Up and down, all the time, even in his sleep. Sometimes he could see the notes, dancing among his fingers like little animated figures from antique cartoons, each exploding into glittering showers when he caught and squeezed it.

The others watched for a few moments, then Anyelet sighed. "I understand The Hunger as well as anyone, but why turn an abomination like him into one of us?"

Rita snorted. "Maybe they thought it was a joke."

"Very funny. If I ever find out who did it, I'll laugh as I personally dig their teeth out." The redhead's sharp voice caught Hugh's attention and he wandered back, performing a clumsy two-step to music that only he could hear.

"I wonder how he feeds," Rita mused. "We don't let him near the people upstairs, and he doesn't have the sense to hunt . . . does he?"

"This damned place is *UGLY!*" Hugh suddenly screamed. He gestured frantically at the pink-and-lavender decor. *"Look!"*

Gregory, a sensitive-looking young man who had once been an accountant, spoke. "We should kill him and be done with it. He's a liability." His thin fingers stroked the collar of his sweatshirt as though searching for a lost tie, then carefully smoothed his sand-colored hair.

"I like him," Vic said stonily. His face had gone dangerously rigid and he folded powerful arms and stared hard at the smaller vampire. "He's *interesting.*"

"Still—"

"If he amuses Vic, let him be," Anyelet interrupted.

Greg shrugged his acquiescence. "Sure. Whatever you say."

Hugh moved in front of Anyelet, his wrinkled face earnest around eternally dreamy eyes. "I remember a place where there were paintings and sculptures from the old country, so beautiful—"

Anyelet started. "Old country? Which old country?"

"—not like this *shit* here, this damned *SHIT* they call decorating—"

"Hey," Vic said. "Calm down, Hugh." The old guy's arms were flailing like wet spaghetti.

"What does he mean, 'old country'?" Anyelet asked again.

Hugh frowned at her. Sometimes even the Mistress—and sure, he knew who she was, all right, she was the

BIG CHEESE, the *MAIN MAN*, or the *DON*, as they
would have said in the old country—even *she* was not so
bright as he would have thought. "In *Italy*, of course," he
said patiently. "Where else?"

"Where else?" Rita mimicked sarcastically.

The Mistress, Hugh suddenly decided, was very beautiful, like a holy woman he had once worshiped but
couldn't think of now because doing so burned holes in
his mind. It was only proper to surround her with beautiful things. He did a shuffling twirl in homage. "Da
Vinci!" he sang merrily. "Van Gogh, Monet!"

"Well, well," Greg said. "He still knows the names of
the artsy crowd."

Hugh stopped by Vic. "Let's go shopping now, everybody's shopping now, come on a safari with me-e-e!" His
cracked voice wailing the altered Beach Boys tune as he
hopped around made Vic wince. Hugh spun and abruptly
dropped to his knees in front of Anyelet, his old bones
making a hollow *thunk* as they hit the floor. "Let me es-
cort you there," he pleaded, clasping his hands. "Its
beauty is surpassed only by yours." He grinned, showing
ancient fangs that barely held a point.

Anyelet gazed at him impassively. "What place is this,
Hugh?"

Instead of answering, he pulled her hand reverently to
his chest, crooning to it as though it were an infant.

"I think he means the Art Institute," Vic said. "That
would make sense."

Rita rolled her eyes. "Nothing Hugh says makes
sense," she sneered. "Besides, why bother?"

Still on his knees, Hugh let out a shrill laugh. "Might
find other stuff, too!" he cackled.

"What?" Anyelet demanded. Her eyes turned sharp.
"Answer me!"

"It's locked." Hugh looked up at her trustingly, his face
old and strangely childlike.

"Are there people there, Hugh?" Anyelet persisted.
"Humans?"

He nodded sagely as Rita's eyebrows raised. "Sure,
lots of them. You should see the Warhol exhibit."

Greg made a disgusted sound. "The old fool is talking

about the paintings. He wouldn't know a human if one bit *him*."

"I saw a body on the railroad tracks," Hugh said sweetly.

"You did?" Anyelet dropped gracefully into a crouch, like a panther settling on its haunches. "When?"

Hugh closed his eyes and began humming tunelessly, still clutching Anyelet's hand. Holding onto her made him feel secure and serene, like Tisbee had once made him feel. Got to find that woman, he reminded himself without pausing. And switch that kid a good one for being gone so long. Fathers are so *unappreciated*—

"Hugh," Anyelet commanded. "Open your eyes and look at me." She tapped his cheek and his eyes, wet and red, opened sleepily. She locked gazes, then went *inside*, deep into the recesses of his mind, searching for the memory he'd spoken of, trying to discover if it was real. Fragments spun and crashed in his thoughts—

a tall woman with dark hair and darker eyes holding a child Tisbee my son can't find them why can't I remember big gray stone buildings I'm not old and the so dark subway what do they mean Alzheimer's where is Tisbee find that boy can't happen to me can't remember what he looks like see that body on the tracks someone shot a hole right through its chest fall and all the leaves whirling around all dried red no food so many colors can't find Tisbee want to get in see the paintings I used to all that music but the door locked reinforced sounds so pretty don't care—

—and Anyelet found it difficult to make sense of them. Severing the contact, she stood and hauled Hugh up; he chortled happily and pirouetted away, careening off a couch and into an end table.

"Someone take him outside before he knocks over a candle and sets the place on fire." Anyelet struggled to sort through the images still flitting in her mind. The man was insane, but apparently he *had* seen the body of a murdered human by the Art Institute last fall, though her guess was that it had probably rotted away by now. But there might be humans hiding in that building, and Hugh was simply unable to convey that idea. It was worth investigating.

"Come on, old one," Vic said. He grasped Hugh's frail-looking wrist with a massive hand. "Time to go."

"Sure," Hugh agreed. "Let's go to the opera!" He tipped his head back and let out a howl that sounded like nothing so much as a dying wolf.

Anyelet watched them go, then turned to Rita and Gregory. "We'll go to the Art Institute tomorrow night." Her eyes matched the glittering candleflames reflected in the glass cases along the lobby walls. "We've been lazy— there're plenty of humans in this city that we should be catching and breeding. The ones here won't last forever."

"Especially with that pig Siebold," Rita interjected.

"True. It's time we considered our future. Our own recklessness will be our suicide." She settled onto an upholstered chair and stared at the candelabra on the table. Closing her eyes, she listened to Hugh's fading, faraway singing, wondering at the things in his mind.

Vic led the old man down the riverfront sidewalk to Wells Street, then gave him a little push toward downtown. "Go on now," he said. "Find yourself something to eat."

"Hungry," Hugh complained. He took a few steps, then stopped and turned back. He smiled crookedly. "Tisbee will fix dinner in a little while. You're invited, too."

Vic looked at him sadly. "Tisbee's gone, Hugh. She's never coming back." How many times had he said those words?

"Gone?" Hugh looked puzzled. "Where would she go?" He ambled away, already forgetting about Vic and the others. Why, Vic wondered, couldn't fate be more merciful and let the sun catch Hugh in the morning? Dark instinct, in Hugh's case, seemed stronger than insanity.

A half block away, Hugh began singing again. The unnatural silence in the city made it easy for Hugh's voice to carry.

"One is the loneliest number . . ."

Vic jerked around as he recognized the Three Dog Night song from decades ago. Where in the hell had the old man learned all these rock-and-roll songs? He couldn't help straining to hear the next line.

"Twooooo can be as bad as one . . ."

Staring after Hugh, Vic realized what he hated most about being a vampire.

He hated not being able to cry.

21

REVELATION 18:2
And he is become the habitation of devils,
and the hold of every foul spirit,
and a cage of every unclean
and hateful thing.

■●■

"One of these days I'll take that bitch down a peg or two," Howard Siebold said loudly. No one answered and in frustration he lashed out with his foot at a battered vinyl-covered chair. He yelped, scowled, and flexed his bruised toe before pacing the ten-foot room once more.

Siebold rubbed his hands briskly up and down his flabby arms, trying to warm the skin through his stained sweater. It was Rita's fault he was cold; if she hadn't pointed out to the Mistress the way he'd beaten the new woman, that same woman would have helped raise his body temperature before he'd come home to this damned little icebox. They would've had a fine time, you betcha. God, how he despised this ancient monstrosity of a building. Eighteen floors—plus a tower if a man was crazy enough to actually climb that high—of little besides cramped, drafty offices and tiny shops split by endless, echoing halls and the occasional cavernous showroom, thousands of rooms smashed into a shape resembling nothing more than a shoebox four blocks square upon which a bored architect had centered a leftover peak. He kicked out again, this time at the empty propane heater. What he ought to do was crawl into his Quallofil sleeping bag and get some shut-eye. In the morning it would be warmer and he could ride his bike over to Morrie Mages Sporting Goods and fill a backpack with propane canisters, and more cooking fuel, too, if the worms on the third floor were going to get something besides cereal and cold soup. He dreaded it, though; it would take him a laboring half hour to get there, and longer to return carrying a load. He wished he had a car, but none of the ones around here would run.

Siebold wished he had *company*. "Shit!" The room was so small that after only a few steps, he had to turn around. He'd already staked out one of the south-side showrooms on the fourth floor—only one floor above the prisoners but still high enough where he could feel comfortable at night . . . most of the time, anyway. A few more weeks and it ought to be warm enough to move to those bigger quarters and get the hell out of this little pit. He'd wintered in a small room because it was easier to heat, but most of the time he didn't need a heater; he had great natural insulation and the sleeping bag was enough unless the temperature dropped below ten or fifteen. He was cold now because he was horny and had expected better.

"Bitch," he repeated, but with less vehemence. The bodybuilder, Vic, was another problem—no love lost there. The guy had never liked him, but after coming out of the woman's cubicle—and with a full belly, too!—he'd looked like he wanted to kill Howard twice as bad. But Vic hadn't said anything, and that was somehow worse than Rita, who never missed a chance to voice her hatred. The way Vic watched him was scary, like the man was just waiting for a chance to . . . what? Howard rubbed his throat and the crusting sores, remembering Rita's open attempt to throttle him. It might be best if he curbed his more . . . *vigorous* appetites for a while and concentrated on trying to breed the women, stop wasting virility on the guys who pissed him off. If he could get a few of the gals knocked up, it wouldn't matter what Rita thought. In warmer weather the prisoners wouldn't be so miserable all the time; not only were his chances better with a healthier broad, they'd be more fun when they had energy to do something besides lie there. Even using self-restraint, Howard thought he could still have fun.

Vic could still be a problem, but the two vampires would obey Anyelet, and Howard was positive she would protect him if he did his job well. He *had* been apathetic and self-indulgent—blame it on the weather—but he'd turn things around.

He wedged himself into the sleeping bag, then blew out the single candle illuminating the room. In the darkness, Howard couldn't resist rubbing his hands together in anticipation.

There could still be hot times in the cool nights to come.

You betcha.

22

●━━●·●━━●·●━━●·●━━●

REVELATION 18:19
For in one hour is she made desolate.

●━━●·●●━━●

I am a dead woman.

Deb didn't know why the thought exploded into her mind, but it spread with enough force and certainty to jar her awake. The noises in the old building were soft and familiar; she could almost *feel* the rightness of the huge stone blocks, the insets of metal and glass, windows and doors, still sense their unbreached security. She was safe. *Tonight.*

But not . . . when? Tomorrow night? Or the next? Deb forced her breathing to slow as she listened to her life's air swelling and ebbing in the dark like a miniature bellows. Waking prematurely yesterday had been a fluke—she had scared herself with her own silly paranoia. Now there was no reluctance to move and no doubt that she was alone in the Art Institute, and although the cot was good for sleeping when she was exhausted, awake it was narrow and uncomfortable; Deb finally sat up, sliding the Winchester under the cot without hesitation. She found her book of matches and lit the lamp, watching the welcome glow spread through the alcove before scrubbing at her face with her hands and looking at her watch: three o'clock. Three hours to sunrise.

I should be afraid, Deb thought. Hell, I *am* afraid. But it won't do any good.

I am a dead woman.

She inhaled deeply, calmer, vaguely accepting. When? The oil lamp's golden light glimmered softly on the burgundy-colored drapes encircling her small, cozy home. "Not tonight," she said aloud. Her voice should have been frightening in the semisoundless room; instead she found it reassuring. She combed her fingers absently through her hair and tried to think. Why this sudden premonition? Her life had changed drastically today—perhaps Alex was the answer. As much as she would like to think he was different, maybe in reality he wasn't. . . .

She didn't believe that. Her game of making sure he didn't follow her when they'd parted had been just that—a game. Her intuition insisted he was trustworthy, just as it had made her leery of John last fall. Her reluctance was just a way of dealing with too much too fast; she was already looking forward to seeing him tomorrow.

Tomorrow. . . .

Her shoulders sagged and she fought the tears suddenly burning her eyes and making a smear of the lamplight around her. Tomorrow would come, but what about tomorrow night? Or the next day?

God, she hated crying, and the flaring pain in her stomach made her want to cry even more. Not because it hurt—she could deal with pain. What really *stung* was knowing that she no longer needed to go to the library or read up on it.

Her ulcer just didn't matter anymore.

The tears splashing her hands sparkled like drops of honey in the gentle light.

I am a dead woman.

23

REVELATION 18:24
And in her was found the blood of prophets, and of saints,
and of all that were slain upon the earth.

To the human eye, the city under tonight's cloud-hidden
quarter moon was a gray haze, downtown a deserted, il-
lusory shadow across the river like a black-and-white film
frozen at its darkest moment. Staring over the east railing
of the Wells Street Bridge, Anyelet smiled widely. This
city wasn't dead at all; she could *feel* the life still pulsating within it. It might seem empty to a puny, light-loving
human, yet let that same fool dare to walk its sidewalks—
her sidewalks. If he or she were lucky, they would be
captured and brought to the Mart by one of Anyelet's
soldiers. Otherwise. . . .

Her calculating gaze swept the southern side of the
Chicago River, following the narrow concrete park along
its base and seeing even through the distant darkness the
tiny buds sprouting on the tree branches. The fancy
stone sidewalks were spotted with granite benches and
matching trash bins between trees encircled by metal
sunbursts set into the concrete. Two years before, office
workers had carried lunches down those steps, ignoring
the transients and winos who made the minipark a place
of residence in the warmer months. Then the riverside
had been unsafe to most citizens at night. Now it was
death, and Anyelet's eyes narrowed as she picked out a
few moving figures in the blackness down there, starving
things that could barely carry their own weight but
whose presence forced her soldiers to move in twos and
threes away from the Merchandise Mart. Anyelet seemed
to be the only one able to travel anywhere alone, which
was as it should be. A year ago it had never occurred to
her that one vampire might prey on another, so desperate

would they become in The Hunger. Before now, she had thought the food would never end, like the queen in the hive, blindly enjoying the fruits of her womb as they catered to her every whim.

But the food *had* run out, and by the time she'd realized what was happening, it had been far, far too late. Chicago, the continent, the *world*, had been filled with her children, and her children's children, *ad infinitum*. In their feeding frenzy, they had doubled each night, conquering this huge city in only slightly more than three weeks. The mathematics had been astounding: Anyelet had reproduced, created a single child, then taken that nativity to the nth power. All those faraway places—California, Hawaii, Asia, Europe, every island and continent in the world—had been victimized as her offspring fanned out, crossing borders and oceans, using boats and those oh-so-wondrous airplanes to take The Hunger to every possible point on this suddenly too-small planet.

And why? She breathed deeply of the night air and gripped the steel railing, listening to the lap of the water as it kissed the supporting walls on each side. Because she had grown *tired*; tired of hiding, tired of being alone and inventing stupid little games so that she could feed without arousing suspicion, tired of forever being the stranger. All those epochs blurred together: here in the twentieth century Anyelet alone knew the real reason Stonehenge had been erected, and while the avenues of her memory were blurred, she could still recall the first night of her solitary existence, her dark and bloody birth upon the Slaughter Stone facing Stonehenge amid a circle of horrified, barbaric priests. After twoscore centuries Anyelet knew the location of countless undiscovered riches still hidden in the sands of Egypt, and the fates of dozens of civilizations in the steaming tropics of South America. In the youth of man she'd had so many opportunities to feed unnoticed, all those wars and atrocities through which she'd slipped unseen—the Crusades, the American Civil War, the death camps of Germany, Korea, and, of course, Vietnam, with its ingeniously camouflaged prisoners of war. So many secrets, blending like melting wax as the years sped uselessly, boringly by. Because at

its most fulfilling, what had her nights been but an endless hunt for the next meal? She wanted fellowship and
servants, the sound of voices raised in adulation and respect, the everlasting degree of *power* that belonged to
her by the very fact of her dark and immortal being.

Finally Anyelet had risen one cool fall night with a
need so great it nearly eclipsed The Hunger, a need to
walk where and when she pleased and choose anyone for
food or entertainment, the burning, irresistible desire to
surround herself with an entourage of immortal companions. Chicago teemed with life, its music and laughter
and screams enfolding her in an endless, vivacious
bloodscent. At the time her reasoning had been so clear:
This was a city of plenty. *Why shouldn't she claim it?*

And so she had. There was little forethought, just a
smug self-confidence that whomever she created would
be hers forever, a multitude of little puppets eternally
dancing on her strings. So many centuries had passed in
her existence yet *never* had she met another like herself,
and the few she'd accidentally created in the dawn of her
being had failed to survive, perishing from stupidity or
carelessness, leaving as their legacy enough evidence to
create the lore and superstition that forced her into per-
petual hiding. When at last she'd sunk her fangs into the
first of the humans who would help her bring down this
city, there'd been no one to guide her, no one from whom
she could seek answers or advice. She'd had only a burning rage and strength of will born of millennia of isolation.

As she had in her earlier dream, Anyelet now spread
her arms wide, feeling an odd mixture of fulfillment from
the man who had pleasured her and unease from the
dream's horrifying end. It was regrettably true that she
had started the chain reaction that had all but emptied
this planet, and her decision had been brash and swift
and devastatingly *unstoppable*. She might call her children an army, but in reality her "soldiers" were simply
the strongest and most obedient of her creations. Anyelet
had once thought mankind was her enemy, but she had
been so very wrong. Her true enemy was also her truest
and most constant comrade: The Hunger. The Hunger

had decimated her world and driven off most of her children, making them skulk into the night like hyenas, disgusting scavengers feeding on rats and whatever else they could find in the sewers, subways, and underground avenues. The ones who remained—Rita, Vic, Gregory, and a few others—were well rewarded, but even they lacked the common goal she'd tried so hard to instill. Cohesiveness was nonexistent while self-serving greed showed itself at every turn. The vampires across the country or the world mattered little to Anyelet, and with each generation her hold became increasingly vague and tenuous, until all that remained—and it would *always* remain—was the inborn sense in every creature Anyelet encountered that she held a power, a *rightness* which could not be questioned. That sense of command would forever exist.

Eventually the outcasts would die off. The rats, diminishing in number, would keep the undead mobile but not strong; they were already tearing at each other to lessen the competition, and each sunrise killed dozens more who had been unsuccessful in the hunt and were too weak to seek shelter. Another six months and most of that garbage would be dead.

The breeze picked up from the north and she lifted her face and flared her nostrils. As Hugh had implied, there were still humans in the city, strong survivors who would make excellent additions to her "farm." With the right conditioning, Stephen, that weak would-be priest, could eventually be persuaded to replace the violent Siebold as the breeder.

The wind again, carrying its scent of weather and lifting her hair. Chicago's hidden cache of food would soon discover that the clouds were bringing more tomorrow than just an early sunset.

In another two days, they would bring snow.

Anyelet grinned, threw back her head, and shrieked joyously at the sky.

II

March 24

Rediscovery

1

"Oh, Father," Jo said unhappily as she stepped outside St. Peter's and gazed up at the still dark sky. "Your will be done. But I sure wish I knew Your reasons sometimes."

She shivered and hugged herself. The temperature was at least twenty degrees lower than last night, with sunrise later because of the heavy, ominous clouds rolling in from the west, and she could smell harsher things coming. Still rubbing her hands up and down her bare arms, Jo headed toward the south branch of the river without bothering to go back for a coat. Her hair was like a blanket anyway, and it wasn't the cold that bothered her but the danger she knew would come with it. Crossing Wacker, she stood at the metal railing on the Adams Street Bridge and looked south. What was happening far beyond the range of her eyesight or imagination? This river led to other parts of the country, warmer climates where perhaps the men and women were not so crippled by nature's cold whims. Did they struggle as hard as the small, pathetic groups here? If so, were they *successful* in those struggles? And who helped them?

I am not alone, she told herself sternly. There are others like me in other places, fighting this evil. I am *not* alone.

The water rippled like thick ink and she watched it for a few minutes. To her right the shadowed recesses of the train tracks of Union Station stretched along the river until water and retaining wall merged into one indistinguishable blur, hiding the creatures of death that dared the sunrise just enough to scuttle amid the concrete supports and stare up at her. Jo could feel their hungry eyes crawling over her flesh like fire ants, but this morning she felt no compulsion to go to them. She twisted and looked at the buildings lining the north waterfront, gleaming monoliths of steel and glass lightening under the growing glow from the eastern sky, marveling that man could build such a structure when as a child she'd hardly been able to stack blocks five high. Tilting her head, she glimpsed the sleek shape of a falcon overhead, one of the peregrines—or perhaps a new generation—freed in the city years ago to help control the pigeon population. There were still pigeons, though not as many. Lazy, trusting birds, they had been quick and easy food when starvation had begun to run its spasming hand among the vampires. Now the pigeons roosted high atop the skyscrapers with other, more timid species and took their chances among their more natural predators.

She watched the falcon until it was out of sight, then began picking her way along the riverwalks toward the Merchandise Mart. Chicago was a sad place now, full of death and immense abandoned buildings, with few corpses to show man had ever existed in this once-magnificent place, and it gave her a feeling of inconceivable emptiness, as if the city had become nothing more than a doll's world cast aside by a bored, giant child.

It was full light by the time Jo walked the northwest curve of Wacker Drive and saw the Mart, the sight of the building enough to make her ache to bring some solace to the terrified people trapped on its third floor. She had only an inkling of their future, but the time wasn't yet right and Jo did not question the things she was compelled to do.

Still, she *could* bring comfort.

She slipped inside at the Wells Street entrance. The west corridor was still deeply shadowed and would stay that way for another half hour, the dribble of light from the doors at either end combining with the high windows on the river side to give just enough illumination to drive the night creatures to their beds. Could they sense her presence here as she could sense each and every one of them? It would be so easy to find the lairs, but she wasn't physically capable of destroying more than one every couple of nights. But there were other roads to victory.

Jo's feet made only sibilant whispers along the scuffed, dusty hallway as she climbed the stairwell at the far end and stepped into the fourth-floor hallway, where only a few feet of stone and iron separated her from the prisoners directly below. No one had been up here in some time and Jo dropped to her knees, her dress and hair making feathery swirls in the silvery dust on the floor. She could *feel* them below, the pain, the hopelessness. How many were there? The rush was too strong and befuddling; she knew there were men and women but no children, though one woman had already tried to destroy the blameless child in her womb, a son fathered in rape by the man who traded their lives for his own twisted pleasure. Another, forced to womanhood at fifteen, carried the seed of a daughter though neither she nor her rapist knew it. One man had wanted nothing more than to serve God, and his torment and self-loathing seethed like hot acid in Jo's heart. Their misery filled her and made her temples pound; her breath shortened as she swept her palms along the floor and hung her head.

"Hear the voice of our supplication when we cry out to Thee," she said quietly. Her echoing voice trembled as she fought to keep going. The pain was monstrous, like a huge animal *chewing* on her insides in a frenzied, useless attempt to escape, making it unlikely she could last more than five minutes without fainting. But comfort, even a little, was never wasted.

Her eyes rolled back as her fingers pressed against the dirty linoleum until flesh and floor appeared to meld.

"Let not your hearts be troubled," she gasped, and *reached* for them.

The floor around her hands began to glow.

He was curled snugly within his blanket, warm and sated and . . . safe. In the seconds before he fully awoke, he didn't remember that the blanket encircling his wasted figure was filthy and crusted, that the floor was bare linoleum and streaked with dried urine and human waste. Then he heard a moan, low and pitiful, and

Stephen's eyes flew open when he realized that the half-human wail was coming from his own mouth. He moved then, pulling free of the dirty trap of a blanket, kicking his sticklike legs until the cruel chain around his ankle stopped him.

Oh, Lord, he thought in despair, why am I still here? Your most merciful deed would be to allow me death. He stood and tried, as he did every morning, to reach the window, as though his chain had magically grown the extra links he needed. If Satan himself had appeared and offered him death or a breath of fresh air for his soul, Stephen didn't know which he would choose. As always, the chain stopped him just short of the glass and he sank to his knees, his face bleak, not understanding how someone as simple as himself could be caught in this web of . . . *lust*. That's what it was—sex. Not the kind that went with marriage vows or even the naughty fumbling that spent itself in the backseats of cars. This was much, much worse, the illicit disease of pimps and pornographers and those who went from peep shows and paper-wrapped magazines to slick, hidden photos of children.

If only he could *die*. What did it matter that nothing waited but hell? Was this not hell *anyway*? He was an unspeakable combination of food and love toy for a creature so evil and suffocating that even the dream of freedom became nothing, every last dream was destr—

Warmth washed over him and his eyes bulged. He felt . . . he felt *healthy*! For the first time in weeks, he stood easily and gave the chain a fierce tug. The smells that hung on the fetid air faded in his nostrils, and for a second Stephen imagined he actually smelled flowers.

Drawing the chain taut, he strained forward and tried to glimpse the corridor beyond the doorway, ignoring the chill slapping his skin as the blanket dropped to his feet. Down the hall he could hear others rattling their chains and calling out in suddenly strong voices. Below the din he could hear Siebold's bellowing, his shouts escalating to roars as the captives clamored from their cells. The clear voice of another man carried from one or two rooms away.

"Hey, mister, come on! Why don't you let us go? We

understand how a guy might do anything to make it. Hell, you're scared, we're scared—we're all in the same trouble here. We won't hold any grudges. How about it?"

And Stephen knew, as warmth and an inexplicable serenity suffused him, that the man *meant* it. If Siebold were to go from room to room and open the padlocks, all these people, who had wanted nothing but to tear their jailer and rapist apart only a few minutes ago, would clap him on the back and walk from this building without so much as spitting on him.

They would *forgive*.

He thought fleetingly of Anyelet and found her only a shrinking black boil in his mind that was easy to shake away.

Howard Siebold appeared at his doorway, his rushed face florid with fear. Standing straight and proud despite the cold and filth, Stephen smiled calmly and motioned to the chain. "We could start fresh," he said. "Rebuild and live in God's light, be it sun or moon, the way it was meant to be." He stared into Howard's eyes. "Would you like to be free again?"

Siebold looked terrified and torn; sweat was pouring down his dirty face to layer another circle of salt crust around his stained collar. Eyes wide, he jerked at Stephen's words. "I can't *do* that! They'd kill me—they'd kill us all! Besides, I don't have the *keys!*"

"Not if we all stayed together," Stephen said reassuringly. "We could make it, Howard. We *could*."

The larger man hesitated, as if this strange feeling of contentment was affecting him, too. "I don—"

Abruptly the feeling was gone. Reality returned in a smothering flood of cruel sensations: cold, pain, hunger—all at once, followed for Stephen by the familiar unfulfilled desire and self-hatred. The sudden draft made his shoulders quake and Stephen was unable to stifle the perplexed groan that slipped past his lips. Siebold blinked at him, then hurried from sight. In seconds the sounds from the surrounding rooms returned once more to whispers of hopelessness and weeping.

Stephen sank to his knees on the stiff, gritty blanket and hung his head in despair.

2

REVELATION 14:11
And the smoke of their torment ascendeth up. . . .

"Wake up," Mera said. She shook his shoulder gently.

"Mmmm," he mumbled. "Just five more minutes, okay?" He smiled into his pillow with his eyes still closed.

"Dr. Bill," she said, "rise and shine."

Bill Perlman's eyes opened and he blinked at the figure crouching beside his sleeping bag and holding a small candle. Calie, her face a dark glow in the flame's light, waited patiently as the soft memory of his wife fragmented and flew away; the gray area before wakefulness had always been his most vulnerable, and the regret that Mera hadn't survived to join this newfound community leapt into his mind with razored claws. And what of his tiny son?

Calie's warm fingers brushed his cheek in an oddly sympathetic gesture, then she stood and offered her hand. "Come on," she said as he struggled up. "Let's get you breakfast and show you around. Then we can check on your vampire."

"Okay." His voice was raspy and he cleared his throat, his face carefully expressionless as she pulled him to his feet and agony flared in his foot.

"Bet that toe hurts, huh?" Calie said in a bland voice. "We'll get you some aspirin."

"Gonna take something stronger than that," Bill muttered.

Calie didn't comment as she led him, now limping openly, down a short hallway. The only light came from Calie's tiny candle and he had no idea where they were in the building or even what time it was; yesterday evening had left his mind little more than a muddled overload. He suddenly remembered his watch and peered at it: nearly six o'clock. Ten minutes more and it would be light.

"This way," she said. "Watch the beam, we're going down a flight of stairs."

"Doesn't everybody sleep on one floor?" he asked.

"No. That way if something happens during the night, there's more of a chance that some of us can escape—unless, of course, we're outnumbered."

"Not an impossibility," he commented.

She shrugged and pushed open a door on the next landing. Voices floated from far down the corridor, where soft light spilled from an open doorway. "It's less likely now than three months ago because of winter and starvation. Most of the ones left are pretty wretched, like that boy you found. Others . . ." Her voice trailed off.

"What about the others?" he prompted.

Calie hesitated. "Others are still well fed," she said finally. He opened his mouth, but they were at the doorway and she waved at it. "Go on in."

Bill stepped through and raised his eyes from where he'd been tracking his careful footsteps. For one long moment he could've sworn his eyes actually *bulged*, like some swollen-faced cartoon character.

There were close to twenty men and women seated around the room, ranging in age from a serious-faced girl of eleven or twelve, the youngest, to a hefty man in his late fifties or early sixties. *A crowd!* Bill thought. *A real, honest-to-God crowd!* The people stared with mixed expressions of caution and curiosity; the best Bill could offer in return was a stupid, rubbery grin. He wanted to say something profound, but his throat clogged in a sudden fit of shyness and he felt a tremor of nervousness when no one returned his smile. He expected everyone to continue staring, but after a few seconds most turned their gazes to Calie. He looked to her for help and she smiled and nudged him forward.

"This," she announced, "is Dr. Bill Perlman. He's going to kill the vampires."

She said it as though she'd never had a doubt.

•   •   •   •

"So," Buddy McDole said, "perhaps we should call you Dr. Van Helsing." His smile was an even mix of humor and gentle sarcasm. The three of them had moved to an upper floor, where they now sat in front of floor-to-ceiling windows overlooking Michigan Avenue; the murky details on the street below were gradually becoming clearer as the sun pushed above the structures to the east.

Bill reddened and gave Calie a sidelong glance; her warm brown eyes never wavered. "I'm afraid I'm far from finding a solution. Calie's statement was premature."

McDole's smile faded a bit. "Hope is never premature, Dr. Perlman. Remember that." Bill watched the older man measure ground coffee into a tiny paper filter suspended from a thin plastic rod, then balance the rod across the rim of a mug and pour hot water through the filter. Bill inhaled deeply as the smell of hot coffee surrounded the trio. "Handy little things." McDole grinned. "Found 'em in a coffee shop. Bet it's been a while since you had fresh brew."

Bill nodded, his mouth watering as Calie sank onto a chair to his right and watched him with silent amusement. "How long have you been here?" he finally asked. He was full of questions but her frank appraisal was distracting.

"We moved into the building last October," McDole answered. "Stocked up enough to last through the snows and stayed put during most of the cold weather." His nubby fingers bounced the thin filter bag lightly over the cup. "It wasn't too bad. A little cabin fever now and then, but we managed to pull through. And we didn't lose anybody."

Bill frowned. "It must be hard when you do."

"More than you realize," the other man said. He slid the filter into a plastic trash bag. "There are practical considerations besides the obvious pain. We used to live in the AT and T Corporate Center on Adams and Franklin. Nice place, big and new, very comfortable. Then Leonard, one of our men—a kid, really—went out screwing around by himself and didn't come back at sunset. We were packed and gone by nine the next morning."

"You *left*? But what if he came back the next day?"

McDole handed him the mug of coffee. "We had to. The best that could have happened was he might have come back and we would've been gone—though someone *was* there until midafternoon to be sure he hadn't gotten hurt and stayed hidden until daybreak. If we had stayed and he *wasn't* all right, he would've returned for sure that evening or the next, possibly with new friends. We would've all been killed. In a manner of speaking." He clasped his own mug in bear-sized hands. "The gamble was too high. The day someone doesn't come back to Water Tower—and I hope to Christ that never happens—is the day we move on."

"To where?" Bill sipped his coffee. "It must take a lot of planning to move all these people on such short notice."

McDole shrugged. "Not really. Everyone is responsible for their own stuff—if you want to keep it, you move it. Most of us have learned to travel light. I've chosen the next place, and the day we move is the day everybody finds out where that place is. Survival makes it a subject that's not open to discussion or vote; the only way to make sure we're going to a safe place is for only one person to know about it ahead of time."

"And if something happens to you?"

"Then Calie has somewhere in mind."

"And if I'm gone," Calie added, "the group will follow Ira's decision. And so on."

"Oh." Bill didn't know what to say. The idea that you couldn't trust someone enough to wait and see if they were alive warred with the sense of responsibility he felt for his fellow man, the Hippocratic oath, his instinct to give everything to ensure the continued existence of someone else. But reality was a nasty slap; he thought of his beloved Mera and how incredibly foolish and lucky he was to have lived all this time in the familiar surroundings of Northwestern. That it had been a necessary risk because of his research was nothing but a transparent excuse.

McDole leaned forward, his face grim beneath its crown of white hair. "But we can't live like this forever, Dr. Perlman. I don't believe modern man will be satisfied returning to the nomadic way of life. We've become too pleased with ourselves and too comfort-oriented. Our own intelligence will never let us revert to a perpetually harsh way of life." He waved at the plush furniture around them. "This won't last forever. More importantly, the *food* won't last forever. One of these days all the pre-packed stuff will be gone, and then what the hell do we do? Attempt to grow our own vegetables? That's a sure way to attract unwanted attention."

"Why couldn't it be done?" Bill asked. "Obviously, it would require a lot of planning—"

"No," Calie interjected. "One irresponsible move, or a spy, and we'd be finished."

"Spy?" Bill frowned at her.

"Sure," she said. "Why do you think we knew about you for a month before C.J. and I came to get you?"

Bill's eyes widened, then dropped to his hands. A month, he thought numbly. Four weeks—four *long* weeks. . . .

He felt movement and Calie was standing beside his chair, her fingers touching his shoulders. "I'm sorry," she said softly. "But it couldn't be helped. We had to be sure."

He nodded, then swallowed his hurt and watched her return to her chair. "What's this about spies?"

McDole set his cup on the floor, then stood and shoved his hands in the back pockets of his khaki slacks. "Some people," he said slowly, "will do anything to stay alive. Having been in some tricky situations myself, especially in the beginning, I can appreciate how desperate a man can get." He gazed out the window for a moment before continuing. "But I'll never know how a man can be a pimp for the lives of his own kind."

"There are people *selling* other people?" Bill leaned back. "I can't believe that."

"It's true," Calie said. "And there's worse."

Bill grimaced. "What could be worse—except, of course, becoming one of them?"

"Being bred as food."

Bill jerked. The coffee splashed unnoticed down the side of his mug and splattered his jeans. "What did you say?"

"The Merchandise Mart is being used as a corral for human flesh," Calie said simply. "Twenty or thirty people are being held prisoner there."

"Well, for God's sake, *get them OUT!*" Bill sprang from his chair. "Or are you going to wait a month, like you did to contact me? Or two? My *God*, what's the matter with you people!"

"We can't." McDole's voice was grim. "Not yet. Calm down—*sit*, dammit, and I'll explain." He waited as the doctor spun and returned to his chair, flinching as the younger man slammed the mug down on the floor in frustration. "The people are watched during the day. As far as we can tell, only one guard cooks and tends them." He hesitated, then decided against detailing the rest of the atrocities the captives endured. He turned away to hide his rage. "There may be someone else, and it's still too risky to get close. The obstacle is that they're all chained and the guard doesn't appear to have a keyring. That's probably kept by one of the vampires."

"Can't you search the building?" Bill demanded. "Or just cut the chains off?"

"We've considered that. But we're not positive there's just the one guard, and we don't know if he or they are armed. To get in, cut the chains, and get everybody out with any kind of speed, we'd have to send almost every one of our men, each loaded with bolt cutters—which might not work anyway—in addition to their own weapons." He shook his head. "Then we'd have to get all those sick people back here with*out* leaving a trail. And it'd have to be successful in a single attempt. How could we leave anyone behind to face the vampires that night? It's just too damned dangerous."

"What about a torch?" Bill asked. "Melt the chains or something."

"We found one of those," Calie offered. "In the Hanley-Dawson body shop on LaSalle."

"Well?" Bill raised his eyebrows at McDole.

The older man looked helpless. "It's a huge, double-tanked acetylene job, but no one here knows how to operate it. I've got carpenters, lawyers—I was a bookstore manager, myself—but no one who's used anything more complex or dangerous than propane. And if you've seen the Mart, you realize it'd be impossible to search for something like a keyring. The building is immense—it covers more than four blocks and it's linked with the Apparel Center, a building which is almost as big, by a skyway over Orleans Street. There's nothing we can do—"

"—yet," Calie finished for him. She slid off the chair cushion to the floor and scooted a few feet until she was at Bill's knees. "That's why we're counting on you."

"What about outside help? It's not like this is the middle of the wilderness. All these people—you must have a shortwave radio set. Have you tried that?"

McDole looked at Calie meaningfully. "Yes, and we still listen once a week but all we get is static. The one time we broadcast, we ended up with some very . . . *unpleasant* voices on the other end trying to wrangle us into giving our location but refusing to reveal theirs. We killed the transmission and seldom broadcast anymore. Like Calie said, we're counting on *you.*"

Bill sighed. "You don't realize how *long* something like this can take." He held out his hands. "Months, years . . ."

"We don't have that kind of time." McDole came to stand behind Calie. "We used to think we could just wait out the vampires, and if we stayed hidden, lack of food and the sun would eventually finish them off." For a second his jaw clenched. "We realized that was a stupid assumption when we found out about this . . . *farm.* I don't know how long those folks have been there—we've only known about them for a week. If we're lucky, we'll find a way to free them. If not, we may all end up down there with them." His face was hard and pale. "We *have* to fight back. If we let ourselves be raised like livestock— God forgive me but it's true—we deserve whatever we get."

Calie stared up at Bill, her face earnest. "Please, what can we do to help? Whatever you need, we can get it.

Blood—*anything*." She turned her arm and stretched her wrist toward him. "It doesn't matter."

Bill's throat constricted at her desperation. Those poor people, caged in an empty, freezing building. He thought of zoo animals, or worse, the neglected hostages in forgotten roadside menageries at the mercy of cruel tourists. His thoughts touched on the guard—what did he do besides keep them there? The likely answers filled him with horror. He'd always felt a sense of purpose, though there'd never been a conscious time limit. Somehow he'd seen himself the lone hero, Charlton Heston in *The Omega Man*, and the sudden responsibility felt like an iron girder. He stood and stepped around Calie, the pain in his foot an unimportant thrum.

"I have work to do."

But the biggest question still loomed in his frantic thoughts: How would he accomplish the impossible so quickly?

3

REVELATION 7:17
And God shall wipe away all tears from their eyes.

REVELATION 2:10
Fear none of those things which thou shalt suffer;
behold ... be thou faithful unto death.

"Hi," Alex said.

He felt suddenly bashful, as though this was a slow-motion repeat of his first date with all its awkward, nearly forgotten feelings. For an instant they reawakened with poignant intensity and he started to grin, then he saw Deb's face. She looked *exhausted*, the skin beneath her eyes so shadowed it looked bruised, making the lighter blue of her eyes and her pale skin glow beneath her heavy black hair. Alex's exhilaration had kept him so keyed up, he felt lucky to have slept the four hours he had; even so, he felt charged, ready to take on the world. But Deb looked ... *sad*.

Instinctively he reached for her hand. "Are you all right? Did you have trouble last night?"

She shook her head and tried to smile, looking miserable instead; he couldn't help noticing she didn't pull her hand away. "No trouble," she said. "I—just didn't sleep well, that's all." She began to walk and he followed, not caring where she was going.

"Me neither," he admitted. He glanced at her. "You don't look so hot. Are you sure—"

"I'm fine," she interrupted. "Bad dreams, that's all." She smiled again, this one a little more sincere. "Let's find something to eat, okay?"

"Sure." He stopped and she followed suit. "You have a taste for anything in particular?"

She grinned suddenly. "Yeah. Eggs."

He rubbed his chin, then realized he'd forgotten all about shaving. Damn—he'd have a "midnight" shadow before noon. Aloud he said, "This is not impossible."

Her eyebrows raised. "No?"

"I can't get you fried eggs and ham, but how about canned ham and egg drop soup?"

She laughed and a warm feeling spread through his chest. "Sounds yummy. Lead the way, Chef Alex!"

Marshall Field's, the gourmet food section again. Deb followed Alex from floor to floor and helped carry the things he wanted until they ended up back on the seventh floor, this time in a well-lit section of the Walnut Room. There he assembled his tools: two food warmers with double candles arranged with matched settings of Aynsley china and Waterford goblets, which he filled from boxes of juice. As the food heated, he wiped the dust from a table and silverware beneath a huge multi-paned window. Deb watched it all with a small smile.

"So," she finally said, "what's the occasion?"

Alex blushed, suddenly realizing how silly and over-blown all this must seem. "I—well—"

"I know what it is," she said.

"What?"

"It's breakfast. For *two*." She stared at him for a moment, then ran a finger carefully around the rim of one goblet. "I think that's a pretty special occasion, don't you?"

He nodded, unable to speak. The immense *emptiness* of the previous months welled like some huge, black shadow; he turned away and fiddled with one of the dishes so she wouldn't see the unexpected moisture that crept into his eyes. He stirred the two dishes, then swept an inviting arm toward the table.

"Your breakfast, madam, will be served shortly. I shall return." He pulled out the chair and she sat, then twined her fingers beneath her chin with a tolerant expression and Alex had to chuckle; Deb looked like the patient patron of a slow restaurant. Two minutes and he was back with a few odds and ends to complement the meal: crackers, olives, a small tin of chopped pimientos for color. He placed everything on the table while she dished up the soup and meat, then he brought out his final surprise.

"In case the *egg* drop soup doesn't quite cut it," he announced, "I've included these." He held out a tiny can.

"What are they?" Deb peered inside.

"Eggs."

"My eye."

He sank onto his chair in a huff. "You never specified what *kind* of eggs. These are quail."

"Oh! Of *course!*" She speared one with a fork and popped it into her mouth. "Umm, eggs that taste like pickles."

"You mean they have to *taste* like eggs, too?" Alex shook his head mournfully. "Some people are never satisfied."

"I'm stuffed," Deb admitted after they'd cleaned up. "Where to now? I think it's time for my two-hour nap."

"Me too." Alex took her hand and led her up one of the stilled escalators. Upstairs was the furniture department, its contents shadowed and not nearly as well lit as the Walnut Room.

Deb glanced around nervously. "It's awfully dark in here, Alex." Her voice sounded pained.

"Don't worry," he promised. "I just thought we'd pick a comfortable couch and relax for a while, digest the meal."

"Where?"

He thought of the areas here that stretched off into near darkness and wondered suddenly if this had been a good idea. He knew she'd barely slept last night and had thought a rest would do her good, but if it only made her skittish—

"How about there?" She pointed and he saw an overstuffed monster of a couch fronted by an ornate coffee table against the waist-high railing of an inner wall. It wasn't actually a *wall*, for that matter, more the tissuelike material that made up Japanese screens; above it, muted daylight bled through the cream-colored squares from the skylight in the roof.

He grinned in relief. "That looks great." Alex felt suddenly drained, as though the past day and a half had sapped him of energy as well as excitement. "I'm bushed." He flounced down. "Come on, sit. I promise not to bite—besides, I've already eaten. Remember?"

Deb looked at him warily, though her expression wasn't as mistrustful as the day before. After a few seconds, she sat somewhere at midpoint on the piece of furniture, watching as he untied the machete from his belt and placed it along the wide arm of the couch with its sharpened edge out. The corridor to the left of Deb was sealed; if by some quirk of fate someone else came, it would be from his right. He hadn't asked, but he knew Deb still had her gun hidden in her clothes and that was fine—in fact, it helped *him* feel safe. His watch said what he already knew: at not even eleven, they had plenty of time for a nap. He propped his feet on the table, leaned back, and let out a sigh. He felt Deb shift but he didn't move; he guessed she was a little uncomfortable but he didn't know what else to do to make her feel at ease. Thoughts crowded into his mind, ideas and farfetched notions he would have dismissed the day before yesterday.

Like doing more than simply surviving. Like *fighting*.

"Pick up your arm," Deb said softly.

Alex peeked sideways, then lifted his arm dutifully. He felt something between disbelief and nostalgia as she slid across the cushion and snuggled against him; he was almost afraid to drop his arm across her shoulders, but she didn't pull away. After a few minutes her breathing deepened.

He felt . . . content. Happy, sleepy, filled with vague battle plans and a new reason to fight. Until now he'd been existing, day to day, hand to mouth, like some sort of urban Neanderthal, and suddenly there was this woman who had struggled through her own private hells and now slept trustingly beside him. What had she gone through to reach the decision that he wouldn't hurt her in spite of the horror of the man she'd had to kill last fall? *Could* he be trusted, especially with the incredible responsibility of someone else's life?

Deb made a sound that was half snuffle and half moan
and he glanced down, wondering if she was already coming out of her nap. It'd hardly been a quarter hour.
"Deb?" he said softly. He carefully brushed aside the
lock of hair that had fallen across her forehead. The dark
circles beneath her eyes made her look like an ill-used
china doll. "Deb?" he repeated.

No answer; the tiny sniffling came again, but Alex
would have bet his next meal that she wasn't awake. He
couldn't stop his fingers from touching the delicate trail
of moisture that slid down one cheek to follow the line of
her jaw.

She was crying in her sleep.

Look at them, Jo thought. How peaceful.
How sad.

Her eyes traced their faces as they slept: the man, not
particularly tall but attractive, with coarse brown hair
chopped unevenly at shoulder length and a fast-growing
stubble trying to take over his sturdy face. If he opened
his eyes, Jo knew they would be brown, warm and honest, overly generous. The American nice guy.

The woman beside him was beautiful. Thick black hair
tumbled across her forehead and down her back, shining
curls that her man would remember longingly in years to
come. She was taller than her companion, a good head
above Jo, and fine dark brows arched above well-defined
cheekbones. In her mind Jo could see the woman's frank
and intelligent eyes, a startling light blue.

They would have made quite a couple.

The woman gasped in her sleep, as if her dreams were
portents of the coming changes in her life. Before her
nightmares could frighten her to wakefulness, Jo touched
a finger to the woman's pale cheek; the sleeper sighed
and her breathing deepened again. Jo watched for a
while, appreciating the sight of two people in trusting
slumber, mourning the sinister vision that enveloped the
woman like a dark and suffocating shroud. The man
would be crushed and God would not spare him the
sight of his lover in her death. But he was strong, and

with a little outside help—and she would see to that—he might, *might* make it.

How bitter and terrible to have this second sight, to know yet be unable to alter—sometimes the tiniest choice meant the difference between light and dark. Perhaps it was all preordained anyway, destiny, and she was just a piece in God's puzzle. Or was He testing her, too?

Tucked in one pocket were a half-dozen of God's most wondrous creations—seeds. In the other was the small flask of water from St. Peter's that she'd filled before leaving the church at dawn. She looked at the seeds and shivered. It was a cold time now, and it would get colder still. Soon the woman would be filled with darkness, denied forever the sight of the sun or the touch of green and growing things. In the time ahead, she would give of herself in ways even Jo could not imagine; it was a small thing for Jo to give something now that the future would not allow her. She studied the tiny dormant pods on her palm for a moment before dribbling a small amount of water over them. Her fingers folded automatically around the wetness and a small crackle of blue, like gentle summer lightning, encircled her hand as she closed her eyes and thought of bright skies and sunshine, singing birds and squirrels running through the grass in a park she remembered from her childhood, the lake, sparkling like a billion glass fragments backlit by explosive light, the warmth and smell of cut grass and the way the leaves of the bushes tickled her fingers and wrist as she ran her hand lightly along the top. Like now.

She opened her eyes and inspected the pair of nearly perfect daisies that had sprouted from two of the seeds. They were almost painful to look at in their simple beauty, and how many months had passed since she'd smelled their sweet fragrance?

During his nap the man had shifted, and now the woman slept securely within the circle of his arms. As Jo scattered the remaining seeds at their feet and deftly tucked the daisies between his fingers, her hand brushed against the woman's dark hair and she stirred and mumbled something. Jo touched her cheek soothingly again, then stepped back.

She wished she could wake them, talk to them, tell them both to run as far and as fast as they could. Instead, she forced away the sting of tears and slipped away from their sadness.

4

REVELATION 4:1
I will show thee things which must be hereafter.

For one blinding moment Louise felt a hot, disorienting rush of terror, twisting her gut and making her body go weak. Then, as she felt Beau's warm little body curled against her, she finally remembered where she was and how she'd gotten here. She sat up, then groaned as the blankets fell away. How long had she slept? She felt draggy and . . . sick, as though she had the flu, or maybe a fever. Beau snuffled and tilted his head at her, then tottered on the edge of the rollaway bed and yipped to be put down. Louise had bedded down in the small office beside the confessionals on the east wall, and ten feet away she could see the vague, slightly lighter outline of the doorway that opened to the main hall of the church.

"Okay, boy," she croaked as she found a new pair of jeans by her shoes. Her tongue felt like her hands, thick and swollen, and the jolts from her fingers as she dressed and picked up Beau were much worse than her knee when she stood and cautiously worked her way to the door. She limped a path down the main aisle and stepped outside, putting the dog on the sidewalk to do his business while she considered Jo's unshakable trust.

Jo—now there was a mystery. How had she managed to survive? It was clear she wasn't the survivor type; thin almost to anorexia, though fragile was a better description of the tranquil-faced teenager, not someone likely to last out the night, much less the winter. And such faith! Louise shook her head and stared dully at the empty street. The temperature had dropped and Louise was already chilled through her jacket, yet hadn't she seen Jo leave St. Peter's hours ago without a coat? The sky was a bleak, gunmetal gray, a reverse of yesterday's pseudo-

spring. Louise dreaded the undeniable return to cold
weather and the threat of snow. On the sidewalk to her
left, Beau turned and began a blind run toward her. She
opened her mouth to tell him to stop, but Jo's sweet
voice intervened.

"You shouldn't be outside."

Louise whirled. "Jesus! You scared me!"

Beau wriggled around Jo's ankles and the slight girl
bent to pick him up. Louise was grateful; it saved her
from having to hold the squirming dog in her hands,
which had leveled off at a painful, continuous throb. If
pain could have a color, Louise would have called it *red*.

"How did you sleep?" Jo asked.

"Okay." Louise tilted her chin to the sky. "That doesn't
look very good. Snow, maybe."

Jo shrugged. "Nothing you or I can do about that."
Her eyes dropped to Louise's bandages. "How're your
hands?"

"Fine," Louise said quickly. "Thanks for taking care of
me." Sudden embarrassment filled her; this porcelainlike
creature had survived without complaint all this time,
and here was tough Louise, with her hands and knee
screwed up and feeling like crap. Nothing in Jo's manner
indicated that Louise and Beau were anything but welcome, but perhaps they were imposing, altering the lifestyle and routine that had kept the girl safe all this time.

As though reading her thoughts, the younger girl
flashed her a wide, genuine smile. "It's good to have
company," she said. "I've missed the sounds of life. Everyone is welcome here." She shook her head, her expression bewildered. "I had expected the House of God
would be the obvious place of shelter, but I guess too few
of us have the beliefs we should."

Louise felt a little dizzy, though she wasn't sure if it
was fever or the strange things Jo was saying. For safety's
sake, she bent her knees and sat casually on the stone
steps. "So, there *are* others?"

"Oh, many!" Jo stroked Beau's ears and looked at
Louise thoughtfully. "You'll meet some of them soon."

Louise frowned. "I can't believe there are a lot of other
people, here or anywhere else. You're the only person

I've seen since . . . since—" She stuttered for a moment. "I can't even tell you how long it's been," she finally finished.

Jo sat next to her. "But why shouldn't you believe? You came downtown because you knew there would be places to hide, lots of food and supplies. Right?" When Louise nodded, Jo continued. "Don't let pride preclude common sense. If you can make it, there are plenty of others, stronger, wiser, better equipped, who've also survived and probably had an easier time doing it." She smiled slightly. "And there are others who seem like they should have died months ago but didn't."

Louise felt her cheeks warm and wondered if the girl had read her mind again. "But if there are others like you say, why haven't they gotten together to fight the vampires? It seems pretty silly for everybody to struggle alone."

"Oh, it is. But look at your own way of thinking. Did you trust me last night? Do you really trust me now? As terrible as it sounds, your instincts are good. There are many reasons to distrust in today's world, and in time you'll discover why." She stood and clasped a hand under Louise's elbow to help her to her feet. "But first you have to heal, and you can start with something to eat."

Louise followed her benefactor into the church, trying to understand Jo's words. Perhaps it was her building fever making it hard for her to accept that Jo already knew where other people were; the girl sounded as if it were only a matter of time before social introductions were given. She tried to rethink their conversation as she moved to help Jo put together a quick meal on a small portable stove just behind the railing that separated the apse from the church's main aisle, then finally just sat and watched after Jo sternly told her to rest. She was just so *tired*, not really hungry, though the chicken soup that Jo heated from water and a dry mix tasted good. Her eyes and ears seemed covered by a dull film, as though she were seeing through a veil and hearing sounds while underwater. Afterward Louise took the aspirin Jo offered, though she brushed off Jo's suggestion that they put fresh bandages on her hands. All she really wanted was more sleep.

"Well," Jo said finally, "you'll probably feel better if you rest anyway." She lifted Beau and guided Louise back to her temporary bedroom, then spread a double thickness of blankets on the rollaway bed and patted it.

Louise nodded groggily. "I'm really tired." Beau was already dozing with his nose tucked between his paws and his belly full of leftover soup, and Louise let herself slide down beside him on the inviting covers. Her eyes closed, then opened briefly as Jo draped yet another blanket over her.

"I'll get more from downstairs," the younger girl said. "It's going to get very cold tonight."

"Sure," Louise agreed. Her voice sounded strange and slurred, as though she'd been drinking.

"You get some sleep," Jo said gently. Louise was already nodding out and barely heard Jo's final words.

"You're going to be amazed at what tomorrow brings."

5

●━●●━●●━●●━●

REVELATION 2:16
[I] will fight against them with the sword of my mouth.

━●●━●

Dr. Perlman found the videotape of the vampire child's behavior disappointing. It revealed nothing except that this particular creature functioned on little besides instinct: eat and sleep. He discovered no wonderful insights or clues, though he viewed the tape so many times that the rubber eyepiece of his battery-rigged camera felt fused into his skull. Still, he didn't give up until the batteries were starting to lag.

The boy could only be described as a beast. When he'd dragged the vampire back yesterday, Perlman had found it impossible not to wonder who the child had been in his original life. Where were his parents, how old was he, and how had he ended up like this? Had he been a mischievous little boy a year and a half ago, a playground bully, or had the one-night transformation taken him from angel to monster? All those questions were unanswerable; while the boy was frozen in eternal childhood, his skin was wrinkled and gray, bagging where body fat had once been plentiful and stretching elsewhere to give him the awful countenance of a mobile, ancient mummy. One thing Perlman noticed right away, though: the small meal had already caused a marked improvement in the vampire's appearance. While his skin was still in a sorry state, it *had* improved; there weren't nearly as many split places in the creases and the face was already fuller around the cheekbones.

Perlman sat back and rubbed his eye where it had been pressed against the camera viewer in between scribbling notes and staring out the window. He could learn nothing more from the tape; what he required was blood and tissue samples, and for that he needed help.

The first thing the video had revealed was the terrible ease with which his "thin little boy" had torn through the carefully crafted bonds. A tapping made Perlman glance around; Calie stood in the doorway with C.J. behind her, looking as though he'd rather be anywhere else. She smiled, her gaze clear and unwavering, and Perlman's thoughts veered for a moment. He forced them back stolidly, ignoring Calie's warm look. "What can I do for you?"

Her smile grew a little beneath her solemn brown eyes. "We came to do for *you*, Dr. Bill." She glanced at C.J., who was studying the walls with a bored expression, then back at Perlman. "Thought you could use some help in your research or something."

Perlman scrutinized his notes. It was eerie the way they'd shown up at just the right time, as if Calie had known he was ready to move forward. He pushed out of his chair, careful not to bump his injured toe as he had earlier this morning. "As a matter of fact, I was thinking just that. I'm ready for a tissue specimen."

"A what?" C.J. asked.

"A tissue specimen. Samples to put under the microscope." The doctor hobbled to a cabinet and began gathering the items he would need: a surgical knife and tongue depressors, rubber gloves, a petri dish and a couple of clean towels. "I'll probably need a hand with him."

C.J. snorted. "Shit. You're going to need more than a hand when you start cutting. That bloodsucker's going to rock and roll."

"I only need a small sample," Perlman said. "Hardly more than a scratch from the skin surface." He paused, then chose another dish. "Though it would be helpful to get a scraping from one of the mucous membranes."

"From his mouth?" Now even Calie looked doubtful.

"Well, that would be best but probably far too dangerous—"

"You're not kidding!" C.J. interrupted.

"—so I'll settle for one from the nasal cavity."

C.J. threw up his hands. "Big fucking difference, Doc! A whole half inch! I'm sure it'll be happy to lie still while we stick a knife up its nose!"

"I think we can do it," Calie said. "He'll have to be retied first, of course." C.J. rolled his eyes. "And we'll still have to hold him. But as long as there's three of us, we should be able to keep anyone from going under."

"Going under?" The doctor stepped into the hallway with the other two. "What do you mean?"

C.J. sighed in exasperation, dipped his fingers into a vest pocket, and pulled out a battered cigarette butt. "*Hypnotized*, Doc." He glanced at Calie and gave a hard shake of his head, his black hair swinging wildly. "I can't believe he trapped that thing by himself and lived to talk about it. What a crock."

"Actually"—Perlman limped behind them down the stairs—"I *had* thought about 'going under.' I had no intention of trying this alone."

"God bless you," C.J. muttered as he came up with a match as they descended to basement level and Perlman pulled a flashlight from the top of a fire-extinguisher box. He snapped it on, but its beam was a disappointing puddle of light; while it was daytime, Perlman couldn't rid himself of the paranoia that the sleeping child had woke and was now waiting, ready to leap from shadows that deepened with every step. Finally they stood at the steel door that led to the bomb shelter. Anything but pleased, C.J. bent and gathered the coil of rope and another roll of the silver duct tape Perlman had placed beside the entrance, then looked at Calie and the older man.

"Ready?"

They nodded. Calie seemed as calm as ever, and though C.J.'s callused hands were shaking, Perlman suspected it was more from adrenaline than nerves. Personally, he was having trouble swallowing around the pretzel-sized knot of fear in his throat; even his breathing had escalated to just ahead of hyperventilation, and he forced himself to inhale and hold it for the count of three. The child vampire's nearly successful hold on him was a nightmare memory that he was afraid would lunge when the door was opened; to put him further on edge, the door screeched like a crypt entrance from a stupid old horror movie as Calie yanked on it and C.J. stood ready with the crossbow.

Nothing sprang from the blackness beyond the door
and Perlman's breath escaped in a rush, but neither of his
companions noticed. He wondered if C.J. was disappointed and thought it would have made the kid happier
to kill the childbeast and be done with it.

"You have another light?" Calie asked. "We're going to
need more."

Perlman cleared his throat and his voice came out
raspy. "Yes," he croaked. "High-powered." He gave his
own flashlight to Calie and handed another to C.J., then
clipped a small battery pack to his belt and held up a
black-case spotlight connected to it by a coiled cord. "So
I can see what I'm doing."

C.J. hit the flashlight's ON switch, then played its
bright beam down the stairs. The backwash made his
face dark and chiseled, like an ancient Mexican god with
deep, glittering jewels for eyes. "Let's do it."

Bill stepped forward but Calie pushed past and was
halfway down before he could protest. "Wait—"

C.J. followed Calie like a magnet, weapon up and
ready. "Come on, you're bringing up the rear."

Perlman clambered down, half hopping, using his
hands to keep his graceless body and the equipment in
his pockets from bouncing against the walls. At the stairwell's bottom, Calie had already freed two of the three
bars and was waiting for him before removing the third.
C.J. stood by with the crossbow, a complicated thing of
strings and metal loaded with a thin arrow tipped by a
deadly, four-sided razor head. For the first time, Perlman
saw C.J.'s crossbow as a real weapon which could kill as
effectively as a firearm, or literally pin a target in place.
He was suddenly very grateful for C.J.'s presence.

Calie didn't hesitate; as Bill took the bottom step she
yanked out the final bar and leaned it against the wall in
a smooth, swift motion. An instant later she grabbed the
handle and pulled the metal door wide.

The three stood, frozen. Beyond the pathetically dim
circles cast by the flashlights, something stirred in a
darkness thick with the smell of decay. "Your light, Dr.
Bill," Calie said urgently. "Turn on your light!"

"What—oh!" He was too terrified to feel stupid as his

fingers fumbled to find the switch. Light, unbelievably bright and piercing, flooded the small room, bringing into sharp black and white the cracked concrete surrounding them. The child vampire was lying against the wall a few feet away, in the same position in which the physician had last seen him on the tape. In places his gray, filth-streaked skin was nearly indistinguishable from the mottled pattern left by the dismantled shelving.

It definitely looks better, Perlman realized instantly. *Healthier.* Fascinated, he studied the creature from where he stood, noting that the gray tint was not as pronounced, the skin, though still loose and hanging, not as flaccid. The scalp hair was thicker, the face fuller—

Daddy! A child's sweet voice cut through his thoughts. *You came back—I knew you would!*

Perlman blinked as his gaze found and locked with that of the child's through transparent eyelids. He tried to pull away but it felt as though he were dragging his eyes over coarse, sticky sandpaper.

This is not my son! Perlman could almost *see* the thought as a physical thing in his mind, cold and indisputable—a given, a fact, something he *knew* was inarguable—

Yet his feet still moved him forward.

Without warning the memories returned, bubbling from some long-plugged well within him: the pleasant smell of baby powder, the velvety feel of tiny arms, feathery hair tickling his cheek next to the infant's gurgling laugh and toothless smile.

"No—"

Perlman thought he heard someone talking, then felt a sharp tug on his head; he dismissed it as insignificant. If there was even the remotest chance that this child was his son, perhaps gone through some accelerated growth because of the change, wasn't he responsible for the boy? Shouldn't he do anything to give comfort—

Pain then, agony clearing Perlman's mind like the sweep of a chalk eraser and literally dropping him to one knee; when his vision cleared he realized he was a scant two feet from the childbeast. He didn't remember crossing the distance, but Calie was crouched beside him with one hand hooked around his elbow, and her face was twisted with a mix of fear, anguish, and sympathy. His foot felt as though he had shoved it into an incinerator and Perlman hissed through his teeth, then cursed as he tried to stand. Floating beneath the swells of pain was a stinging in his scalp that generally added to his misery.

"You all right?"

Surprised, Perlman nodded up at C.J. The teen's face seemed naked for a second, vulnerable and afraid, then it slipped back to its hard, unreadable mask.

"What happened?" Perlman glanced furtively at the vampire and his mouth fell open when he realized that one of his companions had covered its eyes with duct tape.

"You went under," Calie explained. "You didn't hear me or even notice when I started yanking on your hair." She looked ashamed. "I'm sorry, but I had to stomp on your toe to make you come back. I hope it doesn't hurt too badly."

"Only a little," he lied, but she didn't look convinced. "I'll be fine. Really." He struggled with his legs and the injured foot until he was kneeling at the vampire's side, then began pulling out his equipment. "Let's get this over with."

"The man finally has something good to say." C.J. set the crossbow carefully against the wall and took a stance at the head of the child on the floor. "What's first?"

Perlman forced himself to think through the mist of pain as he studied the child critically. "I think we'll do the tissue sample last. How much can he do while he's sleeping? Shouldn't we tie him up?"

"He's getting smarter," C.J. told Calie as he held up the rope and twisted slipknots around the vampire's arms and legs that would only tighten in a struggle. The length of gray rope nearly vanished against the boy's dull skin. When C.J. started to cover the mouth with duct tape, the doctor stopped him.

"I want to get the mucus sample from his mouth," he said.

"Great." C.J. looked disgusted. "Just ask him to say ahhhh."

"Let's not make this harder than it has to be," Calie admonished, then looked at the doctor. "Okay, then. What now?"

Perlman sucked in a breath, then jabbed a hand toward the vampire's face, swiping his fingers below the nostrils just out of touching range. As he had suspected, the child could smell fresh blood even in sleep; as his hand pulled away, the vampire's mouth stretched in a parody of a yawn, revealing a blackened maw ringed with jagged yellow and brown teeth from which strands of rancid saliva dripped. A second later the mouth closed.

"Gross." C.J.'s face twisted. "How the hell you gonna get him to *keep* it open long enough to cut? I'll bet he chomps on anything you stick in there, including your finger."

"He's right," Calie said. "You're likely to lose a piece of your hand if you try it."

"We'll tape his mouth open," Perlman suggested. "I don't need to cut, just run the depressor along the inside of one cheek. I *will* take a little flesh for a tissue sample, and for that we'll turn him facedown so it'll be harder for him to bite."

"Fine," C.J. said. He tossed aside the piece of duct tape he'd been holding and tore six longer pieces, layering them into one thick strand as he knelt behind the vampire's head with the tape spread like a garrote. "We're ready. But you'd better be quick. I really don't think this'll hold for long." Calie grimaced in revulsion as she grabbed the child's ankles to keep it from kicking; the body trembled slightly at her touch, and somewhere beneath the pain still sharpening his senses Bill thought he heard the word *cold* in plaintive tones. He pushed it away and bent to his work, thankful he no longer had to worry about avoiding the creature's eyes.

Slipping on a glove, the doctor pulled a tongue depressor from his pocket and tore it free of the sterile wrapping, then leaned forward. Before he could find an excuse, Perlman again passed a hand over the child's face. When its mouth widened he stared into the moist blackness leading down the thin throat, one glance lasering the image into his memory. All the internal tissues were black, including the tongue, though the doctor thought he could see an undertone of deep red. The front teeth were hideously overdeveloped, especially the canines, but the premolars sloped into the line of malformed gums on both the upper and lower jaws, and molars no longer existed at all, hence the sunken-cheeked appearance.

C.J. brought the tripled strip of tape into the open mouth with admirable speed, hooked it behind the bottom premolars, then yanked down, forcing the jaw open farther. A clot of nasty-smelling fluid sprayed from the vampire's mouth and settled over the skin of its face as it began to struggle sluggishly, trying through the comalike sleep to snap its teeth. Muscles bulged in C.J.'s arms as he fought to keep the head against the floor while at the other end Calie leaned on its writhing legs with all her strength. Perlman didn't need to be told to hurry this time, though he had to fight his sense of self-preservation to make his fingers thrust the tongue depressor into the contorting mouth and drag it along the inside cheek. He was profoundly thankful for the protection of his glove; his thumb and forefinger had reached beyond the child's lips for only an instant, yet they and the depressor were covered with vile-looking, stinking saliva.

"Done!" Bill pulled back and nearly fell in his haste to get his hand out of the creature's range. In eerily synchronized movements, C.J. dropped the tape and yanked his arms up as Calie released the boy's feet; the body spasmed and Bill gasped as the vampire tried to sit up. C.J. crouched, the crossbow already in hand, but abruptly the child's shuddering ceased as it sank back into its daytime trance.

"Halfway there," Perlman said grimly as he snapped the depressor in two and dropped the pieces into one of the small dishes, then turned a cover over it. "The best is ahead."

"I can't wait," Calie said. Her calm was still holding, but she looked a little shaky. He glanced at her, worried, but she grinned wanly. "I'm fine."

Perlman pulled off the soiled glove and nodded at C.J. "Let's roll him over. One, two, three—" And it was done, the clammy coldness of the boy's arm lingering against the nerves of the doctor's fingers. C.J.'s face was stony, as usual, but Calie looked green and Bill couldn't blame her. How could a body that moved feel so much like a corpse?

"Where are you going to . . . take it from?" Calie asked in a hoarse voice. "Do you think it will hurt him?"

"No more than he'd hurt us if he had the chance," C.J. said in a hard voice.

"I don't need much," Bill said quickly. This time he pulled gloves on both hands after setting out a dish. He picked up the scalpel. "I think the best place is the back of the calf. It'll be quick." He felt Calie's eyes on him and shook his head. "I don't know if it'll hurt or not. Even if it does, we don't have a choice. You ready?"

C.J. stooped next to the side away from the vampire's face and placed both hands flat on the boy's back just below the shoulder blades. "Go for it."

Perlman glanced at Calie. She swallowed and gripped the boy's ankles, pulling the legs out straight. "Fast as you can, okay?" She looked ready to vomit.

Perlman inhaled, then gripped the knife and hunched over the vampire's leg. "Here we go," he said, and drew the blade in a fast swipe, carving out an inch-square chunk of flesh.

The beastchild convulsed, then kicked, knocking Calie's hands loose and flinging her against the wall. Incredibly, C.J. maintained his hold, keeping the snarling creature's face pressed against the concrete as the doctor dropped his sample into the dish. The vampire hissed once more and fell silent, its suffering apparently ending as abruptly as it had begun.

Calie sat up, then choked and pointed. "Look!"

Perlman followed her extended finger and gawked. The wound was already healing, the exposed layers of gray flesh filling and meshing before their eyes. He bent closer, enthralled by this instantaneous regeneration; although it had once been a human child, he couldn't help wondering if, like certain species of amphibians, this creature would actually grow an entire new limb if one was lost. The question was fantastic and frightening, and its potential answer scared the hell out of him.

"Well," Perlman finally said as they examined the unbroken skin on the boy's leg, "if it *did* hurt, it wasn't for long." He spent a few seconds studying the dish containing the skin sample, afraid that the flesh would disintegrate. So far it remained intact, and he sealed it and peeled off his gloves. C.J. and Calie watched until at last Perlman looked up and grinned. "That's all, folks."

They exhaled in relief, then Calie wrinkled her nose. "Let's get out of here. I need some fresh air in the worst way." C.J. nodded and Perlman thought he could see a sickly tinge beneath the teen's olive coloring. Though the whole escapade had taken less than twenty minutes, Perlman felt as if he'd aged five years.

"Jesus," C.J. said once they were safely upstairs, "I'm glad that's over. It's sure not something I want to make a habit." Calie looked away and the teenager's gaze found Perlman's carefully bland face. He scowled. "Aw, man. You ain't thinking of doing this again, are you?" When Perlman didn't answer, C.J. showed his anger by kicking the wall hard, just once. "Calie? Shit—that's just great. When do we do it again?"

"Tomorrow?" The question came from Calie.

"Tomorrow," Perlman agreed. "And every day after until we find the answer."

Looking at C.J.'s expression, Perlman was very grateful that the heavy Barnett crossbow in the kid's hands wasn't cocked.

"Well, what did you think you'd find? A miracle?" There was no one in the room to answer and Perlman sat back and ran his fingers across his forehead, then massaged his temples. "Yeah, maybe so." Frustrated, he dropped a hand to the sheaf of notes he'd spent most of the day scribbling. And what *had* he expected? Slice and dice the sample, slap it under the Wolfe microscope he'd power-rigged to a minigenerator, crank the magnification to 100× and *Bingo*! Instant Answer.

Wrong.

What he had was cramped fingers and nearly blackened eyes from sitting for hours with his face plastered against the eyepieces. Still, he had to look again. It was as though he'd discovered some incredibly complex insect that no one had ever seen before, and in a way he supposed that's exactly what had happened. His first glimpse of the sample had been hours ago, yet the doctor was still awed to see that everything was actually where it should be. Incredibly, the cells were pliable and even the right color, as long as the slide was taken from a deeper level of the segment; closer to the surface of the skin, it became dried out, gray, and tough. But they weren't *alive*. They were frozen, trapped in a state of suspended animation from which the vampire's mind could still demand movement, though nothing on the slide was in motion. Predictably, minute colonies of clostridia, common bacterial decay, were scattered here and there, locked into that same permanent paralysis. He could see no fungi and he'd certainly not expected to find any viruses on dead matter. He might as well be looking at a slice of cork.

A blood sample, Perlman thought. Right out of its arm—won't C.J. just love that. And I need to find a way to tie a centrifuge into one of the diesel generators in the basement—now there was an adventure he could cheerfully put off until the next decade. The doctor frowned and drummed his fingers on the table. Obtaining a blood sample might prove nothing but a waste of time, if the blood turned out to be only that of the donor's. Or what if it was absorbed so rapidly that none was left, or no transfer of matter or cells occurred? He wondered if they could open the shelter door and toss in a meal just before sunrise, then chided himself on his foolishness. I'm spoiled, he realized sadly. For years he had simply submitted requisitions and purchase orders to obtain research supplies, samples, and equipment. At worst he'd had to attend a few administrative meetings. Now he'd have to make do.

A small tinkling from his alarm wristwatch—Calie's idea and a damned fine one—made Perlman realize he only had an hour of good daylight left. This makeshift laboratory was sinking quickly toward darkness, and he couldn't very well examine the tissue samples back in his original lab with its wall of large, northern windows. C.J. and Calie had provided three kerosene lamps to add to the battery-powered spotlight, and now the doctor noted that the spotlight's glow had faded to soft yellow and most of the room's wan light came from those lamps. He pushed out of his chair and stood unsteadily; fatigue, the pain in his foot, and yesterday's blood loss still working on him. It was time to wrap it up and perform his final and irreversible experiment. He powered down the generator, pulled the slide from the microscope and carefully covered it with dark plastic, then swept the soiled slides, debris, and damaged samples into the trash; it was vital that he had fresh tissue to work with on a daily basis, no matter how difficult it was to obtain. That done, he snapped on the Mag Lite, extinguished the remaining lights, and hobbled back to his regular lab. Another five minutes' preparation and Perlman was ready.

He estimated that it only took four seconds to get the slide in place and flood it with nearly painful halogen light, yet already the tissue had started to disintegrate. Maybe, he mused, *disintegrate* was an incorrect term, one that implied decomposition. *Dissolve* was more accurate, or *evaporate*. He wished desperately for a higher magnification level. Perhaps a sudden, massive output of enzymes was causing the tissue to digest itself, with the sun's rays as the catalyst. Or was it something more toxic, or a modulator, a type of noncompetitive inhibitor. . . .

The slice of tissue was gone, like a fragment of shaved ice in August heat, before Perlman's questions had even begun.

He sat back and mentally replayed the tissue self-destruction, comparing this viewing with the first experiment he'd performed on the fresh sample hours earlier. He flipped through his notes to make sure of the time— noon. The sun had been at its peak point beneath the gray clouds that had moved over the city yesterday evening. That small piece of flesh, purposely placed under the microscope by the window, had deteriorated at almost twice the rate of the one he'd just witnessed, a noteworthy example in terms of energy output versus re-tention. And more reason to get back to Water Tower, as another look at his watch verified. He stood hurriedly, glanced around, and decided everything could be left where it was overnight. His stomach growled and Perlman grinned; he'd quickly returned to forgotten habits— the days without meals and hours of not speaking to another person when he was heavy into a project. The future was sure to get him plenty of sleep though, since it remained impossible to work through the night. He'd be the most well-rested scientist in history.

Satisfied that nothing was running, Perlman slipped on his jacket and limped down to the first floor, letting himself out and locking up. Someone would be waiting for him at the Water Tower entrance, probably ready to come after him in another ten minutes if he didn't show. The freezing temperature and gusty wind made the empty length of Michigan Avenue desolate, especially against his memories of harried lunchtime crowds and the long-gone horns of the once-abundant taxis. Now it was . . . *nothing*, winding away to a gray, damp haze at either end, making him look forward to the company of Calie and the others, and maybe a hot bowl of canned stew, things that would warm him in body *and* spirit. He was tired, and it was nice to be heading home.

Home.

Now *there* was a good word.

6

"Alex?" Deb squirmed within the circle of his arms and heard him murmur. "Alex, wake up." She used her elbow to prod at his ribs. "Where'd you get these flowers?"

He opened his eyes and smiled; looking at him, she decided she liked the way his grin carried into little crinkly lines around his eyes, which were a deep, puppy-like brown and filled with warmth. Instead of sitting up immediately, he tightened his hold around her. "What flowers?"

She tugged the two daisies gently from his fingers and held them up. "These, you big goof. Where'd you get them?"

He jerked as though she were waving something nasty under his nose, then he was on his feet, gripping the machete and hurrying in one direction, then another, as he peered suspiciously into the afternoon shadows of the store. Deb sat staring on the couch, stunned and very aware of the cool draft where only a second before his arms had been.

"What's wrong?" she demanded. "Did you hear something?"

Another explosive ten seconds passed while she sat frozen, one hand cold against the pistol in her jacket; finally Alex let out a shaky breath and turned with a bewildered look. "Someone else was here," he said, his eyes still probing the unseen corners and making a lie of his calm, flat voice.

"I never left you!"

"Look at this," Deb said. They stood by the store's front entrance, the same one from which Deb had fled the day before. State Street Mall stretched away on both sides, empty, cold, and windswept; occasionally pieces of trash skittered along, pushed by a wind that was becoming frigid beneath heavy, mercury-colored clouds. "Look," she said again, the breath pluming from her lips. "They even have roots, Alex. *Roots.*" The shock had worn but not evaporated; it was mind-boggling enough to realize that there really *was* another person in the downtown area, though Deb knew Alex had already been convinced of that, but to know that someone had stood within a foot of them, perhaps even *touched* them while they slept ... Every time she got to that point, her mind shut down and gave her nothing but a gray, blank fog. It was simply unthinkable.

"I'm sure it was that girl," Alex said suddenly. "The one I told you about."

"Why?"

For a second he looked sheepish, then his jaw set stubbornly. "Because she was ... weird. Crazy enough to come out before sunrise, then just walk right into the arms of that vampire, like she *wanted* it. Yet by the time I got down there the vampire was nearly dead and she'd disappeared." He looked thoughtful. "If that'd been you or me we'd have been killed. I just can't figure it out."

"How can you grow daisies in Chicago in March?" Deb asked wonderingly. She bent her nose to the sweet-smelling blossoms. "Maybe we can plant them. Do you think they'll grow? I always thought they were outside flowers."

Alex sighed, then his expression softened. "I don't know, Deb. Tell you what, we'll go by Woolworth's and get some dirt—"

"Soil," she interrupted.

"Okay, *soil.* And we'll get a pot and stick them in and see what happens." He grinned. "We'll worry about where they came from some other time."

"Sounds good to me." Deb smiled at him. "Let's go." His words brought the sadness creeping back and she strove to keep it from her voice. Alex's warm gaze faltered, then smoothed as Deb put a little more effort into smiling. Her eyes had always been naked little windows into her thoughts; best to turn Alex's mind to other things, because if he pushed, she'd probably spill everything and spoil their too-short time together. "Do you think it'll be safe?" she asked. "I thought the garden stuff was in the basement."

"Then let's try somewhere else," he suggested. "I know—Carson's has a floral shop on the first floor. Probably nothing but dead plants now, but there'll be plenty of light and pots."

"Say," Deb said severely. "How come you know where the florists are in this town? Guys are only supposed to know where to buy footballs and beer."

Alex lifted his nose and gave her a smug glance. "Because, my dear girl, it was formerly necessary to keep my harem in fresh flowers on a daily basis."

"Harem, huh?" Alex dodged the mock swipe of her fist. "Obviously a group of backwoods girls who never had a city woman like me to show them the ropes."

"They were willing slaves to my many charms."

"Oh, jeesh!" Deb snorted. "This *is* getting deep!"

Alex laughed, then shoved his hands into his pockets and began walking backward. "It's getting *cold*." The chilly wind made a soughing noise as it spun between the buildings and past the doorfronts and he indicated the flowers with a nod of his head. "You better put those away or we might as well not bother."

"Pretty nasty, isn't it?" Deb tucked the daisies carefully into a high pocket, then turned up her collar and pulled her sleeves down and over her hands to keep them warm. "Nothing like yesterday."

"Here we are," Alex said cheerfully. "The landmark building of Carson Pirie Scott and Company. Let's get out of this wind."

"I don't know." Deb rubbed a spot on the dusty window with the side of her hand but she still couldn't see much. "You seem to like taking me into dark department stores."

"It's not as dark as it looks," he promised as he pulled open one of the doors and stepped inside. "I've been in here before. It just seems that way because it's lighter out here than inside. Besides, we should get going. With

these clouds, it's going to get dark earlier than normal.
Let's grab what you need and go home."

Deb had been about to follow him into the foyer, but
that stopped her. "Home?" she asked mildly.

Alex flushed a sudden deep red. "I didn't mean it like
that," he stammered. "I would never assume—"

Deb couldn't stop a mischievous grin as she gave him
a playful shove. "You sure embarrass easily for a guy who
used to have a harem."

"It's late," Alex finally said. They were seated once
again on the stone bench in the plaza of the Daley Center. "There's probably only an hour of light left." Huddled next to him, Deb could see him watching her out of
the corner of his eye. Time, it seemed, *her* time, was
passing much too quickly. They were facing west and
Deb tilted her face into the breeze, enjoying it despite
the temperature. Somewhere beyond the buildings, obscured by thick clouds, the sun was settling slowly
toward the horizon, leeching away the rest of the day's
warmth.

"It's very cold," Deb said. Inside her pocket she could
feel the delicate petals of the flowers and she wondered
if life still moved within the slender plants. At her feet
was a shopping bag with a clay pot and a small bag of
potting soil. Would these simple things combine to protect and keep life in the daisies? Deb's thoughts took a
sudden black turn and her stomach twisted in sympathetic pain.

And what will it take to keep life in me?

Oh, God.

Her eyes followed the sleek lines of the Daley Center.
Behind its black steel and darkly tinted windows, if she
wanted, was temporary safety and warmth, and other
things, too, long-forgotten feelings—physical *and* emo-
tional—that a short time ago she had thought she might
never feel again.

For just one night.

I will treasure this memory, she thought. For as long as
I can.

She smiled and stood, then held a hand out to Alex

and tugged him to his feet. He looked at her quizzically and she was glad they were almost the same height; it made it that much easier to press her lips against his. For a moment she felt his surprise as she squeezed his hand, a startled tremor that blurred beneath the warmth and pleasure the kiss reawakened. The muted agony in her belly faded, then winked away like a snuffed candle.

The city around them darkened visibly as its myriad shadows gathered and lengthened to become more inviting to those things of the night she particularly wanted to avoid. She wasn't feeling very brave this evening.

"Stay with me?" Alex whispered against her cheek. "We don't have to—"

"Shhh." She put a finger gently across his mouth. His eyes were wide pools of raw emotion in the fading light. "Let's go."

Hands entwined, warm flesh against warm flesh, she followed Alex across Daley Plaza.

I will treasure this, she thought again.

And I will have no regrets.

The Hunters

7

"You seem very pleased with yourself tonight, Howard.
Things went well today, yes?" Anyelet's eyes, so deep and
black, glittered across the candlelit expanse of the main
lobby.

Howard started and realized that they were all watching him—the Mistress, Rita, Vic, even that creepy little
Gregory. Now there was a type, all right, just like those
finicky little bastards at his old job. They were jealous,
he knew—after all, he had the best of both light and dark
worlds, and they were forever trapped in darkness. Well,
you make your choices.

"Yes." He smiled at Anyelet and nodded his pudgy
head for emphasis. "They did." He could feel Vic's gaze
boring into him, trying to read his thoughts, and Howard
was careful not to meet the former bodybuilder's eyes or
even look in his direction. They could read minds; he realized that now though in the past he'd never been quite
sure. But after what he'd seen Anyelet do to the old man
last night—he'd been hiding just around the corner—
Howard finally believed.

"How many women did you beat and rape today, Howard?" Rita jeered. Coming from her, his name seemed
like a dirty word and Howard flinched.

"I didn't beat anyone," he responded smoothly, raising
his voice to be sure that Vic could hear him clearly. "I
had ... *relations* with three of them." Not bad for someone of his immense weight and as out of shape, too. Did
vampires have sex? He didn't think so—the act would be
impossible for a male since they had no blood to maintain an erection. Howard barely kept his snigger to him-

self. Good ol' American Red: he had it, they didn't. Besides, he'd heard about bodybuilders and steroids and what that shit did to a man's sex drive and performance. That meant Vic had two strikes against him—no wonder the big vampire hated him. Howard almost felt sorry for the guy.

But not quite.

Howard had been saving his next statement for a few days, treasuring it like a special piece of candy. "I think," he said, unable to mask the pride he felt, "that another woman might be pregnant. One of the younger ones." Howard thought he heard a growl come from deep in Vic's chest and his head jerked toward the larger man in alarm. The odd sound was drowned out by Rita's harsh voice.

"It's easier when they're babies, isn't it?" Rita spat. "What a pig you are, Howard!"

"What difference does it make to you?" he challenged. "You only need them for food."

Rita opened her mouth but Anyelet cut her off. "That will be enough." There was a dangerous hint of impatience in her tone. "Howard is serving a useful purpose. Aren't you?" She looked his way.

Rita stared at the Mistress in disbelief. "But just last night you said . . ." The tall vampire lapsed into silence at Anyelet's warning glance and Howard's eyes narrowed. "Last night was a different time," Anyelet murmured. She raised her voice and spoke to Howard. "You say another child will be born? When?"

"It's too early to tell," Howard admitted. "But I'm positive the girl has missed her cycle for at least two months."

"It's probably just stress," suggested Gregory. "I understand that happens sometimes."

"It is *not!*" Howard protested hotly. "She's as healthy as any of them, and she hasn't been giving me any trouble."

"Which is another way of saying you haven't found an excuse to slap her around," muttered Rita.

"But you're sure she's pregnant?" Anyelet interrupted. Howard nodded, straining to conceal the sudden nervous flutter in his stomach. He hated putting himself on the line like this—what if that stupid, nerdy Gregory was right? What if the girl was only screwed up, some kind of mysterious female infection or something? *Jesus*. Rita's words flashed painfully into his mind, like sticking your face onto the glass of a Xerox machine and pressing the COPY button with your eyes still open.

"Good job, then," Anyelet continued. "The ideal situation would be to have all the females impregnated as much as possible and feed only from the males."

"The ideal situation would be if there was food for the taking everywhere, like there used to be," Rita said sullenly.

Howard considered offering his own opinion about the future, then wisely decided to wait when Gregory spoke. "True," the boyish vampire agreed, "but impossible. We would inevitably end up in the same position—"

"I know that, you idiot!" Rita hissed.

Gregory threw her an irritated glance. "Well, you seem to need reminding." The onetime accountant's smile was smug, and Howard imagined computer drives churning in the icy recesses of Gregory's brain. "The ones like you ruined it for all of us, you know."

Anyelet's eyebrows raised. "Oh?"

"Not you," the thin vampire amended quickly. "That's not what I meant at all." He shrugged and brushed at his sweatshirt fussily. "I mean the . . . I suppose a good word would be *gluttons*." He nodded at Rita, who wore an expression of incredulous rage. "The ones like her who took more than they needed and hunted just for fun, depleting everything. That's why we're in such poor shape."

"Who the *fuck* appointed you judge?" Rita shrieked, leaping to her feet. "You annoying little *cockroach*! I could stomp you into the floor right now—"

"Vic," Anyelet said so softly that only she, Vic, and Howard heard the world. Howard cautiously edged away.

Gregory laughed, unperturbed by Rita's threats. "Hardly, dear. You're more mouth than muscle." The air between the two crackled. *Go on!* Howard cheered silently. If Gregory tore the bitch's head off, the dweeby CPA would solve Howard's worst problem!

Rita sprang like a deadly jungle cat, black and sleek and twice as fast as the feeling of scalding water on bare skin. Gregory rose to meet her, either in response or anticipation, his own movement rivaling the astounding killing strikes of the rattlesnakes on the old PBS nature broadcasts. Howard's stunned gaze couldn't even follow the blur as the two bodies hurtled toward each other.

Incredibly, Vic was there, stepping between them before flesh met flesh and collided to a point of no return. One immense forearm wrapped around Rita's shoulders and simply plucked her from midair; when Gregory would have attacked the imprisoned woman, Vic's fist connected solidly with his chest and knocked the smaller vampire back a good twenty feet. Howard's sweat-slimed fingers clenched in disappointment inside his pockets when Vic made no move to further punish the combatants, and he shivered and turned away; it was colder tonight than yesterday and he found it disconcerting to watch these horrific creatures battle without the slightest puff of steamy breath. They never seemed to notice the temperature. "I think I'll go check on the prisoners," he said to no one in particular. There was nothing more to see here anyway.

"Yeah," Rita said nastily. "Keep them *warm*." She made an angry strangling sound as Vic tightened his hold.

Anyelet finally spoke from the shadows. "Yes, Howard," she said in a liquid voice. Her quiet rage made him tremble. "That's a very good idea. I have things to which I must . . . attend."

Rita and Gregory looked suddenly sick, and Howard barely hid a grin as he left the lobby and plodded up to the third floor. Let the Mistress give that vicious bitch something to think about other than antagonizing him. In the meantime, he'd spent a good part of today cautiously searching for Rita's and Vic's sleeping places, and he planned to continue his hunt tomorrow.

Upstairs it was cellar-dark and the oil lamps he'd lit at dusk were nearly empty. It was cold, too, miserably so, and if he didn't drag out more blankets, most of these shit-for-brains would end up with hypothermia. If that happened, they'd probably die and all his progress would be undone; above all he had to look out for the woman and the teenager—he hoped—who were pregnant. Already he could hear moans and teeth chattering—a sound that pissed him off no end—from several of the lightless doorways.

Evening chores irritated him, though he realized tonight was his own fault for ignoring his charges most of the afternoon. He'd planned to be in his sleeping bag by now, warm, full, and in dreamland. All that good—good, hell, he'd been great!—sex today had exhausted him and he'd been too worried last night to sleep well. His eyes had opened at dawn, and with the sun slowly brightening the room he'd had the first inkling that had sent him looking for the hidden rooms where his two enemies spent their daytime hours in helpless slumber.

If he found them, it would be an easy task to kill them both.

8

REVELATION 18:4
Come out of her that ye be not partakers of her sins,
and that ye receive not of her plagues.

"Stephen."

"Go away," he said. He tried to say it with conviction,
with command. Please, God, he begged silently and
squeezed his eyes shut. Save me from this female Satan.
If he prayed fast and hard enough, if he was truly, *truly*
despondent, would she be gone when he opened them?

"Stephen, *look at me.*"

He groaned. An hour ago he'd thought he couldn't feel
any colder or more miserable; now Stephen realized how
wrong he'd been. *She* had come back to seduce him
again and take his soul—*if* he still had one—a few more
miles down damnation road. "Jesus!" he cried suddenly.
"Why have You abandoned me?"

"Stop that!" Anyelet said sharply. Stephen's eyes widened. Had the Savior's name hurt her? Burned her, or
stabbed her right in her evil, hellish heart? He desperately hoped so, but cowardice made him hang his head.
How many saints had died for the Lord? And here he
skulked, too terrified to even say God's name aloud.

Anyelet moved inside the doorway, her scarlet dressing
gown rippling, and Stephen cursed his quickening pulse.
He wondered if she wore anything underneath, then
damned himself again and smacked his closed fist against
his forehead, hoping that the pain would cut through his
already building desire.

"Darling," Anyelet said, "what's the matter? Are you
cold?" Her voice eased around him like oil, swelling
above the damp, frigid air, making his heart race and
stealing his breath.

"Get away," he said hoarsely. "I don't want—"

"Oh, but you *do* want, don't you?" She smiled and stepped in front of him. "I think you want very much."

He closed his eyes again, this time in surrender. She smelled so sweet, like his mother's perfume—what had it been called? *Shalimar.* The memory brought back a dozen others: his parents laughing in the family room as they pieced together a jigsaw puzzle; countless meals in the kitchen; the smell of the bathroom after his mom had patted the final touch of perfume behind her ears. Like now.

Anyelet's mouth was on his neck and he breathed deeply, drawing in the scent of her as his hands, eager traitors that they were, moved to caress her shoulders. Just before her teeth sank sweetly into his flesh, Stephen thought he smelled something else.

Something like . . . rot.

Once again Anyelet had stopped just short of him becoming unconscious, just short of . . . what? Now he felt high, like he'd smoked a little of the weed that had circulated at a party he'd attended in high school, or had maybe drank too much beer. Why couldn't she kill him and be done with it?

He shuddered. Could she read his mind? He knew Anyelet had that ability, but would he *know* if she was doing it? He let himself think longingly of Jesus, His serene and compassionate face, the agonizing Fourteen Stations of the Cross, and of a salvation forever lost. Lying beside him within the folds of her own clean blanket, Anyelet didn't stir. That was good; he loathed himself enough without the chance that she knew how close he was to begging her to change him, to stop this nightly torture and give him her elusive hell.

Stephen stared up at the myriad cracks in the thick paint of the old ceiling. Do I really want that? he wondered. Do I actually want to be like her, to feed on *people*? He ground his teeth at the thought of some man or woman or—God forbid—child, cowering as he approached to fill his unholy appetite. Another question, disgusting and more than morbid, bloomed at the same instant he felt something black and sinister touch his mind: *What would it taste like?*

"Shall I show you, Stephen?"

He gasped as Anyelet leaned forward and hoisted his limp form beside her with effortless strength, then smiled and held out one white wrist. As he watched in blank horror, she slashed deeply across its tangle of bluish veins with a razor-sharp fingernail; blood welled, thick and reddish-black, glistening like a strange and exotic dish.

"Drink!" she commanded.

Stephen shook his head, though try as he might he couldn't wrench his eyes from her tempting offering. Anyelet's cold hand slid sensually up the skin along his spine, then cupped the back of his skull. His vampire lover began forcing his face toward the wound in her skin.

"No!" Stephen choked and tried to squirm away, as much from Anyelet as to escape the diabolic thirst that exploded within him. But her brutal hold was impossible to fight; liquid, cooling and not at all the hot wetness he had expected, smeared his nostrils as she covered his face with her arm. Instinct made Stephen open his mouth to breathe, and the taste of copper and salt filled his mouth and made him gag, then swallow reflexively. Dark hunger filled him and suddenly he couldn't stop himself from clutching her wrist and sucking, his lips and tongue probing the moist gash in an obscene parody of a kiss.

He barely heard Anyelet's amused laugh. "Why, Stephen . . . you're drinking your own blood!"

9

REVELATION 3:17
And knowest not that thou art wretched, and miserable,
and poor, and blind, and naked.

"Good morning!" the old man said cheerfully. "A fine and
lovely day, don't you think? I'd like a nice, hot cup of coffee, I think. And a danish."

Hugh straightened his tie and sat military straight on
his stool in the Pedway Cafeteria beneath Marshall
Field's. The tie, a nice red-and-black-dotted bow-thing
he'd found while rummaging through Karroll's Men's
Shop last night, was more tangled than knotted, but he
was positive it looked just right, though he couldn't be
sure because none of the mirrors worked anymore. Or
maybe he was ill—every time he checked his reflection,
like now, using the mirror behind the refrigerated pie
case, he got dizzy. High blood pressure? He'd have that
checked at his physical next month. Anyway, someone
should tell the manager that the case wasn't working and
all the food in it was black and covered with colored,
fuzzy mold. He remembered that same case being broken some time ago, when the weather was still warm,
and hadn't there been a whole slew of disgusting bugs
swarming inside it? He'd never liked insects and his
mind shied away from the thought. "Excuse me," he said
loudly. "Can I get some service?" He shook his head in
irritation; he didn't know why he kept coming back here.
The service had been bad for months, ever since . . .

Ever since what?

Hugh frowned and looked at the other tables. The
manager was apparently trying to save on electric bills
and Hugh certainly understood that, but he could still
easily examine the entire restaurant. He waited at the
counter by the register—and that was another thing, the

counter was *dirty*, and didn't these damned bastards know about soap and water? Tables and chairs, some up-ended, stretched into the empty western end of the cafe. Was he the only one here? Where was the waitress? He snorted; Tisbee would never stand for this. Why, she'd have—

And where the hell *was* she? He peered at his watch anxiously and the little numbers stretched multifingered hands and waved, moving too fast for him to tell the time. He tried to look at them sternly, so they would behave and let him read the clockface, but they were just too cute and when they started singing a Supertramp song that his son—and where the hell was *he*, besides?—had often played on the stereo, Hugh first began giggling, then dancing, and finally singing in time to the music.

"Don'tcho look at my *girl*friend!" Whirling now, faster and faster, until his concert was abruptly cut when he crashed into one of the Plexiglas windows that separated the cafe from the lightless expanse of the pedestrian way, a tunnel that ran from Michigan Avenue until it connected with the subway and ultimately the Daley Center and City Hall. It branched other places, too, like the Brunswick Building to the south, or the State of Illinois Center, though he couldn't go there because you had to go through the Daley Center and for some reason the doors at that end wouldn't open. His poor little clock people shattered and fell to the floor in jagged pieces when he hit the window, their wonderful rock-and-roll voices exploding into brief shrieks before the silence settled around him again.

"Hell," he said indignantly as he snapped his fingers—one! two! three! "I'll take my business *elsewhere*! I *certainly* don't have time to put up with this *shit*, you know!"

Hugh felt his way out—sometimes it was hard to see where the windows started and stopped, even with his darktime vision—then began skipping toward Marshall Field's. Where the basement entrance to the store and the subway met, he chose the subway tunnels instead, since he was hungry and food could sometimes be found down there if he was quiet and real careful. He crept past the ticket window on all fours so that the dried-up and scary-looking thing inside couldn't see him, then descended the frozen escalator on silent feet, down to that part of the tunnels where daylight had never, ever reached. There were *things* down here, *monsters* that had once been like the shadow things above which he sometimes visited. But these monsters were driven by starvation and insanity, and although in rare, lucid moments Hugh knew that most of his own mind had disintegrated, he was still a world apart from them. Existence in the bottom levels of the subway was all they had left, a place that offered occasional food and solid protection from a sun they no longer had the strength to avoid on their own and the only place Hugh himself could successfully hunt. Desperation had heightened their malnourished senses beyond his, and only an elemental sense of self-preservation kept his constant litany of music silent on these visits and made his movements mostly undetectable. Sometimes the tables turned and he became the hunted instead of hunter, but his better-fed frame generally let him simply outdistance his pursuers. For that, he knew, he had the boy to thank. Every so often his mind would clear and Hugh would find him; then they would talk like they had in the old days and—

There was a vague, sibilant noise in the black void to his right, beneath a bench that dated back to the 1940s when the subway first opened. The sub-tunnels where the actual trains had run were so black that Hugh had difficulty seeing in them, though his mind obliged him with pictures of how they had once been at their worst: dirty water flowing in filthy fountains from broken overhead pipes, mildew bubbling in virulent colors and patterns down the cracked walls; the deafening swell of sound as two trains roared into the same station from opposite directions. The old man froze, wondering if the noisemaker was a rat and his next meal or one of the monsters. For a split second he saw himself as an old and very wrinkled rat, gigantic, white-haired, and funky-looking, and the image nearly made him snicker aloud; then he blinked and recalled where he was. A few more seconds and Hugh picked up a furtive scurrying and the skin of his face split into a grin; the rats were down here, oh yes. Not as many but still some, if you were stealthy and patient and *fast*. That was the problem the monsters had—they were too damned noisy, they didn't know when to keep a *LID* on it, but he did, old Hugh did, and he would by-damned eat tonight.

He slipped off the platform and onto the tracks, laying a gnarled hand against the high third rail, once a shining strip of silver along the ground, now grime-encrusted and loose. There it was, the tiniest vibration, reminiscent of the way the rail had hummed in anticipation of an arriving train. The sound came again, closer, a timid scratching that was cut off by Hugh's swift grip before the rat could escalate its startled whimper to a screech. Despite his speed, the old vampire knew immediately by the plaintive wail and sliding sounds a half block down the platform that something else had picked up on the minute scrabbling of the rodent's claws. Already that same something was dragging itself toward him, and for a moment he lost his concentration—such an elusive thing to begin with—and his hold on the rat, a large gray with jagged yellowed teeth, loosened enough to let it squeal and dig incisors into its captor's hand. So much for stealth.

"Stupid dinner! You're supposed to be quiet!" Hugh raged as he leapt up the catwalk, then fled in the direction of the escalators. The animal issued another thin cry and he gave it a hard shake and felt the neckbone crack; no matter, alive or dead, a meal was a meal.

Another three seconds and he was back on the pedway level and had already forgotten the monster pursuing him. As he wandered along, sucking on the dead rat like an ice cream bar, Hugh wondered again where that damned kid was and shook his head in disappointment. Tisbee was always asking and he was getting hard-pressed to answer her; besides, he had a few of his own questions, the same ones he asked her over and over but which *she* never answered. He passed a telephone, stopped, and carefully replaced its dangling handset; he thought about calling Tisbee, then realized he didn't have any change.

When he'd gone as far as he could, Hugh tossed the drained rat aside and peered through the glass doors at the insides of the basement below the Daley Center, then pushed angrily at the heavy double glass doors. At his left was the stairway leading to the plaza, which tonight was filled with deep shadows cast by the wan moonlight dribbling through the roiling cloud cover. Instead of climbing, he pressed his wizened face against the door and tried to see into the blackness beyond. Tisbee was in there, he decided. He could remember the two of them making a special trip to this same building for some kind of license decades ago, and not long after that they had dressed up in pretty clothes and stood in *that* place, and taken vows, made promises to each other that were supposed to have been eternal.

"You come out of there, woman!" he bellowed abruptly. Hugh pounded on the thick glass, but he'd done this countless times and the see-through barrier remained unbreakable and impassive to his assault; along its edges gleamed a thick, welded seam of dull metal. Enraged, the old man picked up the rat carcass and hurled it at the door, where it exploded and left an art deco star of gray fur and pink intestines that slowly smeared its way to the ground. It infuriated him that this place, like the place that held the beautiful paintings from the old country, was closed to him, and maddened him even more to think that Tisbee—and that damned boy besides—might be inside.

A snarling sound made Hugh whirl and jerk aside as an emaciated vampire, wild with hunger, swung at him. It was impossible to tell if the pathetic thing had been a man or a woman, and that it had made it up the escalator at all was a noteworthy feat. Astonishment at confronting one of those damned *monsters* slowed Hugh down just enough to let the wasted vampire seize his jacket and cling there like some pitiful bat as the old man smacked at it hysterically.

"Let go, you bad thing!" he screamed. "Bad bad *bad*!" His balled fist connected with the creature's head and the puny beast fell away with a soft *thunk*, then spied the door's savage decoration of rat entrails and crawled toward it. Once more the old man fled, leaving the skeletal night dweller searching for a trace of blood among the cooling remains of the splintered rat.

Hugh climbed the stairs with jackrabbit speed, up and out of the subway, away from the twisting, submerged corridors and across the plaza, then back to the hulking Picasso statue, around and around, until the cotton-wadded sky above began to spin treacherously. Vertigo hit, but Hugh's trusty musical friends were there to help him stand upright and point him in the direction of the Mart. It was good to have friends, and Hugh smiled at their company and began to sing from an old rock-and-roll opera as he traveled through downtown in a pattern only he could understand.

"See me, fee-eel me . . .

"Touch me, hee-eeal me. . . ."

10

●━●∙●━●∙●━●

━●∙●━

Something was scrabbling at the window.

Deb moaned in her sleep, a soft noise slightly louder than the coo of a dove. To Alex's straining ears it sounded like a bullhorn, and combined with the monstrosity on the other side of a pane of glass that now seemed hardly stronger than a sheet of plastic wrap, it sent his heart jackhammering within his rib cage. Their sleeping bag was pushed against the south wall of windows, the warmest side and Alex's favorite. The room, once a magistrate's private chamber, was a well-lit study in shades of gray, thanks to a short-lived break in the heavy cloud cover. Alex's eyes flicked to the pale square of light thrown by the sliver of moon, and his breath hitched as he saw the blurred silhouette of a darker, more sinister shape suspended in the center of the moonglow's rectangle.

Beside him Deb moaned again, then mumbled sleepily, as though an uninvited nightmare had joined her in sleep. Alex wanted to touch her, yet he dared not move. They were in the protective shadow cast by the waist-high sill, so far unseen by the creature that was stuck to the outside of the window like a nasty wet slug. What if it could sense, or even *see*, the heat of their bodies through the glass? Or what if Deb threw a hand into the square of light outlined on the carpet? Alex felt a sick certainty that the steel and concrete surrounding them offered nowhere near the armament upon which he'd always counted; how foolish of them not to have moved into a closed inner office earlier—yet the window had seemed so romantic. . . .

As if sensing his fear, Deb's eyes opened abruptly and

she started to sit up. She managed only a muffled *"What?"* before Alex clapped a hand over her mouth and pushed her back down.

"Shhh," he hissed. *"Be quiet!"* She blinked in agreement and he relaxed his grip; her frightened gaze followed his pointing finger toward the window, then narrowed at the curious scratching sound above their heads when it came again. In one smooth movement she had the H&K pistol in her hand and Alex was momentarily shocked at her deadly speed as his fingers slid beneath the sleeping bag and drew out the machete; how strange to have made love a few hours before, their bodies joined stomach to stomach while only a few layers of soft fabric separated them from steel.

More sound, insistent now, almost banging. Alex could feel Deb's warmth, her silky thigh still pressed along his, before he regretfully pulled away. Fear pushed them apart, segregating them into individual machines of survival. Alex's heart pounded heavily beneath the hard shell of his chest, but Deb's gun hand had been so steady it was easy for him to assume she was still calm. Was her mouth as dry as his? In spite of the survival skills honed over the past eighteen months, his palms were greasy with fear-induced sweat. Was she even frightened? There was a flash memory of the murder she'd committed, and while he acknowledged that it had been unavoidable, Alex nearly shuddered. She seemed so in *control* . . . had he become entangled with a woman reduced by her environment to an automated assassin?

He rolled his eyes up to the window again. The thing was still hanging there, though it had slid to where the metal and glass met. It looked thin and cruelly elongated beyond the distortion of the glass as it stopped and began picking at the sill more quietly, as if it had become bored and could think of nothing better to do than stay and idly terrorize the prey it thought might be inside. If it possessed the strength to climb this high, why couldn't it just break in? Maybe its energy had simply run out. The beast gave a screech that sounded more like an annoyed cry through the thick glass, then it was gone. The window vibrated for a moment, as though heavy suction cups had been yanked away, then muted moonlight again flowed unimpeded through the huge window.

Alex felt the tension drain from Deb as quickly as it did from him. Then she trembled and began to cry, her sobs coming in tiny, whimpering hitches that she struggled uselessly to conceal. All Alex could do was hold her and bask in the shameful relief of knowing she was actually capable of tears.

Sometime later—fifteen minutes, a half hour—he kissed her forehead. "Let's move the sleeping bag in case it comes back." She nodded, and he could see her white face in the sparse light, her cheeks still wet with transparent tears in the soft, chilly dimness. They did it quickly and silently, as though they'd performed this basic chore together a hundred times, settling in an office sheltered from the windows that lined the outer walls. It was totally dark here, and the last glimpse Alex had of Deb's face was as she led the way through the doorway, her features pale, like an eerie specter floating on the air currents running past his chilled flesh. At last Deb was beside him within the sleeping bag, her body strumming with unvoiced tension. She reached for him, her hands so cold that he twitched at the shock of her touch; still, her icy fingers traced streaks of flame across his skin. The nighttime temperature had dropped drastically, but Alex hardly felt the difference.

When dawn spilled over the tops of the buildings and daylight began to seep beneath the crack of the closed door, Alex woke her so they could make love again, confident this time that no unwanted audience could use the sounds as the means by which to hunt.

He also wanted to look into Deb's eyes when he told her he loved her.

11

REVELATION 7:14
... and have washed their robes, and made them white
in the blood of the Lamb.

*Louise was in a red world. Everything was thick and
slow-moving, and filled with pain. She could feel it, radi-
ating from everything around her in vicious pulses, each
spear of agony searching for HER, as if she had become
a magnet to which all the suffering of this new existence
must attach. She tried to move quickly through this place,
wanting to flee from something that was chasing her (and
she KNEW, oh yes she did, just what that WAS), but her
body dragged stubbornly against the messages from her
brain, as though the muscles were determined to do only
the opposite, like obstinate children thwarting their
mother out of spite.*

*She fought on, because anything else was unthinkable.
To stay in one spot was to invite death, and she wasn't
ready for that, she wanted to live forever, get married,
have a hardheaded child or two of her own. But those
dreams were tantalizing wisps floating just out of reach,
then dissolving.*

*She pushed on, past the empty buildings in which light
and dark things slept in unknown proximity. Both species
found it imperative to kill the other for survival, one
living—if such could be said—to kill, the other killing to
live. The streets were lined with the shells of cars, parked
years before and never reclaimed. Every vehicle was red,
the ones with smaller windows darker than the others.
More of the dark things rested in these metal crypts and
she dared not wake them lest they join in the pursuit.*

*More pain, stronger now, this time coming from a com-
panion, someone who had joined her in flight and whose
every movement and exhalation filled her with additional*

misery. Jo? Louise didn't think so; she couldn't imagine that Jo would ever run, or even be afraid.

Red buildings, red cars, even the sidewalks were red, deep and shadowed except where vibrant shades of scarlet spilled from the cracked cement, streaming through like hot rays from an alien sun. Louise felt as if she fought a gale-strength wind with every foot, and each step brought a new stab of agony, blossoming cell by cell until it all centered in her hands. At last she looked down, her running mate forgotten or killed, and her hands were the only things in this dreadful place that weren't red. Instead they were yellow and green, an ugly, diseased rainbow that seeped from beneath her fingernails in disgusting, viscous droplets. Her face twisted in terror as the skin began to slough away, revealing more of the clotted matter beneath a cracking surface that had once been the tissues of her body. The pain flared threefold, a hundredfold, but all Louise could think was that she would never be able to survive without them, she would never be able to CLIMB, and God help her if they fell off—

"Louise," someone said. "Wake up. It's only a nightmare."

"What!" Louise came up fighting and gasping for air; for an instant she'd had the insane thought that she'd been sleeping underwater. "Dream!"

"Yes," Jo said soothingly. "Just a dream." Jo's face, lit by the glow of a fresh candle, swam into focus. She felt Jo's touch on her forehead, cool and calming, and the tripping movements of her heart and lungs regulated; at last she could breathe almost normally. But Jesus, she was hot! "How do you feel?" Jo's voice echoed strangely in Louise's ears. Beau's little body was too warm and Louise pushed him away and decided tiredly that it must be the vastness of the church causing the voice distortion, all those empty pews. . . .

"Okay." A robotic answer, conditioned by years of polite response. But how did she really feel?

She felt . . . red.

"What time is it?" she finally managed. The always-unspoken question: How long until sunrise?

"It won't be light for some time." Jo studied her. "How about something to eat? To keep up your strength."

Louise shook her head. "I don't think I could keep it down," she admitted.

"Then you fibbed. You really *don't* feel well." Her hand was on Louise's forehead again, the touch comforting. "You've got a terrible fever, you know." She clucked. "We have to unwrap your hands, Louise. They're probably infected."

Louise's stomach wrenched and she looked at Jo pleadingly. "Maybe I've just got a cold."

"Sure," Jo said amiably. "But they need clean bandages anyway, don't you think?"

Louise thought about her dream, the red world and the sight of her fingers, stripped of their miraculous sheet of skin and bleeding dark pus and the poison of infection. Just a *dream*, that's all. Yet . . .

What would she do if they pulled away the bandages and that's what she found?

She bent her head and examined her hands, appalled to see the once-white wrappings soaked with a score of nasty-colored stains.

"We *have* to." Jo's voice was insistent and Beau whined nervously. Louise wanted to refuse; instead she reluctantly held out her hands.

The pain mounted with each featherlike tug Jo gave the material, as if it were no longer blood that pulsed through the veins and capillaries but a congealed mass of rotting liquid forcing its way through her body and spreading as each finger was released, pushing disaster further into her vulnerable flesh. When the last strip was peeled away, Louise was again teetering on the edge of that raw, scarlet world, as though pain and fantasy had melded at the altar of St. Peter's. Kneeling in front of her, even Jo was at a loss for words when Louise's swollen hands were fully bared.

Beau's nose twitched at the odd and unpleasant smell coming from his mistress and he sniffed along the pew until he found her leg. As Jo dropped the last bandage, he tried to scramble clumsily onto Louise's lap to investigate. When he lost his balance, Louise grabbed for him reflexively; struggling for footing, Beau scraped his claws across the ravaged hands that reached to cradle him.

The red world burst into a special, angry shade of crimson and slammed Louise in the face.

Louise woke to find her spasming hands clutched in Jo's grip, pulled so firmly against the younger woman's thin chest that she could feel Jo's lungs heaving beneath her frail ribs. She tried to pull away and tell Jo that she was much better—her hands weren't paining her anymore and she didn't feel so feverish or dizzy. Then she saw Jo's face and froze.

At first Louise thought Jo's eyes had turned as white as her hip-length hair, then she realized that they'd rolled so far back in Jo's skull that her gray irises had disappeared beneath the virtually translucent covering of her eyelids.

"Jo?" Louise tried frantically to disengage her fingers but it was no use. She wanted to see her hands, but Jo held them so desperately against her body that Louise was afraid the girl would suddenly grab her shoulders and pull her into some terrifying, inexplicable embrace. Five seconds, then ten, stretching to twenty; still Jo hung on. All at once the pain returned with startling intensity and Louise wheezed, then nearly screamed when she saw that Jo's hands were glowing, the light spreading through their entangled fingers until it climbed onto Louise's knuckles, the backs of her hands, then her wrists. "Stop it!" Louise yelled. "Let me go!"

She panicked and backpedaled, trying to swing her arms from side to side like a dog fighting a too-tight leash, but the smaller girl's grip was impossible to break. Blood was rushing through her temples so fast and hard her arteries would surely burst—maybe she was having a stroke and this whole thing, even Beau's frenzied barking in the background, was only the prelude to an eternity of visions signaling her death.

Then her hands *did* explode, and the agony made the red world flare in front of her vision again, expanding a thousandfold into a noxious black cloud that spun wildly until it was nothing more than a fading black dot.

• • •

Louise sighed and groped for the blanket. If she could find the covers, she'd be comfortable enough to catch another half hour of shut-eye. Behind her, Beau was making annoying little cries and she turned over and tried to squeeze her eyes shut tighter. The roll brought the unprotected skin of her cheek against the cold, dirty floor of the church and her eyes flew open.

She scrambled to her feet. "Jo?"

Louise spotted her underneath the front pew where Beau was nuzzling her shadowed face. Louise hurried toward her, then hesitated as she remembered what had happened . . . how long ago? A glance at the stained glass windows told her it was still dark and she had no way of knowing how much time had elapsed since she—and presumably Jo—had passed out, although it must have been a while since the candle had almost melted on its saucer. Jo was curled beneath her spill of silky white hair and Louise's heart missed a beat; what if Jo was seriously hurt? She reached to push the hair from Jo's face and her pulse lurched again.

Her hands were healed.

She turned them over frantically. Nothing marred the skin surface, not even a hangnail; no cuts, no blood, no pus. Neither looked as though she'd ever taken a fall or been ravaged by an out-of-control infection, or even done *work*, for God's sake. She swallowed and turned back to Jo. There would be time to marvel later; right now Jo needed her help. This time she didn't hesitate to brush aside the mass of hair. "Jo?" Louise touched one thin shoulder. "Can you hear me?" The blonde girl moaned and moved slightly, trying to pull herself into a tighter ball, her arms wedged between her knees and her chest.

"Come on," Louise said. She slid her arms between Jo and the floor and flinched at the girl's body temperature. "You're freezing. Let's get you off the floor." She felt strong and healthy and it was no effort to lift Jo to the blanketed pew while Beau twisted underfoot; the teen's head lolled against her shoulder then disappeared beneath the tangled hair as Louise eased her along the length of the blankets. When one of Jo's arms slid to rest palm-up on the floor, Louise gave a small yelp. The hand—and its mate—were split and battered and obviously filled with a virulent infection.

Black dots of shock twinkled around Louise's vision but she resisted; there was no time to freak out. Instead she rapidly tore clean strips from the bottom of Jo's dress to use as bandages, telling herself that a lot of things were different now, and if people who had been drained of blood and died could rise and do the same to others, who was to say that a strange, angelic teenager couldn't have the power to heal? If she wanted reality there was always Beau, crying plaintively and gazing blindly off into space. She washed Jo's hands carefully, wincing each time the younger girl groaned and shuddered, then carefully wrapped each one as Jo had done for her, chewing her lip helplessly when she saw that foul yellow fluid and sticky blood already spotted the wrappings. The stains and mess on the front of her companion's dress would have to wait, and Louise finally covered Jo with two more blankets, then wrapped another around herself and sat next to her, easing Jo's head onto her lap to keep it off the cold wood. Jo's breathing smoothed, and as Louise felt her own head drooping she realized she was still recovering from the last remnants of her own infection. After a time, she slept.

The first thing Louise saw when she opened her eyes was her own breath fogging in front of her face, an amazing thing because she was so warm. The oppressive weight across her shoulders turned out to be too many blankets and she felt movement across her thighs; her hands felt beneath the blankets and found Beau curled on her lap. She disengaged herself and left Beau snoozing amidst the covers as she searched the dim church anxiously, but Jo was nowhere to be found. Back where she started, Louise noticed a small pile on the floor next to the altar; she poked at it curiously and discovered the dress Jo had been wearing and a smaller jumble, the remains of the ragged strips that had covered Jo's mutilated hands. At last Louise spread everything on the floor and settled down Indian-fashion to stare at it in wonder.

The petite dress, the hem torn into uneven fragments, and the equally ragged bandages were a pristine, nearly painful white.

Louise flexed her wrists and fingers, felt the play of muscles and tendons and the warmth of unimpaired circulation as she wondered idly what had happened to the bloodstains on the material.

At length, she supposed it really didn't matter.

12

REVELATION 11:18
And thy wrath is come, and the time of the dead,
them which destroy the earth.

■●■

"Explain what's going on between you two."

It was a demand which, fearing her own temper, Anyelet had waited several hours to make. Although her face was expressionless, she was seething with repressed rage, and these fools were walking a tightrope of destruction.

Both Rita and Gregory started talking and Anyelet felt the old impatience rise, the same impotent frustration of a year ago when her army had started disintegrating. What was left? A handful of soldiers and that pathetic excuse for a human upstairs. So few, yet they still fought among themselves. *Enough*; there was no more time for petty in-fighting. She still admired the Celts of millennia ago and their passionate battles over the best treasures and the most beautiful women, but stupid luxuries such as those were unaffordable in this new age. And here were these two, still yammering at each other and her, neither saying much of anything.

"Shut UP!"

Rita and Gregory jumped, their voices ceasing abruptly. Anyelet brought a hand to her forehead and tried to block the fury building within her, that dark indignation born of loneliness and isolation and nurtured by those who would have hunted her in past centuries. Now she was the hunter instead of the hunted, but for how long? She gnashed her teeth. Like it or not, Gregory's theory of gluttony had left an insidious impression and Anyelet raised her black gaze to a finally silent Rita and Gregory. "You are both worthless!" She spat the words as though they were something foul. "You fight like territorial dogs despite the warmth, food, and safety I've provided. Perhaps you would prefer to take your argument out there." She stabbed a finger at the huge windows that lined the lobby. "Each night Ron and Jasper kill at least two of our 'brothers,' but more creep from the undergrounds like snakes. Is that what you want?"

Both of their faces showed surprise, then shock. "Consider," Anyelet continued, "how it must be to hide belowground and tear at each other for rats, with only enough strength to try again the next night." Her voice dropped to a malevolent whisper. "Would you like to experience the *true* intensity of The Hunger?" Rita met her gaze unflinchingly, convinced Anyelet would never do such a thing—it showed all over her lovely, arrogant face and infuriated Anyelet even more. "Do not fool yourself, Rita," Anyelet said icily. "I will not hesitate to eliminate someone unable to coexist with the rest of my forces."

Rita's face crumbled and Anyelet allowed herself a small, satisfied smile. Rita's days as the favored concubine were ended—so too was her disrespect.

Gregory was looking at both Anyelet and Rita now, terror pulling his lips into an elongated grimace. He permitted himself a reptilian glance at Rita, then returned his gaze to Anyelet. "I can get along," he assured her. His voice was disgustingly close to begging. "It was just a minor disagreement." His eyes flicked again to Rita. "Right?"

Anyelet's former lover nodded grimly. "Sure, we'll get along just fine." Rita's eyes were hooded and darker than normal, and Anyelet studied her suspiciously but let a warm, sincere smile spread across her face. "Well, then," she said heartily, "shall we go on with the plans for tonight?"

"The Art Institute?" Gregory looked relieved.

"Yes." Anyelet motioned to Vic and he moved to her side instantly. "Find Gabriel. I want him to come with us." Vic inclined his head and glided away.

When he and Gabriel had returned, Anyelet addressed the group again. "Is anyone familiar with this building?"

Everyone shook their heads except the teenage Gabriel, who shrugged and made a chewing motion as if he had an invisible wad of gum between his teeth. "I was there a couple of times. Big place."

Gregory frowned. "That's true, it's huge. We should use more hunters or it'll take all night to search the building."

Anyelet considered for a moment, then made a negative motion. "That won't leave enough to guard the humans. Five will have to be enough."

"If we don't have enough, a human could escape," Rita offered.

"That's a chance we have to take," Anyelet said. She glanced at each of them. "Let's go."

The small group followed her from the building obediently, with no bickering or teasing among themselves. Gabriel had always been a dangerous, brooding kid and Anyelet liked that; his youth and speed, which far surpassed the others', would be valuable tonight—besides, his name amused her immensely. It would have been nice to linger under the cloud-laden skies, go to the lakefront and watch the waves pounding the rocks edging the harbors. Anyelet smiled at the snowsmell on the wind, knowing it would help the hunt. Still, she'd never cared for the colder temperatures and had been toying with the idea of moving her group and the humans south, where the weather was not so bitter and it would be easier to keep her stock of food warm and healthy.

Gregory moved in front, leading them south on Wells Street, over the river and its siren call of certain death, all five of them warily scanning the darker blackness of lower Wacker Drive. Here even Vic kept a keen watch, recalling the occasional discovery of severed heads and scattered limbs that were all that remained after a vicious attack by a pack of outcasts. Moving steadily southeast, Anyelet marveled at the cold, empty beauty of the city. Had someone suggested two years ago that she would someday walk the streets of Chicago and find them vacant, she would have laughed. Yet here it was, her fantasy . . .

Backfired.

In a few more minutes they stood on Michigan Avenue, gazing at the stone lions adorning the main steps of the Art Institute. Anyelet had never visited this magnificent place; how much like the blasé hometowner she had been—and still was! While she and her entourage grew placid on the blood of a few sadly overused humans, hundreds of undetected men and women perfected survival skills and plotted ways in which to kill Anyelet and her children. And, of course, there were the outcasts. If she fed them, would they regain their lost sanity? Doubtful; she was surrounded by instability and unfaithfulness. If her plans did not succeed, if the human women could not carry to term and her food stash died off, would her soldiers grow hollow-bellied and slip away, seeking their meals among the rats and birds?

And what of herself?

It was an unthinkable end. *She* had initiated the change that had brought this city, this *country*, this *planet*, to its knees, a victory unequaled by anyone in the history that had been so painstakingly recorded in the now-moldering history books. Because of her, Anyelet, the sonic booms of jets no longer split the atmosphere, the rancid smell of garbage was simply a bad memory, and the surface of the moon would never again feel the footsteps of man.

Because of her.

Who could battle so great a power?

Anyelet gave a mental snort and looked contemptuously at the stone facade of the Art Institute. No one. She had reigned before and would again, beyond when even the massive blocks of this building were reduced to unanswerable mysteries.

"Let's go in." She started to climb but Gabriel's voice stopped her.

"There are other doors where it won't be so obvious."

She cocked her head. "Where do you suggest?"

"Over there." Gabriel led them around the northern corner of the building and indicated a dark metal door at the bottom of a flight of disused steps. "If we use this, chances are a human won't notice."

"What difference does it make?" Rita demanded.

"It will if we don't find anyone and have to come back," Gabriel pointed out.

"*If* we can get in without ripping it apart," Gregory commented.

Anyelet turned to Vic. "What do you think?"

He came forward and peered at the door, which was fitted closely into a metal frame and would have normally pushed open from the inside. There was no outside handle, but his fingers quickly found the three covered steel hinges on its left edge. Each gave a screeching protest as he cracked it apart and forced the concealed pin free; the noise was shocking in a darkness devoid of even the sound of breathing, like the clatter of falling silverware in a quiet restaurant. He tugged on the jutting fragments until the door grated out of its frame and lifted it aside, then scanned the opening. When he spoke, he made no attempt to lower his voice. "I don't think this door's been opened in at least five or ten years. This looks like some kind of storeroom."

"Keep your voice down," Anyelet admonished softly. Hidden by the darkness, her eyes narrowed at his carelessness.

"Assuming there's someone *to* hear," Gregory whispered. They moved inside and began picking a path around dust-covered obstacles. "We might be chasing the ravings of a senile old man."

"Someone lives here, all right." Gabriel's tone was barely audible. "Now that we're inside, I can *smell* her."

"A woman?" Anyelet wasn't really surprised. Her scouts occasionally found females, most strong and unbelievably cunning. She herself had proved to be mankind's most unconquerable adversary. If the woman could breed, Anyelet would be even more pleased.

From Anyelet's right, Rita's muttering confirmed her thoughts. "I'm sure Siebold will be glad to hear that. More *meat*."

Anyelet jerked. What was that? A charge, a *feeling* from . . . *Vic*. Even in the coal-black storeroom, with its filthy piles of jumbled crates and mounds of tattered canvas throws, she could see the giant vampire waiting by a pair of rusty elevator doors with his iron-hard arms folded. Had it been anger? Seldom could she catch the private thoughts of her own kind without their knowledge, and it was unnerving to know that this monstrously sized night creature hid an emotion so intense it was literally *leaking* out of him. She would have to watch him closely.

"How will we get upstairs?" asked Rita.

"Well, since the stairs are obviously blocked"—Gabriel pointed at a pile of debris nearly as high as the ceiling—"we'll use the elevator shaft. Unless you want to move all this stuff."

"Let's not waste any more time," Anyelet cut in. "This building is huge. It may take all night to find her."

Gabriel's eyes were impassive. "I doubt it." He raised his chin and his nostrils flared wide. "She's been here a long time and her scent is very strong. I think we'll catch her within, say, a half hour." He grinned, showing the long, thin fangs of a nightwolf.

Anyelet nodded at Vic, who turned and began prying at the elevator doors. More noise, this time a loud groaning, as though the elevator doors themselves were trying to stall Vic's intrusion. Anyelet ground her teeth; surely anyone inside had fled by now! They could only hope the size of the building would muffle this overabundance of sound. One last scream and the doors yielded, the shaft stretching away to a cold, damp nothingness.

"Well, isn't this handy," Rita grumbled. "Just like the old days."

"You expected an operator to push the button for you?" hissed Gregory.

Anyelet made a soft snarling sound and both fell into a nervous silence. "Climb," she commanded. Already Vic was hauling himself up, muscles working smoothly, and Anyelet reached for one of the cables, adjusting her grip around the slick, oily surface. She began climbing easily, Vic's movements overhead making the cable strum in her hand. The others followed one by one, the thick strands of steel vibrating beneath their weight, causing echoing metal whispers as they crawled up its length like mutated caterpillars.

Anyelet bent her head back to Gabriel. "How far?" Her carefully modulated voice carried eerily in the shaft.

"Next floor up," he murmured.

Above them, Vic paused. "This is as far as we go," he said quietly. "The elevator's blocking us and I can't get a good enough hold to push it out of the way."

"This'll do," Gabriel said.

Vic put one foot on the thin ledge running around the shaft and pried at the closed doors with his free hand, widening them enough to crawl through. Anyelet was out in an instant, crouching cautiously next to the elevator and scanning the foyer. The others streamed from the shaft like a pack of slick cats, then milled uncertainly, waiting for instructions as Anyelet sighed in exasperation. These were not hunters—they were *children*, uneducated and undisciplined. Was it laziness? Or abundance? Abruptly she knew just how Hugh had survived: mind and reason gone, the old man functioned on instinct alone, that wonderful, inexplicable sixth sense that was— *normally*—so heightened in those of the night.

Only Gabriel appeared to have retained a semblance of the valuable skills accompanying his immortality. Now he lifted his nose and sniffed, turning in a slow semicircle before moving down a short hall on their right to a closed glass door. "Through here," he said. "I can smell her clearly." Rita stepped up to examine the door, a double glass barrier with metal bars for handles through which a heavy chain and steel padlock had been threaded and locked from the opposite side. The doors parted just enough for her to slip a hand through the opening and grab the chain.

Anyelet nodded, knowing that some sacrifices had to be made. "As quietly as possible."

Rita began to apply a slow, steady pressure; fifteen seconds later, the chain hung in two pieces. Rita's mouth twisted in contempt as she lowered the pieces to the floor without so much as a rattle. "A fool's effort," she whispered.

"I think they count more on being able to hide," Gregory said softly. "The bigger the building, the better."

Gabriel grinned, his red lips stretching to show fangs as clean and white as a puppy's. "Not this time. Come on." They followed, matching his pace through mazelike corridors and galleries, past dead-end alcoves that seemed to go on forever. Paintings and statues flowed past, a thousand objets d'art representing man's past and the permanently frozen present.

"Gabriel"—Anyelet's voice was barely audible—"can you still follow her scent?"

"Yes," he whispered. His red-blue eyes flickered with anticipation and he put a cautionary finger to his mouth. Another door yielded and he led them down again, following a striking staircase to and through an unlocked pair of doors marked with a plaque bearing the words AR-THUR RUBLOFF AUDITORIUM. His nostrils spread and he forced air into his nose. His expectant leer faded.

"She's not here," he said, not bothering to lower his voice. "Otherwise these doors would be locked from the inside." He pointed to a length of chain and several heavy padlocks pushed against the wall.

Vic bent and fingered the high-quality steel. "They won't be a problem," he commented. He stepped inside and the rest shambled in behind him; immediately their footsteps echoed through the large room. Anyelet admired the woman's choice—even knowing the room would amplify noise wouldn't help them move quietly.

"But she's been here recently?" Anyelet looked around, noting the raised stage and the upholstered seats tilting upward for several stories at a dizzying angle.

"Probably last night," Gabriel responded.

"Maybe she's not coming back." Rita didn't need to be specific, and Anyelet rubbed her tongue across her fangs as she considered the odds.

"We'll check again tomorrow night," she decided. "Just to be sure."

"Be careful not to touch anything," Gabriel instructed. "You can bet she knows every detail of this place."

"I found where she sleeps," Rita called. She had pulled aside a fold of the heavy draperies at the farthest end of the stage, revealing an alcove no bigger than a closet. Inside was a cot bearing a heavy sleeping bag and blankets, a small cookstove, and a few other things, including a chemical toilet that made Anyelet chuckle.

"Check this out." Gabriel carefully lifted the spill of blankets between the cot and the floor. Beneath it they could see the well-oiled gleam of a shotgun stock. Anyelet looked to Gregory, but the former accountant shook his head. "It'll be the first thing she checks if she comes back. Weapons are like security blankets to humans."

"What if we just take out the bullets?" Rita asked.

"Shells," Gregory corrected. "And no way. She'll clean and reload it. Anything different and she'll be long gone before we even wake up. We'll have to leave it."

Anyelet frowned. "That's a tremendous risk."

Gregory spread his hands. "What are the odds she'll return and bed down for the night without going over her gun? Personally I think we'll lose her if we screw around with it."

Anyelet studied the Winchester thoughtfully. "The firing pin—"

"Forget it," Gabriel interrupted. "She'll break it down to clean it. Let's face it—it takes a smart human to last this long. There's nothing we can do about the gun."

Anyelet nodded reluctantly. "All right. Let's get out of here. Make sure to leave everything the way it was, no slipups. And keep the gun in mind tomorrow night."

They filed toward the exit, disappointment robbing them of conversation. Anyelet was looking in the other direction when she sensed rather than saw Vic's lightning movement as he plucked some small trinket from the plastic record crate that served as a nightstand next to the cot. For a moment she was stupefied—he must know his act would likely make tomorrow night's foray useless! Her first instinct was to snatch it from his pocket and demand an explanation, but she squelched the impulse. What was happening? She had lived centuries by herself, existing on common sense and a fierce need for self-preservation, two things blatantly lacking in the obnoxious and sloppy children she had borne. At first the loss of bits and pieces of her army had seemed negligible, but now each betrayal represented a larger percentage, an unraveling of her already-shaky hold over these rebellious offspring. Her lip curled scornfully; perhaps it would be best to kill them *all* and simply start over. In the end, she needed no one but herself.

Outside the sky resembled an overstuffed mattress that had split and was now spewing its dark innards in great, coagulated globs, and Anyelet, Rita, and Gregory waited while Gabriel and Vic carefully repositioned the door. "I'll bring some oil to squirt around the frame tomorrow night," Gregory promised when he and Vic had finished. "It should cut down on the noise."

Anyelet glanced at Vic, but he said nothing; she had the distinct feeling he wouldn't care if the door tripled its racket, and, in fact, he'd prefer that the woman escape. Her eyes narrowed as she realized it wasn't just petty thievery she'd witnessed, but an act purposely warning their prey.

Gregory's low voice intervened on her reverie. "I wonder why she didn't come back tonight."

"It doesn't matter." Anyelet's words were frosty as she gave Vic a long, hard look. "Wherever she is, tomorrow night she's ours."

13

●·●··●·●·●

REVELATION 16:6
Thou hast given them blood to drink; for they are worthy.

●━·●━●

Vic examined the cloisonné box, turning it over and over in his heavy fingers and peering at the butterfly of brilliant colors against its fractured royal blue background. Such a tiny thing, it disappeared entirely when he folded his fingers into a fist.

Such a little thing, indeed.

Anyelet had seen him. It hadn't taken any so-called vampire "gift" to feel her shock, then her repressed rage. He *responded* to others, to their treatment, their impressions upon him, like clay pressed into a mold. He'd grown up a tough Italian kid who'd constantly fought with and against the west side street gangs, and even immortality couldn't erase the mementos he still carried, one wide scar crossing his left side from battling a kid armed with a shattered liquor bottle, another arcing around his neck, this from a fifteen-year-old who'd nearly managed to cut Vic's throat. Hand encased in homemade brass knuckles, Vic had delivered a punch to the solar plexus that had left his enemy gasping and helpless as Vic had pried the knife free, torn open the youth's shirt and carved the word COWARD across the sallow, boyish chest.

Vic still felt guilty about that. And who, after all, had been the coward? Himself, of course, a boy already masquerading in a man's body. His friends would have crucified him for letting the Latin King live, but it hadn't mattered. When he'd staggered into the house covered with blood, his hysterical mother had actually *slapped* him before realizing what she'd done. He knew she'd struck him out of fear and love, but his resentment was quick and helpless as he thought of the constant, uncon-

ditional devotion she gave Vic's nearly bedridden father.
In those days physicians still made house calls, and Dr.
Finocchiaro, a frequent caller anyway, came in the middle of the night to sew Vic's neck back together because
in the old neighborhood you handled your own business
and didn't involve the police. As a result of that night, his
mother had sent him to live with her brother in Rock-
ford, an older man who was as unyielding as a block of
granite beneath a surprisingly mild exterior. Young and
still impressionable, Vic had learned an appreciation for
life from Uncle Mike out of which he would eventually
make a career; all that trouble to save his neck and look
what had happened to it.

Yes, Anyelet had seen, and Vic hadn't cared. Respond-
ing to her anger, in fact, he had mentally *dared* her to say
or do something about it. At least it had proven she
couldn't see into his mind without him *knowing* it,
though with eye contact she could rifle someone's mind
like an open file cabinet. The traitorous thoughts that so
often filled the spaces that before his dark transformation
had held human feelings like love, charity, and forgive-
ness remained hidden; now he only hated in degrees, de-
pending upon whom and what he was thinking about at
the time.

And he Hungered.

Oh yes.

There was no logic behind his theft. The notion of
challenging Anyelet's authority was absurd—he no more
wanted to control this motley pack of animals than he
wanted to crawl beneath the sun and fry, and besides,
she probably held powers that he couldn't even imagine.
He wanted to *live*, and maybe *there* was his subconscious
desire to betray their presence. That unknown woman
wanted to live, too, and he knew that tomorrow the
struggle she'd so valiantly carried on these past months
would end, all because of the ravings of a stupid old man.
Vic sighed and dropped the butterfly box on his cot, then
slipped down a back stairway, indulging in a lazy fantasy
about what he would do to Howard if he caught him
skulking around. Sunup was only an hour away and he
had to make sure old Hugh was inside for the day. The

crazy vampire was probably hungry, too, even if he had
managed to snare a rat or something else for a sort of
dinner. Vic had followed him once, and while the old
man usually caught *some*thing, the meal was never very
large. If he didn't help things along, Hugh would slowly
starve, withering until he became indistinguishable from
the outcasts that haunted the tunnels and connecting
basements of the downtown buildings. Vic would never
be able to bear that.

The ancient vampire was in his habitual spot outside,
standing where the concrete sidewalk met the metal grating on the bridge, peering between the spaces rather
than over the walkway at the water below and playing an
invisible trumpet. At the sound of Vic's approach he
raised his head and smiled with crooked teeth.

"Waiting for Tisbee," Hugh explained. He glanced at a
broken watch dangling precariously from his wrist, then
sucked in a mouthful of air so he could make a blowing
noise. "She's late again," he complained. "Been waiting
here for a year, dammit all." The accuracy of Hugh's
words made Vic start. "Boy's late, too," Hugh continued.
"Supposed to bring me dinner, and the little bastard's not
here. *Shit!*"

"It's all right," Vic said soothingly. "He'll—"

"I'm *hungry!*" Hugh's voice was a sudden, strident
scream through the steel girders of the Wells Street
Bridge. Vic gasped at its loudness, then the old man abruptly dropped his tone back to normal and gave Vic a
sidelong glance. "Have to go to the dungeon soon," he
said cryptically. "The fireball's on its way."

"Yes," Vic agreed. He saw the hollowness of Hugh's
cheeks and the way the skin had shrunk close around his
jaw. Once the old one's mouth had been full-lipped and
laughing; now it was a hard, jagged slash barely covering
the cracked fangs.

"Hungry," Hugh said again. He looked at Vic and for
a moment the younger vampire saw regret in that shriveled expression—regret, and a plea for understanding,
maybe a cry for mercy. A long time ago Vic had thought
he could give Hugh a cure; instead he had frozen the old
man into permanent imbecility.

Vic had purposely fed again a short time ago, taking a small meal from a healthy man only because he knew that Hugh would be hungry and, after all, someone had to look out for the old man. The others were already burrowing into their sleeping places, filled and fat, quick to flee the coming daylight. Last night he'd been petrified during the endless moments of Anyelet's attempt to look into Hugh's mind. Now he knew that no one could see. Or maybe, as in life, no one bothered.

He offered his arm and Hugh fell upon it eagerly.

The least Vic could do was watch over his own father.

III

March 25

The Seekers—
Gathering for the Battle

1

REVELATION 17:18
And the woman which thou sawest is that great city. . . .

C.J. eased the breath out of his lungs, feeling the tension flow from his night-knotted muscles as he stretched. For a few seconds he was enveloped in the tingly sensations, like the time the clinic dentist had pumped him full of laughing gas before pulling a molar that had shattered at the gum from a hard punch to the jaw by his old man. Back then C.J. had figured that feeling was as close to heaven as he'd ever get, because hell waited at home in the form of a fat, lazy man who claimed to be his father and who bathed in beer instead of water.

Now, hell was everywhere.

He rose, stripped, and washed, gritting his teeth against the cold air and colder water. He dressed in loose chinos and a baggy wool sweater, then reconsidered and pulled off the sweater to layer a couple of long-sleeved shirts underneath it. Finally C.J. slipped on his fatigue jacket and stepped into the hall, noting that as usual he was the first to rise. Before he went downstairs he poked his head into Calie's room to check on her. She was still sleeping, her face to the wall beneath the heavy sleeping bag. He waited a few seconds, then backed out and stepped away; two or three feet down the hall he thought he heard a low chuckle and he paused, then kept going. She was always pulling little tricks on him.

Sitting in the small breakfast room, he checked the strings on his crossbow and made sure the flights and broadheads were firmly attached during the twenty minutes it took McDole to show up. Suddenly C.J. was nervous; if the older man said no to his request. . . . Well, he might bitch about it, but he would never disregard McDole's orders.

"Morning." The white-haired man's voice was cheerful. "Feels like December again, doesn't it?" C.J. nodded, reluctant to speak as McDole put a match to a can of Sterno for hot water. "Get down some coffee, would you?"

"Sure." C.J.'s voice came out hoarse and he cleared his throat. McDole watched him curiously as the teen set out their usual coffee makings on the table by the little campstove.

"You have something you want to talk about?"

C.J. sighed inwardly; between Calie and McDole, sometimes it seemed he had no privacy at all. Well, what the hell. "Yeah. . . ." He'd always found it hard to ask for stuff, especially time to himself, and as a toddler he'd learned that asking for something usually caused pain. He was sure his father was either dead or one of those maggoty things in the subways, but the drunkard's lessons still lived on.

"Well?" McDole's voice was encouraging.

"I got something to do today," the dark-haired youth finally managed. "Could someone else help Calie and the doctor?"

McDole studied him, then turned his attention to draining the coffee filters, layering the air with the rich smell of the brew. "If you think it's important, then yes. Someone else can be found."

C.J. hesitated. Was what he wanted to do really *that* important? Enough to put the rest of the people with whom he lived to extra trouble? He hung his head.

"What was it you wanted to do?" McDole asked. "Do you need help?" He offered a steaming mug and C.J. reached for it, his callused hands oblivious to the heat. "I, uh—"

"Well, it's none of my business anyway." McDole's tone was carefully level and C.J. glanced at him suspiciously. Just what was he up to? "You seldom have time for yourself, something we all need," McDole continued. "But if you happen to be outside, you might keep an eye out for that girl we saw the day before yesterday. She looked about your age."

C.J.'s breath drained silently through his nose and he

fought a grin. That sly old fart, he thought admiringly. He knew the whole time; he just wanted to see me squirm.

"Sure," C.J. responded as casually as he could. "I'll keep my eyes open." McDole raised his cup in a toast and hid his smile behind the steam.

"But only if you think of it."

C.J. found the motor scooter, a yellow Vespa bearing a sticker that read VESPA OF CHICAGO and listing an address fifty blocks north, abandoned on the bridge, and he knew stale gasoline had probably done it in. There was nothing to indicate where its owner had gone and he wandered into the congested buildings of central downtown more out of boredom than anything else. It was doubtful he'd find the girl unless she showed herself on purpose, and what was the chance of that? Still, he couldn't give up so soon. Once C.J. had craved privacy and the safety it offered, a harbor away from his father's brutality and the squalor and violence of the housing project in which he'd lived. Now Chicago's empty buildings hulked like great boxes with a million brooding eyes. Did the girl watch him from behind one of the windows that sparkled at every turn?

He ambled along, finally stopping at the White Hen Pantry in the apartment building at Lake and Dearborn. The market's door had already been shattered, but from the dust layering the fragments of glass it had happened a month ago or longer. Water stains crept past the threshold of the cracking linoleum, and while the contents of most of the shelves were still intact, here and there it was evident the rats had been at work. In the early months the rats had multiplied with frightening speed, becoming a major danger to the health and food supply of the humans who'd managed to survive, then starvation had hit among the vampires and the number of rodents had dropped dramatically. They still bred in the deep tunnel system and sewers, though they were seldom seen in the open. C.J. scanned the shelves but the signs of another person—an opened rather than chewed box or an empty can or two—were few and crusted with age. A deli counter ran beneath the southern windows, but he

averted his gaze and breathed through his mouth as he
went past it, and he'd learned long ago not to open
freezer doors. Not much to see and he didn't want to eat
in here anyway. Most of the liquid—ketchup, soda, bottled juice, you name it—from exploded bottles and jars
had dried up; still, the smell was overwhelming.

He grabbed a can of soup that looked free of rust
stains or punctures and a box of Ritz crackers. Outside it
was damned cold and heavily overcast, but still better
than the store, with its smell of rot and crumbling sense
of claustrophobia. Lake Street and its overhead grid of
train trestles cast too many shadows, even in the daytime, and after a minute C.J. moved on, the hope that
he'd find the girl finally starting to fade. He circled the
convoluted Dubuffet sculpture that graced the patterned
sidewalk at the main doors to the State of Illinois Center,
then spotted the granite wall that rimmed the entrance to
the Daley Center's underground garage across the street.
He settled there, a good twenty feet above the entrance,
where he could see the Picasso and the plaza through the
glass walls around the lobby of the Daley Center. Directly in front of him was the fountain, dry and filled
with bits of trash. He still remembered a third-grade
field trip where his teacher had shown them the plaza
and the building when the name had just been changed
from its former title of Civic Center. C.J. pried the can
open and sniffed it, then ate and hoped for the best. One
of these days he and the rest of the underground would
probably end up with food poisoning when the stuff
started to go bad. Most of the jars and cans had burst
over the winter; only the denser items with less water,
like beef stew, canned meat, or thick soup, were left. C.J.
figured they'd end up existing on mixes of dried soup
and lake water. *If* they made it.

When he was through with his lunch, C.J. gathered his
trash, stuffed it in the empty cracker box, and thought
briefly about leaving it on the wall in the hope that
someone would see it and know that there were still people in the city who lived and ate what they'd been meant
to, then he looked up at the dark glass of the Daley Center and changed his mind. What if by leaving this sign of

life he endangered someone's hiding place? He couldn't risk it. He leapt off the wall and took a step to regain his balance when someone behind him spoke.

"Hi."

C.J. whirled and brought the crossbow to firing position with deadly speed; beneath his finger the trigger was only a fraction of an inch away from killing as his heart slamdanced in his chest. The practice and danger of the past months showed in his skill; even with his pulse thundering his aim was steady.

The girl never flinched. "My name is Jo," she said.

"Joe?" he said stupidly. He was acutely aware of everything: the sound of the wind turning the corner of the County Building from the west, a scrap of paper scuttling along the street in its wake like a half-crazed squirrel, the rise and fall of the girl's chest beneath the prominent bones of her shoulders. Somewhere to his left a sparrow twittered. "That's a boy's name." Flash thought for the day, he thought disdainfully.

"It's short for Jovina." She raised a hand and pointed south; C.J. watched her finger float upward, then jerked and stared at her suspiciously, wondering if she was hypnotizing him. Most of the upper half of her dress was ripped away; the rest fell in burned tatters. She didn't seem to notice that one of her breasts, pale and hardly developed, could be seen through the ruined material, nor did the thirty-five-degree temperature seem to bother her. "I live in St. Peter's," she said.

"I've been in there," he said flatly. "It's empty."

She smiled then, and the sight made C.J. think he was going a little crazy, because he'd just met her, only thirty seconds ago, and she was standing here half-naked and weird, yet he was thinking already that she might be okay. "You were there a couple of weeks ago," she said calmly. "I watched you."

"But why didn't you say something?" His cool facade fell away and he looked at the girl in astonishment. How could someone see *him* without him knowing it?

"It wasn't time yet." She turned and C.J. found himself staring at a mass of impossibly long white hair that was nearly indistinguishable from the pallid flesh of her back.

"Can you come with me?" she asked. "There's someone I'd like you to meet. She can't stay with me forever."

"Who can't stay with you forever?" Score another intelligent question, he thought. *Christ.*

"Her name is Louise." Jo's eyes found his and for an instant he sort of got . . . *lost* in them, like fading out or locking into a light stupor when you were tired. Only he wasn't staring into space, he was staring into *Jo*, and when he came back a moment later, he knew without a doubt that he had to do whatever she said. It wasn't a matter of trust at all; it was . . .

The *future.*

He lowered the crossbow.

"Lead on."

2

REVELATION 12:16
And the earth helped the woman. . . .

Amazing, Louise thought. Un . . . *believable*.

Sitting on the front steps of St. Peter's and waiting for Jo to return, Louise ignored the cold and held up her hands, turning both front and back, flexing each finger and enjoying the feel of the wind between each digit. It was, indeed, a miracle that they were healed, but this went even further—every single scar or blemish that had ever been present on her hands was totally *gone*.

The cold had seeped through her clothes and Louise hoisted herself up and went back inside, still peering at the side of her right hand. Before her fall onto the street grating, she'd had a twisted, inch-long scar there, caused by shattering the glass door in the foyer of her building with the heel of her hand the summer she was eleven. Now the scar was missing, and even her fingernails, always so cracked and bitten, were smooth and healthy— long, too, grown to manicure length past her fingertips. As she settled onto the front pew, voices drifted in from the vestibule and Louise glanced up. The sound was so fitting that for an instant she didn't pay any attention, then she realized it was voices, and not just Jo. She jumped to her feet, then stopped uncertainly as she heard Jo tell someone to follow her in.

"Good morning!" Jo called. "How do you feel?"

"Fine." Louise cupped a hand around her mouth to help carry her voice. "Where've you been?" The question was automatic as Jo led another person up the aisle and Louise strained to see. "Who's that?"

"His name is . . ." Jo glanced at the man walking next to her.

"C.J.," he said as he and Jo stopped in front of her. "That's what everyone calls me."

"Hi." Louise couldn't think of anything else to say.

"This is Louise," Jo told C.J. "She came in the day before yesterday."

C.J. shifted his gaze back to her and Louise saw that his eyes were a discomforting golden tan. She tried to smile and knew immediately that it was more of a sick grimace than anything else. For the first time in a year she wondered what she looked like, and she couldn't stop her fingers from smoothing her hair. She'd started using her hunting knife months ago to hack off chunks of it, impatient with the care it needed just to keep it neat. Now her thoughts touched regretfully on the memory of four-inch locks of hair floating to the floor on a bright, long-ago afternoon. Her face—was it even *clean*? She was mortified; her eyes, an unremarkable shade of vague blue, were the only thing left. Big damned deal, she thought miserably.

Oh yes—and her brand-new hands.

C.J. cleared his throat uncomfortably and looked away, his eyes instinctively searching the darker areas of the church nave before returning to Jo. Louise blushed and realized that Jo had lost most of the neckline and front of her dress, and half her childishly formed chest was in full sight. C.J., however, regarded her with an almost clinical interest, much as a boy would watch a small and interesting pale frog. "So," he finally said. He slipped a medieval-looking contraption from his shoulders and placed it carefully on one of the pews. "You've only been here two days?"

Louise nodded and swallowed her nervousness. "Yeah."

"Where'd you come from?" He leaned against the side of one of the benches and folded his arms. "Were you with anyone else?"

Louise shook her head. "No, just me and Beau."

"Beau?"

Louise couldn't wait any longer. "Jo, what *happened* to you?"

Jo looked at her strangely, then made an only semi-concerned effort to pull her dress together. Louise's mouth dropped open when she saw that Jo's hands, so terribly mutilated last night, were as white and unblemished as her own. "Your hands—"

"I think I'll go change," Jo interrupted. Her voice was muffled and sleepy-sounding. "And splash some water on my face." She smiled sweetly. "You guys get to know each other."

Louise quickly scanned the aisle. "Beau—"

"—is in the back," Jo said calmly. "I guess he's tired, too."

"Who's Beau?" C.J. asked again.

Louise had taken her gaze off Jo for only an instant, but the white-haired girl was gone. In another moment Louise heard a door close somewhere in the northern end of the church. C.J. was still waiting, his eyes like some bizarre pair of sparkling yellow stones. "My dog," Louise finally managed. "Beau is my dog."

"You have a dog? Wow." He sounded impressed. "That must've been a trick. Were you always by yourself?"

This time she answered his repeated question with a nod. "Were you?"

He shrugged. "Sometimes." Again he looked briefly at the dark rear of the church; it was a habit Louise understood well. "But . . ." He hesitated.

"But what?"

"There are . . . a few others now," he finished at last.

Louise's tense expression spread into pleasure. "Well, that's great! How many? And where are they? I was starting to think I was the only one left before yesterday, because I hadn't seen anyone else in so long, you know—" She stumbled slightly over the last word and stopped. She was babbling and he was staring at her like she had two heads. And why not? Her face turned scarlet. Where did I get off thinking I was the only person with brains enough to survive? She choked back the sudden urge to cry and closed her mouth.

C.J. grinned abruptly and the smile lit up his face and made him look like an impish little boy. "Hey, don't stop now—you're on a roll!" He glanced around the dim interior, lit only by the richly colored but feeble glow from the stained glass overhead. "Let's get out of here. I'm sure it's holy and all that, but I just don't like dark places." Louise followed him outside without speaking, then was shocked to feel the drop in the temperature in only the last quarter hour. She threw a worried glance at the sky.

"It's going to snow soon."

C.J. jumped at the sound of Jo's voice floating from just inside the door to the church, and Louise dredged up enough courage to touch the sleeve of his jacket reassuringly. The only *living* thing she'd touched for the longest time was Beau. "She's always doing that," she told him. "I think she likes to surprise people."

"Person could get killed that way," he muttered.

Louise thought of the dangerous-looking weapon inside and wondered just how badly Jo had startled him earlier in the day. "Not her," Louise said.

C.J.'s eyebrows lifted and Louise shrugged. She might sound as odd as Jo acted, but she believed every word. Jo rejoined them, wearing a white dress that except for the sleeves was the same as the ruined one. Her porcelain-tinted skin glowed when she lifted her face and breathed deeply of a swirl of frigid wind sweeping the thick sheet of her hair. She turned back to them, her gray eyes a strange reflection of the tightly layered clouds. "We have to get you back to Water Tower."

For the first time, C.J.'s iron composure cracked. "How did you know about that?" he demanded. "Who else knows?"

"I know a lot of things." Jo's soft voice was reassuring. "And only Louise knows—now. You're quite safe." Watching Jo, Louise had the queer notion that the younger girl's eyes changed to a darker, brooding gray that had nothing to do with the snowclouds overhead, like some kind of optical chameleon. It was scary and Louise's belly gave a single, dreadful twist. "Let's go," Jo said. "I'll walk with you, but I can't stay when we get there."

"Why not?" Louise asked nervously. She was distinctly aware that she could be an uninvited intruder into C.J.'s life. He'd never invited her to Water Tower Place. What if—

"Of course you can," C.J. interrupted Louise's jumbled thoughts. "What're you going to do, hike all the way back? By the time we get there, it might be dark. No way."

Jo shrugged. "Then let's not waste time. Why don't you tell Louise about your . . . what would you call them? Family?"

"Whatever."

Louise bristled at C.J.'s snappish response but Jo didn't appear to notice. "Get Beau and your things," she told Louise. "You won't be coming back."

"I won't?" Confused again, Louise glanced at C.J., but he only stared crossly at Jo. A flicker of irritation stirred, warring with uncertainty and the sensation of homelessness she'd had ever since leaving the north side; had he and Jo planned this without even asking her? "Suppose they don't want any more people?" Louise plunged on. "Or—"

"There's room," C.J. said. His tone made it clear that he thought her questions were yet another waste of time.

"I don't want to impose," Louise continued stubbornly. She felt like the unwanted relative during the holidays. "I can take care of myself and I don't have to stay with Jo to do it." Louise was getting angry and embarrassed. What was happening here anyway? One minute Jo was saving her life and performing miracles, the next she was kicking Louise out on her butt.,

C.J.'s expression was rigid. "Get your stuff."

"I refuse to be a burden!" Louise said hotly. "I'm not so stupid I'd go where I'm not wanted!"

"Oh, he wants you to go, all right." Jo's voice was smooth and sweet, like warmed honey. "He's just too shy to say so."

Louise was about to retort when she realized that despite his fighting stance and protectively folded arms, C.J.'s face was deep red. "I–I'll get my backpack," Louise stammered. "Here, Beau! Come on, boy!" She fled to the small confessional office where her dog and small cache of belongings waited; as the door closed behind her she could hear the tinkling of Jo's laughter, the sound light and not at all cruel.

A few minutes later and they were on their way, Beau tucked safely in his customary place inside Louise's jacket as the trio wound through the downtown streets. They were only four blocks from St. Peter's when the snow began to fall in thick, clinging clumps that immediately began to gather in small piles. Louise stopped. "We should go back," she said, struggling to make herself heard above the wind; when she halted, Beau poked his nose inquisitively from a fold in her jacket, then quickly retreated. "Before we leave tracks. It won't matter if they lead back to the church." She looked at Jo knowingly. "We'll still be safe."

Jo shook her head and her companions gaped at her in disbelief. "No. Come on." The young girl resumed her steps, leaving small telltale depressions in the growing layer of snow. Louise and C.J. followed, knowing it would be useless to disagree, petrified about the footprints marking their progress like huge blotches of black paint on a white canvas. In the cold—something that apparently didn't affect Jo—their prints were becoming more defined with each quarter block. How much would it snow? It was barely past noon now; what if it snowed *all day*?

When the crystal-shrouded front of Water Tower Place was finally less than a block away, Louise shivered as C.J. planted his feet firmly on the snow-covered sidewalk and refused to go any farther. "I can't do this." The snowfall that had seemed so pretty now swirled ferociously around them and the sidewalk was crusted over with ice, leaving perfect depressions with each step. "The tracks will lead the vampires right to the front door."

Louise's voice was grim. "He's right." Although she was only three feet away, Jo seemed to blend into the harsh weather and Louise could barely see the white-haired girl.

"What tracks?" Jo asked gently.

Anger twisted C.J.'s dark-complected features. "Are you completely crazy?" he demanded. A clot of snow tried to stick to one cheek and he slapped it away. "We might as well hang flags, for Christ's sake!" His black hair was sodden beneath a crown of quickly accumulating snow. When Jo smiled and touched his arm, he snorted in disgust and whirled to point at the indentations marking their passage, but his sound of derision ended in a shortened gasp.

There were no tracks.

The snow stretched along Michigan Avenue, unbroken and startling in its magnificent blanket of purity.

The blood drained from Louise's face and an absurd thought occurred to her: she and Jo must look like winter sisters right now, Jo, with her flowing mass of colorless, strangely *dry* hair, and Louise, with her snow-covered brown hair and shock-white skin.

"You two go in." Jo's voice was kind. "Louise was ill yesterday and shouldn't be out in this weather."

"What about you? Aren't you coming?" Louise grabbed Jo's hand and clung to it; even without a coat in the subfreezing temperatures, Jo's skin was pleasantly warm.

"But you'll die out here!" C.J. protested. "You'll—"

"I'll be fine."

C.J. and Louise stumbled after Jo as she crossed the final steps to the glassed-in entrance and pulled open the door.

"That's supposed to be *locked!*"

"It was." Jo brushed a new clump of snow from the young man's cheek and Louise's flesh crawled when she saw Jo's eyes darken again to that terrible, brooding shade of gray. For a moment the girl stared at them, then she turned back to C.J. "You just have to accept that. Sometimes you have to accept a lot of things." She glanced at Louise, and the brown-haired girl felt as though she'd been *touched* by a flash of love and . . . regret. Terror swept her for a second. Why would Jo look at her like that?

"Both of you be in Daley Plaza tomorrow at noon," Jo said suddenly. "Don't come earlier or you'll miss him."

"Miss who?" C.J. demanded. He looked ready to explode. "*What are you talking about?*"

Jo's perfect smile, even in the midst of the surprise snowstorm, blanketed them with warmth.

"The key to the Mart."

Louise blinked at C.J. and his return gaze was perplexed. Both teenagers turned back to Jo—

She was gone.

And there were still no footprints.

3

REVELATION 13:14
And deceiveth them that dwell on the
earth by the means of those miracles. . . .

"I wonder if C.J. found that girl."

McDole's voice was loud and startling, but he had to say *something* to break the silence; he and Calie had been sitting here for nearly two hours watching Bill Perlman stare into a contraption he claimed was a microscope. McDole was amazed the doctor had gotten the thing to work, and if he hadn't believed the results would someday be worth it, McDole would've protested about the number of batteries used to provide power for all the lights and equipment the physician needed. He looked at Calie, but she only sat on her stool, rotating slowly and watching the men, occasionally glancing into the darkened hall of the basement where they'd hastily moved the laboratory after the tissue sample had started to disintegrate in the bright lab at Northwestern. They hated being in this dismal part of Water Tower Place, but it couldn't be avoided.

"Damn," Perlman said. He stepped back from the microscope.

"What?" McDole said. "Do you need something?"

Perlman shook his head. "No, but thanks for offering. You two have been very capable assistants. I couldn't have gotten this far without your help—and C.J.'s, too." Still, he looked tired and discouraged. "But today's great experiment was a bust."

Calie rose and peered uncertainly at the slides. "What was the experiment?" The doctor started to answer and she held up a finger. "Keep it simple. Doctors run in your family, not mine."

The younger man looked rattled by Calie's comment,

then began to speak as McDole leaned forward. "Well,
I'm trying to . . ." Perlman frowned. "The vampires are
dead," the doctor began again. "Or they're supposed to
be. We don't know what animates them and probably
never will. Maybe, and I'm very hesitant to say this, it
takes place on a spiritual rather than physical level. However, the only arena in which we have experience is the
physical, so that's where we have to try and tie the two
together." His gaze stopped briefly on Calie and Perlman
looked as though he would qualify his words, then decided against it. "So these dead creatures get up and
walk around—"

"They do more than that," McDole interjected.

"Sure"—Perlman nodded—"but again, you're going
into a new realm." He motioned to them. "Look here.
What do you see?"

Calie positioned herself and studied the view through
the microscope, then McDole took a turn. There wasn't
much to see: a spattering of light and dark shapes around
something that looked brown and dried up. Nothing
moved. "Not much," McDole admitted. "Cells, I guess.
But I didn't see anything alive."

"What were we looking at?" Calie asked.

Perlman scrubbed at his face with both hands without
speaking. McDole could see weariness and frustration
etched in the lines beneath the doctor's light beard stubble. Finally he answered. "Clostridia, one of the most
common bacteria found in dead animals. This bacteria—
which causes decomposition—is a major factor in the cycle of life. The brown spot was a microlayer of vampire
flesh taken from our friend in the bomb shelter."

"But they don't decompose," McDole said.

"Exactly!" Brief excitement broke through Perlman's
tiredness. "But if I could develop a bacterium or fungus,
or mutate a clostridium that could survive introduction
into a vampire's body and reproduce, maybe the decomposition process could finally begin, as it should have
when the body first died."

"Like giving them a big dose of the flu," Calie suggested.

"Not at all. Influenza is a *virus*, not a bacteria. A virus always requires a *living* host; without one, it ceases to function, although it may not die per se. On the other hand, certain bacteria can exist in either living or nonliving environments."

"I'm out of my league here," McDole said, "but I didn't see anything moving under that microscope."

"You wouldn't have anyway," Perlman told him absently. "I haven't had time to isolate the substance which makes the vampire's body a hostile environment, either by indirectly attacking the bacteria or by being highly toxic to the organism. Besides, it's a moot point."

"Why is that?"

"The way I see it—and this is open for discussion, so let me know if you have any ideas—the vampires are not technically *dead*. Although life-force functions—cell division and activity—have stalled, enzymatic action doesn't take place."

McDole shook his head. "I'm lost. One minute you're talking about trying to make them rot like they're *supposed* to, the next you're saying they're not dead, which to me means they're *not* supposed to."

Perlman spread his hands. "I never said it would be easy to use technology to destroy what seems to be supernatural." He gave McDole a wry smile. "Remember the name for them in the old movies? *The undead.* Whether that's legend or someone's imagination, it's very appropriate; they're not alive, but they're not dead. They're like people-sized viruses, parasitically using a host for sustenance and reproduction."

"So what about today?" Calie asked. "What were you doing?"

Perlman powered down the microscope. "I cultured a bacteria in the *Clostridium* genus," he told them. "Nothing spectacular, just a little stronger. Then I gave it vampire tissue. It should have gone wild feeding and replicating."

Calie twined her fingers. "But it didn't."

"I didn't expect it to—not on the first try, anyway."

"But you seem so . . . disappointed," she said.

"I am," the physician admitted. "And a little flabbergasted, too." His fists clenched briefly, then relaxed. "I can work with cells and living and dead organisms, but I'm not sure what to do here." He stepped toward his equipment as though debating continuing his work. "Every time I put the bacteria or any living organism anywhere near a vampire cell ... did you notice the brown cells of the vampire flesh extending past the cell membrane and into the cytoplasm of the bacteria? The bacteria are literally being *transformed* into vampire flesh in an instantaneous, yet invisible metamorphosis. Not dead, but not alive."

"But how can that be?" McDole demanded.

"How can a vampire *be*?" Perlman shot back. "The problem is understanding a new biological function that I simply don't have the resources to research. That's what's happening here—like when two living animal heart cells are placed in proximity to each other and they synchronize almost immediately."

"Synchronize?" Calie asked.

"Heart cells *beat*," the doctor explained. "Literally. Two of them will gravitate to each other and find the same rhythm. The heartbeat of a sleeping human will synchronize with a dog's if he falls asleep with a hand resting on the animal."

McDole looked perplexed. "What's that got to do with the vampires?"

"Maybe nothing," Perlman said wearily. "And I have no idea why blood would effect the kind of rejuvenation it has on these creatures. In a man it would be understandable—"

"*Blood?*" Calie looked dismayed.

"Don't think of it as blood, Calie," Perlman pointed out. "Think of it fundamentally as *food*. Feed a malnourished person and the body begins to repair itself by using the vitamins and energy supplied by the food source. But a vampire's body isn't living, so how does it convert food to energy? Not only does it obviously do so, but apparently a constant food source causes an amazing and rapid improvement in physical condition."

"So you're saying," McDole cut in, "that every time you feed that kid in the bomb shelter he gets stronger, while the person donating the meal ..." His voice trailed off as he recalled the woman who'd offered her arm and a half pint of blood this morning, their prisoner's second easy meal.

Perlman nodded solemnly. "Yes. And while I'd love to have a healthy vampire for my research, the risk is too great. The strength these things possess is immense. Calie can verify that getting the tissue sample this morning was far worse than yesterday, even though you and Ira were there." Calie nodded unhappily. "If we feed him tonight, trying to get a piece of him tomorrow could be disastrous. We simply can't let that happen."

Calie choked and both men turned to look at her. The young woman's expression was grim in her pallid face. "So you're suggesting that we stop feeding him? Isn't that like starving a caged animal?"

McDole looked to Perlman pleadingly. "I suppose it is," Perlman answered. "But we don't have any choice. It comes down to the lesser of two evils—use a once-human child for our tests or watch mankind become extinct." Perlman set his jaw, and McDole was impressed to see him meet Calie's eyes without flinching. "I can't say that it's right or wrong, Calie, just that it has to be this way. The best we can do is put the boy out of his misery as soon as possible."

Calie nodded and stared at the floor, then her glum look brightened and she hopped to her feet. "Are you through?" She sounded impatient. "C.J.'s back."

Perlman nodded, then frowned. "How could you know that?" he asked as he and McDole followed her out of the lab.

Calie didn't bother to answer as they extinguished the last of the halogen camping lights around the room. "Come on, come on!" she said excitedly. "Not only is he back, he's brought company!"

McDole had to laugh at the look on Perlman's face.

4

●━●━●●━●━●●━●

REVELATION 12:6
And the woman fled into the wilderness,
where she hath a place prepared. . . .

●━●●━●

"I've got to go."

Alex struggled up from the sleeping bag, trying to push the last of the night's sleep from his mind. "What?"

"I've got to go," Deb repeated. "I've got to get back to the Institute. It's starting to snow." Deb was already pulling on clothing, her voice a muffled jumble as she tugged a sweater over her tangle of blue-black curls.

"The Institute? You mean the Art Institute? Wait a minute," Alex protested. He began reaching for his own clothes. "If it's snowing, you shouldn't leave the building."

"It just started."

"Deb—" She wouldn't answer, just kept gathering her things and dressing rapidly, blue jeans, heavy woolen socks—already she was lacing the black high-tops he'd found so amusing. He suddenly felt helpless and embarrassed, as though last evening had been nothing but a one-night stand and this extraordinary woman a cheap bar pickup whom he'd never see again. He couldn't let that happen.

"I'll go with you—"

"*NO!*"

Alex stuttered and stopped in midsentence at the ferocity of her voice. "I—I'm sorry," she said then. "I didn't mean to yell. I . . . just need some time, that's all. It's all so much—meeting you, us. . . ." She faltered, then continued. "I just want to go home and—and think things out, get cleaned up and change. I'll come back after the snow melts."

"No, you won't."

Alex's flat statement brought an instant of surprise, then Deb recovered. "Of course I will," she insisted. "Why wouldn't I?" She pulled on her jacket while Alex stood dumbly, his feet still buried in the folds of the crumpled coverings. She'd dressed so quickly that all he'd managed to don was his pair of long underwear; now he felt absurdly exposed and vulnerable.

"You can't even look me in the eye," he said.

Then she did just that, and Alex was sorry for his challenge because the terror he saw in those crystalline blue eyes was paralyzing. Deb pulled her gaze away. "Tomorrow, after the snow melts—"

"What makes you think it'll be gone by then?" he interrupted. He had to keep talking, stalling, until he thought of a way to change her mind.

"Sure it will," she said. "It's almost April."

Alex wished he felt as confident as she sounded. "We've had plenty of spring blizzards."

"After the snow melts," Deb continued patiently, "you can come and ... get me."

Alex's hopes rose, then plummeted again. Why had she paused like that? Would she even *be* there? Perhaps she was already planning to leave—but *why*? "How will I find you?" he asked. A wistful note had crept into his voice. "That place is huge."

Deb was already by the door to the stairwell. Now she lifted the metal bar, pushed the door open, and stepped into the cold darkness; once again he heard that terrible split second of indecision. "I'm in the Arthur Rubloff Auditorium on the lower level. Come when the snow melts. I'll unlock the front entrance." She turned to go.

"Deb—"

"Don't follow me, Alex." Her voice had taken on a sudden, horrible coldness. "Swear to me that you won't."

"But—"

"Swear it!"

"All right!" he snapped. As soon as he said the words, he regretted them. But she was gone and it was too late to retract the hurt and frustration that had taken charge of his mouth when what he should have done was enfolded her in his arms and kissed her, and told her yes, he'd see her tomorrow, and by the way, *did you remember that I love you?*

He scrambled to the door and peered down the stairs, but the stormlight that filtered in from the office would only show one landing down. Far below he heard a faint *clang* as the fire door on the first floor swung shut. Shivering, he went to the south windows, draping one of the sleeping bags across his shoulders as he stared out at the plaza. Sixty seconds more and he saw Deb, first jogging, then flat-out running in those oh-so-funny-looking shoes across slick granite stones already dangerously covered in powdery snowfall.

I shouldn't have let her go! Alex railed at himself. He watched helplessly as she angled across the intersection of Washington and Dearborn and disappeared. Catching her now would be impossible, and going after her to begin with was unthinkable—after all, he'd promised. A stupid, *stupid* thing to do, but done, nonetheless.

Alex could still see the soft outline of Deb's prints a hundred feet below, though they were already filling in and fading. In another half hour it would be as though Deb had never existed at all.

5

●━●☰●☷●━●☰

REVELATION 6:8
And I looked, and beheld a pale horse:
and his name that sat on him was Death. . . .

━●━●━

C.J. and the girl were a dripping mess, so laden with melting snow that it was leaving tiny, tearlike trails down both of their faces. Calie's first thought was for C.J.'s safety, yet there was another, more important question. Even she was too slow.

"How deep are the tracks you two left?" McDole's voice was harsh with fury. "Can they be brushed away?"

"Didn't leave any," C.J. responded immediately. The girl, a pale, pretty teenager about C.J.'s age, said nothing; she looked like a terrified rabbit, frozen by the glare of an onrushing truck. Her dark blue eyes flitted nervously from C.J. to Calie to McDole and back again.

McDole's expression relaxed slightly, though fear was still apparent in the crevices across his forehead. "Are you sure?" He glanced at the girl. "Absolutely *positive*?" She nodded timidly, and Calie guessed the girl was struggling more with shyness than fright.

"Hi," Calie said warmly, and stuck out her hand. "My name is Calie." The girl smiled in relief and Calie saw C.J.'s eyes widen as the expression transformed her whole face. Calie decided that later she'd ask if the girl wanted a trim on that dreadful haircut.

"I'm Louise," the teenager said as she offered her own hand. "I'm really glad to be here."

Calie clasped Louise's hand and the world *stopped*.

They might have touched for a second or a minute, but in the faded light behind Calie's eyes it was timeless, *eternal*, and she was filled with a sudden, terrible sense of terror that exploded briefly in her mind then abruptly fell away to nothingness.

"Calie?"

C.J. was staring at her and she made the mistake of turning her glazed sight on him before breaking the touch with Louise. Despair twisted her gut when she realized that this premonition extended to C.J. as well. She pulled her hand away. "We're glad to have you," she rasped. She could feel Bill's questioning eyes on her from the door of the stairwell, where he'd lingered when she and McDole went to greet C.J. and his new girlfriend.

McDole crossed to the front windows and peered at the maelstrom beyond. Outside the wind howled like an enraged beast, hurling wet snow and ice pellets against the thick plate glass. "I don't understand how you didn't leave tracks in this slop," he muttered.

C.J. set his jaw and looked embarrassed, until Louise finally spoke. "It was Jo," she said. "She ... took the tracks away."

"Jo?"

"You mean there's someone else?" Perlman came into the room. "And you left her out in the storm?"

"She wouldn't come in," C.J. said. "And then she was gone, just disappeared."

"With no tracks," McDole commented doubtfully.

"Jo is ... special," Louise said reluctantly. "She does things."

"What things?" Calie knew her question wouldn't help the girl feel more at ease, but it had to be asked. This mystery person might be a valuable asset to the underground. Calie was not impressed with her own abilities— parlor tricks, like knowing where to find the entrance to a building or second-guessing someone's trustworthiness with more accuracy than the average guy. Someone who could make footprints in the snow vanish was another thing entirely.

"What things?" McDole prompted.

"She can unlock doors," C.J. offered. "How do you think we got in?"

McDole scowled and checked the metal lock-bar across the bottom of the seldom-used front door. It was firmly in place, surrounded by small puddles of melted snow that trailed from the door to the youngsters' feet. In the gray light of the storm, he could see the unmarked snow on the sidewalk outside. "Anything else?"

"She *heals*."

Louise's statement stunned all of them, but affected Perlman most of all. His attention level tripled. "What did you say?" he demanded. "*Heals?*"

Louise wasn't at all surprised at their reaction, though McDole jumped as she proudly held up her hands, then unzipped the front of her jacket and brought out a tiny grizzled dog. She stroked the dog lovingly before she spoke. "Twenty-four hours ago both my hands were cut and horribly infected. She healed them. It's that simple."

The look on C.J.'s face said this was news to him, but doubt never crossed his features. "I believe her," he said. "I think she could do it." C.J's mouth turned up in the self-conscious smile of someone trying to explain the fantastic.

"I wouldn't call that 'simple,'" McDole said.

"Can I see?" C.J. asked. Louise blushed and held out her hands. They gleamed a soft pink, as though the girl had been living in luxury for the last year and a half with two or three servants and a manicurist.

Hardly.

"There used to be a scar here." Louise pointed to the heel of her right hand with a perfectly shaped fingernail. "Not big, but noticeable. Freaky, huh?" C.J., absorbed in his inspection, had yet to relinquish his hold.

Perlman stepped forward. "May I?"

Louise looked to Calie hesitantly and Calie gave herself a mental shake. "I'm sorry, Louise. All these people must be a shock, and here we haven't even introduced everyone. This is Dr. Bill Perlman, that's Buddy McDole." McDole nodded; still at the front door, he looked numb. Perlman smiled reassuringly and C.J. reluctantly moved aside.

"Where have you been living?" the doctor asked in a conversational voice "In one place?"

"No," Louise responded. She glanced at the little dog snuffling uncertainly at her feet The dog's eyes were a milky, blinded white—no wonder he hadn't tried to explore his new surroundings. Calie picked him up; he was soft and warm, wagging his stump of a tail as he licked her face. "Beau and I moved around," Louise continued. "That way we didn't build up any patterns. I started thinking there might be people downtown." She looked tired. "Plus I wanted to stay somewhere for more than a couple of nights at a time. I thought it'd be nice to have a home again."

Perlman stopped his examination of her hands and grinned at her. "Say ahhhh. Don't worry, I'm not going to try and dissect you." Louise laughed nervously and opened her mouth, standing patiently as the physician checked her eyes and ran his fingers beneath her jaw and behind her ears. "Did you know you have a slight fever?"

"Jo said you shouldn't be out in the snow because you'd been sick." C.J. folded his arms. "Was she talking about your hands?"

Louise nodded. "Probably. I felt awful."

"Why don't we get Louise some dry clothes and food instead of making her stand here and shiver?" Calie suggested. "Then she and C.J. can tell us about this Jo person."

Louise looked relieved. "I could use something hot," she said hopefully.

"How about some coffee?" McDole chimed in.

"That sounds great."

"She needs some aspirin," Perlman added. C.J. nodded and immediately hurried up the escalator.

"Meet us in the breakfast room in half an hour," McDole called after him. C.J.'s shout of agreement floated back.

Calie smiled at the girl and tried to ignore the darkness that bubbled up when she looked at those pretty blue eyes. "Come on," she said. "I happen to know a shop in this building that keeps snowstorm hours and has just your size."

She led Louise away, being very, very careful not to touch her.

It was nostalgic, Calie thought later, how old habits still clung, despite the circumstances that had changed permanently. Louise was certainly likable—funny, too. Alone in the breakfast room, Calie was still grinning at the memory of Louise checking the price tag on a sweater that had caught her eye in Lord & Taylor, then almost putting it back. She'd looked decidedly sheepish when Calie had laughed at her. They had all settled early for the night because of the excitement and the dragged-out feeling that a hard winter storm always seemed to bring. C.J. and Louise had answered questions about Jo as best they could, although Louise had apparently met the mysterious preteen only two days ago. Both were determined, snow permitting, to be in Daley Plaza tomorrow as Jo had instructed.

What time was it now? Surely after six. Calie blindly touched her cheeks, feeling her rough fingers move over the pores of her face. The gift of healing, for God's sake—what else could that strange girl do? Could she "see" that something terrible awaited C.J. and Louise? And if so, could this Jo *do* anything about it? It was a maddening question.

Darkness surrounded her now, the dusky light left from sunset effectively strangled by the low-lying stormclouds. Calie rose and made her way to the stairwell by memory, her hands gliding soundlessly along the cold railing. C.J. and Louise were together, bent on obliterating the loneliness that had permeated both their young lives. Good for them—tomorrow might bring horrors undreamed of; so much the better that they found comfort in each other's arms tonight. Farther down, Calie hesitated at the door before hers. Go on to bed, she told herself. He doesn't want to listen to you. She started to step away.

"Calie." Perlman's voice was barely a whisper.

I should keep going, she thought. But she honestly couldn't find a reason not to answer. "Yes?"

"Come in for a while?" he asked. "Unless you're too tired."

"Not at all," she answered softly. "Where are you?" She stretched a hand into the darkness.

"Here." His warm fingers brushed hers, then closed

over her hand and guided her to the corner. She sat, her slight weight sinking into the thick folds of the down bag.

"So what do you think of our newest addition?" Bill asked without releasing her hand.

"She . . ." Calie closed her eyes, glad the lightless room hid the sudden moisture on her lashes. "I don't know," she finally finished.

Perlman said nothing for a moment. Then, "You're not happy she's here."

"It's not that so much," Calie said. Talking in total darkness made her disoriented. "I have a feeling that something . . . *bad* is going to happen to them."

"Them?"

"C.J. and Louise."

"Maybe you're wrong," he suggested. "You've been wrong on occasion, haven't you?"

She found herself clutching his hand. "Never."

Thank God he didn't try to humor her. "I'm sorry," he said simply. He slipped an arm across her shoulders.

Squeezing her eyes tightly shut now, Calie didn't respond. She'd be damned if she'd cry over something about which she could do nothing, although she supposed this was when a person *should* weep. Why shed tears over things you could change? I am not the crying type, she told herself sternly. I won't—

"We all have our times to cry, Calie." The night was like a heavy shroud, and he couldn't see her face as she gaped at him. For years she had anticipated the words of others; finally she knew how strange all those folks had felt. Bill pressed something soft into her hand. "There's nothing wrong with it."

"What's this?"

"A Kleenex." He brought his other arm around, linked hands, and held her. "It's okay. Really."

Her mind reached out automatically and touched briefly on C.J. and Louise; two doors down, the new lovers murmured gently to each other. A terrible, black loss filled her, blotting out everything for a second. At last, Calie's shoulders began to shake.

In the chill and smothering night, Bill Perlman held her, and cried too.

Soldiers of the Night

6

■━■•■━■•■━■

■━•━■

I shouldn't have run out on him like that.

I *had* to, Deb reminded herself. There was this terrible, pressing feeling that if she had stayed with him, as she had so desperately wanted, whatever dark destiny awaited her would encompass him, too. She couldn't bear that responsibility.

The Art Institute loomed around her, a sad place with a thousand faces staring from prisons of antique oil. The storm added to her feeling of despair, muddling the daylight in some places, blocking it entirely in others as she went from gallery to gallery armed with a flashlight and a heavy knife taken from one of the weapon displays in Gunsaulus Hall, randomly checking doors, windows, and closets she hadn't thought about in months. It was impossible to check everything before nightfall and every corner held a shadow that made her jump, every stair a creak that made her glance over her shoulder. She found a sprinkling of dust by one of the elevator doors and pried at them experimentally but they wouldn't budge; the dirt had probably sifted from a slowly growing ceiling crack in front of the elevator.

Back in the auditorium, Deb was beginning to believe that she'd been wrong about the whole stupid thing. Clinging to Alex last night, the memory of his hard body moving so smoothly with hers, seemed like a sweet, faraway dream. If only they'd found each other a year ago! He was probably thinking the worst, and tomorrow morning when she let him in she'd have to explain her crazy behavior as only the hermitlike mistrust and paranoia of the last year overwhelming her. She grinned and started to sit on the side of her cot, then realized that her pillbox, a trinket from her long-dead grandmother, was gone. Just . . .

Gone.

There was no doubt. This wasn't a house full of kids, where Dad always lost his keys and Mom could never find her purse. This was a backstage alcove with at best a half-dozen precious personal items within easy reach. For a time Deb simply stood, letting the fear consume her in one great, hungry tide; then, when she could walk without stumbling, she went upstairs and stared blankly out the window for a while, where huge clouds tumbled their load of frigid entrapment upon the city. The world had already shifted to dusky gray, the buildings along Michigan Avenue fading into a mass of swirling whiteness. The sidewalks to the east would be indistinguishable from the lawns of Grant Park, the landscape nothing more than a white sea of frozen death. Fleeing was not an option, nor was suicide or surrender. Deb *knew* in her soul that she'd be found, no matter where she buried herself in this massive building. Her fingers folded into tight fists. Better to fight; the nightside of this world would not claim her without a fight.

She returned to the auditorium along the quickest route, this time discovering the two broken chains. Although she had no hope of them holding, she carefully relocked them. All these closed doors with their concealed locks—nothing more than a meticulously maintained camouflage that ultimately had not hidden her at all. Yet, if she had made it this long, didn't it stand to reason that others had, too? Alex insisted he'd seen someone else the morning they'd met, and of course, there'd been John last fall. As for Alex himself, surely he'd be smart enough to move his sleeping place when he discovered her gone. And one way or another, she was sure she would be.

But she wouldn't go alone.

Deb tossed the knife under the cot with the Winchester, then felt behind the thick curtain in back of her cot. Her hand closed around the best weapon she'd ever found and she pulled it from beneath a carefully placed pile of scrap carpeting. She had no idea if her hunters numbered one or ten, but this would handle more than a few of them, though it was unlikely they'd resemble the starving creatures hidden in the subways. Alex had told her about those and how they sometimes clawed at the doorways he'd welded shut in the corridors beneath the Daley Center. Her visitors last night were crafty, leaving no trace of their presence other than the foolishly stolen pillbox.

Her Grandfather Kendrick had been a crusty old Irishman who'd loved to hunt and had taught his tomboy granddaughter how to shoot despite his daughter-in-law's objections. Deb had worshiped him in the years before his death and still missed him deeply. What would he have thought of the weapon she now lifted? Its weight tested the slender muscles in her arms, and she was sure Grandfather Kendrick would have been horrified.

But then, a lot of things now would have horrified him.

The Streetsweeper.

Deb hefted it and tested its feel, trying to calculate the recoil on the twelve-gauge semiautomatic shotgun that she'd pilfered from the evidence room at the Twelfth and State police station. She hadn't followed the gun magazines like her Grandfather had, but she did remember the controversy surrounding this weapon; originally army-commissioned, the evidence tag noted that this one had been confiscated in a south side drug raid. She had lugged it back and cleaned it, nose burning from the heavy smell of gunpowder on its barrel. Its round magazine was reminiscent of the old Thompson submachine gun and held an incredible twenty-four rounds, and she thought she recalled a write-up saying the Streetsweeper could fire four to six slugs per pump. Deb loaded it with eight-pellet buckshot instead of slugs, opting for the wide firing spread. The powerful shotgun would probably do a real job on the muscles of her shoulders, but that didn't matter anyway. What would they look like, these creatures coming for her? She thought of her family, her mom and dad and younger brother and sister, all disappeared in the course of a two-day period. Which of them had been the first to change, or the first to return for the others? Or had they all "died" at once? Had she lived at home, she would have perished with them.

Her weapon ready, there was nothing left to do but wait. Her belly gave a painful twist and Deb clutched the semiautomatic closer, seeking scant comfort from the cold, oily-smelling metal. This machine held the deadly power that might, *might*, keep her alive tonight, if that was her destiny.

God help her—somehow she didn't think it was.

7

REVELATION 14:15
Thrust in thy sickle, and reap: for the time is come ...
for the harvest of the earth is ripe.

"That's a nice girl. You just stay there, nice and quiet,
and Howie'll get you another blanket." Howard gave
Giselle—the woman he'd beaten so badly the other night
and whose name he'd learned by eavesdropping on
Vic—a false smile, but all she did was look at him with
a sick, miserable expression. He pushed his bulky body
up and zipped his pants with exaggerated carefulness,
though he would've liked to give her a kick just for fun.
Hell, this was no better than jacking off—he missed slapping the babes around, he *needed* it. For a while he'd
thought he wasn't going to be able to come, and only his
favorite fantasy, a dark little dream featuring selected
girls from his seventh-grade class, had finally taken him
over the brink.

Howard sighed and went to get another blanket, then
grabbed a couple of saltines for the woman as an after-
thought. He'd been trying to take better care of the
women just in case more of them turned out to be
knocked up. He hadn't neglected the men either—maybe
they'd start finding the bitches attractive. There was
plenty of meat to go around and Howard's pulse quick-
ened when he thought of the possible free shows. What
the hell, he could even help.

Giselle was shivering under her blanket and Howard
tossed her a heavier one and the crackers, then plodded
away, thinking only of his room and sleep. All this extra
exercise was exhausting, running around in the morning
trying to find where Rita and Vic slept—yet neither had
even glanced at him before they'd left on their hunting
expedition. Maybe he'd simply overblown their hostility.

Vic was probably safe enough, but Rita? Then again, she was perpetually pissed at the world. Hell, he'd had to co-exist before with people who didn't like him. Why should now be any different? He couldn't let this morning nonsense fuck up his performance. Look at that guy Stephen, the one Anyelet had singled out. The man was a mess—wasting away, crying and praying all the time, yet all those wailed promises collapsed every time the she-bitch stepped into his room. Howard's position was pretty good, considering the options. He glanced at his watch and wondered where Anyelet's little "army" was right now. He knew they'd gone to the Art Institute last night on Hugh's tip—and wasn't that one crazy as clown shit!—and found evidence of someone living in the building, though no one had been found at the time. Odds were if they found anyone tonight, he or she would end up in Howard's care by dawn.

Howard unlocked the door to his room, then relocked it behind him. Lowering his heavy body to the sleeping bag with a relieved grunt, he reached beneath a pile of extra blankets and slid out the little Uzi he'd found in the bottom drawer of a desk in the rear office of the lobby currency exchange. Thumbing through a *Soldier of Fortune* had shown a loading diagram, though Howard hadn't really understood it. But the Uzi was already fully loaded, and if he ever had to put in the extra clip, he'd figure it out. This little toy was to keep the Mart secure in the daytime rather than protect himself from the vampires, who knew nothing about it. For that, it probably wouldn't do a damned bit of good. He turned the dusty Uzi over in his hands for a while before returning it to its place under the blankets. Bored, he drummed his fingers on the floor and let his mind drift back to the hunting trip, wondering who they'd be bringing back. His tongue flicked over his lips.

He hoped it was a woman.

8

REVELATION 11:7
The beast that ascendeth out of the
bottomless pit shall make war against them. . . .

It had stopped snowing an hour ago, and now they stood at the stairs descending to the entrance they had used last night. Behind the group of nightwalkers the snow was like a freshly laid carpet of purity marred only by the measured dips of their footprints.

"Why can't we use the door by the auditorium, or the front entrance?" Rita complained. "Why get all filthy again?"

"She may be a human but she still has ears," Gregory said disdainfully. Rita resisted the urge to slap him, knowing Anyelet watched them both.

"This way is safer," Anyelet said quietly.

Gabriel stepped forward. "Let's go." After dribbling a little lubricant on the hinges, he and Vic removed the already-loosened metal door and set it aside, then motioned for the others to enter the dank storage room. It was easier than Rita had anticipated; she hadn't been pleased with the oil and grime caked on her hands the previous evening and would have preferred to leave the trip entirely to the others. On the other hand, they all stood to benefit from the capture of another human, and survival made sharp motivation. But something about their unseen prey still spooked her; if the woman left that kind of firepower behind, what did she carry with her?

The light in the storage room was as poor as before, though retracing their route through the jagged, shrouded piles was easy, the elevator doors heavy but not as difficult. When they reached the double glass doors leading to a long room filled with the moldering remains of ancient clothes and weapons, Rita finally voiced her doubts. "How do we know she's even here?" she demanded as she looked distastefully at her hands, once more covered in dirt and oil from the elevator cables.

"I can smell her," Gabriel said promptly.

"That's what you said last night," Rita snapped.

Gabriel smiled, unperturbed. "Yes, but look here." He pointed at the doors. "They've been relocked."

"It's a better job this time. It's going to make some noise getting through," Vic commented. He looked at Anyelet. "Faster to just break the glass."

"Do it."

Vic nodded and without further warning punched one panel with a lightning-fast thrust; the glass exploded and even Rita could admire the muscular vampire's strength and speed. They climbed through the frame, ignoring the fragments of glass that tugged at their clothes and tinkled to the floor, then they were in the midst of an array of medieval armor and weapons, swords, maces, other things with straps and chains like nothing Rita had ever seen. She paused as an idea occurred to her. "Why don't we take some weapons?" she proposed. "We know she has a gun." Gregory nodded in agreement.

Anyelet's glance was withering. "We shouldn't *need* weapons against a human, Rita. Must you always be so pampered?" She waved her hand. "There are *five* of us to one woman—isn't that *enough* of a challenge? None of you have the faintest idea of what it's like to hunt for yourselves or die." She scowled. "It's time you learned." The Mistress moved on and Rita looked to Gabriel pleadingly, but he only shrugged and kept going.

Another firmly locked door waited at the far end, more noise that Rita was convinced would warn the woman of their presence. Surely she had left by now—who in their right mind would stay? Even with Gabriel's so-called "nose" it would take hours to search just one wing of this monstrous building—unless they walked into an ambush first. Another room like the weapons gallery, filled with more of humanity's faded history: objets d'art from the Far East, the Orient and Islam, exotic figures with elongated eyes and brilliant colors. Rita barely glanced at them; they depicted nothing but more subcultures of a species that was already passing into extinction. They slid silently around the last display case and followed Gabriel to the left; he turned one hundred and eighty degrees at the final wall separating them from the Arthur Rubloff Auditorium and Rita immediately sensed the difference in the darkness as they crept to the closed doors that were the final barrier. It took only an instant to figure it out: beneath the line of the metal doors, a laser-thin light showed. Sudden nerves prickled at the base of Rita's neck.

"What's that smell?" Vic whispered.

"Candleflame," came Gabriel's reply. "I don't like this."

"Let's do it," Gregory hissed eagerly. "I'll go first."

"No." Anyelet stopped him. The Mistress's gaze paused on Rita and she tensed, then Anyelet motioned to Vic, the movement a blur of India ink in the near-black shadows. "Vic will take us in." The two stared at each other for perhaps ten seconds as the rest of them watched, baffled, then Vic stepped forward and wrapped his massive hands around the door handles. He tugged gently but the doors didn't move; he tried again with a little more strength, and this time they made a quiet, drawn-out sound like the groan of an old man in uneasy sleep.

"Ready?" He didn't bother to whisper.

They all nodded. The muscles in his arms and back swelled suddenly and he *ripped* the doors open in a scream of tormented metal and erupting plaster.

The light from dozens of candles placed around the door blinded them momentarily, and instead of the swift entrance they'd intended, all five hesitated. The woman stood center-stage, holding a large, strange-looking weapon that was nothing like the shotgun Gabriel had discovered under her bed. "Oh, *fuck!*" Gabriel screamed as a harsh ratcheting filled the air and the woman yelled something Rita couldn't quite hear.

Thunder filled the night.

9

■--■-·-■-·-■--■

REVELATION 17:16
These shall eat her flesh, and burn her with fire.

■-·-■

Deb watched five of them flow into the auditorium, casting a pall through the warm light like silent, oiled snakes. She'd lit the candles intentionally, preferring to see those who came for her, their faces, their number, their expressions—did they still have *souls*? She wished she could search each pair of eyes to see if any visage of humanity remained.

And so here they were at last, her future, her *fate*. Two women, three men, all except for one lean and dark, all with eyes that glittered like bloodstones across the expanse of the room. The first to enter shared the same red gaze as his companions but was the only one with any kind of bulk, tall and swollen with muscles; his weight easily doubled her own. She would have little time to defend herself; startled by the flickering light, they were already splitting up, moving with frightening speed.

"Come on in," Deb called cheerfully. Beneath her deadly calm she felt the comforting pull of the shoulder strap as she hoisted the Streetsweeper into position. The noise of the shotgun pumping slugs into the magazine drowned out most of her next words.

"I've been expecting you!"

She opened fire.

She tried to swing the Streetsweeper in a semicircle but the eruption of the first five slugs hammered her off her feet and flung her backward. Only the curtained wall kept Deb from landing on her back and she lost precious seconds just sitting there, the room a throbbing fog of yellow sparkles, her ears filled with a deafening roar undercut by enraged screams. Then she was on her knees, screaming herself and grappling with the cumbersome shotgun as she propelled another round into the magazine. The smell of gunpowder was choking, the weapon already fire-hot in her hands.

Something snarled from the right-hand steps and streaked toward her; she swung and squeezed the trigger. The shotgun pounded against her body again and black spots threatened to blot out her vision; she kept at it, taking the force of the semiautomatic and ignoring the faraway *crack* along the right side of her chest. Between the dancing screen of dots that had become her eyesight Deb saw one of the vampires, a young man with sand-colored hair, take two hits in the face. His head *exploded*, and in spite of the agony pouring through her chest and arms, Deb felt a momentary thrill of vindication. Someone else wailed as the vampire's body did a macabre jig and crumbled to the polished wooden floor, one outflung hand still clutching spasmodically by Deb's leg. She staggered to her feet and kicked it away.

"Come ON!" she howled, then sobbed when her own body betrayed her and sent her back to her knees as she struggled to prime the gun for the third time. Somewhere in the ocean of gray seats a woman was screeching wildly.

"Kill her! Kill her! Look what she's done to my FACE!"

Another woman shouted orders, something about going to the right, and at last Deb found the strength to cock the Streetsweeper. Nearly sprawled on the stage, Deb dragged the shotgun wearily to her left, where another young man was creeping up the side steps, inching along like a giant lizard. He dived for the floor when she sent a burst of firepower at him. She clawed at the weapon, wanting to arc it from front to rear, but she was so *tired*, and the Streetsweeper was so damned *heavy;* the tendons in her shoulders and back trembled and twisted into living things with needle fingers beneath her skin. Deb could no longer lift the gun and barely managed to slide it across the floor by its strap as she scooted backward. The same vampire jerked below stage level yet again as the barrel clattered toward him and she groped for the trigger.

Should she pump another round? Her mind was a

bleary swirl of fragmented sounds and shapes that moved
far too fast. Everything was in motion at once; she'd
killed at least one of the vampires and wounded another.
But hadn't there been five? Of those, one was the guy
who kept popping his head above the stage with reptilian
quickness as he worked closer; if she didn't hit him soon,
he'd simply leap and be on her. And the two women—
Deb could hear one still yowling like an injured alleycat
while the other called to someone named "Vic."

Deb started. Tracking the progress of the lizard-
vampire had slipped her into some sort of semiconscious
trance. Her vague calculations totaled only four—where
the hell was that big guy?

He hit her from behind like a steamroller.

10

REVELATION 6:8
And Hell followed with him.

A bead of sweat rolled down the side of his temple, slow and thick, as though a heavy drop of blood had dripped from the ceiling. As it disappeared into his hairline, Alex felt another creep along the trail left by the first; twenty-five degrees in here and he was lying on a perspiration-soaked sleeping bag.

Enough, Alex decided. He crawled from the bag and stepped cautiously to the door of the small office in which he had stayed last night with Deb. He was fully clothed; last night had been the sole exception to that since he'd decided a year ago last October that he'd live longer if he "disappeared" from what was left of the rest of the world. Now he crept to a window in the corner that was partially blocked by a bookcase stuffed with dust-covered law books; it would hide him on the left but not block his view of the plaza below. Still, he knew not to get too close to the glass; he hadn't made it this long by being careless. The world beyond the building was a cold, uniform gray, bleak and not at all beautiful in its winter fury; the plaza itself seemed to float like some stagnant pool long since leeched of color. Although it was still snowing, Alex thought he could sense a letup in the storm's energy.

He wondered what Deb was doing. Was she cold, lonely—did she even miss him? After all this time, knowing her and loving her last night was like dangling water in front of a man who hadn't realized he was dying of thirst. His last feeling of warmth had been kissing his parents good-bye as they left to visit his mom's older brother in Utah—another foolish mistake. In the midst of the disappearances that were sweeping the city, he'd never heard from them again. He should have kept them close, as well as the teenage twins, Daryl and Jeff, and his . . .

Grandmother.

Bitter guilt flared. He hadn't told Deb about that. While she had killed a man in self-preservation, it had been a *stranger*, at least justifying the act somewhat. His grandmother, snarling with a newfound hunger, had come home to her son's house for her first meal, and thank God his parents hadn't been there to witness the foul-smelling carnage as he'd chalked up his first kill on the machete. He'd almost given up then: Daryl and Jeff would be coming; they had telephoned the evening before to tell him they were going out to look for several missing friends. Standing over the disintegrating mass that had been his own flesh and blood, Alex had known that another couple of hours would bring the "Disaster Duo," as he'd called the twins since grammar school, home for dinner. It was his responsibility to stay and release them from the hell in which they'd become trapped.

Alex fled.

There had been no one to see his shame then, but now? He just wanted to get the hell *out* of this building and go to Deb, and be damned with that stupid promise he'd made.

A break in the wind offered a suddenly unobstructed view of the plaza, and goose flesh rippled up Alex's spine at the footprints stretching across the snow, stumbling blotches interspersed with larger holes and loops, as if the walker had fallen more out of laziness than weakness. Alex inched closer to the glass, holding his breath to keep from fogging its cold surface, straining for a better view. The wind gusted again, then stopped; before the next wave of snow could slap the glass, Alex quickly followed the tracks across the plaza until they vanished directly below and out of his range of vision. He cracked his knuckles thoughtfully, mentally rechecking his lockup this afternoon. Another blast of snow against the glass pulled his attention back outside. Beneath the howling of the storm Alex thought he heard something else then, a *fluttering*—

He flung himself to the floor just as a black, tattered creature resembling a man-sized bat clawed and clung its way across the window directly outside the spot in which Alex had been standing only a second earlier. Was it the same one that had terrified them the night before, checking its territory like a starving wolf? Alex had no intention of tapping on the glass and asking.

Alex lay with his face and hands hugging the icy floor. *Jesus!* he thought as his heart whammed in his chest. If this is what I'm going through, *what's happening to Deb?*

11

●━●━●●━●━●●━●

REVELATION 12:4
And the beast stood before the woman for to devour her.

REVELATION 22:12
And, behold, I come quickly. . . .

━●━●━●

Well, this is a fine mess, Vic thought in disgust. He extricated himself from the unconscious woman's legs and stood; the thick, offensive smell of gunpowder crawled up his nose and he waved an ineffective hand in front of his face. Gregory's corpse, now a headless lump of slowly melting flesh, still twitched a few feet away, and already Gabriel was scrambling across the stage, his expression a study of slavering eagerness.

"Just stay the fuck away!" Vic snarled. Rita staggered down the aisle, screeching and ricocheting from one side to another like a pinball being slapped about by mechanical flippers. Her once darkly exquisite face had taken an upward slug in its cheekbone, destroying her right eye and ear and leaving pieces of her skull an exposed and dripping horror. Her head had a new and impossible shape that now sloped toward the front of her gore-encrusted blouse.

"What do I look like?" Rita whined and clutched at Anyelet. The Mistress pulled away in distaste and hurried toward Vic and the woman, leaving Rita to moan against a velvet-covered seat, hardly glancing at Gregory's body. "Is she dead?" Anyelet asked. She nudged the woman with one toe.

"No way." Gabriel was panting outright. "Can I do her?" His lips stretched and saliva trailed in glistening strands from his top to bottom teeth like a sparkling spiderweb.

"Kill her!" Rita's scream rose from the seats below. "Kill her and leave her for the sun!"

Anyelet ignored them both and nodded at the weapon that had killed Gregory. "What is this thing?"

Vic picked it up. "Some sort of semiautomatic shotgun, I think. Never saw one like it before." He lowered it back to the floor. "Pretty damned effective." He looked at Anyelet. "What about Gregory?"

"Leave him," she said flatly. "I've no time for dead meat."

"And the woman?" Gabriel asked again.

"*Kill—*"

"Shut up!" Anyelet snapped. "I'll make that decision!"

"What's to decide?" asked Gabriel. "You want to breed her?"

Vic tensed. The woman at his feet was far lovelier than anyone at the Mart; what would she do when Howard tried to rape her? Howard might kill her trying—and then, of course, there was the mutilated Rita, still keening in the background like an old woman. He cleared his throat to regain Anyelet's attention. "Don't we need to replace Gregory?" he asked. "There's only a few of us left." He couldn't believe his own suggestion, yet how could this woman, who had fought so valiantly to survive, be shut away and used like some weekly menu selection?

Anyelet studied him thoughtfully. "Perhaps we *could* use some new blood." Her black gaze slid briefly in Rita's direction.

"All *right!*" Gabriel swiftly buried his fingers in the woman's curly hair and yanked her head back, exposing her white throat with its richly filled arteries. Vic's huge hand shot out and covered Gabriel's wrist in a crushing hold. Gabriel yelped and released the woman; her head thumped to the floor and she gave a soft moan as Gabriel cried, "Hey!"

Anyelet glanced at Vic sharply and he released Gabriel. The younger vampire rubbed his wrist in bewilderment. "What the hell's your problem?"

"I just thought the Mistress might want to . . ." Vic couldn't bring himself to say it and a play of thoughts crossed Anyelet's features, then she smiled slyly.

"No. I think she should be *yours*, Vic."

"Why him?" Gabriel protested.

Anyelet cut him off with a glare. "Because that's what I *want*." She smiled again. "I think Vic could use a companion."

Companion? It was something Vic had never considered and his eyes sought the woman collapsed at his feet. Impossible—she'd probably despise him as much as he despised Anyelet. Yet . . . she might enjoy the new "life," as had hundreds of thousands of others. He shied away from the threat of Rita's ugly temperament and remembered instead the lonely nights in the echoing, empty Mart and on the city streets before the outcasts had become such a danger. Could the time stretching ahead be shared with someone?

He had to try it.

Vic picked her up in one smooth movement, feeling her warm skin and already regretting that it would soon be as bloodless and cold as his own. The life within her ebbed and swelled with each heartbeat, her pulse surging against the insides of his arms. Gabriel's envious stare and Rita's more vicious one followed him as he quickly carried his burden down the steps and out of the auditorium, grimacing and averting his eyes from Rita; the wreckage of her face was indescribable and far too great to ever heal. Following Anyelet's instructions, Gabriel swung the woman's weapon over his shoulder, then went to help Rita; in another few seconds, the group joined him at the Columbus Drive exit. Outside the locked doors the snow gleamed, white and unbroken beyond the driveway overhang. Gabriel gave one set of doors a petulant kick and they shattered; in Vic's arms the woman mumbled something, trapped in her own ominous dream.

"Unless you want her screams to draw every outcast for miles," Anyelet commented, "I suggest you get her to the Mart as quickly as possible. Gabriel will run with you in case you're attacked. Rita and I will follow."

Gabriel frowned. "What about the outcasts?"

Anyelet's smile was a dull red slash in the night. "They don't dare challenge *me*."

Gabriel nodded and looked at Vic. Without bothering to speak, Vic held the woman close and began to run.

• • •

It was done.

Vic would have liked to have thrown up, but there was no way his body would allow him that cleansing luxury. He'd learned a lot during the melding of minds as he'd feasted, the least of which was her name—Deborah Nole—and more important, that she'd had a lover as recently as last night, a man called Alex. Still, even as her human body died, she'd fought the meld and kept his location so buried within her that Vic couldn't get to it, and the *will* such resistance entailed was beyond his comprehension. Now she slept beside his own sated and lazy form. He'd forgotten the feeling of fullness, of *completion*, that changing someone brought; it left in him a desire for more, and he hated it, and hated himself, too, for sacrificing the life of this splendid, strong woman on the oh-so-vague chance that his loneliness might be eased the slightest bit. He told himself that he was saving her from worse—Siebold—but what was Vic himself, really? Only another rapist, of a more unspeakable kind. At least in death she would've found whatever eternal peace awaited humankind. Now she simply had . . . *hell*.

And what of Deb's lover, "Alex"? The determination with which she'd protected him even in death told Vic that the woman sleeping unwillingly within his arms, her porcelain-pale flesh forever chilled, would probably detest him from the instant she opened her eyes and felt The Hunger.

Vic sighed and pushed a curl of blue-black hair off her forehead. It was a waste that her sky-blue eyes would turn eventually to black, though at least the bruises his bloodkiss had left on her neck would be faded by dawn. Deborah Nole had never even opened her eyes. What a shame.

He would have liked to have seen her soul before it turned to the nightside.

Three A.M.:

In an alcove of St. Peter's, her face a shining, hopeful oval in the dimness, Jo knelt before the rack of votive candles. She'd lit them all—half a hundred—as she'd voiced her prayers for Deborah Nole, and now they flickered like the winking red eyes of tiny nightthings, forever seeking freedom from their metal cradles.

Like Deb.

Deborah Nole had died an hour ago. Jo had known when it was happening, had felt the life-force drain as surely as her own knees felt the stone floor at the foot of the altar, helpless and bound to the church by a Will not her own as her neck experienced the agony of the beast piercing the other woman's neck. Now Deb, too, was bound.

Jo rose and stood before the basin at the foot of Christ's statue, a stone bowl that had in its time held Water that had kissed the heads of thousands of babies as it cleansed them of original sin and sent them on their way to Jesus. It still held the True Water, and always had; while Jo washed with and drank river water, this basin filled sometime each day of its own accord. Jo drew her hand gently across the width of the basin just below the Water's surface, leaving a tiny, bubbling wake. The church was cold tonight, as was the world beyond its protecting doors; the True Water was always body temperature.

She looked beseechingly at the marble face of the Savior and He gazed back without comment, His expression at once stern and compassionate. Once Jo had seen a music video in which the statue of the Son of God had come to life at the kiss of a prayerful young woman. But there would be no frivolous miracles in the real House of the Lord.

The battle approached.

IV

■·■·■·■

March 26

■·■

Coming Together

1

REVELATION 6:8
And power was given unto them to kill with hunger,
and with death, and with the beasts of the earth.

Two hours since sunup.

Alex pressed a hand against the cold window at the
juncture of the south and east corners of the building.
Was the glass really warmer? Or did it just feel that way
because he so desperately wanted to get over to the Art
Institute? He stared at the plaza below and sucked his
breath in with disappointment. The tracks of his night
visitor were still clearly defined, even from the thirteenth
floor. When the edges started to blur and the first small
puddles of moisture spotted the white-covered concrete,
then he could go. He cracked his knuckles and grimaced;
did "watched" snow ever melt?

Alex forced himself to eat, though the combination of
heated water and instant oatmeal looked and tasted like
badly mixed wallpaper glue, the powdered coffee like the
oven-burned spillover of cheap TV dinners. Both scalded
his tongue; neither drove away the ice in the pit of his
stomach. At least thirty minutes had passed when he
lifted his eyes from the study of an old carpet stain.
Wasn't it actually warmer in the room? He pushed to his
feet and went to the window, then grinned. Small circles
of wet sidewalk finally poked through the snow, like
muddy pawprints across the plaza's white blanket. His
watch said only eight-thirty or so; by afternoon the rest
of the snow would be gone. If he left now, any tracks of
his own wouldn't matter.

He'd been so sure the doors would be unlocked as
promised that he hadn't even brought a tool as simple as
a crowbar. But they weren't unlocked, and now Alex

stood on the concrete steps amid his own trampled footprints and considered the problem. He'd knocked but
gotten no response; maybe he was simply too early. Alex
shivered and stamped his feet, leaving wet dots on the
stone veranda. He certainly wasn't doing any good here,
and he was freezing his butt off besides. Better to walk
around the building and pump up some body heat, he
decided, go down to the south gardens, then around to
the rear and Columbus Drive. By the time he got back,
she'd be up and waiting.

He started out and tried rehearsing what he'd say
when he saw Deb. She was ferociously independent and
he didn't want to be too pushy; Alex was reluctant to admit how insecure he really was, how much he *craved*
company. Perhaps—

Alex wanted to swallow but his throat seemed to be
trying to work around a chunk of chalk that had lodged
at the base of his tongue. In front of him was the Columbus Drive entrance and overhang, its length relatively
clear except for a sprinkling of blown-in snow. In front of
the doors was a sparkling sunburst of fractured glass. His
gaze swept the walkway and halted where the overhang
no longer protected the sidewalk from the weather; a riot
of melting footprints lasered into his vision like the harsh
pop! of an antique camera flash.

He ran, slipping and stomping, through the wrecked
entrance, backtracking along the trail of black blood and
stench until he found the open doors of the auditorium,
still reeking of candle soot and gunpowder accented by
the unbearable smell of slowly rotting meat. Machete in
hand, Alex picked his way down the aisle, gazing dully at
the softball-sized holes torn across the seats and small
chunks of decomposing flesh, finally prodding a soggy
mess he assumed had once been a vampire.

"Good for you, Deb," he muttered hoarsely. A small
cot peeped from behind a shredded length of drapery on
the stage and he glimpsed metal beneath it; when he
pulled it out he found a fully loaded Winchester. He
sniffed the barrel; whatever Deb had used to fight, it
wasn't this shotgun. He swung it absently over his shoulder and wandered among the seats until he was satisfied

that Deb's body wasn't stuffed in some forgotten crevice in the huge room. Then, numb and empty, he simply . . . . . . left.

When Deb had gone the day before, he had admired her confidence, her *trust* in what she'd believed the future held—though he wondered now how much of that trust had been an act. She had made him think that he could do more than just admire that certainty, that he could *believe*. Walking in the slowly warming air, Alex believed, all right. He had every faith in the world that in no time at all pain would fill the empty space that had once been his heart.

2

●━●·●━●·●━●·●━●

REVELATION 20:14
This is the second death.

●━●·●━●

I'm so cold.

Who was this hard, oversized man sleeping beside her? Not Alex; though both men were dark, her lover was lean, with the sinewy build of a runner rather than weightlifter.

He must be one of the Red Things.

There were Red Things in Deb's dreams now. The landscape of her mind welcomed them, sheltered them, hid them from her probing sleep-eyes. They flitted in a vast, shadowy chasm below a strip of brilliant, aqua-colored light, eternally separating her from the peace and warmth of the light itself. The stranger at her side tried to stop her as she reached for it, and she realized that he was doing her a kindness because the light would surely kill her. Still she wrenched free, ignoring his loss and sadness as she went to the light anyway.

Her fingers brushed it and a piece . . . *cracked* away, hung suspended in space for a moment, then hurtled toward her with frightening, inescapable speed.

3

●━●━●━●━●

REVELATION 10:6
And there should be time no longer.

●━●━●

"Damn it!"

Bill Perlman stopped just short of hurling the culture across the room. He sucked in a breath and held it, trying to still the thought that sang in his head on a continual, inescapable basis.

I'm not getting anywhere.

There has to be some way to accelerate the mutation process, he insisted mentally, find the stimulation, the *catalyst*, more quickly. His mind kept veering toward the people trapped in the Merchandise Mart. Suppose he did start the decomposition process again—how would the vampires react? What if instinct propelled them into a feeding frenzy in the belief that their disease could be stalled or arrested by a massive intake of sustenance? Then those people would die and become vampires themselves, a useless and deadly transition. No, they had to be freed *first*. Turning back, he inserted another slide under the microscope, though he didn't need it to show what he already knew: the bacterium was dead, though it had been alive when he'd added the vampire flesh to the culture. By all the laws of science, *Clostridium* should have begun to feed immediately, as it had on the tiny slice of his own skin that had proved the culture was active. But once again nothing moved beneath the lens of his microscope. While Perlman could easily tell the dry, corky structure of the vampire cells from the global-shaped spheres of *Clostridium*, the quivering, twisting movement of only seconds ago had disappeared before he could even readjust the focus. Already the bacterium was forming the same woody, plantlike walls that apparently comprised the entire structure of the childbeast.

Perlman sat back and sighed. Even if he added blood, the vampire flesh absorbed it faster than he could get the slide into position. Nothing changed the view under the lens, and now even his subject was gone, since this morning he'd allowed the dangerous childbeast to be killed—a terrible thing to witness—and carried out into the sun. He told himself they were being merciful, though the boy's screams still rang in his mind and refuted his self-righteousness. Now he needed another subject but McDole was hedging, hinting that Perlman's capture of the boy had been an amateur miracle. The doctor would've gone out alone again, but the bitter truth was that he thought the older man might be right. In the end, he had no subject.

And no progress, either.

4

REVELATION 8:11
And many were made bitter.

11:30 A.M.:

Hours and hours until the bloodsuckers came out. And come out, they will, Alex thought. He waved the bottle of Smirnoff's, then toasted the unseen sleepers of the city.

Come to Papa.

He held up the vodka; only a fifth of the bottle was gone, not much considering that fourteen months ago he could've easily put away two six-packs. Two more inches of booze would make him pass out, but he wanted to do it right, so when he started feeling drunk, really *blasted*, he would guzzle the liquor like a cold lemonade at a company picnic. He shivered and took another swig, then made it two. He had to make sure he drank enough to keep him unconscious past dark. He didn't want to feel it when they got him.

A gust of wind hit the branches of the small trees surrounding his bench, making them shake as if in reproach. Fuck it, he thought. Let's be honest. I'm sitting in front of my *house* and Deb knows where it is. I'm not waiting for some unknown bastard to come and bite me in the neck. I'm waiting for *Deb* to come and bite me in the neck. He giggled. *Love at First Bite* . . . do I look like George Hamilton?

Hell no. I don't even have a tan.

"So," he said. His voice sounded loud and hollow as it floated across Daley Plaza. "Who did you think you were? Fucking Adam and Eve?" He regarded the plaza sourly and drank again. Sad little spots of moisture were all that remained of the freaky, one-day snow. "Shit. Like you were going to repopulate the world, asshole." Where *was* Deb? Was she a vampire? Or . . . *dead*? He couldn't decide which was worse, and it frustrated his muddled mind that there was a decision in there somewhere that he could have made instantly had he been sober. But not now. Long black hair, ice-blue eyes. What color were her eyes now? Maybe they were . . . *red.*

He frowned at his bottle, wishing he had some o.j. He didn't want to get drunk as fast as it seemed to be happening, because quick wasn't necessarily *thorough.* Maybe he could do a better job if he had a mixer, which would mean he could drink *longer,* something that made perfect sense to him. A thought flared in his brain: What if she didn't find him down here and something else did? Time to go upstairs.

She won't be Deb anymore, a vague voice in his head reminded him.

"Who said that?" Alex glanced around and stood, then laughed at how his eyesight was warping. "And so what if she isn't? Who the hell am *I*?" He gulped another mouthful of liquor as he staggered past the Picasso. Rage hit him as he made the corner closest to the door, and if he'd had two bottles, he would've hurled one at that ridiculous, looming statue.

"*I'll tell you who I AM!*" he screamed. He whirled haphazardly, the bottle flailing wildly and barely missing the metal doorframe as he fumbled through. "*I'm no-fucking-BODY, that's who!*" His voice choked off until it became a sob, then a gurgle.

"Nobody," he said again.

He slid down the cold frame, propping the glass door open with a booted foot. Sure, he toasted the open door with a numb wave, I'll drink to that. He turned his head with an effort and studied the Picasso statue swaying unsteadily across his vision. Wasn't it supposed to be a woman? Sober, he'd always thought it looked like an abstract horse; drunk, it didn't look like anything for which he could find a word.

Being drunk, he decided, was okay. He felt as if he'd been given a gigantic shot of Novocain, though certain parts of his body remained strangely sensitive. For instance, the muscles surrounding his mouth seemed to have frozen and words were becoming a real mess. He shrugged; without Deb, there was no one to talk to anyway. Other parts still felt normal, like his rump and his spine, which were freezing against the doorframe. And there was the shotgun he'd been dragging around since his visit to the Art Institute, digging into his side and making his ribs ache. Don't need it anymore, he realized; don't *want* it. He pushed it away with a nerveless hand, ignoring the clatter as it fell beside him. He scrunched up his face to see how much was numb as he inspected the Smirnoff's bottle; nearly half of its contents had disappeared. Had he really drank all that?

He swiveled his head to the right and tried to see into the building, but his eyes didn't want to work. Should he go up? He shook his head, the movement making him grin stupidly. Too much work, too many stairs. If he stayed down here, she could find him right away, though he should at least go *inside* so he wouldn't be an open appetizer.

But his muscles ignored his mental commands and his jerky efforts spilled him on his right side as he dragged himself not quite through, losing a helluva lot of booze in the process. He thought his foot might still be holding the door open, but did it really matter?

He squinted at the ceiling, wishing it were already dark. Wishing it were over.

I can't go on, he thought sadly. Not alone. I just can't.

"I'm waiting," he said clearly.

He sobbed slightly.

Then passed out.

5

REVELATION 22:4
And they shall see his face. . . .

REVELATION 11:14
The second woe is past; and, behold,
the third woe cometh quickly.

"This is asinine," C.J. said impatiently. "What was Jo talking about, 'the key to the Mart'?"

"Well," Louise said, "she did say *him.* And she was always saying weird stuff about the Mart." She caught him peeking at her and blushed. They were retracing yesterday's route, headed for Daley Plaza as Jo had instructed. Almost all the snow was gone, the sidewalks nearly dry.

"Like what?" C.J. suddenly looked interested.

"She called it the 'Building of the Damned,'" Louise answered. "She never explained herself, but half the time I didn't know what she was talking about anyway."

C.J.'s face brightened. "'Building of the Damned'—of course!" he exclaimed. "She's talking about the people on the third floor!"

Louise shoved her hands in her pockets. "What people?"

"There's probably twenty people being kept there as food by the vampires. We haven't figured a way to get them out yet."

Louise's mouth dropped and for an instant she forgot about Daley Plaza and Jo. "*Food* for the vampires? Oh, God, C.J.—that's *horrible!*"

"I know. But we're working on it." He scanned the sky out of habit as they came around the Daley Center, but it was a clear and beautiful blue. "That's why I was willing to make this trip, though we could be putting our time to better use. For one thing—"

Louise grabbed his sleeve. "Look!"

"What?" He followed her pointing finger, then sprinted to the slumped man wedged between one set of lobby doors. Not far from the guy's limp hand was a half-empty bottle of vodka that had rolled against one of the floor-to-ceiling windows, and tossed aside was a Winchester shotgun. Louise picked it up and tilted it over one shoulder.

"Stupid fool," C.J. hissed. He nudged the man's foot. "What the hell is he doing?"

"Hey, mister!" Louise said loudly. She shook the stranger's shoulder, but he only mumbled, his fingers clutching briefly at his missing liquor bottle.

His head lolled to one side and C.J. snorted. "Key to the Mart, my ass. This guy's so polluted he couldn't grope his way out of a can of Coke if somebody pulled the ring for him."

The drunken man's face, pale and framed by dark hair, was as calm and trusting as a sleeping baby's. Louise shook him again but got no response as C.J. kicked the bottle of Smirnoff's in disgust, watching it spin to the middle of the lobby and spew its contents onto the floor with a soft gurgling; the tang of alcohol immediately surrounded them. "Well?" she asked.

C.J. gave an exasperated sigh, then bent and pushed his hands under the man's arms. "We've either got to wake this joker up or carry him all the way to Water Tower. Help me stand him up." He grunted as they hoisted the unconscious man to his feet and struggled to hold him in place.

"What now?" Louise panted as she grappled with the man and the shotgun at the same time.

"We walk him," C.J. answered grimly. "Yell at him, slap him, find some water and douse him—whatever it takes."

She peered at the stranger's loose features, zonked out in blissful, oblivious dreams. "What do you suppose he'll say when he wakes up?"

In the strange, tinted glare cast by an old restaurant window they passed, C.J.'s face was greenish and cynical. "He'll probably say we should've let him die."

•   •   •   •

Five seconds after he opened his eyes and watched the
ceiling tilt crazily, Alex rolled on his side and threw up.
Somewhere in the midst of his retching, his brain registered that someone was holding a plastic bucket beneath
his face. His stomach gave a final, painful spasm and he
sagged back and closed his eyes again, groaning at the
roller-coaster action in his head. Nausea threatened again
and he sucked his breath in through ground teeth, in and
out, in and out, until it subsided to merely a horrible case
of seasickness. Gradually the swaying of the world
slowed and he forced his lids open, though the sunlight
streaming around him seemed to have spear-tipped fingers aimed specifically at his head. Jesus, he had a headache! His hand felt as though it weighed thirty pounds as
he reached to wipe his sweat-drenched face. Three feet
away was a man in a white lab coat, holding a stetho-
scope and watching him.

"How do you feel?"

The man's voice echoed in Alex's hung over hearing,
and sounded angry. What was this place? For a crazy moment Alex thought he had dreamed the whole thing—the
empty world, the vampires, Deb—

Deb.

"Where am I?" he croaked. "And who the hell are
you?"

"I'm Dr. Bill Perlman." The man came forward and
used his thumb to pull Alex's eyelid up. "And you're
safe."

Alex shoved the doctor's hand away and struggled upright. "I don't want to be *safe,*" he snapped, then grimaced as the pounding in his head increased to drum
level. "What time is it? I have to get back to the Daley
Center." Snatches of memory floated in his mind: stumbling along the street, forced to walk by two kids he'd
wished would just leave him alone. He tried to stand but
his knees buckled and he sat hard again on the couch.
The sunlight pouring through the huge windows in this
place was like visual barbed wire.

Dr. Perlman folded his arms. "Why? So you can finish
your little suicide attempt? It's a good thing you passed
out when you did, you know. You could've died from al-

cohol poisoning, or been outside at nightfall if the kids hadn't found you. That was a very stupid thing to do, mister."

"I don't remember asking for your opinion," Alex said hotly. His stomach roiled and he dropped his head between his knees until the urge to vomit passed. Finally he was able to look up. "Just show me the way out and point me in the right direction. We'll part company and be happier for it."

"I'm afraid that's not possible," Perlman answered.

Alex did throw up then, aiming instinctively for the bucket at the side of the couch. The stench of the vomit already in it made him retch even harder, until he thought the next thing to come up would probably be pieces of his stomach. By the time he was through he had slid to his knees and was staring stupidly at the floor. Something white crossed his field of vision: a wet washrag; he grasped it and wiped his face, thankful for its coolness against his burning skin.

"Why can't I leave?" he finally managed. "Am I a prisoner?"

The older man chuckled. "Of course not. But even if you made it all the way back there without collapsing—which you won't—leaving you for the vampires now that you've been here would pose too great a danger for us."

He looked at the doctor blearily. "Us?" The thought was ridiculously comforting; at least he wasn't alone in the hands of a madman.

"Quite a few." The doctor watched him for a moment, then handed him a large glass and a couple of tablets. "These will start you on the way to feeling better."

Alex obeyed automatically as a white-haired man hurried into the room. "How're you doing, son? You were in sad shape when they brought you in."

"He could've died of alcohol poisoning," the doctor said again in a sour tone.

The other man nodded absently and offered his hand. "I'm Buddy McDole. What can we call you?"

Alex returned the handshake without enthusiasm. "Alex Nicholson."

McDole studied him curiously. "You don't seem very

happy to see us, Alex. I'd think you'd be pretty interested to find other people. What's the problem?"

Deb.

Alex hung his head, then an irrational hope occurred. "Say," he asked quickly, "you people haven't been to the Art Institute, have you? Maybe last night? You don't have a woman here named Deb?"

Perlman and McDole glanced at each other. "No, I'm afraid not," McDole finally answered. Alex's face crumbled momentarily, then his features melted once more toward stoniness.

"You lost her, didn't you?" Something in Perlman's voice stabbed hard, and before he could stop himself, Alex went to pieces.

The story didn't take long to tell, and sounded pitifully short and overdramatic out loud, especially considering his attempted suicide this morning. It must seem ludicrous that he had tried to kill himself over a woman he'd known only two days, yet there was a faraway look in Perlman's eyes that kept Alex from feeling like a total lunatic. At last McDole spoke. "I'm real sorry, Alex. It must've been horrible to find what you did, and I know my words probably aren't much comfort. But there *are* reasons to go on, there *are* other people, and a life for each of us to live." He nodded toward Perlman sitting quietly a few feet away. "The doctor is working on something that will kill the vampires—"

"We hope," Perlman interrupted.

"—off entirely. It's just a matter of getting it started and testing it out."

In spite of his sick, tinny headache, Alex looked interested. "Something that could kill them? What?"

"A bacteria," Perlman answered, shooting McDole an exasperated glance. "But don't let Buddy get your hopes up too fast." A hint of sarcasm crept into his voice. "The work is pretty slow, plus I don't have a test subject anymore."

"We'll find another one tomorrow," McDole assured him.

"Another what?"

"Vampire. The doctor has to try the bacteria on a real vampire to see if it works, and keep trying until it does," McDole explained.

Alex frowned, the movement making his temples throb. "You actually had a vampire *in* the building? How did you control it?"

Perlman shook his head. "Not here, in a bomb shelter at Northwestern. Tried the bacteria before and after feeding—"

"You *fed* it!"

"I had to see the effect feeding would have. We tossed a little bag of blood into the shelter during the day and videotaped the results." Perlman stared at the table moodily. "It was a little boy. But after two feedings he was so much stronger and dangerous that we . . . put him out of his misery this morning."

Alex was silent as his stomach twisted in protest at the dark idea swelling in his mind. The thought had a thousand razored edges that still couldn't prevent him from reaching for the one chance that he might—

"Deb will probably come to the Daley Center tonight," he said hoarsely. "We could catch her."

—see her again.

"All right." McDole looked at the group. "Are we ready? Do we have *everything*? We can't come back." Alex glanced at the others and tried to think logically about what he was carrying and what he would need. He couldn't; eclipsing everything was the memory of Deb as she had been yesterday morning. Would she still look the same? Would she talk to him, or would she be more beast than human? *Would she even come?*

He forced his sickly, hung over thoughts back to the present: McDole, C.J., the dangerous-looking teenager who'd helped bring him here, and Elliot, a sturdy-looking blond man in his mid-twenties. Although C.J. had a compound bow, they weren't carrying much else in the way of weapons, and for that Alex was grateful. Alex had refused to bring the Winchester, but Elliot carried a gun, a heavy blue .357 to be used only in the worst emergency. Their agreed goal was to capture Deb alive as quietly as possible, then be back at Water Tower by seven in the morning so everyone here would know the group was safe. Seeing was going to be a problem; while the sky was clear, there would only be a quarter moon, not enough light to help anything. Each had a small flashlight, but they didn't dare bring anything too bright. Stuffed inside McDole's backpack were dark green trash bags and several rolls of duct tape, along with a coil of nylon rope and a folded canvas tarp. Alex tried to keep himself from picturing Deb wrapped and bound in plastic and nylon rope, then hidden under the canvas; he didn't want to know what the duct tape was for.

McDole glanced at him and Alex nodded, then followed the men out the Michigan Avenue entrance. He would've never guessed a group of people this size could live together safely in one place, or even that this many people still lived at all. His eyes followed the marble front of the building up to its roofline and gave him a rush of dizziness as a result. The doctor had promised Alex would be well enough to be of use tonight, and also assured him that the walk itself would help clear his head. Concentrating on his steps, Alex willed himself not to think of the black side of his little dream, the chance that Deb would become nothing more than a vicious animal subjected to Perlman's experiments. Could he live with himself, knowing he had set her up for this?

And what would he do if they had to kill her?

6

■■●■●■●■●■

REVELATION 6:4
And there went out another horse that was red;
and power was given unto him to take peace from the earth.

■●■●■

That woman was staring at her again.

Louise shifted uncomfortably on the carpeting, then stood and went to the window. She couldn't see much of Michigan Avenue, and certainly not all the way to Daley Plaza, where C.J. and the others, including the drunken man they'd found this morning, had gone for the night. In another half hour the people here would move to the center of the building where life-signs couldn't be detected from the outside. A shudder danced along the muscles of her shoulders and she asked her question without turning.

"Do you think they'll be all right?" Louise's voice was too loud and the six or seven people in the room started. Most bent back to their tasks, and Louise took it as a bad omen that no one offered immediate reassurance. When she turned to face them, Evelyn was knitting something for her unborn baby, fingers working steadily. The other woman, Kate, was buried in a book called *Organic Gardening* and absently twisting her yard-long red hair. Calie was the only one who didn't have anything else on which to concentrate except Louise, and it was she who finally answered.

"They'll be fine." Her gaze stalled on Louise once more, then moved to a spot on the ceiling.

"Good evening, ladies. Almost time to turn in, isn't it?" Perlman's voice was cheerful but his face was grim and tired as he limped to a seat on the couch next to Calie.

The woman brightened. "How're you doing? Any progress?"

He shook his head and spread his hands. "I told you

it would take time. With this kind of equipment, who
knows? Things'll be better when the guys come back
with this vampire."

"Why do they have to go there?" interjected Kate. The
gardening book forgotten, her tone was tight with worry.
"Why not just catch one in our own neighborhood during
the day?"

"Because"—all eyes turned to Calie—"they hope—and
they realize it's farfetched—that the woman they're going
after will recognize Alex and cooperate."

Evelyn snorted. "That's the most ridiculous thing I've
ever heard. You talk as though this vampire still has a
heart, or a soul, or whatever you want to call it." Her
fingers snagged in her rhythm and she muttered impatiently. "Why couldn't they go in the daytime?"

"They don't know where she sleeps," Dr. Perlman explained. "And if Alex isn't there tonight, she'll probably
never be found again."

"They should've waited and searched for her when it's
safe, anyway," said Kate. "This is way too dangerous."
She looked at all of them. "What if they don't come
back?"

"They will," Calie said confidently. Her face still betrayed her concern.

"We don't have the time to hunt all over downtown,"
Perlman said. "If there's a chance this woman will cooperate and cut some of the research time, we've got to try
it."

"What kind of work are you doing?" Louise asked timidly.

He answered readily. "I'm trying to develop a bacteria
that will kill the vampires, but so far everything is killed
by the vampire instead of the other way around."

Louise knew her next statement might damage any
chance of these people accepting her, but it was too important to remain unspoken. "Why don't you . . ." Her
words trailed off unwillingly. Louise didn't feel right
here, didn't feel *welcome*, especially by Calie. Calie's behavior had deteriorated, and while she wasn't rude or
mean, Calie was . . . *aloof*, as though she was trying to
gently "cut" Louise from the herd. The doctor was as

friendly as when C.J. had brought her here, yet Louise hesitated.

"Why doesn't he what?" Kate looked at her curiously.

"It's all right, Louise," Calie said. "No idea is too outrageous to at least discuss."

Louise swallowed, feeling heat climb across her cheeks. "I just wondered if Jo could help somehow."

Perlman rubbed the side of his nose, then cupped his chin thoughtfully. "I don't know," he said finally.

"You're supposed to be open-minded," Calie chided. "You shouldn't discount Louise's suggestion so quickly."

"I'm not," the doctor protested. "To be honest, I've been thinking about that since Louise's claim that Jo can heal. It's just that . . ." He looked away.

"It's too fantastic," Louise finished for him. "Right?" He nodded reluctantly. "I know how it must sound, but I'm living proof that she's not a fake. She saved my life." Louise held up her hands. "But I wouldn't expect any of you to take my word for it. Just ask *her*."

"And you think we can find her?" Perlman questioned.

"Sure. She lives in St. Peter's."

"There's no harm in trying," Calie said.

"All right," Perlman said after a moment. "I'll go over there after—*if*—we get the new vampire settled. It's just that the concept is so irrational—"

"Ir*rational*?" Calie was smiling widely.

Perlman looked flustered. "You know what I mean." He inclined his head toward Louise. "Or maybe you and C.J. can try to find her." Louise nodded as the group gathered their belongings. "Right now, it's time to put down." He gave them all a final, solemn glance. "I'm not a religious man, but if that brings you comfort and . . . *belief*, then remember our guys in your prayers tonight."

Deceptions

7

REVELATION 6:17
For the great day of his wrath is come;
and who shall be able to stand?

"So what's the plan?" C.J. asked. "It'd be pretty stupid to leave this door unlocked."

"We're not going to," Alex said. "Deb knows where I am. If she shows up, and if she's . . . changed, she'll find her own way in."

Great, C.J. thought. *Deb knows where I am.* Nothing like staying emotionally detached. They followed Alex inside and waited while he locked the door, then led them down a corridor to a stairwell door beside a bank of elevators. Another lock rattled and Alex swung the door open, its hinges making a loud and ear-stabbing screech. He gave them a grin that was still a little green. "My alarm. Ready to climb?" They started up without comment as he relocked the door then passed them, his legs conditioned to the stairs.

"How much farther?" McDole panted.

"Thirteenth floor." Alex tried to sound cheerful.

McDole groaned good-naturedly as their flashlights made small, bobbing circles with each step. "So," Elliot said after a few more flights. "These stairs must've been a pain in the butt."

"Not really." Alex's face was a gray and black shadow, his voice strained. "Normally it barely winds me. I figured the higher you were, the safer—especially with the vampires getting weaker. Here we go." Another door screamed in the darkness as though it had sand in its hinges. "Here's where I live, folks. Not much to see, I'm afraid."

C.J. stepped through cautiously, looking left and right along a dim inner hall before walking soundlessly on the parquet flooring to a better-lit outer corridor evenly spaced with northern windows, making a mental note that he was leaving the only close location of a stairwell. "What's above you?" he called back to Alex. "Have you ever been upstairs?"

"Yeah," Alex said as the rest joined C.J. "Nothing much different from here."

"The doors?" McDole wondered.

"All locked." Alex scrubbed at his face as they turned and moved toward the south end of the building. His eyes were bloodshot and watery with pain; he didn't look ready for a confrontation.

"And there's no one else in the building?"

Alex shrugged. "If there is, they're invisible or they move at night when I can't see them. I've never heard anything."

"I hate to break up the conversation," said C.J., "but darkness is a-coming. We'd better pick our places."

"C.J.'s right," McDole said. "Where would she expect to find you?"

Alex stopped at the doorway to a small office and stood there unsteadily. "Here," he said at last. "She'd probably look here first."

C.J. poked his head in and frowned when he saw the tiny office, bare except for a few miscellaneous items. "No way. There's no room in here to get clear if she—" McDole cleared his throat and C.J. blinked. "Uh—if we have to."

"Where else?" Elliot asked. He and McDole both looked unhappy with Alex's information. "Someplace a little bigger?"

"Yeah," Alex said. "Over here." They rounded another corner and found themselves facing the south wall. Heavy drapes covered most of the windows next to the bookcases; here and there Alex had cracked the material to let in the light.

"This is better," C.J. said. "That office back there is a death trap."

McDole turned from the windows and held up a clay pot. "Where did you get these flowers?"

Alex swallowed. "Deb and I found them in Marshall

Field's," he answered quietly. He pulled a chair from under a desk and sat heavily. "It doesn't matter."

An uncomfortable silence fell, then C.J. clapped Alex on the shoulder and pointed at the ceiling. "Come on, guy. You ever been up there?"

Alex twisted his neck upward. "I told you already. All the doors—"

"Not upstairs, up *there*. In the ceiling." The teenager scrambled atop a desk and raised one of the large tiles in the dropped ceiling. "This is a great place to hide." C.J.'s voice was muffled by the layer of tiling as his hands groped overhead and found a hold. "I'm surprised you never thought of it."

Alex stood with McDole and Elliot and peered at C.J. as he hoisted himself into the hole. "What're you going to do if the ceiling collapses?" he called.

There was a few seconds of soft scuffling, then C.J.'s head poked out. "It won't, as long as you make sure to put your weight where the supports are anchored into the main beams. Use your flashlight to find them." He glanced at McDole. "It ain't gonna be the most comfortable place in the world."

"I think I'll stay down here," McDole said. He eyed Alex and Elliot. "Alex can go up over here," he pointed to one spot, then another. "C.J., you position yourself there." He turned to Alex. "You're positive the doors will make a warning noise?" Alex nodded. "Okay, then, two people up, two down." He studied the office area carefully, then pointed to an alcove created by a couple of filing cabinets. "I'll stay here, and Elliot can hide in the secretarial station at the corner. We should be able to hear her come in"—McDole glanced at Alex to be sure—"and see her when she gets here."

"Not much of a moon tonight," C.J. interrupted. "That'll be tough."

"We'll have to make do. Switch on the flashlights only if absolutely necessary, and then only for a second or two. If something else sees it . . ." He didn't have to finish.

"So we have her surrounded," Elliot said. "Then what?"

"Then we grab her, I guess." McDole's words made

Alex's face go white. "The idea is to take her alive, right? Maybe we can talk to her."

C.J. let out a long breath. "Oh man, this is going to be a trick."

"We can do it," McDole said firmly. "If we all work together. We have to be able to count on each other at every second. There's no room for backing out, okay, Alex? Hesitate and someone could die." Alex nodded curtly.

McDole steeled himself. "Then everybody find your place and get comfortable." He looked at his watch.

"Four minutes until sunset."

8

REVELATION 14:7
For the hour of his judgment is come.

Darkness.

The last tendrils of light faded, drawing away all but a wisp of the day's warmth. This room, larger but unfamiliar, was closer to the outside walls of the building and the sweet pain of the sun; both he and the woman still felt its faraway kiss. Vic felt the micromovement of her skin as her eyelids opened, heard the whisper of her lashes in the blackness as she blinked. She paused, as though listening for something, and he tensed.

When she screamed, he was ready for it.

It took almost a quarter of an hour to soothe her hysteria. "It was only a dream," he murmured over and over, "that's all. Just a dream." The first nightsleep had been the worst for him, and for Deb, too; he tried to slip into her mind and help her through it, but he was a novice at creation and a bumbler at making decisions about other people's lives anyway.

"I couldn't hear my heartbeat," she sobbed. "I couldn't find it!"

"Shhhh, it's okay." Guilt weighed on him like a steel yoke and his lips pulled into a thin line. "It's okay," he said again, as though he were some kind of repetitious recording. She felt good in his arms, though he couldn't forget the lost heat of life within her flesh, now gone forever. But she was beautiful this way, too: her light blue eyes with faint traces of black-red lights dancing in their depths; china-white skin beneath the India ink spill of hair across her shoulders and down her back. The first time she fed, those stunning eyes would start a slow change to red, and eventually the once-sparkling blue would slip away for eternity.

Cradled in his arms, Deb finally stopped her tearless crying. He should have known she wouldn't be afraid; inside was much the same woman who'd faced them in the Art Institute, defiant and brave, stubborn as hell. Her gaze flicked around the room and rested briefly on the pillbox, then she pulled away and stood, her lovely face glowing like a ghostly death mask. She picked up the pillbox and studied it, then closed her fist around it. "I'm hungry," she said softly. Her eyes grazed him, then slid safely to a point above his head.

Vic hadn't expected her to ask so soon. "I can take you to food," he offered. He tried to take her hand but she stepped out of his reach.

"Not *that* kind," Deb said. The fist clutching the pillbox made a hollow *thunk* as she smacked her breastbone. "I'm hungry *here* . . . Vic." There was the slightest hesitation as her memory supplied the new fact. "I want to hear the sound of my heart. I want to feel the rush of my *own* blood pulsing through my arteries. *I want to be warm again!*" She tossed the trinket at him and he caught it automatically, the cloisonné butterfly glimmering on his palm.

He turned his back and stared stonily at the wall. "I can't help you with that."

"Why did you do this to me?" she demanded. "You're not—" She stumbled, searching for the right word.

Vic whirled. "What? *Normal?*"

"Yes!" she shot back. "You're not like you're supposed to be! You don't like being what you are, so why did you have to *make me like YOU?*" Her voice was so full of anguish it was nearly a wail, and Vic fought the urge to cringe.

"Because I was . . . lonely," he whispered.

"You took my life because you were lonely?" The question was harsh and disbelieving. "I'd understand it better if you said you were *hungry!*"

"I thought you might stay with me," he pleaded. "I thought we could be—"

"What?" she asked. "A *couple*?" She turned away, her expression miserable. "Oh, I just don't believe this."

"They would have killed you, or worse," he said.

"Better that than this."

"You don't have any idea. There *are* worse things." He folded his arms.

"Being one of the fat man's playthings at least leaves *hope*!" She rolled her eyes at his startled look. "It's as easy for me to see into your mind as it was for you to poke into mine."

"It wasn't that easy."

"And it never will be," she snapped, "not as long as I have one ounce of—can you believe it! I almost said *life*!" Her shrill laughter teetered on the edge of control.

"Anyelet will want to know where Alex is," Vic told her quietly. "If she even gets a hint that he exists . . ."

"I don't plan on meeting Anyelet." Deb tossed her head proudly.

"What?"

"I want you to let me go, Vic. *Please*," she said at his openmouthed stare. She tentatively touched his shoulder. "I don't want to stay like this. I'd rather die."

"No, you wouldn't—" he began.

"Yes I *would*," Deb insisted. She made a swiping motion and looked down at her body. "This is . . . I don't know. *Dirty*, somehow. This feeling, this Hunger—it's evil and you know it. All those people chained up. . . ." She groaned. "Just . . . turn your back, all right? That's all I ask."

"That's out of the question." His voice was hoarse with disappointment; when he started to reach for her, his hand was trembling and he squeezed his fingers shut instead.

"I'm sorry, Vic, but I can't *be* what you want. I can't fill the emptiness inside you, or be the balm for all your horrible shame about Hugh." She stared at him, and this time it was Vic who pulled his gaze away. "*I can't fix you.*"

"But where would you go?" He looked terrified. "You can't change what you are, Deb." It was the first time he'd spoken her name. "At least here there's safety, and food, too, even if only when necessary."

"I won't feed on another person." Her voice was so low he almost didn't catch her words.

"But you'll starve!" he exclaimed. "You'll end up like one of the outcasts, living in the subway—"

"I won't let it come to that."

Vic let his knees bend and lower him to the blankets on which he and Deb had slept. He ran his fingers over the soft surface, then picked up the little pillbox. Only one night; he'd been hoping for so much more.

He closed his eyes, then dropped his face to his cupped hands and stayed that way for a long, long while, thinking about all the nights of eternity and about a woman whose courage would give her the strength to do what he couldn't face.

She didn't say good-bye.

9

○•○•○•○•○

REVELATION 11:11
Life entered into them, and they stood upon their feet;
and great fear fell upon them which saw them.

○•○•○

The night held a terrible beauty.

She'd never noticed it before and was loath to admit it, but the nightside had incredible advantages that seemed to exist for no other reason than enhancement. Night vision, for instance. At first, she'd assumed it was only to see things (*people*, her mind whispered snidely), yet the stars glittered like a spread of sequins on black satin, sprinkled from skyline to skyline. Never had she seen such a nightsky, even in open country. Scent, too, heightened to enable her to find prey; instead she concentrated on the other smells it brought: the damp smell of the river, the slight scent of green from the tiny buds on the trees, the dark stench of decay drifting up from Lower Wacker and the subways. She moved quickly in the middle of the street, avoiding the black pits of doorways and parked cars and the manhole covers that pocked the streets at regular intervals.

The doorway to the Daley Center was locked, of course. The subway on her right and the parking garage on her left made her nervous, the danger of being attacked from two sides at once tripping alarms in her head. She circled quickly to the north, slipping by the yawning darkness of the garage so swiftly she was only a shadow among a forest of others. Glancing around carefully, she began to climb. At the fifteenth floor Deb stopped and peered at the ground; for a second she thought she saw something move, but at this distance even her eyesight couldn't clearly distinguish anything in the blackness a hundred and fifty feet below. Her fingers gripped the smooth metal effortlessly, clinging to the steel as though each were tipped by an invisible suction cup. She let one hand drop to her face, and dangling from the side of the building like an oversized bat, inspected it in the darkness. She could feel its massive new strength, ugly by its own purpose. There was a new emptiness, too—the ulcerous pain in her gut had been replaced by a ... *Hunger.* But she had existed with pain in her belly for a long time in life, and she could do the same in death. She tried to see her reflection in the window glass and nearly lost her grip when vertigo slapped her; it passed as soon as she looked up instead of straight ahead, and she wondered if a fall from this height would kill her or simply leave her as a pile of fragmented, twitching bones. There was no other way in and Deb broke the window as gently as possible, trying vainly to direct the shattered glass to the interior of the building.

Two floors below, she might find Alex. The mind block she had erected to avoid Vic's discovery of Alex's whereabouts had been an experiment with a new toy; now would come the true test of her will. She forced the fire door at the thirteenth floor, smiling ruefully as it screeched in the darkness. Was he even here? Surely not; the man would have to be as much a fool for staying as she was to think he actually had. Still, she followed the corridor, her shadow cutting through the strips of moonlight thrown by the sporadic breaks in the draperies. At the last corridor she stopped; suddenly she could *smell* him, his scent magnified a hundred times by the memory of their lovemaking only a few nights ago. The place smelled of other humans, too, and she raised a shaking hand to her forehead. What was she doing here? What did she *really* expect to happen? Would she *talk* to him? Her bitter laugh cut sharply through the room. It smelled like Alex had joined up with others; more likely he'd find a way to kill her. But that would be all right, too.

She took two more steps and someone dropped out of the ceiling.

She crouched and snarled reflexively, trying to back away before realizing someone else was behind her.

"Deb?" Alex's voice was a mix of terror and longing;

the sound of it filled her with more pain than she'd thought possible.

Another voice, young and unfamiliar. "Alex, don't go near—"

"Deb, *look out!*" Alex yelled. A third voice shouted angrily as something hissed viciously and leapt on her from behind.

She rolled with it on her shoulders, whipping her head back and forth to avoid the talons trying to puncture her eyes. There was a lot of pain, stinging sensations that surprised her in a detached way; she really hadn't expected pain in this new existence. She got a hand twisted in a hunk of filthy hair and the thing snapping at her neck shrieked as she yanked its head sideways and wrapped her other hand around a bone-thin arm slick with disgusting fluids, jerking the creature away and flinging it to the floor. It was on her again in an instant, clawing at her arms and ripping at the clothing covering her skin. Deb struggled with it more out of annoyance than fear, knowing it was too weak to survive a true battle with her.

Then it was—gone. Suddenly freed of its weight, she took a stumbling step backward and stopped. "Hey," she began, "where—"

The screaming started.

The beast was on top of someone else, a young man bellowing in agony as the thing chewed at his arm, wrist, wherever it could get a bite. Alex and two other men grappled it without success as the smell of blood filled the air and awakened a dark need that Deb ground her jaw against. She came up behind them and easily pushed the youngest one aside; he batted at her angrily before he realized who she was.

"Stay back!" he cried. "You—"

Alex howled.

The nightthing had bitten him, and rage exploded in Deb as she plucked the older man bodily from the fray and shoved him behind her. Fury reddening her vision, and she buried her fingers in the creature's scalp. It opened its mouth and squealed, and Alex, his wrist splattering blood, rolled aside, then dropped to his knees next to his companion as the other men scrambled forward and Deb jammed her other hand under the beast's jaw, the sound of Alex's agony still pounding through her mind. The rich smell of lifeblood was turning the outcast into a slavering maniac, and the realization that it had torn into her lover's flesh infuriated Deb even more. When the outcast tried to clutch at her, she roared and dragged the scrawny thing clear of the floor and brutally flung it against the wall. The instant it regained its feet, something faster than her eyes could track split the air and sank solidly into its chest. Pinned to the wall, the nightbeast gave a long, thin wail, shriveled nails scrabbling at the shaft in its sternum. It convulsed and howled again, then went limp.

Deb whirled. *"Alex?"*

"Don't move, lady." The teenager's voice was cold and emotionless. "If you do, I'll kill you." The weapon that had brutalized the outcast was aimed at her heart, a broadhead arrow already loaded.

"No!" Alex scrambled to his feet and reached for her. "Deb, are you all right?"

"Stay away!" she hissed. His hand was thick with blood and the scent of it crawled up her nostrils like the lure of hot soup on a frigid morning. Despite the arrow pointed at her, she retreated a few steps from the man she'd lain heart to heart with the night before last. "Don't come near me. I'm not . . . *safe*." He hesitated, then looked stupidly at his gore-covered hand and dropped it to his side.

Against the wall, the vampire thing's crusty skin was beginning its slow, smelly disintegration and Deb grimaced. The older man cleared his throat. "So you're Deb," he said. "I'm McDole, that's C.J. The fellow on the floor there is Elliot."

"What's next?" Deb asked sarcastically. " 'Pleased to meet you'?" She glared at Alex and stamped her foot, furious. "What are you doing here? I would've expected you to have more brains!"

"Then why did you even come?" Alex snapped. "I suppose I was just your first easy dinner!"

His words hurt, as did the horrible probability that they could have been true. "I don't know," she whispered. She covered her face with her hands. "I guess I was hoping you'd . . . kill me."

There was a stunned silence but McDole was quick to recover. "You could do a lot more good alive," he said. "You could help us, if you had a mind to."

"Help you what?" Deb's voice had turned hopeless.

Alex looked pained and averted his gaze to Elliot, who was watching them warily and meticulously applying a ripped piece of his shirt to the wounds on his arms and leg. Alex's bleeding had already stopped, the redness more like a black paint spill in the sparse moonlight.

"We're working on something," McDole offered finally. "Something that will even the odds a little."

"Kill us, you mean," Deb said flatly. Her laugh was brittle when McDole pressed his lips together and nodded. "And you want me to be your guinea pig? You know, for a moment I actually thought he came because he loved me—just one more girl in the harem, right, Alex?"

Alex winced. "You don't have to do this," he said in a low voice. "I won't let them force you." C.J. scowled at him, but Alex shook his head. "It has to be willingly or not at all."

"But we *need* her!" Elliot exclaimed. "The doctor—"

"Never mind," McDole interrupted tersely. "Alex is right. We don't have the right to force anyone."

"This doctor," Deb said curiously, "what would he . . . *do* to me? Or do you even know?" Her eyes, so full of red moonlight, sparkled with sudden interest. Or was it pain?

McDole hesitated and Alex jumped in. "Not much, I think. Take samples of skin to study, stuff like that. He's trying to . . . I don't know, make a disease or something."

Deb's gaze fell to her hands again, remembering their terrible strength and the guilt-free ease with which she'd forced her fingers through the flesh of the outcast's head. If she refused their offer, she knew these men would do the unspeakable and let her go free, while her own kind killed at will and blandly accepted the depravities Siebold forced on the people at the Mart. Even Vic, the most misplaced of them all, had stolen her choice of eternities. So what was left? She could either feed or deny

her Hunger and face the starvation Vic had warned
would lead to the existence of a creature like the stinking
mess sliding down the plaster to her right.

Better to die.

But not before this foul thing that had become her
body did something worthwhile. She turned to face
McDole.

"I'll do it."

10

REVELATION 2:2
And thou hast tried them ... and hast found them liars.

■●■●

Anyelet's face was a collage of fury and amazement.

"She didn't want to stay," Vic repeated. His arms were folded defensively across his chest; the other vampires were wearing shocked expressions and backing uneasily out of Anyelet's reach. Even Rita, whose mind had crumbled since the gunshot wound to her face, had stopped hissing and babbling about revenge and retreated to a far corner to stroke the suppurating flesh of her face and mumble quietly.

"And so you granted her permission to leave," Anyelet said slowly.

"No," Vic replied patiently. "I didn't. But I didn't have the right to forbid it either."

"But you DID have that right!" The larger vampire stood his ground as Anyelet strode around the room. She spun back to him. "Tell me where she went!"

"I don't know." Vic kept his gaze carefully directed at her chin.

Her hand streaked forward and she slapped him, a blow that would have snapped the neck of a normal man; his solid body didn't quiver. In the recesses of the room, Gabriel, Ron, Jasper, and Warner, a young man pulled from guarding the outside to replace Gregory, cringed and sighed.

"I don't *know*," Vic insisted. "She wouldn't tell me."

"Then let me show you how you *should* have gotten the information!" Before he could jerk away, Anyelet wrenched his face up and snagged his eyes. Then she was *in* him, searching, reading, *demanding*, and it was incredible how strong Vic's mind was, because even now she could feel him desperately trying to push her out.

She gave an ugly mental chuckle as she found something, a tidbit to be saved for later, but the laughter died when she discovered he really *didn't* know the woman's whereabouts.

A fraction of a second after she pulled out, the cords of Vic's neck muscles relaxed and recognition flowed back into his eyes. "You—you—" He struggled with the words.

"Fool," she sneered. "Did you really think you could fight? Your bumbling alone should have told you to leave her to me." She pushed past him. "Stay away from me tonight, *Vito*. My patience is at an all-time low. And besides," her eyes glittered dangerously, "if something should happen to you, who will take care of Hugh?"

Anyelet paced angrily around her room. With Rita gone mad and Vic untrustworthy, she no longer had anyone who could be trusted to follow orders or with whom she could intelligently discuss her plans for rebuilding. All that effort to create an army and companions and she'd ended up alone anyway. She plopped onto her bed and tugged at her hair in irritation. This woman, Deb, made her nervous. Vic was an amateur at forcing his way through someone's mind, but once there it should have been impossible to hide anything, and the kind of willpower it took to resist was astounding. Weariness settled over her and she sighed and climbed under the comforter. Outside the sun was rising, bringing bright death to more of those traitorous fools who had once been her soldiers. In spite of her fury, she smiled; it took more than willpower to survive. No doubt the outcasts had finished off the inexperienced woman as she'd wandered the streets of the city.

Nightsleep took her.

V

— · — · — · —

March 27

— · —

Sacrifice

1

●━●●━●●━●●━●

REVELATION 19:20
And the beast was taken. . . .

REVELATION 16:8
And power was given unto him to scorch men with fire.

●━●●●━●

Alex was taking Deb to her death.

He knew it, she knew it; perhaps that was why she struggled even in her sleep, writhing in his arms like a sackful of energetic snakes. Squinting against the glare of the sun, the group turned east on Wacker Drive. The golden rays sparkling down the length of the river were blinding after the still-shadowy inner streets and he gritted his teeth as Deb twisted in his grasp, the coldness, the *emptiness*, of her skin seeping through the layers of plastic and canvas.

"Need help, Alex?" McDole offered for the second time. C.J. was using one hand to support Elliot, who hobbled along with a pained expression.

"I'll manage," Alex responded grimly. Deb turned again and he almost lost his grip; his stomach wrenched when he thought he heard her groan.

"She's in a lot of pain."

The four of them whirled and Alex did lose his hold on one end, swearing desperately as Deb's feet thumped to the sidewalk, the sound like that of a dropped corpse.

"Jesus, Jo! You scared the crap out of us!" C.J.'s face was gray. "Stop sneaking up on people!" She didn't answer, just watched Alex as he struggled to pick up Deb's dead weight once more.

"Here," McDole said. He bent and hoisted the bottom of the bundle into Alex's arms and the five of them began to walk again. "So you're Jo."

"Yes." She studied Alex, but it didn't matter; part of his

mind realized that he'd seen this girl from the window several days ago, but he no longer cared. There was a muffled sound of agony as his bundle moved sluggishly again, and saltwater stung his eyes. Deb was nearly *vibrating* in his arms, as if she needed to break free of her sleep and escape the sun. Jo slowed until she was beside him, then lightly touched Deb's covered head. "Sleep," she whispered. "Forget for a while."

Alex felt the tension drain from Deb's body before he'd taken three more steps. "What did you do?" he demanded. "Did you hurt her?"

Jo shook her head. "Bad dreams. She'll be all right now." The girl caught up with McDole again and Alex watched her go with dull eyes, then let himself sink back into his thoughts. Where was Deb now, the *real* Deb, the one he'd lain skin to skin with in the Daley Center? He'd seen shades of her last night, but he'd also discovered a new Deb, too—a woman of immense power and terrifying speed, a killer far beyond the scared survivor who had once shot a man plotting to betray her. He felt sick inside, in his stomach, in his brain. His heart was nothing but a burned-out piece of coal.

"Alex," McDole interrupted his thoughts. "Jo's coming with us to help."

Alex nodded automatically as the white-haired girl slowed again, this time to examine Elliot's wounds; he imagined her telling the man he'd be fine in a few days.

"Alex," McDole said gently at his side. "Alex, I'm so *sorry*. Is there anything, anything at *all*, that I can do?"

Alex shook his head and increased his pace. He didn't want McDole to see the tears dripping on the shroud that covered Deb's body.

"Don't touch her!"

Perlman threw his hands up and stepped back as Alex started to grab for his machete. "Sure, Alex. Whatever you say." He glanced warily at McDole; for once the older man seemed to have run out of words. Alex's expression was dangerously rigid, his eyes wild and suspicious.

"Hey, man," C.J. said, "the reason we *did* this was so that the doc could—"

"Shut up!" Alex snarled. He clutched Deb's silent body closer. "Just ... *shut up.*" His voice dwindled and he bent his head as if meaning to kiss Deb's cold lips through the covering. The others looked at one another uneasily.

Calie drew in her breath and spoke. "Shall we take her downstairs, Alex? Where it's dark and she'll be more comfortable?"

"Down ... stairs," he repeated. His eyes, the circles beneath them like smudges of mud, flicked to Perlman and he tightened his hold around the woman in his arms. Within the thick wrappings, Deb began to stir. "No," he decided. "I've changed my mind. I won't let you use her."

A shocked moment of silence, then Deb moaned in her sleep, a faint, dry sound of despair. Calie had a sudden, horrible certainty that Deb could literally hear Alex make this monumental choice on her behalf and was helpless to stop him.

"*Alex.*"

All gazes turned in Jo's direction as she walked to Alex and gently brushed his cheek. "You're upsetting her. Can you feel it?"

Alex's breath hitched miserably. "But he'll ... *do* something to her. He'll *hurt* her."

"He won't mean to. And you know it's what she wanted, the only thing that will bring her *comfort*. Would you deny her that?" He hesitated, then shook his head, and Calie saw moisture trickle onto the canvas wrappings. "Let the doctor take her, Alex. He'll put her where it's dark and she can sleep quietly for today." Jo motioned to Perlman and the physician came forward carefully. When Alex didn't resist, Perlman set his jaw and slipped his arms beneath the body, lifting it from Alex's hold. The younger man stood for a second with his arms extended, as though his lover were still safely nestled within them. Perlman hurried soundlessly away with C.J. and Louise following.

As they watched Perlman go, Alex's face was a mask of

anguish. When the trio disappeared down the stairwell, Calie felt Jo's gaze on her as the teenager guided Alex to a chair and McDole fumbled about the small table on which sat the makings for his ever-present coffee. For a long time after McDole had placed a cup in his hands, Alex said nothing, then his gaze lifted and Calie cringed at the haunted look in his brown eyes.

"It's going to hurt her, isn't it?" he asked in an almost inaudible voice. "I told her it wouldn't, but it will."

Calie opened her mouth to reassure him, but Jo stopped her. "Yes," she admitted. "What she's become cannot be undone without a price."

"But it wasn't her choice! Why does *she* have to pay?"

"I don't have all the answers, Alex. I wouldn't *want* to. I do know the final gift for Deb is the peace that would have been forever lost. She doesn't want to exist like this. You know that." As he nodded and stared once more into his cup, Jo went to the window. "I'm going back to St. Peter's now," she said in a soft voice. The girl glanced at Calie and McDole. "He'll need something else to give him a sense of purpose." Her smile was kind, and despite Alex's misery, Calie wanted to smile back. Jo walked to the door, then nodded toward Alex again.

"You know," she said, "he's just what you need to get those people out of the Mart."

Then, as always, she was gone.

"What people in the Mart?" Jo's parting words had caught Alex's attention, momentarily pulling him from his self-pity. He watched numbly as McDole peered down the stairwell. "Forget it," Alex finally said. "I've been through this before. She's good at disappearing."

Relenting, McDole spun a chair in front of Alex and straddled it, leaning his arms across its back. Calie sat on the floor a few feet away. "There's something I've been meaning to ask you," McDole said. "What did you do about the lower level and the subway entrances into the Daley Center? How did you keep from being overrun by those things in the tunnels?"

Alex frowned, as though the answer was obvious. "I

sealed the doors, of course." He scrubbed at the harsh stubble on his chin.

"But aren't they glass?" Calie asked. "You mean you boarded them up and none of the vampires tried to break through?"

"Don't be silly," Alex said impatiently. "The glass is unbreakable, but wood would've never held. I welded them shut. What's the matter?" McDole's mouth was hanging open and Calie was grinning widely.

"Well"—Calie's smile grew even bigger—"you really *are* the key to the Mart!"

Fury and Torment

2

REVELATION 8:9
And the third part of the creatures which had life, died . . .

"WHERE IS SHE?" Anyelet roared.

Silence. The others, cowering little rats that they were, had hidden in the recesses of the building, away from her rage and the tantrum that had enveloped her since she'd risen. She spun and pummeled the walnut-paneled wall; the wood shattered and pelted her with splinters, irritating her even more. Anyelet started to swing again, then stopped and touched her shaking fingers to her temples. Last night she'd been convinced that the woman would be dead by morning, ripped apart by outcasts or cooked by the sun and her own inexperience. Anyelet kicked petulantly at an end table, then flopped onto one of the loungers. Her dreams had destroyed that peace of mind, plaguing her with a creeping, faceless thing that chased her through a maze of streets darker than any she'd ever seen, a nameless, terrifying creature that forced Anyelet awake at dusk amid the ruins of her own shredded comforter. A creature Anyelet was *positive* represented that woman.

She glanced around, disgusted. Broken glass was everywhere, slivers and bits of wood and plaster, overturned furniture—all this and she still didn't feel any better. Her head lifted at a sound drifting down the main corridor, echoing and vaguely musical—Hugh's voice, cracked and ringing with nonsense as he sang along with a band only he could hear. Anyelet cursed in a low voice; she didn't need this insane old man simpering and slobbering over her like some brain-dead slave, and besides, he had told them about the Art Institute in the first place.

She stopped. She was not so enraged that she would

seek revenge for his innocent act, but then ... there was Vic, wasn't there? And he needed to be punished, not only for letting that woman go, but for warning her of their attack to begin with. Had it not been for Vic, Gregory would be alive, Rita would be sane, and this *Deb* would be fully integrated into the nightside instead of haunting Anyelet's dreams.

Vic's deepest secret, so easily plucked from his mind.

"Mistress!" Hugh cried as he rounded the corner. He ran to her, dropped to his knees, and hugged her feet. "What can I do for you?" he begged. "Just tell me—anything!"

Anyelet stepped away from his clutching hands and motioned him up. Immortality had not been kind to Hugh: his ancient face was drawn tight, The Hunger stretching his mouth and eyebrows taut while his fingers were little more than steel twigs with razored ends. He pushed to his feet and beamed, lost in his own mind and humming, then smiling with childlike pleasure when she opened her arms.

"You'll be my friend?" he asked happily.

"Of course," Anyelet said as she drew the old man into her strong embrace. She smiled evilly.

"What else?"

3

●━━●●━●●━●●●━━●

REVELATION 2:2
I know how thou canst not bear them which are evil. . . .

●━●●●━●

Alex was coming down the stairs.

She could *sense* him in the rhythm of the heartbeat she could already hear. He wasn't alone; the second set of footsteps, quiet as a cat, belonged to that boy who wisely chose a compound bow as his weapon. Others waited at the top of the stairs so that Alex might have some privacy with their guinea pig, the doctor among them, fidgeting in his eagerness to play his medical games with her body, as though she were a toy that felt no pain.

Deb squeezed her eyes shut. Didn't they *realize*?

The bars were thrown on the door and thin light spilled into the room. "Deb?" Alex's voice was hoarse.

"I'm here." Her response was cold. "Where's the doctor?"

Alex hesitated. "Upstairs. You—you don't have to do this."

She stepped out of the corner blackness, her presence enough to silence him and make C.J. finger the bow as the distance between them dwindled to only a few feet. "Yes, I do."

She was on C.J. before he could breathe, the bow in her left hand as her right easily lifted the snarling teenager from the floor. She dropped him with a little shove that made him stumble backward, then tossed him his weapon. One flight above, the panicked doctor and the others clambered down the stairs.

"It's okay!" Alex yelled shakily. The footsteps faltered. "Just give us a minute!"

"Do you see?" she hissed. Her eyes were glittering slits in the flashlight glow. She grabbed his collar just long enough to give him a single, hard shake. "Do you see what I've *become*?"

"I could be like you." C.J. gasped as Alex stretched his hand out, but she slapped it away.

"You don't want that." Her face, so pretty to begin with, was exquisite in its icy pallor as she motioned to her belly. "There's nothing here but a black, hungry hole." She turned her back, her pain too great to share. "You don't know what this is like. It blots out the most precious memories, and nothing compares—not drugs, starvation, not even desire. It's all that and more, rolled into a dark, ugly addiction that never, *ever* leaves you." She laughed bitterly. "I even dream in red!"

"Deb—"

"Don't touch me!" She twisted away. "Don't *ever* touch me!" She glared at them. "And don't come down anymore with less than four people, and *always* be armed!"

"But you wouldn't—"

"Oh, *wouldn't* I?"

Alex stared at her, then whirled and stormed up the stairs with C.J. backing out of the room after him. She heard the babble of voices above, then the clang of the bars as C.J. locked her in.

Then there was only the darkness to comfort her.

4

REVELATION 21:4
For the former things are passed away.

It was ironic, Vic thought, that he had spent his entire night searching the building and skulking along the streets around it, hunting for Hugh as the old man continually carried on his blinded search for Vic's mother and Vic himself.

He ran a hand through his hair and peered at the shadows by the river's edge. His father should have been here by now, looking for Tisbee, never recognizing Vic, waiting for an easy meal. He scowled as he remembered Anyelet's mindrape of last night; it was obvious she'd discovered that Hugh was Vic's father, but then what? It would serve no purpose for her to harm Hugh—except, perhaps, to strike at Vic.

Damn her, he seethed. With Deb gone, the only thing he cared about in this world was that stupid old man, and the thought that Deb may have already created her own dark lover made him tremble with jealousy. A wave of sickness hit and he staggered, then stumbled back toward the Mart's refuge of dark rooms. Dawn's pink light was leaking into the sky, making this morning the closest Vic had come to seeing the sun since the day before Anyelet had killed him. But he could close his eyes and still see its burning brightness in his mind.

His huge fists clenched and unclenched despite the weariness seeping through him as he slipped into the back stairwell. After all this time, was his father truly dead?

If so, perhaps Anyelet would like to see the fatal beauty of the sun for herself.

5

●━●●━●●━●●━●

REVELATION 13:3
And her deadly wound was healed;
and all the world wondered after the beast.

●━●●━●

Silent blackness, like floating deep in a midnight ocean. Calie's whisper seemed amplified a thousandfold. "This is unbelievably dangerous, Bill."

It was the first time she'd ever said his name without the "Doctor," so frightened was she that she'd forgotten her own joking formality. Perlman stretched his hands timidly along the wall; he knew the route by memory, but he'd traveled it in the dark only once before, during Alex's visit. Now it was nearing midnight.

"How're we doing?" McDole asked quietly from behind.

"We can almost use the flashlight," Perlman answered. "Careful here, eight steps going down." Every instinct screamed that they should all be barricaded in for the night, not crawling through Northwestern's basement like blind lizards in a subterranean cave, yet if his research was to continue, he had no choice. "You people shouldn't have come," he murmured. "I could have done this without putting everyone else in jeopardy."

"No way, man." C.J.'s voice drifted to him. "Besides, remember what she said—no less than four people at a time."

"This must be terrible for Alex," Louise said softly from her place in front of C.J. "No wonder he decided to stay upstairs."

"Was it bad for him earlier, C.J.?" Calie asked.

For a few seconds there was no reply. "Yeah," he finally said. "Yeah, it was."

"I'm switching on the light," Perlman announced. "Cover your eyes." The sudden glow of the flashlight made the hallway more ominous, as though shapes danced just beyond the small circle of light.

"You're sure the light can't be seen?" McDole asked nervously.

"Positive. We're in the center of the building below street level. It's uncomfortable to be moving around at night, though."

C.J. snorted. "*Uncomfortable?* Jesus, Doc. Even I could think of a better word than that."

"Ten steps down to the shelter," Perlman warned. "Ready?" C.J. moved to his side and cocked the bow. At his nod, the doctor pulled the bars free and opened the door.

"*I've been waiting for you.*"

Perlman shivered; Deb's voice was like a blast of cold air. He swallowed and spoke. "I'm going to turn on the spotlight, all right?" He waited a few moments, then hit the ON button.

She looked ghastly. Since their earlier visit, the skin across her cheekbones and nose had tightened perceptibly, sinking into deep hollows next to her mouth. Her pallor was so pronounced that he had to squint to be sure she had skin at all, and blue veins wandered across her face and hands like fine ink trails disappearing beneath the neck and sleeves of her clothes. She resembled something from a 1920s silent movie: black wig and alabaster makeup around a red slash of lips and soulless eyes.

Deb kept her gaze downcast, but her words were heavy with sarcasm. "If you want to get anywhere in this research of yours, *Doctor*, I suggest you stop being so nervous around your ... just what am I? Your patient?" She grinned and he saw that her teeth were revoltingly long and sharp, and as blinding white as a young dog's. Her smile evaporated. "What should I do?"

Perlman glanced at the others. He suddenly felt like a mad scientist hovering over a poor, helpless victim, though his "victim" could effortlessly kill them all, regardless of C.J. "I ... I'd like a tissue sample, please, a scraping from inside your mouth." He stepped toward her hesitantly with a wooden stick, but she snatched it from his grip.

"I'll do it." An instant later she handed him back the moistened stick and he sealed it into a plastic bag. "What else?"

This was very hard. He'd spent the last eighteen months, except for a few days with the vampire child, convinced that vampires were walking corpses, and as such could be sliced and dissected at will.

Right.

"I need a piece of skin," he blurted.

Deb laughed. "Is that all?" She raised an arm and pushed back her sleeve, revealing a roadmap of harsh blue veins. Perlman fought nausea as she sank two fingernails into the skin, curled them under, and pulled free an inch-wide chunk of flesh. "Watch," she commanded, and held out her arm. In spite of himself, Perlman was fascinated to see the newly opened wound meshing rapidly, growing edge to edge as though an invisible darning machine were busily filling in the hole. In the thirty seconds it took to seal the scrap of skin in a bag, the bloodless injury was gone.

Deb turned to face the wall. "No one asked how I . . . died," she said quietly. "I fought, you know. Killed one and mutilated another so badly that even being undead won't fix her." She looked at the floor, then thoughtfully ran a hand along her side. "Broke a couple of ribs during the fight, but they're healed." She raised her face suddenly. "Do you know that there are people being held in the Merchandise Mart?"

McDole looked startled, but nodded. "Can you tell us anything that will help us free them?"

Deb shrugged and leaned against the wall. "Not much. They're on the third floor, chained in little rooms. There's a fat man watching them during the day. I don't know if he's armed."

C.J. spoke up. "Is there a keyring or something?"

"No. The leader of the group is a woman named Anyelet. She chains them up, then tosses each key into the river."

"I knew it was too much to hope for," McDole muttered.

"How many are there?" asked Louise.

"Vampires or people? I have no idea of either," Deb answered. "I never saw anyone there but the man who did this to me. Everything I know comes from him. Ten, twenty, a bunch." Even with her gaze fixed on the floor, Perlman thought he saw red lights of hunger burning in her eyes. "You should get them out."

No one said anything for a minute. "Well," the physician said at last, "what I'm going to do now is give you something to ... eat, then take another sample and see if—"

"That's out of the question," Deb said flatly.

The doctor scowled. "The research won't be complete if we don't. We could miss something vital—I have to be able to see how blood affects your body, what kind of change it causes."

"I'll *tell* you what it'll do!" Deb snapped. "It'll push me right over the *edge*, that's what. I can *smell* each one of you, and I feel like I haven't eaten in *weeks*. You think this is *easy*?" She waved her hand. "I see the way you all look at me, like I'm something *dirty*." She hugged herself so hard her fingers nearly punctured her skin. "Well, I *am*. But I won't let you make me any worse."

"But—"

McDole cut him off. "Let it go, Bill. What if she feeds, then ... you know." He looked unhappily at the others.

Calie nodded. "Try working with what you have now," she suggested. "If you need more, we'll talk about it then."

"It's not open for discussion," Deb said icily.

"I meant we'd find another way," Calie said smoothly. She took Perlman's arm. "Let's let her alone now. I'm sure us being in here is probably a strain."

Perlman opened his mouth to argue, then shut it abruptly. Protesting was useless; it was obvious the others would overrule him. Besides, he was again enveloped with the absurd notion that they all thought him some sort of maniacal hacker. "All right."

They shuffled out, C.J. waiting with the bow while

Perlman pulled the door shut and reengaged the bars.
Just before the metal door met the frame, Perlman
thought he heard Deb whisper something and paused
automatically, then slid the bars into place. He climbed
the stairs bemusedly behind his mute companions. What
had she said? Something like,

By all means, leave me alone. . . .

VI

March 28

Enlightenment

1

REVELATION 11:6
And have power over waters to turn them to blood . . .

REVELATION 9:1
And to him was given the key to the bottomless pit.

Perlman had been awake for hours.

He was more at home here at Northwestern and had risen and felt his way through the darkness to wait outside his old lab until it was light enough to enter. All his notes were here, carted back yesterday when Deb had been placed in the bomb shelter; by sunrise he'd been rereading the most important ones and now he flipped absently through his notebook. He really needed to draw a half-pint of blood and put it in the shelter for Deb to drink when she awoke, but the others would never agree. How was he to accomplish anything without cooperation? All he could do was keep trying to strengthen the bacteria. He had isolated the toxic substance that helped, ironically, to keep vampires from visibly decomposing. How many times had that smell permeated his clothes during med school? The answer should have been obvious; perhaps formaldehyde had simply been too *easy.*

He'd never seen *Clostridium* survive a formaldehyde immersion, yet he couldn't give up. So far his cultures were strong and successful, but only until he introduced them to a piece of vampire flesh. Then they . . . *changed.* They stopped living, but he couldn't say they died because they, like the vampire, never decomposed. They just ceased to *function.* He leaned back and stretched. Did the answer lie in feeding Deb or was that only another blind turn? It was certainly worth a try.

"No, it's not worth it at all."

Perlman's breath jammed in his throat then released as

he jerked upright. "How did you get in here?" he demanded.

Jo sat daintily on the edge of the doctor's desk. "Do you think Deb's soul is worth the price of your curiosity?" The girl's face had a strange glow in the growing northern light as she smiled sadly. "You've heard of Pandora's box, I assume."

Bill gestured angrily at the piles of papers on his desk and the culture dishes with their failed contents along the countertop. "Well, I'd welcome a different suggestion," he snapped. "Or maybe you'd prefer to explain to my uncomprehending mind just what it is about a vampire's *dead* body that enables it to invisibly manufacture a toxin which nullifies any decomposition bacteria it encounters." He slammed his palm on the desktop. "I'd love to have your input."

"All right," Jo said. Oblivious to his anger, she wandered to the far end of the cultures and peered at the dishes that still contained living cultures. "It won't make any difference to your work if you force Deb to feed." She glanced at him, her stone-gray eyes unreadable. "Except it will destroy her. For eternity." She picked up the nearest petri dish.

"Hey," the physician protested. "Put that down."

"The Bible tells us that bread is the staff of life," Jo commented. She set the dish back on the countertop and looked speculatively at the equipment around them, then pulled a small golden flask from her pocket and held it up for Perlman to see. "But what is flour and yeast without water? No more than a fine white powder—with potential."

Bill frowned. "I don't follow." He had thought that Calie, with her unsettling sense of second sight and quiet, almost desperate passion was the strangest woman he'd ever met; now he realized how naive that assumption had been.

"That's what you have here," Jo said patiently. "Powder, in the form of your germs—"

"Bacteria."

"Bacteria. You just lack the proper ingredient, or *catalyst*, to get it going."

Bill gave an exasperated sigh. "You're not making sense. You don't know anything about bacteria or how they grow. Bacteria require a medium that's conducive for growth and reproduction. A source of carbon, vitamins and salts, oxygen—"

"Exactly," Jo interrupted. "You're growing your bacteria in the wrong medium. Try this instead."

"What is it?"

She gave him a sidelong glance. "Water, of course. From St. Peter's."

"You're kidding." When she didn't answer, he glared at her. "I don't have time to play corny games, young lady. Your belief is touching, but I need results, not faith." He folded his arms. "Maybe you think I'm cruel, but the only way I can see to progress is to feed that woman in the bomb shelter and see what kind of metabolic changes take place."

Jo smiled ruefully and unscrewed the flask's top. "You won't even try it? I thought scientists would try anything."

"It won't work," he insisted. "Not only is it a waste of time, it'll ruin a perfectly good culture. Not enough of those things I mentioned a moment ago are present in simple H_2O. This kind of bacteria use dead organic matter as a food source, not water."

"I realize that," Jo said gently, and for a crazy instant he believed she knew exactly what he was talking about. "All you need is something to get it going."

"Exactly. And water just isn't it."

She turned her back to him and leaned on the counter, looking down at Perlman's cultures. "Well," she said at length, "let's try just one, shall we?" Her slender fingers quickly twisted the top from the closest dish.

"Absolutely not!" Perlman exclaimed. He scrambled up and tried to reach around her. "I'm down to only two pure cultures. If those are contaminated, it'll take a week to be sure I have another pure—*stop that!*"

Too late; she'd already splashed a couple of drops of water into the open dish. "There," she said with satisfaction. "Fifteen minutes, and it'll be ready to give to Deb."

"Damn it, Jo! Now I only have one dish! That means

I can't do anything until I'm sure a pure strain will grow from it!"

"You don't need them anyway," she said. "Look."

"Don't be absurd," he said curtly. "You can't see a saprobe without a microscope." He smacked a closed fist against his forehead. "God, I can't *believe* you did that!"

"Can't see a what?" Jo asked mildly.

Perlman sighed. What good would it do to be angry with this child? "This bacterium is a saprobe," he answered patiently. "An organism that can exist in a low air environment and uses nonliving animal matter as food."

"Ah," Jo said. "That's what these are?" She waved her hand at the dishes. "And the dead animal then——"

"Decomposes." It was a simplified but basically sound explanation.

"What will this do to *living* things?" She picked up the dish to which she'd added water and brought it close to her nose.

"Nothing," Perlman responded. "If it's present at all, it's a symbiotic relationship." Jo looked at him quizzically. "The person would only be a vehicle for movement," he explained. "A protective carrier. Like bats—they carry hydrophobia but don't contract the disease themselves, yet the fleas living in their fur do."

"Ah," Jo said again. She went to the other end of the counter and began unscrewing the tops from his discounted cultures and pouring tiny drops of water into each.

"Jo, those are dead," he said. "Nothing will do those any good." For safety's sake, he hurried to the counter and whisked away the petri dish containing the last pure culture.

"That one's already been done," she commented as she twisted the top back on the flask, then shook it lightly. "Still a little left." She set it on the counter.

"What do you mean, 'already done'?" he challenged. "You never even opened it!"

"Nevertheless." She smiled at him. "Men of science are always so . . ." She touched a finger against her mouth pensively.

"Skeptical?" He held up the second dish and examined

it, then mentally cursed as he realized what he was doing. There was no way it could be contaminated.

Could it?

"Why don't you put this one under your microscope?" She offered him a dish.

"There's nothing to see," he insisted. "The bacteria that were there were absorbed by the vampire skin I added, and most of that dissolved in the daylight when I brought it up here."

"Would the bacteria still be in the stuff that's left?" she asked.

"Of course, but it's dead. It looks like burned paper."

"Will you show me?"

"Look," he said. "These cultures are ruined—"

"You have something more important to do in the next five minutes, Dr. Perlman?"

He pressed his lips together. "Fine." He took the dish from her and made a quick scraping, then pushed the slide under the lens. "Put your eyes here, turn this knob to focus the view."

She obeyed, carefully adjusting the focus, then studying the slide. "I thought you said these bacteria were dead."

"They are."

"Doesn't look that way to me. But then I'm not a doctor." She raised her gaze to him. "Care to see?"

To humor her, Perlman stepped up and peered through the viewer, then gasped. The slide was covered with moving, familiar *Clostridia*, yet each was encased in a sort of thickened, protective plasma membrane, or a sheath of the type found in iron bacteria. "What happened here?" he asked in bewilderment. He fumbled the slide free, then hurriedly prepared another from the newest of the culture dishes. "This is incredible!" He straightened, then picked up her flask, fumbling at the unexpected warmth of the metal. "What's *really* in this?" he demanded. He dropped it back on the counter. "You mean that all I needed was *water* and all this work meant *nothing?*"

"It contains water, Doctor, as I said before, but don't ever think your efforts were wasted. After all, the water's always been there, hasn't it? Without you to make the bread and yeast, it would still be just ... water." She turned to leave and for an instant the sun transformed her hair to a sheet of glowing white. "You can go downstairs and give it to Deb. She's sleeping quite soundly, so it's safe for you to go alone. Don't ..." She hesitated. "Don't let Alex know just yet."

Though he wanted badly to turn and glance at the windows, Perlman could only stare after Jo as she stepped out the door and disappeared down the hall. How *odd*, he thought as he finally turned to the panes of glass that had been the lab's source of daylight for many, many months. How pretty the sun's rays had been as they'd highlighted her hair. Though he knew he should hurry down to the shelter and Deb, it still took a few minutes to pull himself away from the windows.

Everybody knows the sun doesn't shine from the north.

2

●━●●━●●━●●━●

REVELATION 13:7
And it was given unto him to make war. . . .

●━●●━●

"We want everybody ready first thing in the morning," Alex said. "Make sure all your equipment—weapons, flashlight, whatever—is set out tonight. We should walk into Hanley-Dawson no later than eight. There we pick up the torch and the tanks and go on to the Mart."

"What time will we get to the Mart?" asked Elliot. He and the others looked at Alex expectantly.

"Nine o'clock," Alex guessed. "It's not that far." His gaze searched out McDole. "You're sure the torch works?"

"Well," the older man said, "we know it's got pressure. Elliot fiddled with it—"

"—but I really didn't know what I was doing," Elliot finished. "I figured if I kept going I'd probably blow up the place. I never used anything but propane in shop class."

Alex's forehead creased. "We'll find out tomorrow. An outfit like that is bound to have a couple of spare tanks anyway." He looked around. "What else?"

"How long to get the chains off?" McDole asked.

"I can't answer that without knowing what they're made of. My guess would be only a few minutes each."

"And the people won't get burned?" Ira asked.

Alex shook his head. "It's a directed flame. For the sake of speed I'll go through a couple of links away from the skin, and we'll cut the rest off when we get back here."

McDole held up a hand. "Getting them loose may not be the hardest part," he reminded them. "We still don't know how many people are actually there. It could be fifteen or thirty. No one's seen them all, not even"—his gaze flicked to Alex—"Deb. Chances are they're probably weak and sick. They may or may not be able to walk, and they'll probably get frantic when they see us." He laced his fingers on the table. "We don't know what we're getting into here. The guard may be armed and he may fight. Every decision you make will be critical, so be careful and be *sensible*. No heroes—we don't want to hold any memorials next week." They all nodded grimly.

"What if it's still raining?" C.J. asked from the window. "Do we go anyway?"

"No." At Alex's surprised look, McDole thumped a knuckle against the map spread on the table. "It's just too risky. Cold, wet weather will triple the odds that we'll leave a track or imprint somewhere that could be followed, and God knows what it'll do to the travel time."

"And dragging those folks through the rain won't help anything," Ira commented.

"Exactly." McDole sat back. "The object is to get everyone back here alive and safe, and if we have to wait for a dry day, then we wait." He leaned forward again, his expression grave. "We can't leave *anyone* behind, understand? Or we'll have to move both the people here and the ones we rescue."

"Christ," Elliot muttered. "How could we leave anyone anyway?" His mouth was tight. "Imagine being there and watching everyone else escape, knowing you're the only person left to face those creatures. Talk about a nightmare!"

"So we're set?" Alex looked at them, then glanced toward the door. "What's that?"

"Sounds like the doctor." McDole rose and walked to the stairwell, then his eyebrows lifted. "He's mighty excited."

There was a clattering on the stairs and Perlman burst into the room. "We've got it!" he cried. He waved a syringe and McDole flinched away from the swinging needle.

"What?" Alex asked warily.

The physician grabbed his arm and grinned, his eyes wide and wild.

"The way to kill the vampires!"

• • • •

"This is it." Calie and Louise joined the group as Perlman raised the syringe for everybody to see. "Suspended in a glucose solution. It's safe, effective, and I tried it an hour ago. I've actually seen it work."

"What does it do?" Louise asked.

"It makes them decompose, the way a human body does when the person dies," Perlman answered. "The way they should have when *they* died."

"That's great," McDole said doubtfully. "But what do we do now? Ask if they want a shot?"

Perlman chuckled. "Watch." There was a collective gasp as he plunged the syringe into his arm, dispensed its contents, then drew out the needle. From his pocket he pulled a small packet containing an alcohol-soaked piece of gauze and dabbed at the spot. "I just became a passive carrier."

"It's not going to make you sick, is it?" Calie's face was frightened.

"It's not going to make anyone sick—anyone living, that is. To put it simply, it feeds only on dead flesh. In or on a living organism, it stays dormant."

"How can you be sure?" McDole queried. "Don't you need more time to research or something?"

"I'm sure because I know my work," Perlman said. His face was sincere. "Besides, I've already tried it."

Alex started. "You have? How?"

The room went silent.

Finally, the doctor answered. "I gave it to Deb early this morning, Alex. The process has already started."

Alex made a choking sound. "But we—all of us—you never even *asked*—"

"Jo told me to," Perlman said, as though it was all the reason needed. "The credit—and I mean *credit*, not blame—goes to her. She actually . . . I don't know how to describe it. *Made it work*, I suppose. Everything was stalled until she showed up in the lab right after dawn."

"I wonder how she gets in," McDole said absently.

"Who cares?" C.J. came forward. "What matters is that this germ of yours *works*, right, Doc?"

Perlman nodded vigorously and Alex looked sicker than ever.

"How long does it take?" Elliot asked innocently.

"Not very." Perlman took a deep breath; the truth was unavoidable. "At the rate it's going, the process appears almost retroactive. I'd say . . . less than a day." Alex looked stunned and Perlman forced himself to continue, regretting his bold, insensitive announcement. "On some the process may be faster because they haven't—"

Alex bolted from the room.

"Alex!" When McDole started to go after him, Perlman's voice made him pause.

"Let him go," he said. The physician suddenly felt very weary, and *very* guilty. "There's no way to stop him from going to the shelter, and it doesn't matter anyway. Not only is Deb still sleeping, she's considerably weaker than she was last night. He'll be safe."

"Oh," Calie said softly. "She's . . . *dying.*"

Perlman hung his head. "Yes."

"Is she in pain, Bill?" McDole's voice was filled with dread.

Perlman went to the window and stared out at the rain, thinking of how Michigan Avenue had once looked on a gray, wet afternoon like now. Then it had been all lights and shine on the streets; now it was dreary and deserted. "Yes," he said finally.

"God," Louise said in a small voice.

"She never hurt anyone." Calie's words were quiet.

Perlman's eyes fixed on the floor. "No," he agreed. "She never did." It was a cowardly thing to think, but Perlman was glad he wouldn't be at Northwestern when Alex opened the door to the bomb shelter.

Neither Alex nor Deb deserved what he would find.

3

●━●・●━●・●━●

REVELATION 18:9
He shall see the smoke of her burning.

●━●・●━●

Alex was afraid to open the shelter.

He was filled with the dread that came with seeing Deb as a vampire, a creature that preyed on human beings for food, or would have, had she been less strong-willed. But the real truth was that he knew what he would see would tear him apart.

The smell smacked him as soon as he pushed open the door, ugly, thick, like a rotting frog forgotten on the back shelf of a biology-class closet. He fought the gag reflex and won only by pinching his nostrils hard enough to bring tears to his eyes as he breathed through his mouth. His other hand closed around the spotlight and snapped it on. He regretted it instantly.

The light, bright enough to illuminate a room twice the size of the shelter, showed everything in lurid, horrifying detail. Deb was on the floor, twisted atop a blanket Perlman must have given her, curled protectively as though trying to hide beneath the still-luxurious waves of her hair. Part of her face was visible, as were the hands that clutched her knees against her chest. Alex's breath hitched miserably.

Skin slick and swollen with mottled decay, covered with a fine sheen of noxious-smelling slime, she looked like a melting, unformed fetus.

"Oh, Deb," he whispered. She moaned lightly, as though she'd heard him say her name. Her head turned toward him for a moment, then returned to face the wall; the agony Alex saw there was nearly unbearable. He wanted to sink to his knees and scream, pound on the wall, *anything* to get this horrible *hurt* out of him, and even then, how did *she* feel? Had anyone considered that she might be in *pain*?

His fists bunched uselessly as she sighed in her sleep; Alex could have sworn she sounded . . . lonely.

He didn't care about the danger when he joined her on the floor, took her in his arms, and rocked her like a baby.

4

REVELATION 12:2
And she being with child cried . . .
and pained to be delivered.

"It's a boy," Bill Perlman announced. His smile was wide but shadows of exhaustion ringed his eyes.

There was a burst of applause. "That's great!" McDole said heartily. "It's about time we had some good news around here!"

"Wasn't he early?" Calie asked. "Are they all right?"

"Mother and son are fine," Perlman assured her. "He could be a little bigger, but for being a month premature, five pounds is a damned good size."

"Five pounds!" Tala was amazed. "Wow—that's no bigger than a sack of onions!"

"He's fine," Bill repeated. "But since you're all here, I want to let you know what's going to be happening in the future."

"Great," C.J. muttered. "Crystal-ball time." He rolled his eyes despite Calie's severe look.

"We have a new addition, though I can't tell you his name since his mother hasn't decided. She did ask me to immunize the child."

McDole looked puzzled. "Immunize?"

The doctor folded his arms. "Like me, Evelyn and the baby are now carriers of the bacterium that was tested this morning, which I've called V-BAC for lack of imagination."

"Is that really safe?" It was the first time Alex had spoken since he'd returned from Northwestern a couple of hours earlier.

"Completely," Dr. Perlman said. "And desirable. In fact, I recommend that everyone be injected."

C.J. chewed on the inside of his cheek for a moment,

then cleared his throat. "The way I understand it, this bacteria thing isn't going to save us if we're caught by a vampire, so why bother?"

Perlman raised his forefinger. "That's where you're wrong. It *will* save you—in a way. Will it stop an attacker from killing you? No." He looked around the room. "But the vampire that attacks you will become infected and die within twelve to twenty-four hours." He lifted his chin. "As a carrier, you'll already have V-BAC present in your body. It's doubtful you'll last long enough to become one of them, and if you do, you won't be strong enough to attack anyone else. You'll be gone for good by the end of thirty-six hours."

"It'll keep us from becoming vampires ourselves?" asked Ira, his face bright with interest. "Or at least from staying that way?" Perlman nodded.

"I'm all for it." Heads turned at Louise's enthusiastic words. She stood and rolled up her sleeve. "You got the needle? Stick it right here, Doctor." She tapped the inside of her elbow.

"Me too," C.J. said suddenly. "I'll go for it."

McDole looked thoughtful. "And you're positive it won't hurt living humans. Isn't medicine normally tested for years before using it on human beings?"

The doctor nodded again. "Yes, but these aren't normal times, are they? If there'd been any doubt, I might still have tried it on myself, but never on Evelyn and certainly not the baby."

Alex finally looked up from his study of a map of the north Loop. He had returned to the group a half hour earlier only because of the desperate need to free the prisoners in the Mart; until now he'd stubbornly avoided joining the conversation. His clothes smelled of death and the others shifted nervously. "Did you say you took your first shot at the same time you gave one to Deb?"

"Yes, and I think Jo herself somehow . . . *ingested* a dose before that. My second shot was just for demonstration."

"Well," Alex said in a thick voice, "I've had a firsthand view, and the doctor looks a helluva lot better than Deb does." He turned back to the map.

"Wait a minute—does this mean someone has to literally *sacrifice* himself to spread it?" Calie asked with wide eyes.

"Not at all," Perlman responded. "V-BAC is like any common bacteria—it *is* a common bacteria. Spread by touch, airborne, surface contact, anything a carrier touches, spits on, sneezes on, whatever, receives a sizable dose. This bacteria is not only strong and incredibly durable, it consumes food and reproduces at an amazing rate." He grinned self-consciously. "It sounds nasty, but if you people take these shots, then walk around spitting on the sidewalk for a couple of weeks, V-BAC will easily spread throughout the city—especially if we inject it into leftover food and toss the scraps in the subway entrances and sewers for the rats. That'll take care of those things down there." Perlman gave them a pleased smile.

"We could be free of the vampires within a month."

Disintegration

5

REVELATION 9:21
Neither repented they of their murders. . . .

●━●●

"Fucking *liar* anyway!" Rita screeched.

The small mirror shattered as she brought her hands together with a *crack!* then flung the pieces aside. She felt around the long countertop until her fingers found something else—a drawer—and pulled it open. She stared uncomprehendingly at the lengths of stainless steel for a few seconds before her fogged brain told her what they were and where she was. Carving knives . . . of course. She was in one of the deli restaurants on the second floor.

Rita frowned. What was she doing here? No matter; she lifted a ten-inch blade and examined it. For a moment she imagined she saw her reflection dance along its length, just as she could have sworn she'd seen herself in the pocket mirror. If I'd had one of these, she decided, that bitch wouldn't have gotten me. Why hadn't Anyelet listened? Her lips pulled back and she stifled a cry at the pain that shot through her cheek. To show pain was a sign of weakness, and that would never do; anger, though, had always been impossible for her to hide.

Rita tucked the knife into her belt and sidled out of the restaurant while her fingers caressed her face, trailing over the lumpy scar tissue that had formed over the dirt, grease, and gunpowder embedded in the surface, sinking occasionally into a few still-open spots that continuously trickled moisture down her blouse. I'll change clothes, she decided. Then I'll get a phone book and find a plastic surgeon. After all, I run a modeling agency and I have to reflect my clients—it's all so damned *competitive* now. She skittered across the corridor and leapt the last of the steps. That mirror, she told herself, had been

. . . mistaken. Something had been wrong with it, a man-
ufacturing flaw that had caused it to wickedly hide her
reflection. She would stop and get a new one at the drug-
store, one that wouldn't—

She tilted her head at a noise, trying to refocus her
thoughts, then smacked the flat of her palm against her
forehead in impatience, the pain of the blow causing a
low growl in her throat. There *was* no agency, not since
the night she'd crossed paths with that redheaded demon
two years ago in Mother's, a Rush Street area bar. A half-
dozen drinks and Rita had left with the seductive, deadly
woman, taking the first steps of her one-way trip to hell.
And was that Anyelet now? She had a few things to say
to that slut, all right, and she'd start with a pointed re-
minder of her suggestion about weapons. Someone
coughed and Rita grimaced; not Anyelet at all, but
Siebold, lumbering around like an overweight, overstuffed penguin. Another disgusting bodily sound as he
stepped out of a side hall, then froze. He turned to hurry
away.

"Wait!" she commanded. He stopped, flinching when
she circled him as he stared at his dirty shoes. "What are
you doing here?" she demanded. "Spying on me? Did
Anyelet tell you to?"

"No," Siebold said quickly. "I was just g-going up to
look in on the people, that's all."

"Yeah," she sneered. "Gonna give some lucky lady the
pleasure of your company tonight, huh?" Once so immac-
ulate, Rita flicked a filthy fingernail beneath his chin.
"And what's this? Big man with a little gun?" She
laughed nastily as she poked at a small semiautomatic in
the front of his belt. Howard said nothing, but an idea
suddenly sparked in Rita's mind. She grabbed his shoulders and twisted him to face her. "Look at me. I said *look
at me!* Tell me what I look like."

He glanced hastily at her face and back down again.
"You look . . . all right."

Rita stopped, uncertain, then relaxed her grip and
patted his arm. "Come on . . . Howard. You don't have to
be afraid. I've always admired honesty in a person—you
know how I always say what's on *my* mind. I respect that

in another person. And, of course, I'm not having much luck trying to use a mirror. Help me out."

"You look fine, really," he insisted.

"Don't *lie* to me!" she screamed suddenly. She pushed her face close to his and he squeezed his eyes tightly shut. "If you don't open your eyes and tell me the truth, you fat, fucking worm, I'll rip them out with my fingernails!"

"All *right!*" he yelled. He scrambled backward, her insult making the words spill recklessly from his mouth. "It looks pretty bad, okay? Like ground meat!" Sweat beaded on his forehead then streamed to his collar, and he fumbled the Uzi out and aimed it threateningly. "But remember you told me to be honest! You *told* me to!"

"Yes, I did," Rita said sweetly.

She crossed the space between them in less than a second and buried the knife in his gut. He squealed and squeezed the trigger spastically, the spray of bullets catching Rita across her chest and collarbone but not stopping her. Still, they hurt and she made him pay, cackling at his shrill scream when she twisted the blade and heaved upward, splitting his rib cage from sternum to throat. His blood, thick and red and repulsively plentiful, spurted in a dozen directions but Rita ignored it. She yanked the carving knife free and watched Siebold fall heavily to the floor atop his stupid, pathetic gun, a corpulent, sodden mass.

"Fucking liar."

6

REVELATION 19:18
That ye may eat the flesh of men ...

Bloodsmell.

It hit Anyelet as soon as she entered the main corridor, drew her irresistibly to the far end where a group of her soldiers were jostling each other for a spot on a body sprawled across the floor. Mingling with the smell of fresh blood were other scents, too: grease, dirt, sweat—
Siebold.

"Who did this?" She waded through the cluster, yanking them back from their places by whatever was handy, an arm, a handful of hair, anything. Ron was holding a small Uzi clear of the mess while he suckled heartily on a spot of flesh squeezing through the torn fabric covering one knee; another idiot, Werner, literally had his face buried in the hole of the dead man's chest. She pulled him up and flung him aside with a sound of disgust.

Werner wiped his face on his sleeve, smearing the gore down his arm. "We don't know, Mistress." The others murmured in agreement. "We found him like this." He pointed to the slash that ran from Siebold's neck to his crotch and giggled. "Field-dressed!"

Anyelet scowled and dismissed them. "Go back to your feast." They fell hungrily on the body and she moved away. Rita? Probably; it was a waste of a good breeder, though the man had been an annoying shit and caused more grief than he was worth. Now there was only one other person who could be trusted to guard the humans during the day.

"Good evening, Stephen." Anyelet set a candle next to the door.

He said nothing, merely watched her watch him.

"Where's Siebold?" he asked at last. "He comes around for his final check at dusk."

"Howard is . . . indisposed." She glided to his side and touched his cheek; he jerked away. "Why do you fight?" she asked when he shut his eyes. He stood there, shoulders rigid as he waited. She smiled slyly and dropped her hand. "Howard won't be coming back."

Stephen's face lifted. "What?"

"Would you like to *do* some of the good you're always whining about?" she continued. "You could care for these people during the day." She faced him. "I want you to take his place."

Stephen's face went scarlet. "Don't fool yourself, Anyelet. I may whore myself for you, but I'll never be your in-house rapist."

"Of course not," she said easily. "I'm just offering you a limited type of freedom." His eyebrows raised and she nodded. "Come and go as you please during the day, darling. No chains. I'll trust you to return each night."

"Why?" he asked suspiciously. "Why should I?"

She shrugged. "If you don't, you'll spend the rest of your life knowing you abandoned these people when you could have helped them. No one else stands between them and us." Her eyes glittered wildly in the candleflame. "It makes no difference to me. One of my soldiers can easily handle this chore. Of course, it's not likely we'll be as receptive to their needs." She ran her tongue over sharp, white teeth. "Howard made two of the women here pregnant, you know." Stephen's expression filled with horror and Anyelet chuckled. "We were quite pleased." She stepped to the door and picked up the candle. "I thought your care would be better, but if you'd rather not—"

"Wait! I—I'll do it—on one condition."

Anyelet glowered at him. "*I* make the rules, Stephen. Be very careful when you tell me your 'condition.' "

He stared at the floor. "I just want you to stop . . . *touching* me. Like you do."

She laughed heartily. "As you wish. I've grown bored with you anyway." She stepped out the door, then turned and gave him a wry smile. "Interesting," she said, "I didn't think you'd be strong enough to ever say that."

• • •

Well, Anyelet thought, Stephen won't be much good at defending the cache of food, but at least he'll take better care of them. Short of cutting off their feet, she didn't believe he was resourceful enough to free them. There was still the problem of breeding, but it was a minor one; cut off from her, Stephen would probably end up as horny as Howard, though not so brutal. Besides, once he cleaned those people up, it would be easy to entice one of the males with a less-than-savory mind into indulging. It always was.

She wandered thoughtfully downstairs and stared at Howard's body, drained and pasty-faced in death, his skin pocked with bite marks. She should tell someone to get it out of here and dump it in the river, then gather a group to search a few of the nearby buildings. That odd-looking State of Illinois Center was a possibility, or the courthouse. She shrugged; except for an occasional moan from the third floor, the Mart was silent. Rita and Vic had disappeared, and the cluster of soldiers who'd glutted themselves on Howard's blood were probably sprawled sluggishly in their rooms. She turned and went back to the main lobby, her thoughts of the other night returning. This so-called "army" was useless—lazy, disorganized, and above all, disobedient, a group of sad and ignorant stragglers. She would grant them this one last night of indolence, but that was all. Then there would be a change for the better, or she would destroy them all and start over.

Perhaps her first new companion would be the holy man himself.

7

REVELATION 2:11
She that overcometh shall not be hurt of the second death.

"Please ... don't."

Alex stepped inside the door of the bomb shelter.

"You were here while I was sleeping," Deb whispered. "I felt you."

"Yes." He took another small step.

"Why did you come back?" Her voice was thick and bubbly, her lungs clotted with liquid.

"I ..." He couldn't answer.

She laughed sadly. "You came to say good-bye."

He didn't turn on the spotlight this time. Instead he set his flashlight on the bottom step outside, giving only enough illumination to make out her location. He wanted to remember her as she had been, not as this terrible smell proved she was now. He sucked a breath in through his mouth and moved closer; her eyes, watery and red, were the only thing that showed clearly. He didn't know what to say.

"It hurts, Alex," she whimpered suddenly. "I didn't expect it to hurt this much."

"Oh, sweetheart." Before she could protest, he was kneeling at her side. "I'm so sorry."

"It's a success, right?" Every attempt to speak was a gurgling, fluid-filled moan. "You guys'll be all right now?"

"Yes." He put his arms around her shoulders and pulled her onto his lap, his heart kicking when her skin shifted sickeningly under his hand. Everything about her was wet and bloated; what had they done to his beautiful onetime lover?

"I didn't want you to come. I wanted you to remember ... you know."

He surrendered to the tears filling his eyes. "I do," he assured her. His throat was trying to lock up on him. "And I always will." It was true; his mind's eye showed him a reelful of shots: Deb when he'd first met her, holding him at gunpoint with her face frightened and determined; Deb sitting across from him at Marshall Field's, laughing as she ate pickled eggs; Deb yet again, her expression glowing with passion as their bodies entwined in the moonlight. "I love you," he said hoarsely.

"I love you too," she said gently. She gazed up at him and he felt his heart crack as the reddish lights in her eyes visibly dimmed. All traces of the hungry thing that had tried so hard to claim her had fled. Her mouth was a darker slash against the blotched gray shadows of her face.

"Bury me in the sun, Alex," she said clearly.

And she was gone.

Alex hung his head and sobbed.

8

REVELATION 13:15
And cause that as many as would
not worship the beast should be killed.

"Oh, no," Vic said brokenly.

The smell of death had brought him in. The hope he'd experienced when he'd found Howard's body in the hallway faded as he realized that the fat man's corpse was too fresh to give out the scent of decay he was picking up. Since Hugh only entered the building when someone else was inside, last night Vic had barely glanced at the lobby before taking his search outside. Had his father, skull and torso crushed beyond repair, been stuffed so carelessly between these display cases even then? He raised his head wearily and his gaze found Anyelet, lounging on a couch a dozen yards away, her expression smug.

He crossed the distance and stood over her. "He was just an old man," he said furiously. "He was my *father*."

"He was your punishment," Anyelet pointed out. "The next time, you will be loyal to me before you indulge in foolish sympathies." She rose, her eyes flashing. "You belong to me, Vic. I *made* you."

"What is that?" he spat. "Some kind of big deal? I belong to *myself*. You're nothing but a cold, vicious bitch who kills for the fun of it!"

She threw back her head and laughed loudly. "I never claimed otherwise! You're the one harboring grand delusions of humanity! You're a *vampire*—start acting like one!"

Vic turned his back. "I should kill you," he said quietly.

"*What!*" Her mouth fell open and she jerked him around to face her. "How *dare* you—"

He punched her, watching as though he were someone

else as the knuckles of his fist met her jaw with all of his
strength. Anyelet hurtled through the air, brightly colored clothes making her look absurdly like a tossed
beach ball. She crashed against the far wall at shoulder
height, then slid down and sat there, stunned and stutter-
ing.

"She-bitch."

He turned and walked out, his stride growing to a full
run by the end of the hall. When her howl of rage clamored through the building, he was on the tenth floor and
still climbing, headed for a secret storage room in which
to hide and lick his wounds.

"I want him killed," Anyelet said fiercely.

She glared at the vampires shuffling their feet nervously. How pathetic! Even insane, Rita was a more effective hunter than these soft fools, though now she
tended to forget things from one moment to the next.
Perhaps there was hope for Gabriel and Werner, but Ron
and Jasper were just standing there like automated man-
nequins waiting for someone to throw the ON switch. Two
weeks ago only Rita, Gabriel, and Gregory would have
been enough to complete this task.

Werner dug his fingers deep into the filthy hair that
hung to his collarbone. "I dunno," he began, "Vic's awfully big—"

"*I don't CARE!*" she screamed. "You just do what I tell
you!" She snatched the nearest vampire by the collar, and
the middle-aged woman with teased blond curls made a
mewling noise as Anyelet shook her. "What is going on
here?" she bellowed. "Do I have to kill one of you to
prove that *I MEAN WHAT I SAY?*" She pitched the
woman aside.

"We'll find him, Mistress. Don't worry." Jasper shot the
sprawled woman a glance and everyone mumbled their
agreement.

"Good," Anyelet snapped. "Now move it. And don't
stop looking until you find him or the sun comes up."

They scurried from the room and in a moment she was
alone again, still boiling inside from Vic's blow. She
closed her eyes, then opened them again. Rebuilding was

impossible, and she'd finally come to accept that. Not only were the humans depleted nearly to extinction, her so-called children had become so numerous that they had lost that fine sense of obedience that was so critical. Unlike them, she had lived on the blood of rats and wild animals successfully for centuries, and could easily do so again—and *not* end up like those bedamned nuisances in the subways. Hiding from the sun and from mankind was a simple thing when she could slip deep into the earth and lower her metabolism for literally centuries at a time. There were things to attend to first, though: Rita and the others could not be left to destroy what was left of mankind, if only to ensure a land of plenty when she reemerged.

And, of course, there was Vic. She rubbed her jaw absently, feeling along the line of bone to where the ridges were almost healed. Her eyes darkened; had his aim been six inches higher, she might be lying dead next to Hugh. A few feet away amid the lobby's ruined furniture and cracked plaster, the old man's body rotted silently on the floor.

Her eyes narrowed to slits as she headed for the sub-basements to join the search. It was time to start cleaning house.

VII

March 29

Liberation

1

●━●━◠●━◠●━◠●

●━●━●

"Why was Calie acting so strange?" C.J. asked. He and
Louise were posted at the door to the Hanley-Dawson
body shop; he could hear Alex and the others talking inside. LaSalle Street gleamed with moisture, but the
warm sun was already spreading dry patches on the
pavement.

"I don't think she likes me," Louise commented. "She's
acted funny ever since we met."

"Calie acts funny anyway." C.J. poked his head inside.
"What's the holdup?" he yelled. "We should be halfway
there!"

Perlman came out of a darkened doorway grasping a
flashlight. "We can't find another tank of oxygen," he
complained as he wiped a grimy hand across his nose.
"Alex says the one on the cart is nearly empty and it
might not be enough."

"How do you know there *is* another one?" Louise
asked.

Perlman shrugged. "Alex says there should be. He—"

"I found it!" came a muffled voice from downstairs.
Perlman hurried back down and in a few more minutes
the men lugged a heavy cart and tanks onto the main
floor.

"I never heard of such a thing," Alex grumbled. His
eyes were swollen and ringed with purple shadows.
"Why the hell would they put the extra setup in the
basement? It should've been in the body shop."

Ira hustled into the room with Kyle, a redheaded man
in his late forties. "I can't find any spare parts," he told

Alex. "They're probably locked up in someone's tool-box."

"I thought you just needed the oxygen tank," C.J. said. "That's the big one, isn't it?"

"Yeah, but the acetylene tank on this one is in better shape," Alex pointed out. "We're better off using the newer equipment." He looked peeved. "It wouldn't hurt to have a spare piece or two, though. I could take the extra one apart. . . ." He shook his head. "Never mind. We don't have the time."

Elliot pushed experimentally on one of the cart's wheels. "This thing's a wreck. We'll be lucky if it doesn't fall apart."

"The other one's worse," McDole said. "Stuff's been beat to hell and it's rusted besides."

"We'll make do." Alex shoved the Winchester awkwardly into his belt and grabbed the cart's handles. "Let's just go. We're an hour behind already."

"I don't understand why you had to come." C.J. pushed his hand into the pocket of his jeans. "We could've handled this."

"I never said you couldn't," Louise said. "But Dr. Perlman agreed that having a woman there is going to help calm these people if they start to freak out. You guys are just too . . . I don't know. Efficient, maybe. All business and no softness."

He snorted. "There'll be time for that tomorrow." There was a sharp metallic clatter behind them and someone cussed. The teenagers halted and turned back. "What's wrong?" C.J. asked.

"One of the wheels snapped off." Elliot grimaced as he inspected the left side. "Damn, I *knew* this would happen. Can we carry it?"

"We'll have to." Alex was already sweating from dragging the heavy cart along the bumpy street. He gave Elliot a meaningful look as the blond man started to grab a tank. "Don't try it; we don't need a drip trail from one of those bites. C.J., take the other end of this oxygen tank; Buddy, you and Ed take the acetylene. And look out—these suckers are *heavy*."

C.J. handed the bow to Louise, then grunted as he hefted the end of the oxygen tank. "Oh, man," he groaned as they began a slow trek toward Wells Street. After a block, he had to ask. "How much farther do we have to go?"

"Too far," Ed, a thinner man in his forties, panted.

"It'd be easier if these things had handles. There's nothing to hold on to. Let's rest," McDole gasped. He and Ed lowered the acetylene tank to the ground and McDole sighed. "Sorry, guys."

"Doesn't matter," Alex said. "We needed a break anyway. These tanks are bastards—all that concentrated weight."

Despite his complaints, C.J. didn't even look winded as he squinted at his watch. "Are we going to be able to pull this off?"

"It's still early," Louise protested.

"At this speed we won't get there before noon," C.J. pointed out.

"That's still enough time," Alex said as he let out a slow breath. "Cutting the chains should go quick. It's getting back to Water Tower that worries me."

"As long as they can walk, we'll be all right," Perlman interrupted. "To be safe, I'd say we need at least two hours to get them from building to building."

Alex scowled. "You're really trimming down my time. If there's more than ten or fifteen, or if something goes wrong . . ."

Perlman spread his hands. "I'm just trying to make a safe estimate, that's all. Better to say we need more and have time left over than to run out."

"All right." McDole squinted and grasped his end of the tank, looking relieved when Perlman took a position in the middle. "Let's go, folks."

"Jesus," C.J. hissed as he and Alex edged through the doors and peered into the dimness of the Mart's main hallway. "What's that smell?"

"Rotting meat," Perlman answered softly from behind him. "Someone dead."

Alex inched along the wall for a few feet, then waved

them in. "Clear so far—oh, *God*." He looked pained as the others filed in. "Here's the smell."

"Wasn't this the guard?" C.J. asked, wrinkling his nose. "You think no one's watching them now?"

McDole studied the remains of the man on the floor. "Yeah, this is him," he said in a low tone. "But I wouldn't count on there being no one else up there." He glanced at them. "Don't get reckless."

"Let's go," Alex said. "Which way?"

"Third floor in the back," said Frank, a black man nearly McDole's age. He nodded toward the dead man. "That's where I've been seeing this guy move past the windows." His dark eyes were hooded and angry. "Seen him do a lot of other things, too." He cleared his throat gently, then spit a glob of saliva onto the corpse as quietly as possible. The others stared at him and he lifted his chin in defiance. "I didn't do that for you, Dr. Perlman. I did it for those poor people upstairs."

"Let's go," Alex said again. "We're wasting time down here. Kyle, you know where you're going?" Kyle nodded. "Then lead the way."

2

●━●◦●━●◦●━●◦●━●

REVELATION 22:5
For the Lord God giveth them light. . . .

●━●◦●━●

"I'm *sorry*," Stephen said again. The woman just stared at him, her face dirty and blank. "You have to understand," he pleaded. "There *aren't* any keys. She throws them away."

"Then kill us and get it over with, damn you!" a man yelled from the next room. He banged on the wall furiously.

Stephen clapped his hands over his ears, squeezing his skull. God, how he wanted to free them! He'd thought he could help them stay warmer and feed them better, let the women start healing now that Howard was gone. But he had been so terribly wrong. They talked to him like they'd never talked to Howard, and asked things of him that he just couldn't do. He would free them in an instant if he could. Other than that . . .

He was not a murderer.

"Please," he offered the pale woman a cup of hot chicken soup made from supplies he'd found stacked in an empty cubicle. "It'll make you feel better." But she just sat, staring at the skirt and jacket he'd given her instead of putting them on. He was afraid to try and dress her, afraid she would think he was Howard all over again. "You should put those on," he prompted, "so you can be warm." Still, she just . . . sat.

He sighed and went on to the next, and the next, and the one after that. The response was the same: people so numbed to abuse and the cold that they were unable to respond to what little help he so desperately tried to give. One young man grabbed him and shook him, then released him in disgust; another threw the hot soup in his face and told him he was no better than Siebold.

When the brown-haired man and the kid with the bow stepped out of the stairwell, Stephen had slipped into a confused, mumbling prayer.

And he truly believed God had finally heard him.

3

●━●━●━●━●

REVELATION 16:1
Go your ways, and pour out the vials of the wrath of God
upon the earth.

━●━●━

"This guy's brain is oatmeal," C.J. said. "Look at him."
The man still sat on the floor and muttered about God
and the hellbeasts that ruled the earth.

"Forget him," Alex said shortly. "Look at this." He was
standing at the door to the first of a long row of tiny offices; inside, a teenage girl gawked at him and struggled
frantically to wrap herself in a robe that still bore manu-
facturer's tags.

"It's all right, miss," McDole said in a soothing voice.
"We've come to get you out of here." His words simply
didn't register. "I said, we've come to get you out of
here!" he repeated loudly.

The hallway *erupted* with sound. The startled group of
rescuers rushed from room to room, trying to calm the
frenzied people as cries of "Please!" and "Help!" mingled
with sobs and other entreaties, and as they finally quieted, the group realized just how poorly the prisoners
had been treated. Most suffered from ongoing exposure
and shivered constantly; no doubt more than a few were
in the early stages of pneumonia, and almost all of them
had muscle and tissue damage from the chains tightly
encircling their ankles. They were malnourished and
weak, and Perlman was infuriated when he discovered
how badly some of the women had been beaten. When
he reached a cubicle containing an obviously pregnant
woman, he whirled and strode back to the man on the
floor. "Why is that pregnant woman tied?" he demanded.
When he received no answer, he raised the man's eyelid
with his thumb, released it, then slapped the man
sharply. "Snap out of it! We need answers *now*!"

Surprisingly, the fellow did try. "She—" He frowned, as though it was difficult to concentrate. "She doesn't want the baby," he finished at last.

Perlman glowered at him. "Why not?"

The man blinked and realized they were all staring at him. "Because of Howard," he explained. "It's his."

"Who's Howard?" Alex asked.

"It must be the dead man downstairs," Frank said. "He made it a daily habit to . . . have relations with the women."

"He *raped* them?" Perlman was so enraged his face was turning crimson.

"He called it breeding," the white-faced man told them. He struggled to his feet and gazed blearily down the hall. "They aren't doing so good."

McDole put his hand on the man's arm. "What's your name, son?"

"Stephen. I'm a . . ." His words faded away.

"What?" Elliot prompted.

Stephen's eyes fogged. "I . . . don't know. I can't remember."

Alex clapped his hands briskly and everyone turned their attention to him. His face was determined. "Let's get these people the hell out!"

"You have to go *faster*!"

Alex pushed Stephen away. "Stop it! I don't have time to listen to you!" he snapped.

"Stephen," Perlman said from behind the emaciated young man, "can you help over here?" Stephen hurried to Perlman's side and began helping with a woman whose expression was dazed as they pulled a heavy sweater over her head, then pushed her feet into a pair of sneakers. Stephen had been foraging haphazardly in the wholesale outlets on the higher floors, running up and down with armloads of mixed-up clothes and shoes. A good thing— none of the rescuers had even considered there wouldn't be clothing available for these people to wear. At the far end of the hallway, Louise was sitting with the pregnant woman and rambling on in a calm voice, talking about how nice it would be for them all to walk around free in the sun again. Stephen hadn't been lying; when the doctor had tried to untie her, she'd gone into a rage and started screaming at him to perform an abortion immediately. He finally had to sedate her and leave her bound; it was a good bit of foresight that he'd thought to bring several Tel-E-Ject syringes of diazepam along with the syringes of V-BAC. Injecting everyone, including Stephen, had been quick and silent; most just sat there and accepted the shot. It was unnerving.

"Doctor—" Stephen tugged on Perlman's sleeve. "Don't you know what time it is? There're five more to go."

"We *know*, Stephen," McDole answered as he hurried by, pulling a man and two women toward the stairs. "We're going as fast as we can. There're more people than we expected and the chains are tougher."

"Go *faster*," Stephen repeated. His face was starting to show a fine edge of panic.

A few doors away the loud hiss that had backgrounded their conversations over the last several hours stopped. "We're ready!" Alex called. A scraggy-looking man stumbled out and squinted, then grinned and yanked on a baggy pair of jeans. "Four now," he croaked. "I'm Nathan. What can I do to help?" He hastily pulled a sweatshirt over his head and shoved sockless feet into a too-large pair of Nikes.

"See if you can find someone who's strong enough to pair off with you and take the pregnant woman out," Perlman suggested. "She might not be able to walk. I had to drug her pretty heavily." Farther down the hall, the hiss of the torch started again.

Nathan raised a finger. "We'll only have to carry the lady downstairs," he said. "Then we'll grab a cart from Walgreen's and push her the rest of the way if we have to."

"Great idea." Perlman pointed to the woman struggling to her feet. "Can you take her, too?"

Nathan nodded. "She'll come around. How many more?"

McDole began counting on his fingers. "Still four, including her." He tilted his head toward the sedated wom-

an's cubicle. "Think she's calm enough for Alex to go in
yet?"

"Sure," Perlman said. "But we'll go with you, just in
case."

"Once she's loose, that'll make three left," McDole said
with satisfaction.

"Free!" Alex yelled. A sallow-faced young man tripped
out of a room, then fell to his knees.

Perlman ran to his side, then clucked worriedly. "This
guy's in pretty bad shape, Buddy. I don't think we should
wait any longer for the ones that are ready to leave."

"Hey, Alex!" Buddy yelled.

"What?" Alex and Elliot paused in the midst of dragging the tanks on to the next room.

"The far end." McDole waved his finger. "The pregnant
one. It's getting late."

"I *know* that, damn it!" They spun the tanks awkwardly, then hauled them to the far office as the doctor
and Nathan hurried down. Alex fired the torch again, filling the air with a blast of light and heat as he pulled his
welding goggles over his eyes. "Look the other way!" he
called over the torch's noise.

Stephen was doing another check, his face wild.
"There's two more." His fingers twisted around themselves. "A man and a woman."

"It's okay," McDole assured him. "We've got plenty of
time."

"Less than an hour!" Stephen cried. "And some of the
stronger ones wake up early!"

"We'll be fine," McDole repeated, though suddenly
he wasn't so sure. Would they really start moving before
the sun completely set? He eyed the long hallway, noting the darkening shadows forming in the windowless inner cubicles.

C.J. looked up from his guardpost at the stairwell. "We
gotta get going, man." He peered nervously down the
stairs. "At least get 'em out of this dark building. It'll be
a lot lighter outside."

All three jumped at the sound of shouting and McDole
ran to join Alex and Nathan in the last office. Louise was
backing out of the room. "She bit me," she said angrily.

"What's the matter with her, anyway?" In spite of the sedative, the freed woman was kicking at Perlman.

Alex reached around the struggling duo and twisted the torch off at the tanks, then slid his hands under the woman's shoulders and lifted her bodily from the floor. "Stop it!" he yelled, his nose inches from her own. "If you hold us up any longer, you'll get us all killed! Is that what you want?"

"I don't want to have that monster's child!" she cried. Tears were streaming down her face. "I don't—"

"We'll worry about that later, all right?" Nathan grabbed her chin and forced her head to stop its jerking. "Right now, let's just get out of here *alive*. Now come *on!*"

"You've got to hurry!" In the hallway, Stephen's voice was almost a scream.

Alex and McDole lugged the tanks into the hallway and the younger man's eyes flicked warily to the fading light. He turned to Elliot and Nathan. "Get the ones downstairs and go. McDole and I'll follow with these last two."

Elliot looked skeptical. "I don't know—"

"Just *go*. There's no time to argue!" He gave the blond-haired man a quick push. "The less people who have to run, the better!"

"Go ahead, man." C.J. pulled on Elliot's arm and guided him to where Nathan, the pregnant woman, and four others waited. "Kyle and Frank left already, and these folks will need someone to show them where to go. You're elected."

"What about you guys?" Elliot demanded

"We're armed," C.J. reminded him. His gaze stopped on Louise. "But take her with you."

"Forget it," Louise said. "I'm staying right here."

"Listen—" C.J. began.

"Don't tell me what to do, hotshot." Her tone clearly said *stubborn*. "I make my own decisions." C.J. closed his mouth.

"All right," Elliot said. "We're taking off. But you guys ... *Jesus*." His eyes were wide. "Be careful, okay?" He turned to the former prisoners. "Let's go, folks."

As they hurried past, Stephen hovered around the torch like a panicked moth. "Come on, come on!" He looked ready to vomit. "They'll be coming any time!"

Alex's forehead glittered with sweat. "The sun won't set for another forty-five minutes," he said.

"It doesn't matter!" Stephen insisted. "This building is so dark that once it drops below the skyscrapers on the west, they're already starting to wake up. They'll get up, but they just won't go outside!"

"Christ," Alex muttered. "Buddy, help me get this thing over there. How many are left?"

"Only two," Louise told him. "A man and a woman. They look like they're in okay shape."

"That's something—Stephen, will you get out of the way!" He gave a hard pull on the acetylene tank and jostled it close to an anxious woman already dressed in an oversized sweatshirt and denim skirt. "Buddy, get this guy outta here, will—

"Oh, *damn it! OH, SHIT!* I can't believe I *did* that!"

"What's the matter, Alex? For God's sake, *what's wrong!*"

The dark-haired man was frantically twisting a T-shaped handle on the tank of oxygen and glaring at the pressure gauge. He hissed as his fingers fumbled at it, then dropped helplessly to his sides. "We're *fucked.*" He looked dazed. "I didn't back off the pressure. I blew the diaphragm in the regulator."

"You what?" Louise asked. Her face was ashen. "Can't you fix it?"

Alex shook his head, spun, and pounded a fist against the wall. "What a stupid, *stupid* thing to do!"

"Can you bypass it?" McDole suggested anxiously.

"I wouldn't get enough oxygen to make the flame hot enough. It wouldn't *cut.*" He buried his fingers in his hair as the chained woman, her arms and face mottled with ugly bruises, moaned softly. "It's useless. We've got to find another way."

"I've got bolt cutters," C.J. said. He produced a small but new tool from his jacket and handed it to McDole. "Brought for an emergency."

"Let's see those." Alex snatched them from C.J. and

bent to the chain. As with all the others, the end of the chain was padlocked to an old-fashioned radiator as immovable as a table-sized block of lead. "This is hardened steel. I don't think these are going to do it," he said grimly as he fought to make the edges meet through the metal link. The muscles in his arms swelled; there was a loud *SNAP!* and he blinked, then his face twisted as he held up the busted pieces of the cutters. "Too small to handle it."

"*Go,*" the woman said suddenly. She squeezed Alex's wrist. "Come back tomorrow or something."

"You can't do that!" Stephen wailed from behind them. "Don't you see? Anyelet will kill her and the other one, too! You *have* to take them with you!"

"C.J., guard those steps," McDole commanded. He looked at Alex and Stephen, then motioned for Louise. "Everybody grab the chain," he said grimly. "Our only chance is to pull this radiator right out of the floor."

4

Vic sat up and tried to shake the nightfog from his brain. A babble of voices drifted through the pipes and the thick old walls, barely registering in his sensitive ears. Anyelet and the others wouldn't be awake yet; better-fed than Vic, they fell more deeply into nightsleep and stretched it out, knowing that awakening would bring the constant nag of The Hunger. He was always the first to rise, and tonight the chorus of voices and the stench of Howard's room, where he'd decided to hide, forced him awake while the sun was still sinking.

The noise grew and realization hit him. Humans— louder, more rushed than they should have been. He eased into the hallway and stood indecisively. He should flee; Anyelet had surely given orders to kill him, and as strong as he was, Vic would never survive an attack by more than three of his own kind.

But all that noise . . .

Someone was downstairs trying to free the people Anyelet had kept prisoner for so long. The others would sleep for only a little longer; as it had Vic, the noise would tease even the laziest vampires early from their nightsleep.

But he had a few minutes' jump on them and his mouth stretched in a dark grin. Running with the gangs of his youth had taught him that revenge could be a never-ending game.

Trade-Offs

5

●━●·●━●·●━●·●━●

REVELATION 22:9
For I am thy fellow-servant. . . .

REVELATION 16:4
And the third angel poured out his vial upon the rivers
and fountains of waters; and they became blood.

●━●·●━●

"Oh God, oh God!" Stephen was crying and babbling, his
frail hands little help as the others pulled savagely at the
chain where it looped through the radiator.

"Shut up!" Alex hissed. "At least try to be quiet!"

The woman yanked frantically on McDole's sleeve.
"Get out while you still can! It doesn't matter about us—
for Christ's sake, just run!"

"One more try," McDole said stubbornly. "One, two,
three, *heave!*"

"Damn it!" Alex rattled the chain in fury. "Why can't
we—"

The woman caught sight of something over their
shoulders and gasped as Alex whirled and raised his fists
instinctively and McDole cried out in surprise. Alex had
an instant to realize how foolish hand-to-hand would be
against the huge creature that faced him, then the
muscle-covered vampire grabbed both him and McDole
and tossed them aside. Louise bared her teeth and drew
a black pistol from her jacket, planting herself between
the cowering woman and the vampire. She raised the
gun and cocked it, then yelped at the stinging pain in her
fingers; he'd yanked the weapon from her hand so
quickly she hadn't even seen him move.

"Hey, you son of a bitch!"

The creature spun and snarled as Alex primed the
Winchester and fired from only six feet away. The slug
opened a crater in the vampire's right bicep and he bel-

lowed and tackled the dark-haired man, leaping the distance in the space of a breath. Louise screamed as Alex took a vicious crack in the face and dropped the gun; before McDole could react, Deb's Winchester was in the vampire's hands.

"Get back," he growled, and swung the barrel at McDole. "Farther, damn it!" He glowered at the two men, then motioned at Louise. Thin reddish fluid dribbled from the hole in his arm. "Get out of the way." When she refused to move, he grimaced, snatched her arm, and pushed her behind him, sending her stumbling into the arms of the two men edging up from the rear. Alex sprawled on the floor and lost his grip on the machete he'd pulled from his belt; it went skittering out of reach as McDole landed heavily on one hip and gasped. C.J. pounded toward them from far down the hallway.

"Vic," Stephen entreated. He held his hands out. "Please—"

The former bodybuilder ignored Stephen and hefted the woman to her feet, then grasped the chain a foot away from her ankle and literally *tore* it apart. He shoved the terrified woman into Stephen's outstretched arms and streaked into the next cubicle as Alex gained his bearings and dived for the machete, then dropped it again when the vampire hauled the final prisoner from his room and threw him at Alex and McDole.

"Get the hell out of here," he hissed. "Before Anyelet—uh!" His face slackened for a second, then his eyes widened and he grinned. He sank to his knees and pitched forward.

"Vic!" Stephen cried. He ran to the vampire's side and struggled to turn him over, face filled with dismay at the sight of C.J.'s arrow buried so deeply in Vic's back that it protruded through the front of his chest. Alex helped roll him on one side, hoping frantically that this unexpected ally would survive, but Vic raised a hand and waved them toward the open stairwell door behind them.

"Go on," he rasped. "I unlocked it." Alex had a flash memory of how horrible Deb's voice had sounded just before her death; this man's was exactly the same. The vampire sucked in air and coughed; a gout of black-red heartblood gushed down the front of his white polo shirt. He looked down at it and smiled. "Good," he said in that awful death rattle. "I hated being like this." His head lowered to the floor and he was still.

McDole pulled the woman to her feet and yanked on Alex's arm. "Let's get out of here," he said urgently. "There's no telling how many more are coming. What the hell are you doing now?"

Perlman was yanking a syringe from his pocket. "Leaving them a present." He ripped off the wrapping and squirted its contents onto the vampire's chest. "Done— let's go."

"Oh, man," C.J. said. He crouched, looking toward the main staircase unhappily.

"We are in some *serious* shit now."

6

REVELATION 20:13
And Death and Hell delivered up the dead which were in
them.

C.J.'s bow found its second kill of the day.

The vampire, a young, clean-cut man who might have
been a store clerk in his former life, gave a loud gurgle
as black, oily fluid spewed from his mouth and nose onto
his shirt, dripping from the arrow embedded in his chest.
He dropped to his knees and the two following him up
the stairs bared their teeth and ducked behind him, then
yanked his twitching body upright as a shield.

"This way." Stephen jabbed a hand toward the stairway
door Vic had used. "This will—"

Gunfire shattered the plaster above their heads. C.J.
spun against the wall with a yell as buckshot peppered
his right hand and he dropped the bow, then grabbed it
again.

"What the hell has he *got!*" Alex cried. The woman Vic
had freed crawled frantically for the stairwell and Alex
planted a hand on her backside and shoved her forward,
then rolled and brought up Deb's Winchester, pointing it
toward the vampires at the end of the hall.

"Shit!" the vampire holding the gun raged and primed
it again. "I can't control the aim of this bast—"

Alex fired, pumped, and fired again and again, his aim
wild as he pushed himself backward along the floor. One
of the creatures reeled with a howl.

"Motherfucker shot my *ear* off! He almost killed me!"

His companion hurled the semiautomatic shotgun
across the hall in fury. "Cocksucker's empty!"

The other vampire, one side of his head spurting
blood, pulled something from his jacket and tossed it to

his friend as he swiped at the fluid spilling across his eyes. "Try this."

"*Go!*" Stephen screamed. He dragged the woman the rest of the way, then swung the thin man who'd been released last around and tossed him bodily into the stairwell. Louise and C.J., his right hand punctured in a dozen places and nearly useless, stumbled forward and fell into the doorway as submachine gun fire hammered through the air.

"He's got an Uzi!" yelled McDole. "Keep moving!"

Alex pumped the Winchester again, then swore as the chamber came up empty.

"Got you fuckers now!" cackled one of their attackers. The linoleum in front of Alex splintered as bullets streaked across the floor and McDole stumbled into the stairwell. Stephen, his face red with exertion, leapt after them and slammed the metal fire door, throwing them into darkness as the bar-lock slipped smoothly into place. A second later the vampires began pounding on the other side.

"This will lead you to the main floor. Turn left when you come out; you'll have to go all the way down to the Wells Street doors. Don't go right—the Franklin Street doors are locked. Now *go!*"

No one needed further urging. They tripped blindly down the stairs, C.J.'s bow dangling worthlessly from his left hand.

"Come on!" McDole demanded when Stephen made no move to follow. "That door won't hold much longer!"

"I'm not coming."

"*What!*"

"You're wasting time—they won't hurt me anyway. Get *going!*"

McDole was unprepared for the hard shove the man gave him. He stumbled backward, fighting for balance on the dangerously dark stairs. When he regained his footing, the hallway was silent except for the pummeling on the door, and McDole knew he'd never find Stephen. "Last chance!" he said desperately. When there was no answer, he fumbled after the others.

On the first floor, the deepening darkness made the

hall seem endless, made their shambling, terrified steps little more than attempts to run on ice. When they finally flung themselves through the main doors and onto the Wells Street sidewalk, McDole groaned. Only a trickle of daylight still bled along the tops of the buildings, not nearly enough to keep the vampires inside. At the far end of the hall behind them, the stairwell door banged against the wall as the two vampires spilled out. The underweight man Alex had been pulling along whined in fear.

"Take this!" C.J. shoved the bow into Alex's hands. "I can't shoot anyway. You've got enough time to break into the alley entrance of another building. Choose a small one, barricade yourselves in, and the bow will give you even odds."

"Where are you going?" Alex's face went white. "Wait!"

"The only chance you guys have is if something takes their attention away from you."

McDole grabbed his arm. "A decoy—absolutely not!"

"You don't have any choice!" C.J. wrenched his arm free and suddenly waved both hands high above his head. *"Hey, you rotting little fuckers!"* he screamed. *"See if you can catch someone who'll fight back!"* He laughed then, an insulting giggle teetering on hysteria. "Go!" he shouted over his shoulder as he sprinted in the opposite direction. He glanced back to be sure and saw the group finally flee northward and cut between two buildings, then realized Louise was running alongside him. "What are you doing?" he cried. They wrestled in midstreet as he tried to force her to turn back.

"Stop it!" she yelled. "We've got to go *now!*" She sprang ahead, her slender legs pumping frantically over the Wells Street Bridge. He chased after her, shouting angrily.

"It's too late for that, C.J.," she panted. He followed her pointing finger and saw the two vampires burst onto the sidewalk. "And how many more are coming?"

"Oh, *no,*" he hissed as the two nightbeasts turned toward the direction in which McDole's group had fled. He jumped at a sharp *crack!* when Louise pulled the pistol she'd retrieved upstairs and fired it, knowing she couldn't hit anything from this distance. The vampires' heads whipped toward them.

"What's the matter?" Louise taunted loudly. "Afraid you can only catch the *old* ones?"

Even from a block away, the teenagers could see their nasty grins as the vampires surged toward them.

C.J. clutched Louise's hand and they began to run in earnest.

7

REVELATION 13:2
And the beast which I saw was like unto a leopard.

"Come on, Gabriel, speed it up! The shits are getting away!"

"Not likely." Gabriel's bloodless face gleamed in the growing dusk as he smiled widely. Ron grudgingly slowed his pace to stay with him, the discovery of both Jasper's and Vic's bodies and the danger of outcasts enough to keep him from going after the two humans on his own. Besides, catching them too quickly would spoil the fun.

"Shit!" cried Ron as their prey veered east off Wells Street and disappeared around a corner.

Gabriel did increase his pace then, easily passing the heavier vampire and angling wide around the side of a building, then sliding to a halt and peering east. A block down Congress, he saw the two teenagers slip into a doorway and heard the faint tinkle of breaking glass. By now they must be nearing exhaustion; there was no way a human could keep up that kind of speed. Ron joined him and they quickly checked the shadows for outcasts, then eased along the side of the huge Board of Trade Building until they found a door to a small shop where shattered glass speckled the concrete. Inside, he guessed the humans would head straight up.

"They're really getting desperate!" Gabriel laughed.

"That or they think we'll lose them in the building," Ron said.

"Not a chance," Gabriel responded. "Let's go."

The two of them darted into the building like hungry, oversized cats.

8

●■●·●■●·■●·●■●

REVELATION 18:20
For God hath avenged you on her.

REVELATION 15:4
Who shall not fear thee?

●■●·■●

By the time she shot up the stairs and tripped over Jasper's body, Anyelet's vision was red with fury. "What's going on here?" she bellowed. *"Where are my humans?"* She skidded to a stop behind Stephen and reached for him with razored fingernails, then hesitated. Crouched over someone on the floor, he ignored her as he tucked a blanket tenderly around the body. Stephen's loose clothes were dotted with blood, though he didn't seem to be bleeding himself, and instead of the usual moaning and whimpering there was only silence; inside the door of a room a few feet away sat two smelly metal tanks and an abandoned welding helmet. She shoved him angrily. "Who is this?" she demanded. "And what have you done with my humans?" When he didn't answer, Anyelet bent and yanked the blanket away; Vic's peaceful face came into view, his mouth a slack, crimson hole. She tugged harder and the blanket jerked free, splattering her hands with droplets of the heartblood leaking from the lethal chest wound.

"You tell me where those humans went, damn you!" She twisted her fingers in Stephen's baggy shirt and hauled him to his feet. *"TELL ME!"* she shrieked as she shook him furiously. "Tell me or die!"

"Th-he-ey ca-ame an-nd got-t th-hem." Stephen's voice wobbled with his body, but he seemed unconcerned at her rage. "They didn't say where they were going."

She flung him away before her temper made her strangle him outright; he bounced against the wall and tripped, then sat staring at her and rubbing his shoulder. "Why didn't you go with them?" she hissed. Her fists were clenched so hard her nails were opening deep gashes in her own palms.

"Because I wanted to stay with you, of course."

She gaped at him for a moment, then whirled as Rita and four more vampires hurtled into the hall, goggling in amazement. "Get the others," she ordered, "and search for the humans. They'll head north to avoid the river and Lower Wacker."

The middle-aged woman Anyelet had raged at the previous evening looked at her apprehensively. "I think we're it, Mistress. Gabriel and Ron are usually here before us—"

"Then the four of you go!" she shouted impatiently. "*Move!*" They fled down the stairs.

"Stephen, snap out of it." She crouched next to him. "We have a big problem here." He just kept massaging his shoulder and smiling. "All these hungry vampires and no more food," she continued. She touched his arm, then dropped her hand. Why was he still *smiling*?

"You can use me," he suggested. He offered his wrist. "You can *all* use me. Not that it makes any difference anyway."

She stood. "You're not making sense." She resisted the urge to slide into his mind; right now he reminded her of Hugh, or Rita after her face had been blown apart, and she would deal with him later. She spun at a tumble of sound and saw Rita and the others shuffling backward up the stairs, scrambling over each other in their haste to get away from something. Werner, the last one, toppled and fell, then did an awkward crawl away from the stairs until the wall stopped him. He cowered against it, shivering and gawking with bulging eyes at the empty staircase. Rita, the scars on her face a livid purple, snarled at the stairwell and huddled a few feet away.

"*What*—" Anyelet's roar was cut off in midsyllable.

A white-haired girl stepped from the shadows.

The taste of fear, so unfamiliar, was like acid in Anyelet's mouth. To her shame, she found herself also retreating from the girl, and she forced her feet to stop their ridiculous backpedal.

"Who are you?" she demanded. The girl locked gazes with her, gray eyes—*like Stephen's!* Anyelet thought in surprise—blazing as Anyelet yanked her glare away at the stab of physical pain. Anyelet took another involuntary step backward as the girl moved closer, ignoring the other vampires as they hissed and yelped like whipped dogs, then stopped in front of Stephen where he had begun crooning a wordless hymn to Vic's dissolving corpse. Her hand slipped under his chin and raised his head; Stephen's eyelids fluttered, then his clouded eyes cleared and widened.

"Werner!" Anyelet shrilled. She stabbed a finger toward the young woman. He responded immediately, sidling around to the right to come up behind the girl. Her head turned, the movement like a slow-motion bullet, and Werner froze when her eyes tracked him; suddenly he whirled and clapped his hands over his eyes with a cry.

Turning back, the girl bent and dipped the tips of two white fingers into the blood splashed across Vic's shirt, then touched first her own forehead, then Stephen's. Her fingertips left a mark like blood-soaked holy day ashes. "It's your burden now, Stephen," she said softly. "Time to go."

Anyelet's face twisted as Stephen nodded, a semblance of sanity returning to his face. How had this twit known his name? The girl glanced around the hall, the only spot of color on her body the small streak of crimson on her forehead. Then she stared at Anyelet again, and Anyelet could have screamed at the swelling of pain those crystalline eyes brought to her head. The girl smiled sweetly, and when she spoke, her whisper was like the damning moan of funeral bells.

"The angel of death has been born."

9

■■·■·■·■·■■

REVELATION 12:14
And to them were given two wings of a great eagle,
that they might fly.

■■·■·■■

"This is the end of the line, C.J. *C.J.!*"

"*No!*" He sprinted in the opposite direction, then
stopped unsteadily at the edge of the small terrace. Below the sidewalk was like a black flood; here and there
the light of the moon highlighted the far rooftops. He
stretched a blood-flecked hand toward her, then dropped
it helplessly. "I'm—oh, *God*, Louise." His glance skittered over her shoulder to the door, barricaded with only
an empty, rusted oil drum. "We should've gone up to the
next level—I should have *known* better—"

"Shush." She pressed her fingers against his mouth. "It
wouldn't have made any difference. We knew that when
we pulled them away from the Mart, didn't we?" He
flinched as something knocked playfully against the other
side of the door.

"*Hellooooo . . . Anybody home?*"

Louise gripped his arm tightly, pulled the pistol from
her jacket pocket and offered it to him.

"You know that won't help!"

"I don't mean for them," she said urgently.

C.J. squeezed his eyes shut, then tugged her farther
away from the door. The small section of roof wasn't
much; once the beasts beyond the door got tired of playing, it would be only seconds to the end. With each half-
lazy thump, C.J.'s heart gave a sledgehammer pound of
its own. "I can't do that," he said hoarsely. "Can you?"

She opened her mouth, then shut it. "No," she whispered. The pistol clattered to the tarred surface. Her
eyes were terrified sparkles as she looked at him pleadingly.

"I don't want to be like them."

"Me neither." C.J. stepped to the terrace edge and peered over. A hundred feet below, the sidewalk was like a tempting, dizzying trampoline.

Louise followed his lead, then shot a frightened glance behind her as the metal can gave a scream of protest when the door began to force it aside. A small moan slipped from her throat. "Suicide?"

"No," he said grimly. Behind them the door rebounded against the wall as their pursuers finally beat it open. From up here, the last of the daylight was a lost purple smudge in the west.

"Salvation." He held out his hand, and she took it and squeezed. His fingers slid forward and they locked wrists.

Silent, they stepped off the edge of the world and flew like eagles.

"Shit, man," Ron said in disgust. He picked up the limp wrist of the girl, then let it drop. He and Gabriel had tried to get at least something from the bodies, succeeding only in getting their clothes and hands sticky with blood. Anything worthwhile was splattered across the concrete. "These guys are nothing but dog meat."

"Yeah." Gabriel grabbed his arm. "And here come the dogs." A small pack of outcasts was slinking along the sidewalk, growling and snapping, their tongues black and dripping at the smell of blood. Soon they would be scratching and fighting amid the remains like hyenas.

Ron and Gabriel fled into the darkness, leaving the bodies to the scavengers.

10

REVELATION 16:6
For they have shed the blood of saints and prophets. . . .

"Kill her!" Anyelet hissed. "Do it *now!*"

No one moved. Anyelet's face went purple. "You're all imbeciles! Rita!" she barked. Rita's head snapped up, her puckered, twisted face jarred to attention. "You take care of it! The rest of you come with me before the humans get too far—"

White fire encircled her wrist and rocketed up her arm as the girl's hand shot out to stop her. Shrieking, Anyelet tried to twist away from the hand clamped on her as the other vampires gasped and wailed but made no move to help. She felt like she was being *electrocuted*, her thoughts crisped in her mind before they could finish. At last she managed a sharp backhand that sent the girl reeling into Rita's waiting arms. Something blue *flashed* and Rita screeched and flung her away.

"She—she *burned* me!" Rita yowled. "I can't touch her!"

"Then *use* something, you fool!" Anyelet bellowed. Her remaining soldiers were no more than frozen statues.

"Yes, Rita . . ." The girl cocked her head, as if trying to hear something. The stench of burning flesh and charred cotton filled the hallway. "Why don't you use your . . . *knife?*"

"*DO IT!*" Anyelet roared, and shoved Rita forward. Rita stumbled, then righted herself and drew the carving knife from her belt, its blade still crusted with Howard's blood. She gnashed her teeth and advanced on Jo as Anyelet and the others closed around the two women like wolves.

Jo smiled serenely and closed her eyes. Then she spread her arms wide in a welcoming embrace, soundless as her lifeblood splattered the dead who gathered.

VIII

March 30

Aftermath

1

REVELATION 22:11
And he that is holy, let him be holy still.

"We have to move," McDole told Ira and Calie. "I know we've only been back a couple of hours and it's going to be difficult with all these new people, but tell everyone to be ready by ten o'clock." Beneath his anguished eyes, his cheeks were hollow from lack of sleep. Last night had been difficult beyond words; while Alex's choice of a hiding place had proven wise, the darktime hours had been filled with terror as they dragged painfully by in the wait for dawn. "We'll give them one more hour—"

"That won't be necessary."

McDole spun, nearly tripping over the chair behind him. For a moment he couldn't even speak. "How did you get in here?" he choked out. "How did you even *know* where to come?"

Stephen smiled calmly at the older man and Calie, who was staring at him openmouthed with Beau cradled in her arms. His face darkened. "C.J. and Louise won't be coming back," he said in a low voice.

Calie sobbed, just once, then lifted her chin. "They . . . they didn't—"

"No," Stephen answered simply. "They didn't." McDole sat heavily onto the chair and stared at the floor.

"Calie." Dr. Perlman hobbled into the room. "I'm having a hard time—" He stopped at the sight of Stephen. "I thought you'd . . ."

"Be dead? No, not yet." He gazed at the doctor, his eyes an odd mirror of Jo's. "I came because I . . . had a feeling you needed help with Renata."

Perlman started to say something, then dismissed it. "Come with me," he said. Yesterday's frantic exercise made him limp heavily as he led Stephen down a long hallway, then up a flight of stairs into a room converted to a makeshift hospital ward. Calie and McDole followed glumly as the doctor showed Stephen to the far end, where the pregnant woman they'd rescued yesterday strained against restraints. "We had to tie her again. I can't even hold a logical conversation with her," Perlman complained. "She won't listen, she won't talk." Perlman looked haggard. "Listen, I'm a bacteriologist, not a psychiatrist. All I know for sure is I can't keep her sedated; it's bad for both the baby and her."

Stephen stepped to the woman's bed. "Renata," he said gently, "Dr. Perlman wants to discuss the baby with you."

"How do you know everyone's name?" McDole asked in the background.

Calie shot him a puzzled glance. "Wasn't he with you at the Mart yesterday?"

"It's evil!" Renata shouted suddenly. Spittle sprayed from her mouth. "The child is a monster!"

"Not at all," Stephen said soothingly. "Howard is *dead*, Renata. This isn't his child, it's *yours*." His fingers stroked the damp hair from her sweat-drenched forehead. "A baby, blameless, at the mercy of someone else." He paused, then leaned close. "Do you remember what it was like to be at someone else's mercy, Renata?" She stiffened. "Think of a child subjected to that kind of hatred." The woman's hands gripped the bedrails until the fingernails showed white; she began to cry.

"Then"—Stephen let his hand drop briefly to the small swell of her stomach—"think of a child raised under opposite circumstances, how a . . . *boy* might grow into a fine man if he were cherished and taught to love others in a healthy way." His fingers found the sheet strips around Renata's wrists and began untying them; Perlman shuffled nervously. "*Your son*, Renata. You might name him . . ." Stephen's gaze flicked to McDole and Calie, then back. ". . . Clement Judd, after that brave young man who gave his life to help free you and the others." He stopped and studied her. "That is, of course, if you decide you want to keep the boy after all."

Silence, heavy and fearful, settled on the small group as they all stared at Renata. For the first time since her explosive arrival yesterday, her hands were free. Perlman looked ready to leap if she made the slightest movement.

"It's a boy?" Renata asked in a small voice. Her hands folded tentatively around her stomach.

"Yes." Stephen backed away and motioned for the others to follow.

"You're sure—" Perlman began, but Stephen waved at him to be quiet. On the bed, Renata sat up and looked around; after a second she poured herself a glass of water from the bedside pitcher, then picked up a small hand mirror from the table and frowned at her reflection.

"She'll be okay," Stephen assured Perlman. "She just needed to remember that the villain was Howard, not the child."

"Clement Judd?" Calie raised her eyebrows.

Stephen gave her a distracted glance. "A nice name, don't you think?"

2

●━●━●━●━●━●

REVELATION 22:3
And there shall be no more curse.

━●━

Where will I be twenty years from now?

Alex straightened and stretched the muscles in his back. Will I remember the smell of soil and the way the sun broke through the clouds to shine on the park?

Will I remember *Deb?*

He picked up his shovel and leaned on it. Grant Park was, of course, deserted, the Art Institute a gray fortress at his back. A fitting place for Deb's grave; she had loved the Institute, and how many people could've claimed they had worked *and* lived there? Soon the small mound of upturned earth would fade into the surrounding lawn, covered casually by grasses that would probably grow long and wild for centuries to come.

The sun pushed through in earnest as the cloud cover scattered and the temperature climbed noticeably. Deb's final resting place was in the sun, as she had requested, but he thought it looked sad and plain compared to the greening spread of the surrounding park and the eternal beauty of the woman it held. Alex tossed the shovel aside and thought of the tiny white daisies that Deb had so cherished.

He knew just where to get seeds.

3

REVELATION 22:5
And there shall be no night there; and they need no candle,
neither light of the sun.

"We'll have quite a few babies around here within a year," Perlman told McDole. "At least two of those women are pregnant, maybe more."

"Not enough to repopulate the world, Bill," McDole pointed out with a wry grin.

"No." The doctor shrugged. "But it's a start. Besides, once it's obvious that the vampires are gone, I bet we find a lot more people than even you realized."

McDole sat back. "You really believe in that V-BAC."

"Without a doubt."

McDole stared out the window morosely. "Too bad it didn't come last month, or last winter. Then maybe—"

"Don't." Perlman placed a hand on McDole's shoulder. "There're too many 'what ifs' that we could torture ourselves with, and too many of *those* would've changed anyway."

McDole's forehead creased. "Where did Stephen go? He's disappeared already."

"He's one of those 'what ifs,'" Perlman said. He turned and grinned as Calie reached past him and shoved a squirming bundle into McDole's hands.

"Don't look so glum, boss," she said cheerily as McDole gaped at the tiny red face of Evelyn's son. He couldn't help smiling as the baby squinted and waved a miniature fist. Calie folded her arms. "That's better. You wouldn't want your namesake to actually *look* like you, would you?"

"It's hard, isn't it?"

Perlman glanced up as Calie sat beside him on the

curb just outside the open door to Water Tower Place, little Beau snuggled in her arms. The late afternoon sky had turned cloudy and dull, but the temperature was a prelude to warmer weather. It was a sign of faith that McDole had left the doors to Water Tower Place wide open. Perlman grimaced. "I beg your pardon?"

"Don't pull that polite baloney on me, Doc." She gave him a sidelong look. "You're forgetting the most important thing you've said today."

"What's that?"

"You're forgetting to forget the 'what ifs.'" She scratched Beau's ears. "You're moping and feeling sorry for yourself, thinking about your wife and son, C.J. and Louise, and Deb, too." When he didn't answer, she continued. "She's the worst, isn't she? Because you never expected to think of one of those monsters as a human being."

He sighed, then frowned. "I don't recall telling you I was married," he said, "or that I had a son." He turned to face her.

Calie smiled. "It's time to start looking *forward* instead of backward, Bill. Time for a new life." She stood, then bent and kissed him briefly on the lips, her brown eyes twinkling. "Remember, there *is* life after death."

4

●━●:●━●:●━●

REVELATION 19:2
For he hath judged that which did corrupt the earth . . .
and hath avenged the blood of his servants at her hand.

●━●●━●

There were sounds of dying in the Mart tonight.

Rita didn't want to hear them. She couldn't find
Anyelet and guessed that the Mistress hadn't woken yet;
lately it was safer to let Anyelet alone than disturb her
anyway. She put her hands to her face and they came
away covered with gray-green globs of melting flesh, and
Rita frowned at the mess dripping from her fingers and
shook it off. Why did she have such a headache? Was it
even *possible* for her to *be* sick? Everything about her
hurt—her face since the gunshot wound, her arms since
that weird teenager had burned her last night and been
gutted for her punishment, leaving the hand that had
wielded the knife blackened and peeling. There was a
smell in this place, too, the smell of tainted meat left too
long in the warm air. Beneath the baggy sleeves of the
stained copper robe, her skin itched ferociously, as
though it were alive with a million invisible insects. She
stumbled past the currency exchange in the first-floor
hall and thought longingly of plumbing and hot water;
she was so dirty and—

She tripped over something on the floor and sprawled
facefirst. Was Howard's body still here? She tried to
stand, but her bones and muscles hurt horribly, and finally Rita just sat next to the body, ignoring the smell
and squinting in the darkness, her vision gone the way of
her beauty but not so much that she didn't detect traces
of life within the smelly, blackened pile next to her. She
peered at it curiously, couldn't stop her finger from giving it a tentative poke.

It groaned, then raised a head in which the only recognizable things were the leaking, reddened eyes belonging to Gabriel. A few seconds later he hauled himself up and grabbed the doorframe, his body making sucking, liquid noises when the flesh pulled away from the floor. A hole that might have once been his mouth opened and he gurgled.

Rita screamed and fled, the skin of her own arms sloughing away beneath her clothing. In her haste she toppled against the opposite wall, then backed away in revulsion when she realized the viscous mass slipping down its surface was part of her own skin. She careened out the front doors and fell, the sidewalk's rough surface shaving away most of her palms and fingers, leaving exposed bone to gleam in the wan moonglow. Shrieking, she scrambled up and ran, into the darker streets of downtown and away from the Mart and its infestation of death.

At Wells and Lake, Rita collapsed, her strength gone. The shadowy refuge of a diagonal doorway on the corner beckoned and she dragged herself toward it. She shouldn't be out here by herself and in this condition, so close to the subway entrance only a few yards away. But she couldn't go back to the Mart, she couldn't—

They came up the stairs like moist, deadly spiders to drag her down and into the tunnels, a new and private hell.

5

REVELATION 10:9
Take it, and eat it up; and it shall make thy belly bitter,
but it shall be in thy mouth sweet as honey.

REVELATION 18:14
And the fruits that thy soul
lusted after are departed from thee.

Try as she might, Anyelet could not drive the beast from
her dreams. It wrapped rotting arms around her with a
lover's intimacy as she whipped her head from side to
side in a vain attempt to escape the fetid kiss of its lips
against her neck.

Then it *was* gone, driven away by that girl, the one
with the silken, silver hair whose blood had splattered
everyone last night and blistered their flesh like fire,
leaving them all screaming and sick. And having this
child-woman in her mind, her gaze burning with holy fever, was far, far worse than the nightbeast who lusted after Anyelet with a Hunger that eclipsed even her own.

She woke in Stephen's arms, not knowing how he'd
found her room or why he would return after so effectively slipping away the night before. The feel of his flesh
should have stirred her dark need immediately, and yet . . .
There was no Hunger.

Anyelet tried to sit up and found she couldn't. The
hand she brought to her face was wretched and stank of
decomposing flesh. She stared at it in horror, then shrank
away from Stephen, but he seemed unperturbed by the
smell or sight of her. "What's happening?" she croaked.

He looked at her in pity and pulled her back against
his chest, smoothing her hair and cradling her gently.

"It's time to die, Anyelet."

• • •

How strange, Anyelet thought blearily, to lie next to the body of the white-haired girl who had brought destruction down upon them all. Stranger still to be moving and thinking, yet so resemble the girl's quickly disintegrating corpse next to which Stephen had placed her on the Franklin Street Bridge; now he leaned against the railing somewhere off to the side like a silent, ancient sentinel. She could hear the water lapping sweetly below, feel the breeze on her burning skin. The sun, she knew, would find her in the morning.

No matter. She would be dead by then.

Death, a concept she had not considered applying to herself since . . . when? Something else that didn't matter. All that did was *now*, on the ground with her cracked, oozing lips drawn in pain as her body ate itself away. Not long ago she had stood on the other bridge and laughed at the stars; in the morning the sun would laugh at her. What would its golden rays feel like upon her flesh? She would never know.

She closed her eyes and let the true darkness take her.

IX

—•—•—•—•—•—

March 31

—•—

Salvation

REVELATION 17:14
These shall make war with the Lamb,
and the Lamb shall overcome them.

The lake under the morning sun was stunning, an undulating sea of fire stretching to the horizon. Stephen had never been to the southern shoreline before, and he had started this trek hours ago to put distance between himself and the silent bodies of Jo and Anyelet. He would have liked to have buried them, or even spilled their remains into Lake Michigan and let the cleansing waters absorb both good and evil. Instead, he'd had to leave them on the bridge for the scavengers—the birds, the insects, and yes, the rats—and this was not something he wanted to stay and see.

Stephen turned south and began walking, barely noticing the sparrow that flitted around his head and finally landed on his shoulder for a free ride. The weather in the south was warmer, the daylight more intense; it was a climate where the smallest things of the earth might flourish that much faster. There were still darker things and frightening times ahead.

But not for long.

X

May 5

Evolution

■ ● ━ ● ━ ● ━

REVELATION 21:23
And the city had no need of the sun,
neither of the moon, to shine in it;
for the glory of God did lighten it.

REVELATION 21:25
. . . for there shall be no night there.

━ ● ━

"Beautiful, isn't it?"

Calie smiled her agreement as Perlman pulled her into his arms and hugged her. "Yes." She studied him for a moment. "Are you happy now, Bill?"

He glanced at her, then nodded. "As happy as I'll ever be," he said finally. "More than I would've thought possible."

"We are, too," she said. "And it's because of you and all your work."

Perlman rubbed a thumb along her shoulder. "Not just me," he reminded her.

"But impossible without you." She looked at him seriously. "I always wondered, what *really* made you so determined to develop that bacteria? Was it Mera? Your son?"

Perlman shook his head. "They were gone months before I got the idea." He smiled dreamily and Calie followed his pointing finger across Michigan Avenue, then up to the sky and its vivid sprinkling of tiny lights.

"I just wanted to see the stars again at midnight."

Epilogue

PROPHECY . . .

REVELATION 20:3
And cast him into the bottomless pit,
and shut him up . . . till the
thousand years should be fulfilled:
and after that he must be
loosed a little season.

REVELATION 20:5
But the rest of the dead lived not
again until the thousand years were finished.
This is the *first* resurrection.

REVELATION 20:7
And when the thousand years are expired,
Satan shall be loosed out of his prison.

ABOUT THE AUTHOR

YVONNE NAVARRO is a dark fantasy writer and illustrator who lives in a western suburb of Chicago. Her first short story appeared in *The Horror Show* in 1984, and since then her short fiction and illustrations have appeared in over forty anthologies and small press magazines. She has also authored a reference book called *The Reverse Name Dictionary* for writers and parents-to-be. This is her first novel.

JOHN SAUL

*John Saul has produced one bestseller after another:
masterful tales of terror and psychological suspense.
Each of his works is as shocking, as intense and as
stunningly real as those that preceded it.*